Bitter Passage

A story set during America's epic 1849 gold rush

Betsy Morris

Elizabeth Buechner Morris

ISBN-10: 1463687079
ISBN-13: 9781463687076

"Join the Reinhardt family in this well-crafted novel on a lengthening, hardening, and shaping overland trek. Entrepreneurial and domineering, Hermann will never rest content until he tries his luck in the gold fields; compassionate and resilient Frida struggles to finds her persona; sons Otto and Fritz quickly grow to manhood, along different paths, while 3-year old Lily glows with innocence and joy. Elizabeth Morris's detailed and accurate research allows readers to feel exhilaration and anguish, step by step, to California." Dr. Robert J. Chandler, Historian, Wells Fargo Bank, retired

"This story of the western pioneers is a story of courage, perseverance, and hope. It is a story well told by Elizabeth Morris in *Bitter Passage.*" Kerry Tymchuk, Executive Director, Oregon Historical Society

"Bitter Passage presents the world of gold rush-era America in all its complexity: urban gangs in New York, slave auctions in St. Louis, the grueling overland trail to the shiny promise of California. Elizabeth Buechner Morris's novel is gut-wrenching, heart-warming, and a unique re-telling of the classic family immigrant tale." Rishi Reddi, Author of *Karma and Other Stories*

"Elizabeth Morris follows a family of German immigrants to the gold fields of California. River crossings, parched deserts, sick children, overburdened animals, encounters with Indians—Morris captures it all in vivid prose. The gold-crazed husband is blessed with a strong, resourceful wife. His tragedy is that he doesn't realize what real gold is. What has become a five hour plane trip for us was a life-changing experience for the Reinhardt family. Reading this novel helps us reconnect with the struggle and determination of the 49ers. It also breaks our hearts. This is a good thing." Claire Keyes, Author of *The Question of Rapture*

In all things it is better to hope than to despair.

Johann Wolfgang von Goethe

Cover Artwork:

Albert Bierstadt, *View from the Wind River Mountains, Wyoming* 1860 (detail). Museum of Fine Arts, Boston

To Monty

Pitt River
Fandango Pass
High Rock Canyon
Lassen's Ranch
Bidwell's Bar
Cutoff to Lassen's
Black Rock Desert
Humboldt R.
Hudspeth's Cutoff
Junction California Trail
City of Rocks
West End of Sublett's Cutoff
Soda Springs
Big Sandy River
Independence Rock
South Pass
Devil's Gate
Mormon Ferry
Fort Laramie
Scotts Bluff
Chimney Rock
Courthouse Rock
Platte River
Ft. Kearney
Republican River
Sierra Mountains

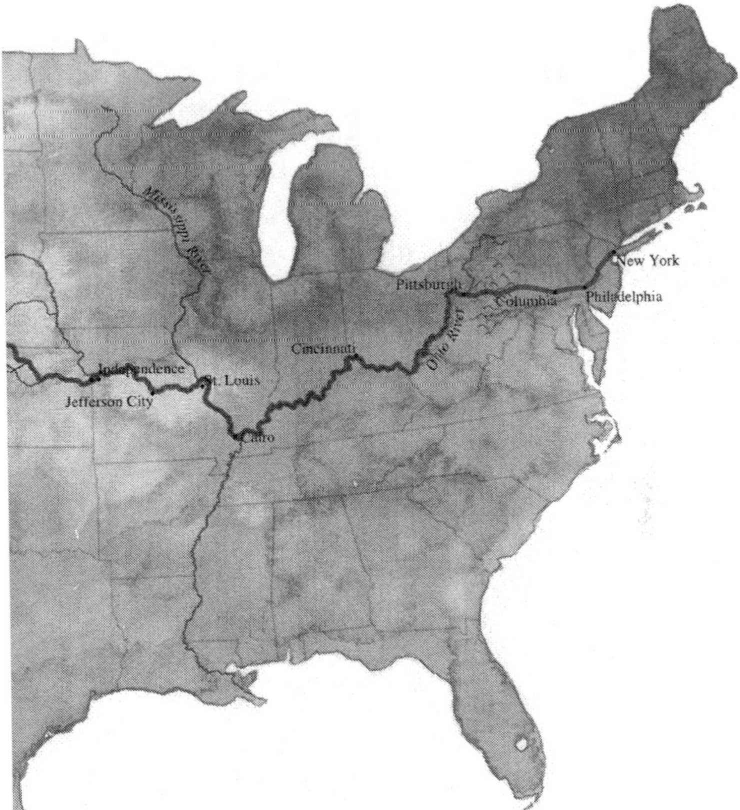

Mississippi River
New York
Pittsburgh
Columbia
Philadelphia
Ohio River
Cincinnati
Independence
St. Louis
Jefferson City
Cairo

Chapter 1

Although it is sometimes better not to begin at all, if a beginning is made, the journey and its end often depend on the quality of the start. And so it is important to describe March 20, 1849, as it was in New York on a winter day with no promise of season's change. Hoary clouds had slumped over the city for a week, concealing warmth and fostering the cold winds that funneled into the harbor and through the city. Frozen ruts in the streets made access difficult, and those who could, stayed by their hearths and stoves. Day and night had little distinction one from the other but for the noises of the daytime street – drays and beer wagons, peddlers, and cattle going to slaughter. It had rained some part of every day and in the early mornings steps and stoeps were slick with ice.

Our clothes and belongings were damp; only those few items that could be hung by the stove in our rented rooms were dry: the baby's gowns, our mittens and stockings. We hoped for some sight of a warming sun at day's break, a signal of change, an omen for our start, but the wind continued on in its course, and blew before it newspapers, feathers, and the stink of decay that was forever present along the East River. Each soggy newspaper headline seemed to announce the same news: Gold Found in California. And we would go there too, headlong toward our fortunes.

My sons had been glad for the distraction of our preparations. All winter their schooling had been repeatedly interrupted as they and their classmates were smoked out of their basement classrooms by incessant, choking charcoal fumes. Our few rooms and narrow piazza could not contain their teenage exuberance, especially as the bundles and cases filled our drawing room and spilt over onto tables and chairs.

My smart boys were admirers of Vater Jahn. His reputation had spread from Berlin to New York. Otto and Fritz were not interested in his efforts to unify all Germany, but they and their friends embraced his ideas of the virtue of exercise and fitness. They worked vigorously to establish *ein Turnplatz* based on his teachings. Often in the chill of winter they would arrive home sweating under their woolen coats, following complicated exercises with Indian clubs. *Meinen jungen Amerikaners,* my husband called them, proud of their energy and their discipline. He was less satisfied with my self-discipline, scolding me in the dining hall in front of the other boarders for spending too much time looking at myself in the cheval glass.

"*Mein Gott,* Frida! What do you see to admire all the time?"

What I saw there I could not speak of with my husband. He didn't see that I was not young and strong in the ways that I had been when we came to New York, nor in the ways that he and Otto and Fritz were. I had kept my figure and looked fit, or so it seemed, hidden from shoulders to toes under winter brocades. My hoops and falsies hid my swollen ankles and thin shanks and concealed my own worry about my stamina for the forthcoming adventure. I stood straight and still before the glass, knowing that my clothes were not travel clothes, that my shoes were not walking shoes, that that woman was not the dreamer she had been during our *Auswanderung* ten years ago. I wasn't the same person who had occasionally twirled in front of that mirror, admiring a new shawl or parasol.

In the glass I also saw our books crated for storage. I could take only a few with me, and I lamented that I must leave behind the books brought from my father's house in Gelsenkirchen. I would miss Byron's poems - for it was patriotism that inspired my husband and me to challenge the old restrictive ways and ultimately to propel him to bring us to this country of freedom. My volumes of Herder, Goethe, Kant and Schiller were packed in cartons to remain in New York. Their soft leather covers reminded me of my tutor, *Herr* Bender, who had tutored my father and his brothers before me. For most of my childhood he boarded with us and was as much part of our household as my mother's sewing box or old Rosa, who shuffled in every day to cook and clean for us. Many evenings *Herr* Bender would sit with us at the round table in the parlor. In the winter there would be a heavy carpet over the table and a foot-warmer with hot coals underneath to keep our legs and feet warm. He would take turns with my parents and me reading these volumes aloud. Often he would tell us about the *Burschenschaft* he had belonged to at University. When I was small, he would brush the tips of his fingers across the shiny scar on his cheekbone, and divert me with stories of his fencing bouts. As I grew up, I became more interested in the same ideals of freedom, democracy, and tolerance that he spoke so eloquently about than in his feats of daring.

During the summer of my nineteenth year, my father invited me to join him on a trip to Köln for a literary soirée. We would stay a week, taking in the sights of that city and stopping off to visit Dusseldorf on our way home. It was there at the soirée, discussing Goethe, that I first met Hermann Reinhardt. He and I were the youngest guests present and were seated side by side at the opening dinner. He told me that his father and uncles had sent him from Hesse to Köln as a representative of their local *Zollverein* chapter to identify trading partners for their woven linens. He explained that Köln continued to have certain customs restrictions, and he hoped to influence the business community to relax them.

"Am I boring you with all this business talk, *Fräulein*?" he asked.

"Not at all *Herr* Reinhardt. I am well acquainted with Friedrich List, his proposals regarding free trade and his *Zollverein* movement. I confess that I am surprised, however, that your family has sent you here for this purpose, as you seem so young!" I felt a little color come to my cheeks as I spoke.

"I am twenty-two, and I graduated from Ruperto-Carola University in Heidelberg two years ago. In fact, I'm staying here in Köln for two weeks with a university friend." He told me that he liked to sing and was a guest member of a singing club with his friend. I told him that I also liked to sing and that I played piano.

When the literary discussion was over that evening, he approached my father and me. "I have tickets to see a traveling show of Dürer's drawings and prints tomorrow. Would you be my guests?" We agreed and made plans to meet the following morning. As we walked to our lodgings, I asked my father if he thought Hermann was handsome. "I haven't known many young men, *Vater,* I would appreciate your appraisal. He seems good looking enough to me. I like his reddish mustaches and his blue eyes, but he is quite ruddy; I'm not sure how I should feel about that."

My father laughed, "*Tochter,* I think he is quite handsome. Also, I think he is smart and idealistic, just like you. He is very light skinned, like all Hessians, and so I think he gets burned from the sun!"

During my week in Köln Hermann joined us several times at the opera. We would have a late supper afterwards and twice took a walk in the park by ourselves while my father enjoyed his pipe. We also spent two evenings at his friend's house enjoying each other's musical company and drinking beer. He had a fine baritone voice, and he and his friend took turns playing piano while the other sang Lieder. Hermann coaxed all the anguish and drama possible out of *Die Winterreise* and *Der Erlkönig.* My father and I joined them singing *Ein feste Burg ist unser Gott.*

He called me *Schwartzi*, teasing me about my dark eyes, but I found he didn't like being teased himself when I chided him once for being off key. *Schwartzi* was not a word known in my area; he must have picked it up in Heidelberg, I thought.

I overheard his friend telling him that he should marry me. He said that I complimented his light skin and hair and that I was of good stock. He also said that I had absorbed my father's liberalism and would be a good partner in the movement.

It came then as no surprise that Hermann asked my father for my hand on our last day before returning to Gelsenkirchen. My progressive father had always treated me with the utmost fairness and broadmindedness. He answered that he would have to confer with me first. While Hermann was not openly affectionate, I was attracted to his intellect and progressive determination. And, I liked his singing. I thought that a man who was musical would be a harmonious partner – supportive, guiding, and perhaps a bit challenging. And, I had never before had a suitor.

I asked my father for his advice. "Why don't we go home and talk this over with your mother," he answered. We can invite *Herr* Reinhardt to stop in Gelsenkirchen on his way home to Hesse. May I suggest that to *Herr* Reinhardt?

"I think I should be the one to speak with him, *Vater*; would you agree to that?"

That evening Hermann and I went for a walk together. It was warm and still, and I went out with only a light shawl. He pointed out certain stars to me, and I showed him Venus low in the eastern sky.

"*Herr* Reinhardt," I began.

"*Schwartzi!* Will you not call me Hermann? You must know that I have respectfully asked your father for your hand. This week together has been a very happy one for me, and I hope for you too. I was hoping he would give me an answer this evening. I was even hoping it would be *Ja*."

I took his arm. "Hermann, I will deliver my own answer to you." I felt my cheeks and neck go red. "I thank you for your proposal, and I am enthusiastic about it. I have had a happy week also. I think we have much in common. My one concern is in leaving the place and people that I love. May I ask you to wait? I cannot make such a decision without my mother meeting you and hearing her opinion of your proposal." I invited him to Gelsenkirchen.

A week later he came and stayed with us for three nights. I walked out with him throughout our little town, introducing him to family and friends. The first evening my mother played piano and we all sang. Hermann took all the harmonies adding depth and color to our usual evening recital. The second evening we sat with *Herr* Bender around the table and discussed Byron's poetry and regional politics. The third evening Hermann and I went for a walk again, and I told him that my mother liked him and agreed that we were compatible. "I would be proud to be your wife."

His work was in Giessen, a small town near his family, and I followed him there by carriage several months later, escorted by my parents. Nothing in my own sheltered life readied me for the trip that divided me forever from all I had known. The newly bared branches of the trees rattled overhead as our carriage stopped first at the burying ground on the outskirts of town so I could say my last farewell to the dead as I had been saying the same to the living.

Frightened of bandits, we went with two drivers so that we could travel through the night, stopping to rest the horses in daylight. For four days we went east, occasionally missing the proper road and having to retrace our way to find it. We slept fitfully in the carriage and ate only what my mother had packed in a large basket. We arrived in Giessen exhausted and dirty. Hermann had arranged for lodgings with a friend in the village.

In a week of frantic activity, my parents and I met his family and prepared for a wedding. On the next Friday Hermann and I were married and I became *Frau* Reinhardt in the *Stadtkirche* with my parents and his many relatives as witnesses. I wore my mother's wedding gown. It was the color of a dove's breast, with velvet inserts around the bodice and seed pearls embroidered at the neckline. It is carefully packed and stored in New York along with our books and other treasures.

Hermann and I were both nervous. I couldn't hold my hands still and my mouth and lips were dry. When I glanced at him once during the ceremony, he was licking his lips, as I was mine. Only when we had walked back down the gray stone steps of the church did he take my hand and smile at me.

His parents hosted a small luncheon for everyone, where Hermann toasted our future with beer made by his uncle and thanked my parents. His grandmother made a presentation to us of the family Bible; it is now in our carton of books in New York. We treasure it both as a family heirloom and as a storybook without equal. She told me his grandfather had fought to suppress church control, as had both of mine; yet cautioned me to respect the rituals of the church. I agreed and pointed out that we had sought its blessing for our marriage.

My dear mother-in-law gave me a cape of velvet and ermine for the occasion. I was as nervous about keeping it out of the mud on our November wedding day as I was about becoming a wife. With no brothers, I knew little about young men. I wondered what we would talk about all our lives and whether I could be mistress to a fine house and mother to the children we would have. But not once had I thought about the intimate side of our lives.

Once on our trip from Gelsenkirchen, my mother had held my hand. “Frida, the night that you and Hermann marry you will sleep in the same bed.”

“*Ja, Mutter,* I know. It will take some getting used to.”

“Then you understand?”

“*Ja, Mutter.*”

Hermann and I had not even kissed until the night before our wedding when our friends and families gathered for dancing and toasts before the quiet ceremony. That kiss was hard, not at all what I expected, and Hermann’s hands on my shoulders were like clamps. In bed that night, I touched my sore and slightly swollen lips, then turned my attention to my mother’s beautiful dress hanging in my room, shimmering in the watery moonlight. That night was long and sleep did not come to me easily.

Chapter 2

Hermann had been established in Giessen for almost two years as manager of his family's linen mill. Even though he was young, he was respected in the business community and was active in the newly chartered *Zollverein* there.

With several other businessmen, he also had become active helping strangers from the eastern provinces – Silesia, Saxony, and Bohemia. Whenever he could, he offered them work in his linen mill for fair wages. Some evenings he and the other businessmen met to consider ways to help these workers by providing lodging for their families and schooling for their children.

He was busy, and I was alone a great deal that first bleak winter, and I was deeply lonely. I had never had a spirit of *wanderlust* as a young woman, and I missed my parents and old friends severely.

"Here's my *Schwartzi!" Hermann* would announce each evening when he would come home for supper. "What will we eat?" I would serve us soup and bread or perhaps smoked eel and crackers, and I would tell him what I had read that day.

"*Gut, Gut!*" he would say and often suggest another book or tract. Soon our conversation would dwindle; either he would go out again to a meeting, or we would sit by the fire and read to each other.

It was a long time before Giessen felt like home to me. When I had my own babies, and neighbors stopped to greet me on the streets and paths and to admire my sons, I finally came to feel less lonely and to like living in Giessen.

I made a few friends over the years, and with them I joined Hermann and the others helping settle the immigrant families from the East. By then our village had built a small resettlement house. When our two sons were born, just two years apart, they came there with me while I served soup and taught the women to knit and embroider. Hermann and I settled into a comfortable routine of work during the week, outings and exercise on Saturday afternoons by the banks of the Lahn when the weather was mild, and *gemütlich* visits with friends in the beer halls on Sundays. Hermann bought me a fine piano, and when Otto and Fritz were six and four, I began their lessons.

When we could, we went to lectures; one of them was about a society in Saxony that helped German-speakers immigrate to America. Giessen was now overcrowded with easterners trying to find work, and Hermann and I started a similar society, hoping to urge immigration on them. The idea was to send a seed group to America. As they became established, they would help the next group, and so on. In this way the Germans in America would retain their language and customs, at the same time spreading the ideals of socialism.

At the resettlement house I talked with women who hated Giessen. Their husbands had no work and were too proud for handouts. The women received food for themselves and their children and most smuggled something for their husbands, waiting outside. Those women loved the idea of a country with land to spare, where their husbands could prosper. Each time I went, they asked for more information. I told them what I knew and about the ships leaving from Bremen, but not one of their husbands wanted to be in the first seed group to cross, and the idea died.

Hermann and I discussed this dilemma. "I don't understand these people, Frida. If I had nothing, as they, I would eagerly pursue such an opportunity. Sometimes I envy their freedom. In some ways, we are less independent than they are. My father and uncles depend on me to run this part of the business. The community expects my participation."

"And mine, Hermann."

"And yours, *Schwartzi*, of course. We don't enjoy the privilege of broad choice; we are harnessed to Giessen."

Later I thought over Hermann's choice of words. These poor families were absolutely harnessed, actually confined, by their circumstances. Didn't Hermann recognize their struggle to meet each moment's needs? How could they think about emancipation when they had to bind their children's' feet in rags against the chill?

As I packed our final trunk in New York the night before our leaving for California, choosing which of my boots and shoes to take and which to leave home, I thought of those women. Wasn't it surprising, I thought, that I had never considered coming to America myself at that time. I mentioned them to Hermann that night and said that I saw certain similarities between them and myself.

"Don't be a fool, Frida," he said. "You are educated, you know music, art, history, and literature. You have fine clothes and important friends. Those women were hopeless. When I hired their husbands, they were nearly useless."

He was right; they were common countrywomen. They were the dregs, these families that came to take the jobs no one wanted. They were yokels, rustics, outcasts. They lived where they could: in caves, under bridges, and in abandoned buildings. Only the lucky few were actually housed adequately through our efforts. But they were good people, and I was unprepared for my husband's harsh words. I wondered what was becoming of his ideals.

I remembered two sisters in particular. Both were about the age that I was in 1849, when I left New York – close to forty. They each had one dress, loose fitting to do duty when they were with child. Each had a hat and a cloak of wool. They had one pair of boots between the two of them, and shared them equally, the other wrapping her feet in rags during cold weather. I can't remember how many children they had, but there were many, in spite of sad stories of children dying of exposure or consumption. When I last ladled them soup and spoke to them, one had a small baby and her sister was pregnant yet again. Those helpless women, paupers really, who couldn't read or write, who had never heard *Das Liebesverbot*, who had no hint of Chopin, Schubert or even Schumann, fought for sustenance every day and still they were willing to take on the burden of hope to relieve their distress. "Some day, *Dame*," said one of them to me, "life will be easier in our country."

I last saw them from my carriage on a late winter's day in calamitous rain. One had a blackened eye. They crossed the road quite close to me, slipping in the mud and filth. A rabble of children pressed around them. A lean spotted dog followed, its ribs barely concealed by its thin skin. The older children, all bare-footed, were weighted down with odd pieces of wood or scrub. I passed on to my home and there and then Hermann informed me that we were going to America.

I thought of those women as I readied all of us for a long overland journey to California. I remembered their fearlessness and willingness. If only I had such nerve and heart for our adventure.

Chapter 3

I had some measure of nerve then, in 1839, when Hermann announced he had purchased passage on the *Maria* sailing from Bremen to New York. I had been that morning to visit Hermann's cousin, Antonia, with the boys. She had become my dearest friend in Giessen. We had much in common: small children, a love of literature and music, an obligation to relieve the misery we saw around us, and, of course, a family tie. Antonia looked quite like Hermann, rosy and plump, with reddish lights in her blond hair. I always think of her with bits of hair straying from under her cap, looking as though she'd just come in from a long walk in the wind. She did her own cooking and got great pleasure from serving meals to crowds of neighbors. She always chided me to eat more, saying my slenderness was related to my nervousness. If I saw her looking grave, I had only to run my finger across her forehead, and the lines would disappear, and Antonia would laugh and turn the conversation to a bit of news or to a word game.

That day Antonia and I had made small almond cakes – *Pfeffernüsse* - with all our children helping. I had flour in my hair and on my clothes. The boys did too. We were surprised to find Hermann there in the middle of the afternoon when we got home. He burst out of the house when he heard us approach and fairly ran across the yard to greet the boys and me, swinging each of us up and down with energy and charm not often displayed.

"*Liebchens*!" he cried, "I have news – wonderful, wonderful news. We leave in a month for America! Our future is there; the future of you boys is in America, not here." My boys caught his excitement like a ball in a game and became boisterous like their father. The three were soon flushed as they spun each other about the yard. Otto and Fritz were infected by their father's feverish mood, a condition they had only seen previously in the beer hall, but that day sharp and penetrating, kindled by hope not by drink. "Frida! Join us!" Galvanized by their intoxication, I danced too, and none saw the fear, disappointment, and rage that reddened my cheeks as much as their own.

Later, when the boys went out to tell their friends their news, I sat and drank coffee with Hermann. "Why have you made this decision without me?" I demanded.

"I wanted to surprise you!" he answered. He went on to tell me what I already knew: that Prussia and the whole German Confederation were stuck in the past. There would never be freedom of commerce or politics. He was convinced that nothing could be done, that nothing *would* be done. He was tired of fighting for reforms. "America! Frida," he kept repeating. "We can do anything there. We can import fine linen there or try something new. I have contacts in New York and in Baltimore – journalists and businessmen."

I had never seen Hermann like this and was bewildered by my own feeling of dread in the face of his excitement. Further, I was hurt and disappointed that he had been considering this move without discussing it with me. Our marriage, I realized, had settled into one like most of our neighbors in Giessen: we were both preoccupied with our roles in the family and the community, and no longer found time to read or make music together or even to talk about our own future.

"I am not a rolling stone like you, Hermann! You have moved, moved, moved your whole life! You have not been fair to me or to our children. I don't want to go!"

But the tickets were bought.

We first saw the *Maria* at night, lying next to the quay, but so far below us that only the masts were visible to us. None of us had seen a sailing ship before, only pictures in books and in the broadsides that made their way inland to Giessen. The reflection of our lamps reminded us that water was below those tall spars, and presumably the ship itself, but further discovery would have to wait until daylight. The dock itself was a jumble of barrels, bundles, and cages of live geese, chickens, and a pig. We located some help and unloaded our wagon, leaving our own belongings alongside the rest on the quay. Hermann paid a man to watch over our parcels and furniture through the night.

We had a restless night in a nearby inn; I worried most about my piano spending a night in the open air, but also wondered about the figures we had passed along our route –

little groups of tired men and women and children, their trudging feet raising puffs of dust from the roads. A few pulled carts; most carried all they owned as they too made their way to Bremen with dreams of a better life. Probably some would never make it, as the heavy payment of their scant energy would prove to be more than they could spare, and they would drop by the wayside with no plan and no resources. No doubt they had seen the same placards as we had nailed to the chapel gate in Giessen, advertising passage on the ships that carried wheat and cotton from America to Europe, that had room in their holds for emigrants on the way back. Like us, they had official documents and identity cards in their pockets, covered with stamps and precious signatures. We also had skills, education, and letters of introduction and credit. And, most important at that moment, we had reservations on a ship built for carrying passengers, not goods.

By morning my mood had shifted – thanks, I suppose, to my youthful inability to stay worried for long. I was as excited as Otto and Fritz to get a good look at *Maria.*

Hermann made the final arrangements with the Port Captain and other authorities, and when we arrived at the ship, the tide had floated her to eye level and flying from the highest mast was a bright blue flag with white center, indicating the imminent sailing of our ship. Five men were gently hauling my piano into the hold. They had wrapped it in cloths, tied carefully around, and my worry was assuaged.

We stood on the quay in the August sunshine and watched as a pig, trussed up in a net of ropes, kicking, squealing, and relieving itself, was hoisted by a hook on a crane and swung over onto the ship. People around us clapped and shouted at the entertainment, calling to the pig to spare them from being its target.

The boys and I, still laughing at the pig, swarmed onto the ship's deck eager to experience the boat and the sea. Hermann had reserved a cabin that opened on the upper deck. It had four bunks for our family. We were privileged, I realized, as our fellow passengers were not so well situated, many being below decks with no port lights and little ventilation.

We sailed with the tide at midday, and the city passed by us as the sailors covered the hatches with canvas and cleared the decks. All passengers were on deck, admiring the view, the day and each other. The Captain's wife was making the passage with us, and she stood beside me pointing out the sights on both sides of the River Weser. She was young and said she and Captain Huber were newly married. She enchanted Otto and Fritz and they eagerly took a tour with her. She showed them everything, including the insides of the lifeboats. "We never need them, of course," she said to us all. "But we're proud that *Maria* is one of the first ships to carry lifeboats."

I will always remember the tremulous light on those long August days. It seemed as eager as we were. One day when there was no wind at all and *Maria* stood still as a heron at river's edge, the men and older boys climbed down ropes to the sea and ducked and dipped like fowl, splashing and yelling at each other. Other days we passed close enough to the Frisian Islands to take on milk and cheese from Dutch *koffs*. Further on we passed herring boats from Denmark and cod fishers from Norway. Each of them was distinct, but without help from my new friend *Frau* Nora Huber, the Captain's wife, we would not have distinguished them ourselves. My sons spent their days in the sun, working the ship's lines with the sailors, while Hermann paced the deck, usually in company with another passenger, always questioning, scheming, and planning our new life. Nora and I played cards or read, and in the evening I played the piano in the ship's saloon, and some of the passengers sang the old songs of home.

In two weeks we got to the Straits of Dover which were crowded with ships large and small entering or leaving the Thames: luggers, pinkies, and barges. At night we could see lights on shore to both port and starboard as *Maria* made her way west. The voyage had been so fine that I had almost been able to forget the painful month of sorting, packing, selling, and saying good-bye. I thought my heart would soften like cheese left too long in the sun when I said good-bye to Antonia; I begged her to come too, to follow us some day, and she promised to talk to her husband Erich about it. She took our sweet dog, as old as Otto, and our house cats; Erich said he would watch over our house until it sold.

And my heart did break when our carriage and wagon train stopped in Gelsenkirchen for one day and a night with my parents. They had not met their grandsons, the distance being too great between Giessen and Gelsenkirchen for casual travel, and these twenty-four hours were to be their only occasion together, and my only time with them as a mother. Our welcome and our farewell were concurrent but not harmonious as they and I clung sadly to each other, every minute of the hour reminding us that our destinies would be forever apart.

After a fine goose dinner on board one night, Captain Huber recommended that we all watch to starboard after dark, for we would see the tall Eddystone lighthouse, and that it might be the last light we would see until we entered the Narrows at New York. We let the boys stay up, and we did see Eddystone Light. The men toasted our calm sail thus far and gave thanks to the Captain for safe passage to the Atlantic and the beginning of our ocean voyage. And on that August night in 1839 I lost sight of the European continent.

Chapter 4

My courage wavered when, in the morning, we could no longer see land. *Maria's* motion was different as the ocean's long swells monotonously lifted her stern and slid beneath the hull, slating the spars and sails against the great masts. There was no hope of daily diversion; we expected to see no ships or boats or any living thing for one month, possibly two. Nora was determined to learn navigation, and spent much time with her husband, the Captain, and with the chief mate. She was a clever girl and desired to be of help. With our little boys busy pretending to be sailors all day long and my husband occupied with the other men, making connections and plotting our future, I was freer than I wanted to be. I had my embroidery and some books with me, but I could not fill an entire day with these activities. And, besides, I found that even a good book lay unread on my lap, as I mused on the colors of the sea and the architecture of the clouds. Even at night, when I thought I would pick up my reading, I would instead listen to the lap of the waves, the splash of the ship through the sea, and sit quietly in the silky dark, promising myself I would read the next day.

I had learned the names of many of the sailors on our trip thus far and had observed them as unusual and curious in their manners and clothes. All were sunburnt in their faces and hands, and toughened by their work. All wore wide trousers, stained and worn, but not dirty. In fact, the cleanliness of the ship was a surprise to me. Decks were holystoned weekly, and bedding and clothing were hung out in the sunshine every day. There was no idleness aboard; the Captain's discipline required every man to be at work upon something. Maintenance on the ship itself never ended. The men scraped and painted the topsides, patched the sails, and guarded against wear with elaborate parceling and marling of lines. To this day I cherish a plaited ring made for me by the sailmaker, an older sailor who had made the crossing twenty times, but had never been ashore. Johann was his name, and he gave me an old palm thummel that he cut down to fit my hand. I spent many hours with him on deck learning to sew the heavy canvas, to sweat on the eyes, hoops, and other attachment points, and I often patched the clothing of the sailors.

In spite of long voyages away from home, there seemed no time or place for sentiment among the men. In fact, I seemed the only one aboard still clinging to memories of my home. My mind wove my life in Giessen into my thoughts at sea. I could stand at the rail with my eyes closed imagining Giessen's fine promenades and its narrow streets near the old castle. Mid-morning I would sometimes imagine myself at market, speaking with friends, paying respects to neighbors, and buying from favored market stalls: beets, squash, onions, cabbage. I would plan imaginary dinners, perhaps using the leftovers from yesterday's imaginary dinner: ground pork mixed with potatoes and spiced with thyme, served with beet greens doused with vinegar. I could make an imaginary strudel, and at the same time greet a sailor or a fellow passenger.

Hermann did not look back. He ignored my evenings of sentimental music, in favor of standing in *Maria's* stem at sunset and imagining our future in the romantic rays in the west. Hermann was resolute, steadfast in his belief that his decision was the right one.

Once when I went out to stand with him under the heavenly protection of Orion's sword, he said, "Frida, isn't this wonderful! I don't think I have ever been happier. I feel the roll of the ship in every bone and sinew. It is making us all stronger."

"Certainly the boys are toughened," I said. "Only a year ago, Fritz was so shy he would not let go of my hand when we were in town. Now he's six and as independent as his brother."

"On calm days he has climbed the rigging to the first yard. I am proud of him," said Hermann. "And of Otto too. He told me he wants to be a sailor when he grows up. Imagine! He'll outgrow that idea soon enough."

"He asked Johann to make him sailors' trousers out of canvas scraps. I thought I'd make a pair for Fritz too."

"Ah, well, we can indulge them for now Frida. Soon enough we'll be in New York – a new city, a new language, and back to school for them. I want them to learn Latin and the sciences."

"They're just boys, Hermann. Wait a bit."

"But, they're my boys."

Chapter 5

One afternoon I approached Johann with an offer to help, but found him rolling his needles and scissors into the pouch he called his *hussif* and putting it away with the threads and assorted yarns.

"A blow is coming, Missus, the Captain warns that the glass is dropping quickly."

"The glass? What is that?"

Otto and Fritz were with me then, and Johann explained to us that the pressure was dropping in the barometer in the Captain's cabin, and that signaled stormy weather.

"Look at the water, boys, and feel the gentle wind on your cheek. This is a fresh breeze, no more, but in the night the wind will increase. When you awaken tomorrow the sea will look quite different. Tonight missus, put away anything that might break, and if you have oilskins, make them handy."

Going to our cabin that night, I stopped at the rail where Hermann was once again embracing the spaciousness of the wild and scenic west. He too knew of the up-coming storm and saw valor in its potential; I saw foreboding in each wave, black against the sky's last light, a prelude to the attack to come.

"I love the sea," he said to me.

I awoke in the night, and by some small light reflected into our porthole, saw bunches of our clothes on hooks, erratically dancing against the wall. The water in the carafe was apparently defying all laws of gravity, now laying at one diagonal, then at another. A small sliver of soap slipped to the floor and skidded around our small space. Fritz awoke too and, quickly shedding his cloak of sophistication as a sailor, climbed into my bunk and under the bedclothes with me. We listened as *Maria* produced new sounds lurching and trembling, glad for the warmth of the other.

"Are there ghosts, *Mutter*?"

I knew he worried about the shrieking and wailing that was all around us.

"It's the wind, *Junge*. Remember how high you and Otto have climbed in the rigging? Now the wind is there. Sing with me, Fritz, but quietly so as not to disturb your father and brother."

And we whispered our favorite songs, even the Christmas ones, the familiar words helping us to be brave together. Even so, I wondered if we would be spared as I had heard of many ships having anxious passages, and of some that never reached the American shore. Johann had told me that in the rhythm of the sea, the seventh wave was always the largest. Fritz and I started counting, as *Maria* rolled from side to side. A spittoon came loose somewhere amidships, and thundered across the decks until its apparent dive overboard. The lashings on a sail must have come free as we suddenly heard the crack and slap and then the rip of canvas. And once, following a seventh wave, we heard the crew shouting that a hatch cover was adrift. It came to me then: our ship would flounder and sink. How unfair it was. I hadn't wanted to leave Giessen; had never thought once of going to sea. My children would never see America, would never be adults. I would have no more children, no daughters. As our trunk came adrift from its tie-downs and scraped noisily across our small floor space, my cries were lost. My sweet boy knew and held me close as I held him, his smooth cheek against mine. "Sing, *Mutter*," he wept.

By the meager light of dawn, we dressed as best we could lying propped in our bunks, for standing was not possible. Hermann fought against the wind to open our door, but his obstinacy was weaker than the gale's. As he cursed, the door flew open as our side of the boat rose on a swell to meet him, and he stumbled, holding the door open with his body. At that moment I was struck in the face by cold salt water, the leading edge of a wave that traveled across the deck and into our cabin. As the ship settled into a trough, we all saw what we had previously only heard. The sea was heavy, monstrous, but also quivering as the howling wind blew away the insubstantial wave tops. The ship's spars were bare, some sails fastened tightly down, others blown out to rags. The lifeboat near our cabin was gone, as were the crates lashed further aft with the remaining geese and chickens. At that moment the Cook came by, clutching the rail.

"Go back inside," he bawled. We did as we were told, and he followed us in. He told us that new tarpaulins had been stretched and made fast over the hatch and that the pumps had kept up with the water in the bilges. He said that only one headsail was bent, and that the Captain was keeping the ship's head to the seas to keep the decks as clear as possible. For our safety, he urged us to stay in our bunks and left us with a canvas bag with bratwurst, bread, some apples, and, to our surprise, marzipan for the children. The confines of our small space were too much for my husband, and in spite of the danger, he joined some of the other men in the saloon. I tried to read to the boys, but the ship's movement made that impossible, and instead I told them fairy tales: *Hänsel und Gretel, Struwwelpeter,* and *Hans Guck in die Luft*. They'd known the stories from babyhood, and after a while Otto told us *Rapunzel* and with Fritz's help he also remembered *Die Bremen Stadtmusikanten.*

That is how we passed that long day. In exhaustion we slept most of the second night, and by the following morning we could go on deck. Our sailor friends looked older, the experience of the night etched in their faces. All were unharmed, save my carpenter friend whose cheek had been bloodied by a block gone wild in the wind. The deck still heaved, and I felt like a baby learning to walk again. The chaos of the storm was evident all about us, but our fine crew was cleaning up. I saw Johann lighting his pipe. He saw me and gestured forward, "See, Missus, your repair in the sail's leech held!"

Chapter 6

This was the first gale I had met, and I wished it to be the last. Even so, some small seed deep inside me swelled and grew a bit with the knowledge that we had made it, that I had made it.

"*Mutter*! It was exciting, wasn't it? I wasn't so scared. I knew the Captain would bring *Maria* through. I was brave, *Mutter*, I could have helped with the sheets and halyards or dripped oil on the waves."

I knew what Otto meant. It had been both terrifying and exhilarating, and the small heat inside me was of pride that I didn't panic or swoon and that I helped the boys. I felt safe on *Maria's* decks. As Giessen had become my home and haven, now *Maria* was too. Nora was a friend, and so were others aboard.

This leads me to speak of Adolph Spies who became my husband's closest confidant and remained so through all our years in New York. Adolph had immigrated to America three years earlier. In New York he married the young widow of another recent emigrant. He had gone back to Germany at the behest of his employer, the *New Yorker Staats Zeitung,* and was returning to his new home on the *Maria,* prepared to write a story for that newspaper on the causes of the ever-increasing wave of newcomers from *das Vaterland.*

Adolph carried a notebook in his vest pocket. The frequent putting in and taking out of that small book had frayed the pocket's edge. I offered to repair it for him, but he laughed and said it had been repaired many times and not to worry. He often quoted from those pages, referred to statistics kept there, or jotted an idea or a name. One night at dinner he pulled it out to verify the price of mutton in New York and minutes later to check some facts about the disastrous fire of 1835. Neither Hermann nor I could believe the varied information that he kept in that small pad. Adolph was quite a remarkable man, brimming with the energy and optimism that appealed to Hermann.

About the American President he had much to say, "*Ach, Fuchs*," he would begin.

The first time I corrected him, "Adolph, isn't the President *Herr* Martin Van Buren?"

"*Ja, ja*, Frida, Van Buren, of course," he laughed. "But the Americans call him The Red Fox. But he's not foxy enough for me, or for the country. Most people see no end to this depression."

Even when he told us about the unemployment, the rioting in the city streets, and the tension between rich and poor, he would somehow lead us and other listeners to consider the opportunities arising because of these problems.

Hermann's stated reason for going to America was to escape the restrictions on commerce in Prussia. Often he stated that we were "going to New York to insure a rich future for Otto and Fritz." That was part of it, but Hermann himself saw New York as a gateway to the markets of America. I knew he had become bored working in his family's business and relished the challenge and adventure before us. And I suspected that he thought success and riches would be his for easy taking. He told me he might import linen from the family business back in Prussia, but the more he talked with Adolph and the other men, the more he saw opportunity all around him. For several days he and Adolph planned a business they would run together. They would hire and train men to police the streets of New York. Adolph explained that there was strong resistance to a municipal police force, of the kind newly formed in London. New Yorkers were not so sure that they wanted to risk their republican liberties by supporting a professional police force, which seemed in the abstract no different than a standing army.

"But," Adolph explained, "They want protection of their homes and businesses from the gangs and ruffians threatening them."

I wondered what my husband knew about such a business, but when we were alone one night and I asked him about it, he told me that I was way behind, that now he had given up that idea and was thinking of building houses in New York.

"Adolph tells me that the *Daily Advertiser* and the *American* have advertisements every week for land that has been foreclosed by the banks. Since we owe neither debts nor patronage in America, we can take advantage of this depressed time. There are newcomers by the thousands in New York every month, he tells me; they need housing."

"Let me guess!" I teased. "Those facts jumped right from Adolph's pocket notebook to your head!"

"Ja, Ja, Schwartzi!"

Adolph had explained to me that New York houses were so close together that they had small yards or none at all and that families lived quite publicly. I wondered about wells and gardens and chickens and geese, things that I had in own yard at home and had taken for granted. Where would we live? That question haunted me, and now I wondered too about water and other necessities. At least if Hermann was in the building business, we would have our choice of neighborhoods and a large lot with space for a garden.

But a few days later, as I lingered in the saloon after dinner, I heard Hermann talking to a man about opening a beer hall together where German speakers could meet their own kind and listen to their own music and eat their own favorite foods. I realized that Hermann was just trying different ideas in his head. I hoped he would settle to something that would support our family when we got to New York.

When we had been fifty days and nights at sea, the Captain gathered all the passengers and crew together after the midday meal. He told us that our trip on *Maria* was almost over, and he gave credit to his wife for fine navigating. He ordered his men to make the ship festive and invited us all to a party that night. The passengers gave him a loud *three cheers* and all of us spent the afternoon planning our dress for the night's activities.

Otto and Fritz helped the sailors scrub the rail and decks with heavy canvas and then the holystones and handstones were brought out and every nook and crevice was cleaned with fresh sand. Next the head pump was manned to wash the sand overboard. Meanwhile the brass was brightened at the stanchions, wheel, forecastle, and bell. Otto sprang into the rigging, up the shrouds, and out on the yards as nimbly as a monkey and helped furl some sails to make our motion easy. Fritz and the cook's boy mixed dough for cakes, and someone rolled out a large barrel of beer and secured it to the windlass.

Johann brought out all the ship's flags, and together he and I strung them about the deck.

We gathered on the deck in the day's last light. The sailors joined the passengers, and together we all cheered the sun as it dipped again behind the western horizon. The Captain ordered the barrel open, and soon beer was being ladled and mugs passed to passengers and sailors alike. Captain Huber gave a speech of thanks for a sound ship: "To *Maria*! A fine sea boat, and tight as a drum."

"To *Maria*," we all cried. One passenger brought out his violin, two sailors had concertinas, and a third had a collection of noisemakers I'd never seen before – castanets, tom-tom, and rattles. He passed them out, and soon a motley orchestra was gathered. I was glad I had laid out a frock coat for Hermann and round-abouts for the boys. I wore my finest silk gown. It was gray with ruchings and blue ribbons on the bodice. Usually I wore it with a lace *fichu* for modesty's sake, but tonight I substituted a scarlet silk shawl that had come all the way from China by way of England. Hermann's family had given it to me as a going-away gift. When they gave it to me, I wondered if I'd ever wear it in New York, it was so bright and luxurious and quite unlike anything I had ever worn before. I loved its gentle caress on my bare arms. I had kid slippers that matched my dress and wore them in spite of the evening's chill.

I have held the memory of how my family looked that night. Fritz, only six years old, could not stand still. His curly light hair and his clothes were in immediate disarray. His nut brown, sunburnt face was like his brother's, although his features were rounder and his figure squarer. Both boys had the same pointed shoulders that I had. Otto had slicked down his dark hair with water, and a few drops dribbled onto his collar from his flat cheeks. Hermann and I looked prosperous in our finery, but more than that, I think we looked happy. Hermann's boyish eyes sparkled in his tanned face, and he seemed to walk on the tips of his toes as though about to dance. I was accustomed to holding my hands quietly, as they were large, and I didn't like to draw attention to them. But that night, I remember that my hands fairly danced about, adjusting my shawl, my hair and the shirts of my husband and beautiful sons.

There were, of course, more men then women making this trip; some of the men planned to send for their families when they were settled, others were young, single, and beginning their adult lives in a new country. All had dressed in their finest for the party. Some were wearing embroidered vests with silk cravats and even a few were wearing evening slippers. The women on board had all dressed up, as I had. Bonnets with feathers, flowers, and ruffles came out of hatboxes, a bit of petticoat lace showed beneath silk dresses. Even the poorer women had changed out of their muslin dresses and were gaily dressed. The sailors were all in clean stockings and shirts and all had shaved or trimmed their beards. The Captain had shed his uniform for a frock coat and silk top hat. We all mingled freely, listening to our musicians as they learned how to play together and sometimes singing with them.

Hermann was excited that night and as joyous as I had ever seen him. He had combed his hair and whiskers carefully, but soon they were flying as he danced about. His cheeks were flushed, and I was reminded of his cousin, my wonderful friend, Antonia. We danced together many times, often singing along with the band when they played an old favorite, like "*Ach! Mein Lieber Augustin.*" My sons made a circle with the other children, and danced around the adults, making up steps as they whirled faster and faster. Many times Hermann kissed me and pulled me close, right in front of everyone. The crowd thought that was wonderful and clapped for more, and Hermann obliged them.

I glimpsed my image in a glass as we parted for a moment to catch our breaths and to drink a beer. I was flushed too, and I think it was more than the dancing and the beer. My skin was ablaze, ignited by Hermann's hands on me while we danced. His touch was warm, even hot, and though it was rough, it both calmed and excited me. Of course my husband and I had intimate moments, moments when he had been quite lustful, even ravenous in his desire for me. Usually his craving was consummated quickly, and he would roll off to his side of our bed and lie panting and gratified until asleep. My own appetite would not be sated, and when his breathing was quiet, I would indulge myself. Seldom had I felt the heat and pressure of his hands like that night at the party on *Maria*. Emboldened, I interrupted Hermann in a conversation with the Captain and suggested another dance. "Later, *Meine Liebste*. Now, you go ask your sailmaker friend for a dance."

Instead, I went to the rail, and watched the phosphorescence on the waves caused by our ship's passing. Johann had explained that it was light without heat caused by the movement of millions of small organisms against each other. They were brilliant in the ship's wake, but soon settled down or died, and, only one or two boat lengths behind us, the waves were dark again. Otto joined me, "I watched you dance, *Mutter*. Will you dance with me now?" I took his two hands in mine, and kneaded his palms, as I would bread dough, feeling the life there; then we joined our shipmates for the last dance of the evening. Our makeshift band began to play the Star Spangled Banner, and the crowd quieted. One of the young sailors unfurled an American flag from the end of a boom. Most of us didn't know the words, but we knew the tune and hummed along. I heard Hermann's fine deep voice behind me. He surprised me, singing out the last line in English, "...the land of the free and the home of the brave."

Chapter 7

"Land Ho!"

I had never heard the cry before, and didn't immediately understand its meaning. The wind seemed to sweep the words out of the sails themselves. From atop the highest spar came the call again: "Land Ho!" All heads were turned; all eyes were on the western horizon. I looked too. There was a wisp of gray astride that fine line between the blue of the sky and the black of the deep Atlantic. All pretensions were put aside, and just like the night before, all hands and all passengers began singing and talking at once. The Captain rang the ship's bell, and when the sailor who had called out hit the deck, he gave him a gold coin.

We had slept late that morning, worn out from our gay time the night before. The boys dressed quickly and left our cabin to find some breakfast. I sat on the side of our bed and brushed out my hair from its evening plait. Even one hundred strokes could not restore its usual dark luster after so many days in salt air. I fondled the small locket at my throat. In it were the twisted tresses of my dear parents' hair, a last memento given to me when we said good-bye months earlier. Hermann still lay abed. I softly touched the familiar thick mat of hair on his shoulders that spilled over the collar of his nightshirt. I was sure my stroke would cause him to awaken and to remember the warmth we shared dancing. I leaned over him and breathed in the smell of the bedclothes and kissed his nightshirt sleeve, as soft as my own lips. But my touch went unnoticed and Hermann slept until I had dressed and gone to find my own bread and tea.

I saw him come on deck twenty minutes after I did, and he saw me, but he went to talk with Adolph, and I continued my conversation with Nora and finished my second cup of tea.

"Your husband is consumed with plans for his life in New York, I think," she said.

I agreed with her, "I only hope he includes me the way the Captain includes you in his life. My husband is a man with much energy, of all kinds. It seems that he prefers to be the captain in our family."

She asked how we had met; I knew she was really asking what attracted me to Hermann.

"We met at a lecture, and our common interest in music and books, as well as our mutual progressive sympathies, were obvious to both of us. Also, I thought he was elegant and blooming with good health. I liked his strong face.

"After we were married, we both believed that we could make a difference to people less fortunate than ourselves. Our goals were similar, but our methods were different. I liked working with people, helping in small ways by providing food for their stomachs and sometimes for their soul – music, and paper and crayons for their children." I told her about the two sisters sharing one pair of boots. "Hermann, at that same time, met with other men of our town and formed a local branch of a socialist political party. As a woman, I wasn't invited to join them."

"When we married, I told Hans I would be his co-Captain, not his mate," said Nora. "He laughed at me and said he hoped I would be both."

At that moment the sailor's cry was heard from high in the rigging, and I watched Hermann and some of the other men pass the flag of Prussia between them, each burying his face into the black and white and passionately kissing the eagle's image.

Until now I had been distracted by packing and planning, by seas and storms, and by new friendships. Seeing before me the tableau of men fervently and emotionally bidding *auf Wiedersehen* to all that was familiar made me feel quite weak. I must have spoken or made some noise, for Nora put out her hand and lay it on mine. "Frida! You're shaking with cold. Wait here, I'll get blankets to wrap ourselves."

I joined the men, gathered on *Maria's* starboard side, and reached for the flag. Adolph had folded it into quarters, and he passed it to me. I clasped it as they had, seeking in its folds for some clue to link my past with my uncertain future. I found only loss and despair of the sort experienced at a grave's side. A mournful cry rose in my throat, and I turned from the men and walked to the ship's other side. What was to become of us, of me?

Alone at the larboard rail and gasping to control myself, I felt quite giddy – almost faint. The scene in front of me, the ocean and bright sky, seemed to burst with color, far more brilliant than it had before. The sun shone scarlet and magenta along with its dazzling gold. Accompanying the light I thought I heard the clangor of a trumpet and a tattoo of drums filling the air. The light was warm and I wanted to bask in its heat. Was it my imagination? The sound and the light were accompanied by waves of smells: first snuff, then mustard, brine, lilies, garlic, and the hot breath of horses.

Even as I experienced these exaggerations and recognized them as my own fancy, my memory conjured an image of my home in Giessen with the windows flung open and the bedding airing in the morning light. There was laundry on the line and I could smell its freshness over and above the sharp and savory smells of the brilliance surrounding me. My solitary apple tree shone with its abundance, and as I watched, the neighborhood children, friends of Otto and Fritz, caught falling fruit in their caps and aprons. Out of the corner of my eye I saw Werner Hulshoff, our butcher, walking with his wife. He had a baby pig under one arm and a fat rabbit under the other; his wife gestured to me and held up *Kirschtorte* for me to admire. I closed my eyes, smelling the warm cherries and the buttery dough.

I took a deep breath, savoring this vision. When I opened my eyes, Nora was back with warm robes, and the cook was with her, passing a tray of *Linzer Torte*, "Today, *meine Frau*, not made with raspberries, but with cherries! These are Danish cherries bought off a boat in the North Sea and preserved by me for today's jubilation."

Not wanting to seem impolite, I took a cake from the cook and the blanket from Nora, although my breakfast was stuck high in my throat and I was suddenly warm: a trickle of perspiration moved down my back.

"I'll be right back," I said to Nora, with as much joy as I could muster, and made my way to our cabin, tears starting from my eyes. Compared to *Maria's* deck, our room was dark, and smelled only of dirty clothes and a forgotten apple rotting in some pocket. Overwhelmed and exhausted by my dazzling experience on deck, I fell onto our unmade bed, and wept. Whether I cried for homesickness or the loss of my transient vision, I am not sure. But I remember that I had nowhere to look for comfort.

I slept and was not missed by those on deck, agitated as they were with our impending landfall.

I've remembered that short, bittersweet moment on *Maria* in 1839 all these years. And I have wondered if something similar would happen on the overland journey to California. Would I miss New York as I did Giessen? Would I be transformed again, as I was transfigured approaching New York's harbor? Would I mourn for the loss of my life in New York? I wondered how I would hold us all together, our little family – now including our dear Lily - so far from its old ties. Hermann had assured me that this trip to the California gold fields would be easy, would be an adventure. He promised we would go slow and take it easy because of the baby.

Back on *Maria* my sweet boy, Fritz, noisily entered our cabin. "*Mutter*, I've brought you some lunch. It's *Schweinsfilets* and *Sauerkraut* today, and it's good! Why are you in here, *Mutter*?"

"Because I am so excited, *Junge*, just like you!" He laughed, believing me, and helped me to eat my lunch, finishing most of the pork himself. We heard a cry from the passengers and sailors on deck and went out to see three ships passing us, each with three masts and all sails set. The Captain recognized the last one, and ordered the ship's bell rung as a greeting to the *Europa*, bound for Hamburg. One young sailor, still affected by the gaiety of the evening past, stood at the bows and pretended to dive into the ocean to swim over to the eastbound ship, calling out his girlfriend's name: "*Greta, Greta, ich komme!*"

Adolph was beside me. "For me it is not quite as thrilling this time as the first!" he said. "That time I snuck aboard a ship in Bremen in the dark of a rainy night. I had with me only my clothes, papers, one blanket and almost no money.

"When the boat sailed the next day I was discovered almost immediately. I begged the Captain to let me stay on board, offering to work at anything at all. As he had sailed two seamen short of full compliment, he grudgingly let me stay, offering passage and food as compensation for my labors.

"It was a winter passage and cold and stormy the whole way. My job was to chip ice from the rigging – too much weight aloft could roll the boat. In borrowed gloves and doubled coats, I crossed the ocean swinging aloft with a hammer tied firmly to my wrist. Sometimes my cold fingers could not detect its handle in my hand, and to drop it onto the deck could have meant a terrible injury to someone below. On my off-watches, I often helped the cook, since the galley was the warmest place on the ship. The cook had gone to sea to escape the inevitable when he got the wife of his previous employer pregnant. His employment had been as chef in a restaurant in Hamburg's finest hotel. So, incredibly, we had excellent food on that voyage. He loved to bake, and made many loaves each day of pumpernickel or *Bremer Klaben*, with almonds and currents. Every evening he made soups out of anything in the galley: potatoes, onions, pumpkins, lentils, bits of fish or meat. He taught me to cook. Someday you will come for dinner at my house, and I will make you some *Käsesuppe*, as he taught me, with a good New York cheddar cheese, and with it we will drink a strong dark beer."

Adolph continued, "When that ship, *das Rhein*, got to this point, just entering the Narrows of New York Harbor, I stood at the rail as we are now. I was so used to being cold that the biting wind hardly affected me at all, although it kept most of the passengers in the cabins. My whole body sagged from fatigue, and I could hardly wait to get ashore. The weather had been gray and wet for most of the long crossing, but that day a weak sun came over my shoulder and lit up the ocean around us as if a hundred chandeliers were lit in the rigging. I thought I heard music and the soft swish of dancing slippers on the waves. It was a moment I'll never forget, although until this moment I've never told another person – why, they might think me insane!"

Adolph took a deep breath, still staring at the land fast approaching. I nerved myself to tell him of my own experience, but at that moment Hermann joined us and my courage drained away.

Adolph clapped my husband on the back, "My friend, do you see that land there? It is Governors Island, and just behind it we will see the piers of New York and Brooklyn. Do you know that almost 200,000 emigrants come through here every year?" He consulted his little notebook. "In fact, last year it was 176,000. Every single one came for opportunity." Hermann turned him away, and arm-in-arm they entered the saloon for a glass of sherry, leaving me alone again at the rail.

I wasn't alone for long, as most of the passengers and off-duty seamen were all coming on deck to enjoy the spectacle of entering the harbor. We had got quite used to having the ocean all to ourselves; now, surrounding us were ships flying flags from Spain, Mexico, Brazil, and many other places that I could not recognize. Otto joined me to point out steamships of all sizes in the harbor, as well as sailing ships and even rowing boats. He gave me a glance as though to ascertain that I recognized his brilliance, but all I saw was my sun-browned boy, jumping from one foot to the other.

As the city itself came into view, I was struck by how charming and picturesque it seemed. There were many spires and cupolas and buildings of four storeys or more. Smoke drifted from a thousand chimneys and joined the low clouds over the city.

Hermann and Adolph joined us, and Adolph pointed out specific sites: on our right side a large windmill right at water level. "It's the Anchor Gin Distillery," he said, "a very important place in the city! And there is Castle Garden and the Battery."

Fritz had joined us too, "Look at the cannons," he cried, "and what are those ships?"

"Those are frigates. They're steam powered. They protect the city," answered Adolph.

"Against what?" asked my husband.

"A Coast and Harbor Defense was formed during the war with England; even after the Ghent treaty was signed, the Americans have been on their guard. But there's no need. The hooliganism in New York is in the streets, not the harbor!"

Maria had seemed quite stately to me on our ocean crossing. Now, threading slowly amongst steamships and ferries and fast packets, she seemed slow and dowdy. I turned my attention to New York passing by as we made our way up the North River. Adolph pointed out some of the docks: Pollock's, Swarthwout's, Lake's, and others. He showed us the Bathing House, and soon after a small boat came to meet *Maria* and took her lines into Rhinelander's Dock.

Pandemonium, held in check until this moment, burst forth, as sailors on the yards furled sails and others tended lines; passengers ran from one side of the ship to the other, hoping to recognize a face in the crowd meeting the vessel. Trunks, cases and bundles were brought to the deck at the same time that the hatches were uncovered and along with a stench of rotting vegetation from some forgotten bundle, out came furniture, trade-goods, coils of rope, and carefully-crated stained glass destined for some new American church. I hardly knew which way to look or what to do. I had finished most of our packing; the rest would only take minutes. I couldn't imagine leaving *Maria* without a final conversation and *auf Wiedersehen* with some of my new friends on board. I turned to find Johann, but at that moment Hermann called out to me, "Hurry, *Schwartzi*, we'll disembark with Adolph. He'll set us off in the right direction."

Without a proper good-bye or a thanks, I hustled our remaining belongings together and joined my husband and sons on the gangplank to New York City.

Chapter 8

Adolph herded us off the ship and into an unfamiliar landscape which assaulted all our senses. He led the boys and me to a solitary tree at the street end of the pier and told us to wait while he and Hermann went off to find our belongings and to hire carts. My agile, adventuresome sons were as astonished as I was by our surroundings, and they stayed quite close to me. Vendors of every description approached us, but I had no money with me and no means of telling them so, as I spoke no English. One woman with a pan of baked pears balanced on her head was angry that we didn't buy from her. She bid us welcome to her city by purposely tilting her tray and spilling a fine line of sticky syrup down my sleeve. Pigs rooted in piles of garbage near us; they seemed to belong to no one, and their pink backs and bellies were gray with city soot. Porters with licenses pinned to their caps pushed carts through the throng, some calling for business, others for a passageway. We would have been run down if not for the protection of the tree we waited beneath.

Two small girls in bare feet and ragged skirts turned cartwheels, then begged for a penny. Otto grabbed my hand and pointed: a young woman, perhaps the mother of the two little girls, apparently had stolen the watch of a well-dressed gentleman near us who had been distracted by the antics of the girls. She was running our way with the man running after her, yelling "*Halt, halt*!" She was too fast for him and disappeared into the crowd; later we saw the same little girls again tumbling on a crowded street corner. Cattycorner from them was the same young woman, this time with a dark shawl over her head.

As the familiar sounds on *Maria* faded, alien ones took their place: metal screeching against metal, rhythmic pounding, repetitive thuds, and sharp whistles – their source unknown to us. At the same time we could hear ship's horns, church bells, and the growl of heavy wagons on the stone streets. The noise of New York seemed a threatening force, very different from the insubstantial noises carried by an ocean breeze. We heard many languages, all of them loud, as vendors, porters, passengers, sailors and citizens called to each other. Above it all, I could hear my own heartbeat, and when I looked at my boys, I saw that they were standing with one hand on their hearts, just as I was. I've always known our heartbeats measure out our lives, one beat at a time, but that process is silent and rarely heard as it was that morning.

We were also assaulted by smells: grease, burned food, animal waste, and baked sweet potatoes as a vendor came by. I reached for my handkerchief to cover my nose, and looked up just in time to see my piano swing out of the hold on the end of ropes from a dockside crane. It hovered high in the air, gently twisting as the breeze found it, then began its descent, too quickly, I thought. I couldn't stand to look and asked Otto to tell me when it was safely on the ground.

Where is America? I thought to myself. I peered into the city as best I could, trying to find its heart. All I could make out was a tangle of small streets, crowded with stores, houses, and warehouses, all apparently leaning against each other. Ash cans and debris littered the narrow sidewalks; above, dirty bedding and ragged clothes oozed out windows. *Where is America?*

Two hours passed as we stood, not daring to leave the sanctuary of our tree to go find the men. The crowd thinned, as the vendors moved elsewhere and some passengers, with all their goods in hand, left to begin their new life. I told the boys they could sit down, as they were tired of standing, although I worried what they might sit in. I myself leaned against the tree, wondering if I would be under this spare small tree all day and night.

By the time Hermann returned to us, I was feeling weak. I thought perhaps I had eaten too much at breakfast, as I seemed to be bloated and had a pain in my stomach, as well as a slight dizziness in my head. Hermann bustled us into a hired carriage with Adolph. "We'll go directly to Der Rosenkavalier. It is a coffeehouse down town. You can find some lunch there and get cleaned up," Adolph said. "The new Astor House is near by; and you can inquire there for rooms."

That carriage ride rivaled the worst of our long passage by sea. Several times I asked Adolph to have the driver stop while I got down from the carriage and was sick in the street. Not one person stopped to help me or even to inquire about my circumstance. Some stepped around me. One shopkeeper charged out waving a broom in his hand, "Not here. Not here!" At one such emergency stop, a group of filthy children encircled me, mocking me with their pantomime of my condition before Hermann could shoo them away.

The smells of this foreign city, combined with the noise, were making me sicker. After we passed an open-air slaughter house, I asked Hermann to inquire if there was a closer place we could stop where there might be facilities for women to rest, but he scowled at me and pointed out that our belongings had all gone ahead and that we must keep up with them. I think Fritz was not so well either. He was very pale, and laid his head in my lap, forgoing the new sights all around us.

Meanwhile Adolph kept up a commentary of the sights: "That steeple above the roof tops is Brick Presbyterian Church, thought by many to be New York's handsomest spire. And there, Hermann, see that small structure on the corner? It's for City Watch. At night a patrolman can take refuge from bad weather there. But everyone says they sleep during their watch. Otto! Take a look, that boy there is no older than you and he's rolling that barrel of beer home to his family!" He told us about someone named Bridges who laid out the city like a chessboard, but left Broadway and the old city as they were.

"Frida, did you expect to see people in such fashionable clothes?" I raised my head and looked out from the carriage and saw a jostle of conveyances of every sort. On the sidewalks I saw women in hoop skirts and men in top hats greeting each other. There were workingmen in leather aprons and dandies in silk waistcoats. I also saw pigs, chickens, geese and turkeys, but no farmyards. What an odd place we had come to. For a moment I forgot my nausea, "Adolph, why are all the horses' tails docked short?" I asked.

"For bedding, Frida; they use the hairs for bedding. Not everyone can afford goose down!"

We arrived at Der Rosenkavalier, relieved to find that the carts with our trunks, cartons and my piano were waiting for us. Adolph made us comfortable in the large paneled dining room, and after pointing out the large Astor House Hotel down the street, he bade us good-bye and left for his own home to see his wife and family whom he had not seen for several months.

I excused myself to wash up. There was a Negro girl cleaning the privy. She interrupted her work so that I could use it. When I finished and went to the washstand, she poured out warm water for my comfort and held out a clean white cloth for washing. I took my time, cleaning my face and neck and scrubbing hands and wrists. I felt refreshed and somewhat steadier. "*Danke Fräulein,*" I said to her. She smiled shyly at me and dipped her head.

When I came back, Hermann had ordered a large *Schlachtplatte* for us all to share. I knew I could not eat all those meats and sausages, and did not want to smell sauerkraut at such close range. I asked for some soup and a small *apfelwein* to settle my stomach. The waiter brought me a bowl of *Kartoffelsuppe*, and when he put it before me, I suddenly realized that we were speaking German and eating food from home. So surprised was I at that revelation that tears sprang from my eyes, and though I tried to hide them with my handkerchief, Hermann noticed and declared that I must be suffering from the vapors. When the waiter returned with bread, Hermann pointed me out with a thrust of his chin: "*Krank*!" he said.

When I remember that day, I realize that he was right. I was sick – sick and tired. I was nauseous definitely, but that may have been due to the carriage ride or even from being back on solid land after the sway of the sea. I was also weary beyond anything I had ever experienced before, including childbirth. But more than weary, I was worn out – worn from change and worry. I felt melancholic, almost despondent. And, it had all come upon me in just the short time since leaving *Maria*. I wanted more than anything to be alone, free to cry. I wished to cry so long and loud that my sweet parents in Prussia would hear me. I yearned to make such a fuss of wet tears and breathless gasps that Hermann would notice and would curtail his gleeful buoyancy. I wanted to go home to see my old dog and dig beets from my garden.

Fritz slipped off his chair, dropping his napkin to the floor. He put his arms around me and snuggled his face to my neck. "*Mutter!* What is it?" As if he had caught the sadness from me, his face crumpled and he began to cry too. I thought Hermann would be sympathetic to the two of us, but he went on talking to

Otto, "You will come with me while I inquire about rooms at the hotel, Otto. We'll want to get settled quickly and begin exploring, eh?"

When my parents bid me *auf Wiedersehen* two days after our wedding day, I turned to my new husband and clung to his chest weeping. He patted my back with one hand and tried to make me laugh by retelling a joke he had heard. I couldn't concentrate on the story and couldn't stop crying either. "Frida! Enough now. We are husband and wife; your allegiances must change. Stop your crying and be strong." Even though I tried, I couldn't stop crying. I'll never forget what he said: "Frida! You're not trying hard enough!"

So, while Fritz and I wept together, neither sure of our reasons, Hermann and Otto finished their meal, and *ein Strudel* besides, and left us to look for lodgings. When they returned an hour later, Fritz was asleep across two chairs. His shirt and pants were rumpled, his socks pooled at his ankles, and lines of soot showed on his face and hands.

I had washed my face and my panic had subsided. With all the fortitude that I possessed, I greeted Hermann with a smile and Otto with a hug, hoping that movement would mask the trembling in my limbs and the quaver in my voice.

Hermann had liked Astor House and had already met the hotel's manager. "What a small world, Frida! He is also from Hesse!" He wanted me to see it before registering.

We woke Fritz, and I took both boys to the washstand to clean them. There wasn't much to be done about their wrinkled clothing, but the Negro girl had left a pile of clean cloths and a pitcher of warm water. I started on Otto and gently rubbed him clean – ears, neck, face and hands. With my fingers, I dampened his fine dark hair and arranged it as best I could without a comb. While he straightened his own socks and tucked in his shirt, I did the same for Fritz, using another clean cloth for him.

Together we walked down the street. I held one hand of each of my sons and realized that my trembling had subsided.

Astor House was new and was quite the most remarkable building I had ever been in. I am sure it was as large as a palace; certainly it was larger than any building I had seen. On the first floor were several dining rooms, a bar, and many reception rooms, appointed in silks of every hue. The manager escorted us up the grand staircase to the second floor where Hermann had rented rooms for us. To my astonishment I found my dear piano, without a scratch, positioned between tall windows that overlooked Broadway, and on it was a basin of asters - red, orange, and purple. We would have three rooms, a parlor and two ample bedrooms. I agreed to Hermann's choice.

Our parlor was furnished with fine pieces and a fire was set in the grate, ready to be lit. Our bedrooms, like the parlor, were high ceilinged with crystal chandeliers hung from carved moldings. The boys' bedroom opened onto a piazza that ran the entire length of the building. These quarters were such a comfort after the hard pavements of this inhospitable city, where there was not a single flower in bloom, not a familiar landscape, building or face, that all four of us fell into the commodious chairs in relief.

We didn't know then that the Astor House would be our home for the next ten years. We would leave for the new California El Dorado from under its ample marble portico on a damp, gray afternoon in 1849.

Chapter 9

New York seemed nothing more than a giant marketplace. Commodities arrived in the city by one conveyance or another, were repacked, and shipped out again by another. Meanwhile, people arrived from everywhere: Europe, the southern states, and some from South America. If they were lucky they found employment within this confusing trading environment. If they were less lucky, they joined the throng of wanderers, who, on the verge of destitution and starvation, would do any work for any small relief. If they were not lucky at all, they begged.

The piers, warehouses, markets and stations were the palaces of New York, and its princes were those men who controlled the trade of goods, not those who packed and carried. Within a month, Hermann had met many of them, and by Christmas we were regular guests at Dr. Cheesman's house on Broadway where we met the Greasons, Russell Isaacs, the Tallmadges, and young Miss Gardiner of Long Island.

At one such dinner, Mr. Isaacs was my dinner partner. He spoke a little German, for which I was grateful. We attempted to discuss the excellent rabbit *ragoût* and vegetables *Provençale*, but the language did not come easily for him, and when dinner was over, he was glad, I think, to turn me over to Miss Gardiner. She linked her arm in mine, and we joined the other ladies in the fine parlor. She was younger that I by ten years at least and exceedingly poised and charming. Although we could not communicate in words, we both made every effort. She admired my dress and shoes; I admired hers and remarked on her locket, indicating that I wondered what was inside. I expected to see a portrait of a loved one, perhaps a *beau*. Instead, when she pried it open, I saw a miniature landscape of a beautiful house and garden with a path to a dock in the foreground. I indicated that I wondered where the actual scene was to be found.

She laughed, as though I should know, and began to explain. I nodded and smiled, but in truth the only word I understood was "dog." She squeezed my hand and signified that I should wait there a moment. She returned with the Cheesman's German-speaking housemaid, who translated for me that her family lived on an island that they had purchased from the Indians for some blankets, ammunition, and one large black dog! Graciously she invited me to visit sometime during the summer with my family. When the ladies reclaimed Miss Gardiner to make a fourth at cards, I continued talking with the housemaid, glad to have a companion. Later, when the men joined us, Hermann was horrified and pleaded the late hour to whisk me out of the room and home.

I was unused to the life that I came to lead in New York. It was evident that renting a house in New York would cost more than boarding at the Astor House, and we determined to stay there. I had no domestic duties beyond seeing to the good health and welfare of my husband and sons. With the boys in school and Hermann usually out, I had time on my hands, and other than needlework, piano, and reading, I had not enough to keep me occupied. At home I had been a hard worker, keeping a garden and fowl, cleaning, cooking, shopping; simultaneously having time for my friends and working with poor women and their children. I was strong then; when I looked in the glass, I saw a young woman with color in her cheeks and strong muscles. During that first winter in New York, when I looked in the mirror, I saw a thin pale face reflected back at me, and I wondered if my very blood had slowed in its circulation.

As I became bolder and more familiar with our neighborhood, I ventured forth to see the city, one block at a time, always retracing my steps exactly, afraid of getting lost. I wrote out a few phrases, which I carried in my bag, but in truth I was shy about speaking any English, and hoped not to use them:

Ich kann nicht gut Englisch sprechen
I cannot speak English well

Ich habe mich verlaufen
I am lost

Wo ist Astor House?
Where is Astor House?

There were other families living in the Astor House; many had come from Prussia, and I met the women and some became my friends. As soon as our closeness would ripen, however, they would move to another section of the city or another part of America. My heart would break each time I said good-bye to another friend.

Even though Otto and Fritz went to a school nearby taught in German, they began picking up English almost immediately. One afternoon in January when I opened our front windows to clear the smoke from our parlor, I saw Otto run out the front door with his ice skates over his shoulder. He joined a small group of boys, and while I watched, I saw one of them throw a snowball at a very fat lady with a baby in her arms. It wasn't Otto who threw the missile, but, with the others, he laughed and called out to the woman a word in English as she brushed herself off and picked up the satchel she had carried in her free hand. When I asked him about it that night, he claimed he was scolding the boy who threw the snowball. I knew my son was lying to me and that he was being changed by this new city and its ways; I also knew that I was unable to confront him with the truth, as I had not learned the language and knew not what he had called. "*Ach! Jungen!*" said Hermann, when I told him the story that night as we lay in our bed, "Otto's a good boy, Frida, don't make him into a Mama's boy."

I lay awake that night in worry, as I had aboard *Maria*, but this night I didn't worry about weather. What else did I have but my family? I had to hold us together. If I lost the smallest thread of connection to these boys whom I loved with all my heart and who were, with Hermann, the only thread of memory to our old lives, what would become of me? The day we drove away through our old garden gate and crossed the fields to begin our new life, I knew the one thing that would sustain me would be our family's closeness. I could envision Hermann's dream for our sons to be strong, productive citizens of America. And, I could imagine us all together at a dinner table in America or playing a game on the rug, remembering our friends from Giessen, perhaps reading a letter from home.

Instead, after only a few months, I found myself yearning for home and for ways to occupy myself, while my boys began to fit into this new community and my husband made new connections while planning for our financial well being. I was frightened of our separateness and recognized in myself a new lethargy. I had a set place at home; here I had none. I was invited out with my husband some evenings, and enjoyed the melodies played on home pianos. Without English, though, I could not join the discussions at those *soirées*, and the women did not invite me on my own. Somehow Hermann was picking up English and seemed to understand it quite well. I promised myself that I would take lessons as soon as Hermann found employment and we had a steady income.

Some days I sat by the window for hours, listening to the sounds of the city, and wondering what caused them. At home I knew the source of every noise of the village. Some years earlier in Giessen I had a small white goat. She stayed near the house and didn't need to be tethered. When strangers came by she would bleat loudly until they passed, but when my dear friend Antonia came to visit, my goat, knowing that Antonia would bring her a turnip, would trot up to my kitchen door, and I would hear the clicking of her hooves on the cobble stones there, announcing Antonia's arrival, long before the knock on the door.

It was only when Adolph came to our rescue once again that my life in New York began to take any shape of its own. Adolph's wife, Anna, had been pregnant with their third child when he left for his trip to Germany. Upon his return, he found her bedridden, warned by her doctor to stay in bed until the child was born or risk losing it. For that reason, we saw nothing of Adolph and did not meet his wife or family until February when we were all invited for a Sunday dinner and to see the new baby and meet the family.

As it was a clear day, we determined to walk to their home on Liberty Street, and all dressed in our boots and warmest clothing. Upon turning into their street, I could not have been more surprised. On both sides were shops and other establishments with signs advertising their wares: shoes, leather, dry goods, silk goods, parasols and umbrellas, Osgood's wholesale clothing, and others. Hermann sent Fritz ahead to find number fifty-five. We entered a plain door next to Comstock & Andrews, purveyor of straw and silk bonnets, and walked up a dark flight of stairs. I had walked about New York enough to have seen that the commercial establishments had apartments above, but I had not thought what it must be like to live there. Adolph answered our knock and invited us in. It took us a while to disencumber ourselves of our cloaks and scarves, before entering the parlor. I had never seen a finer place. Satin draperies – sunflower yellow - hung at the windows and divided the parlor from what I supposed was a dining room. The wallpaper was French, and the walls were hung with fine paintings. The two older children sat together on a piano bench and practiced a Chopin *rondo* with four hands. Anna rose to greet us with a warm smile, "*Willkommen!*" She held out both hands to me, and the warmth of her heart and her home flowed into my tired body and soul as warm molasses onto snow.

I had brought a blanket I had embroidered for the new baby, and within minutes, with our heads bowed over the blue and yellow pattern, she and I were as friends. Fritz and their daughters, Clara and Duda, ran upstairs to play; Otto was engaged with a sketch book of New York sites; Adolph and Hermann laughed over something while pouring sherry. I felt utterly at home for the first time in New York. A door opened and a uniformed nurse brought in the baby. Anna asked me to hold him while she went to ensure that all was well with dinner. I took her place by the window, noting that it had begun to snow, and that the street scene below looked quite pretty. Baby Willem stared up at my face and, with his small fist waving in the air, caught my first tear.

Chapter 10

As I look back and evaluate our years in New York, I realize that we got our bearings that Sunday in Adolph and Anna's parlor. Until then, I awoke every morning with a dull sensation of unease. It was physical: sometimes a headache, other times a heavy feeling in my limbs. Once I felt something in my heart, as though it were shriveling. I believe it was because I had no tasks or responsibilities. Sometimes I wished to be ill, since at least that would be more remarkable than idleness.

Adolph promised to introduce Hermann the very next day to Mr. Hammacher from Holland, to discuss the importation of linen from Hermann's family's mills in Prussia. He and Adolph also talked again about the starting a private police force in New York. Anna and I made plans to take the children to the park the next weekend, and she told me about a neighborhood center where she worked one morning each work and invited me to come to observe.

Fritz went home with a stack of books in German, loaned to him by Clara; Otto had a broadside from Adolph about a gymnasium where "strong minds were encouraged in strong bodies." It was open on Sundays, when, because of the emphasis on church and family, most places in New York were closed. It offered activities for boys six years and older. When we got back to our rooms that night and I told the boys about going to the park the next weekend, they begged to go on Saturday afternoon, after school, so that they could investigate the gymnasium on Sunday; of course, I agreed. Hermann surprised us all by offering to teach the boys a card game before they went to bed. I sat at my piano, listening to their laughter and quietly played some of Schubert's lighter songs.

That week marked the start of happier days for all of us. Hermann was gone each day and some evenings. When he was home, he was filled with enthusiasm for the people he had met. One night the boys begged to be excused early from dinner to complete a game, and he and I lingered over dinner and then took our coffee in one of the small parlors in the Astor House. He told me about his plans to import linen as well as other fabrics from Eurpe and the East. Mr. Hammacher had known the van den Bosch family in Amsterdam and had corresponded many times with Jan van den Bosch in Indonesia. He believed van den Bosch's connections in the East could benefit in the importation of silks and cottons.

"Frida, Hammacher and I are talking about becoming equal partners. I would negotiate with suppliers and government agencies to import fabrics. Hammacher would warehouse the goods in New York and arrange wholesale distribution or retail sales. I have told him I would draw up a contract for his review. There is much to consider; I confess, I am having trouble getting started."

"Why don't you borrow a paper and pen from the front desk? I could help you."

Hermann took notes while I made suggestions. I recommended that the first section of the contract would declare that Hermann take all the risks involved in importing the fabrics. He would buy the goods at his own expense, pay for transport, and arrange for shipping insurance where necessary.

I suggested that the second section state that once the merchandise arrived in the warehouse in New York, it would become Mr. Hammacher's full responsibility. He would cover the cost of storage and all charges relating to sales and distribution.

The last part of the contract would state that they split the profits equally.

"It's good – a good contract! I would not have made it so simple. Hammacher will agree to this, I'm sure," said Hermann.

Hermann put his arm around my waist on our way up the stairs that night, and said, "Frida, we are good partners. I know this has been a hard time for you – a shock, in fact – leaving our familiar village and coming here. You have probably wondered if you would ever be happy, really happy again. My promise to you is that we will work together to be useful in this community. I will be prosperous, our sons will flourish, and you, my lovely wife, will have friends and will work to bring the best of our homeland to this city." He kissed me at the top of the stairs, and it was quite unlike that first stiff, bruising kiss of many years earlier.

To our surprise, Otto and Fritz had put their game away and themselves to bed. "*Ein klein Schnaps, Schwartzi*?" he asked, and I agreed.

Hermann was tender that night. He led me by the hand into our bedroom where only one candle was lit. We stood together before the cheval glass. Hermann looked over my shoulder while slowly unbuttoning my dress. As he removed it and worked awkwardly at my laces, he spoke in a voice so quiet I had to strain to hear him even in that quiet room. "I am a lucky man, Frida, to have you."

By the flicker of the candle, I saw myself, glowing, in chemise only - my petticoats and corset in a jumble at my feet. Hermann was flushed too; his leather boots, trousers and vest at his own feet. He kissed me again more hungrily this time, as though devouring me. His arousal was obvious to me, and he moaned as he caressed my shoulders and back.

"Will you blow out the candle?" I whispered, and he did, and took me to bed. Twice that night we made love. As long as I live, I will remember that. Hermann's lust was loving, and he aroused me slowly with his large hands, gently as never before. When my culminating moment was the same as his, I cried, tears flowing into my hair; we both knew these were good tears of relief and joy. This was a new beginning. We slept entwined, and the next day Fritz and Otto, aware that something was going on but not knowing what, kept their eyes on us and behaved themselves throughout the day, even remembering to put away their playthings.

Chapter 11

Now our days passed more quickly. My sons were doing well in school, and going to the gymnasium most afternoons. Otto was tall for his age, his length being in his legs. He liked working out on the rings and on the pommel horse. In no time he could effortlessly perform undercuts on both sides.

Fritz went to the gymnasium too. He liked the group exercises; but, reading was his favorite activity. For a six-year old, he was a good reader. Usually he liked me to read stories aloud to him the first time. Then he would sit by the window, usually on the floor, reading them over again. At night when I would put them both to bed, Fritz would sometimes ask to tell a story to Otto and me. He liked to blend the tales he had read – to take characters from a pirate tale, for instance, and introduce them to the Bremer Town musicians.

When I asked him how he would like to celebrate his seventh birthday, he said he'd like to have Otto and Clara and Duda be in a play that he would write.

Will you make the costumes, *Mutti*? I'll tell you what I'll need."

I agreed, and the next day he handed me written instructions – most of which were drawings – as follows:

2 pirate hats	2 sets of wings
2 eye patches	1 ermine cloak
2 swords	2 crowns
1 parrot	1 alligator head
1 beard	1 beautiful lady's dress

On his birthday Adolph and Anna and their children joined us for a festive lunch. The children could hardly wait to get upstairs. We were instructed to come up in a half hour, which gave us a chance for *ein schnapps*. The play, "Bluebeard and the Princess and the Scary Alligator," was a jumble of leaping, dancing, swashbuckling, murder, and mayhem. I'm not sure who won or lost, but at the end, the children were flushed and happy, the adults were worn out from laughing, and we all went downstairs for ice cream.

I stopped worrying about how this city was influencing the boys. Even though the newspapers were full of stories of the Bowery B'hoys and other gangs, of gambling and prostitution, our lives took on an agreeable routine.

I began going to the neighborhood center with Anna. She liked being with the children while their parents were otherwise occupied. At first I sat on a bench by the door observing, feeling shy and awkward, knowing so few words of English. One afternoon an older woman, with gray hair severely pulled to the back of her head and secured under a tight cap, was nearly overwhelmed cleaning some little ones at the basin. She brought over a howling baby and a warm damp cloth and dry towel, and dumped the lot in my lap, giving me an encouraging pat on the shoulder. I had brought some hard biscuits in my pocket, and as I stripped off the baby's dirty clothes and diaper, she soothed herself with the biscuit. I found clean clothes for the baby in a hamper. When her mother came back to pick her up, she could hardly recognize her own daughter.

When the first shipment of linens arrived in New York, Adolph and Anna and the Hammacher family joined us at the Astor House for a celebration. The kitchen served us *Pfefferpotthast* with warm *pumpernickel* bread and a *Dortmund bier* and cider for the children. Kees and Rosa Hammacher had four children – three boys and a girl, all older than ours, but the children large and small enjoyed each other. We were all quite amazed that their children, who spoke Dutch at home, also spoke German and English. Anna had brought along her baby nurse, who took all the children to our apartment after our lunch, leaving the adults to enjoy each other long into the afternoon. Rosa gave me the name of her seamstress, for which I was glad, since our clothes from home were showing wear, and the boys' were straining at the seams.

Adolph and Hermann engaged Kees in their deliberation about a private police force for New York. Kees had several stories of his own of local constables ignoring crimes in order to make money by collecting debts or foreclosing on mortgages. He told one story of having to offer a reward to a night watchman if he would catch the person who was climbing his wall and stealing the clean clothes drying on the line.

"*Mein Gott!* Isn't that what he was being paid to do! A reward too – ridiculous!" said Hermann.

The three men determined to engage other like-minded neighbors in their cause. When I asked Hermann if I could join the group, he turned to me and said sharply he would talk to me about it later.

When our guests left, he told me never again to involve myself in his affairs in front of others. Further, the police force idea was for men to work out. He preferred that I work with Anna at Assembly House, the neighborhood center. That night, for the first time, Hermann went to the hotel bar. I went upstairs, read with the boys, and then we three went to bed without a *schläft gut* from Hermann.

I wished that I had argued with him that night, persuaded him to include me and other women in this newly forming committee. I believe that my influence might have induced a less provocative outcome. But I had become complacent around my husband, now that I was content in my own activities. I was eager to keep peace between us. I had gone several times to the neighborhood center and was enjoying my work there. The work of the center was necessary because of the lawless situation prevailing in New York – the same problem that the men were confronting in their own way.

Most of the families who came to Assembly House were there because of the street violence. Some of the families had no head of household at all, their men having been senselessly murdered during the terrible riots of a few years earlier. Others were destitute because of drunken brawls or robberies, which had left the men lamed and unable to work. Assembly House provided one meal each day to these families as well as occupational training to the men, women and older children. Men and boys learned masonry and woodworking. Women and girls could take cooking and sewing lessons so that they could get work in kitchens or as seamstresses, in order to stay off the streets. The paid staff at Assembly House helped find jobs for those who were ready. The volunteer staff helped with childcare and meals, and there was a group forming who wanted to offer lessons in music, the arts, and most important, in speaking and reading English, as many of the clients came to Assembly House without that ability. I was asked to teach a music class to children and to consider directing an adult singing group. While I planned how to accomplish these classes, still speaking little English, I worked in the kitchen, learning to stretch the donated food as far as possible. One cabbage, with the addition of a potato for thickening, could make a soup for twenty-five people.

It was at Assembly House that I began to pick up a few English words. The first ones I learned were those that had no easy translation into German. For instance, the mothers did not want their daughters to become "good-time girls," and didn't want their sons to be "roughs."

One day I was asked to go with a committee of three others to Mulberry Bend to talk with the women in that neighborhood about starting a community house like Assembly. They wanted a German speaker along. It was there on Worth Street I saw my first street fight.

In front of a polling place two large groups of roughs were yelling and threatening each other with swords, tools, and bats. As we approached a rock was thrown from somewhere in the crowd, and both sides roared and fell upon each other.

When our leader, Mrs. Louwen, saw the scuffle, she ordered our driver to turn around, but already we were surrounded. One brute, with fists as big as cabbages, grabbed our driver by his jacket and threw the man aside with the same ease I would use to toss out the weeds from my garden at home. The driver ran down an alley, and we did not see him again.

A group of seven or eight men took our horse out of harness and began rocking our carriage to turn it over. All of them were huge and strong and looked ferocious, but also despairing, and for a moment I wondered why. Two had chains wrapped round their fists, and all were grunting as they tried to tip us over while at the same time fighting off a group in black shirts, who were hitting them with sticks and ropes. "You have no business here," I heard someone scream. "Get out! Go home!" was the outcry. Was it directed at us? I wasn't sure. One of the men thrust his head into our carriage. The red stubble on his cheeks and chin was flecked with spit, and he bared his teeth and snarled like a mastiff on a chain.

Another man was hit on the side of his head by a shovel, and his cheek was laid open from ear to chin. His blood splattered across our front window, momentarily blocking our view down the street where a crowd was gathering to encourage and cheer on the gang members. The man turned and caught the shovel wielder, grabbing him with both hands. With blood flowing freely over his face and neck, he bit off his foe's ear, and spit it to the gutter, both men bellowing in pain and rage.

The three other women clung together in the carriage, screaming. I was nearest to the door to the carriage and stood up, bracing myself with arms and legs. I spoke in as calm a voice as I could to the crowd. I said that we were from another neighborhood, that we'd come to meet some of their neighbors in a nearby church. Hearing German or perhaps seeing only women, or maybe it was my tone, caused the men to hesitate. In that moment I grabbed the arm of the woman next to me, and jumped from the carriage. The others followed and we ran down an unfamiliar street. No one chased us, and, even though we could hear the battle behind us, we stopped under the sign of a cigar maker to catch our breaths. All of us clung together, wild-eyed and trembling with fear. Mrs. Louwen was gagging from the stench of the streets, and another woman gave her a camphor-soaked handkerchief. I had lost a shoe and my stocking was tattered. I pulled it off.

"How do we get out of here? How do we get home?" No one knew the direction we should take to find our own neighborhood, but I remembered that the afternoon sun had been behind us as we made our way to Mulberry Bend and urged everyone to follow me toward the sun, and in that way we made our way back to familiar territory, disheveled, tired, and relieved.

"Frida, you are our savior!" said one woman.

"Without you, we would be back there in the gutters, bleeding, or worse," said another.

I believed her. No one in Mulberry Bend would have come to our aid. We had to save ourselves. I was proud I had taken control.

At dinner that night, I told my family what had happened, warning Hermann and the boys away from that part of the city.

"Weren't you scared, *Mutter*?" Otto asked.

I admitted that I was scared. "But, I also felt quite strong leading the other women back here."

"Did it remind you of the storm at sea?" asked Fritz.

I knew what he meant; I felt that combination of alarm and exhilaration. I knew my cheeks were flushed from the excitement.

"There, Frida," said Hermann. "You see, this police force idea I have been talking about is a good idea. This is a lawless city. You were in Five Points, the neighborhood of some of the worst gangs: the Bowery B'hoys, the Plug Uglies, and the Dead Rabbits. They fight over votes, and no one dares to stop them. Even the newspapers seem to encourage them with their lurid coverage. You are lucky to be alive and lucky not to have been robbed on your walk home. This is not just drunkenness; it's much worse."

I regretted telling the story of this incident to Hermann. I knew not to expect sympathy from him, but I did not expect that the next day he and several other men in the Astor House and in our nearby neighborhood would begin patrolling our streets at night. Within a month he hired forty young men and begun training them in fisticuffs and in the use of arms. In another month he had signed up paid subscribers from the homes and businesses in our neighborhood. Hermann and a few of the other men, including Adolph and Kees appointed themselves Captains, and took turns going out with the men at night.

Chapter 12

The pace of our lives picked up then, as did the success of Reinhardt, Hammacher and Company, and did not slow down for several years until April first, 1849 after we had left New York and made our way to Pittsburgh where we boarded a steamer. By then we were citizens of America who had taken the oath and proudly received our certificates. We spoke English well, although in the family, we continued to speak German. We were confident and were as engaged in the building of a new country as were all the rest leaving for California.

Otto was in his last year of school when we left New York; he spent his evenings working in the police force office, begging to go on patrols with the men. Sundays he and his friends promenaded on Broadway admiring the girls. He told Hermann that he wanted to become a *crusher*.

"A what?" I heard Hermann ask him.

"A policeman, Father. I've been studying the ways of the pickpockets and groaners. At my age I can infiltrate the roughs and identify their leaders."

"No! Listen to me! You will study at a university and then enter the family business. Perhaps you will be the one to expand sales westward. I will hear of nothing else. Policeman! *Ach, verboten!*"

Meanwhile Fritz at sixteen had read and reread all my favorite books in German as well as James Fenimore Cooper, Washington Irving, Charles Dickens, and many others in English. As sections of Nicholas Biddle's *History of the Expedition Under the Command of Captains Lewis and Clark* had been reprinted in a local weekly, Fritz had cut them out and made a scrapbook for himself. He also kept a self-drawn map of North America on the wall of the room he shared with Otto, and on it, he plotted Lewis and Clark's travels from St. Louis westward. In tiny handwriting, he wrote a shorthand version of their trip on the map, for instance: "041305 bflo & br trks," was written just west of Fort Mandan. When I asked him what that meant, he gave me a withering look: "April 13, '05, buffalo and bear tracks. Isn't it obvious?"

Most of his friends were boys who had crossed the Atlantic to New York just as he had, and their favorite activity was playing ship's captain out on the *piazza* in all weather. On the foulest days they would surge back into our rooms, flushed with adventure and often drenched from rain or snow. Occasionally, they would play inside, plotting adventures across the American West. For a while, after reading *The Pioneers*, Fritz toyed with the idea of changing his name to *Bumppo*! He had caught the excitement of western expansion, as Hermann had. Hermann, of course, was interested in the fortune awaiting in California, while Fritz was attracted by the adventure of traveling across the country, meeting Indians, dispatching wild beasts, and sleeping under the stars.

His best friend was Charles Kramer, and through the boys' friendship, Hermann met his father Carl Kramer, as well as Carl's neighbors, Hans-Jürgen Topp, Albrecht Brantlach, and Robert Aulich. These families had all come from Prussia more recently than we had, and all were still finding their way in America.

Robert Aulich had been a choirmaster before coming to New York to work in his brother-in-law's brewery. The first time I met him, he told me that at least half of the baggage he had brought from home was sheet music. "I could not risk that it might not be available in New York," he said. He was only twenty-four then, but he looked much older. He had a way of covering one ear with his hand and tilting his head as though straining to hear only the perfect notes. He was short and overweight and would rock up onto his toes to accentuate a point.

"Do you sing?" he asked me.

"I do sing," I answered, "but I prefer to play piano."

"Aha!" he said, rising toward me onto his toes. "I will remember that!."

Hermann had been extremely successful in his import business. Not only was he importing all the linen that his family in Prussia could provide, but also cottons from England and Indonesia and silks from Canton and Shanghai. He even imported *organzine* from Canton for a mill in Connecticut, and he went there several times to confer on weaving methods. Once I went to Connecticut with him and was astounded at how much like home it seemed. The hills and river valleys were like Giessen. The churches and homes were mostly wood, but were laid out as ours had been. I mentioned to Hermann that it seemed so clean and safe, compared to New York City.

"And dull," he answered.

Chapter 13

It had taken me longer than Hermann and the boys to settle myself in New York, but with Anna's help, I met other women. I never gave up my work at Assembly House, but with my new friends I also began a social life quite unlike any I had experienced at home. I met with a group weekly to discuss books. It was very hard for me in the beginning, since we read American authors and occasionally Europeans, but always in English translation. I don't think I added one single thought or word to the discussions for the first six months! Then, as though overnight, English became my language. Later, when someone would ask me who had taught me to speak English, I would answer, "James Fenimore Cooper, Henry Wadsworth Longfellow, and Edgar Allen Poe!" It was true; in fact, I think Longfellow and Poe and other poets were my best teachers. In order to find the meaning in their words, I had to first unravel the language. My vocabulary blossomed, and I slowly discovered the fascinating nuances of the idiom and the effect of clear speaking and writing.

On the first anniversary of my joining the literary group, I introduced the group to Poe's *The Fall of the House of Usher*. It was our custom that the presenter would stand before the group. Nervously I stood and, referring to my notes, reminded my listeners about Poe's life and works. Then I excused myself for a moment, and when I returned to the room, I had wrapped myself in a shroud like garment. I told the mysterious story from Madeline's point of view, as though she were telling the story to her twin. I became so caught up in my own small drama that I did not once silently translate a German word into English. My friends stood and clapped after I invoked the final scene in the moonlight and then collapsed to the floor, hidden by my shroud. Anna helped me to my feet and embraced me. The rest gathered around and congratulated me profusely. I felt genuine happiness, coming from recognition but mostly from my own small personal success.

"This performance of Frida's gives me an idea!" called out one of the ladies. "I propose that we expand our purpose. Let's continue to meet once a week to discuss our readings, but let's meet a second time to investigate New York. "We'll go to theater and to dance."

"I've never been to Brooklyn," said someone else.

"And music, paintings, and lectures," I added.

"You plan our first outing, Frida, will you? Asked our chairwoman, Mrs. Land.

I couldn't refuse and suggested the National Academy of Design. I'd heard that many of Mr. Cole's paintings of the Hudson River Valley and the Catskills were there, and I'd wanted to go myself. In fact, I had asked Hermann to take me a week earlier.

"No time, no time," he answered.

Six women went on this first excursion. We spent an hour viewing Mr. Cole's *The Voyage of Life* series, and were fortunate in having a student explain it to us. He thought it was quite a sentimental, romantic group of paintings, but I knew about romantic paintings and argued that I thought Cole was less sentimental and more dignified than some of the other paintings displayed, especially the Doughty's. The Academy had chromolithographs of Cole's work for sale, and I bought one as a gift for Fritz. The other women told me they were very impressed with my understanding of art. Mrs. Land asked if I would consider being in charge of our non-literary outings.

"There is so much I want to see in New York!" I exclaimed. "It would be fun for me to plan trips, but I'm afraid I would run out of ideas. Perhaps Mrs. Topp would be willing to work with me?" Kalli Topp was a neighbor. I had met her several times on the street with her husband, Hans-Jürgen Topp, one of Carl Kramer's friends. I knew she wrote poetry and was determined to have something published.

She agreed. "Let's give ourselves a name," she suggested. "What do you think of the Literary Adventure Group?"

"Do you mean L.A.G?" laughed another lady.

"As long as L.A.G. means linger; as long as it indicates that we take our time over our adventures, then I agree," I said.

"Oh, Frida! You understand English better than any of us! Said Mrs. Land. "L.A.G. we'll be!"

Over the years, with these same friends, I investigated most of New York. With them I crossed on the ferry to Brooklyn for the first time and saw the Chinese junk, *Keying,* when it first came into New York harbor and tied up at The Battery. I browsed the collections at the Gallery of the Fine Arts and the American Art Union. I went many times to the Broadway Tabernacle and Niblo's Garden for exhibitions and lectures. I read everything that was published, from Dostoevsky's *Poor Folk* to Edward Lear's *Book of Nonsense*.

At the Tabernacle in the winter of 1846 with Kalli Topp, I attended my first anti-slavery rally. When I told Hermann what I had learned there about the potential spread of this immoral practice to the new territories and that I wanted to take an active role in that movement, he agreed; although I knew it was not because he particularly supported the movement, but that he was too distracted by his own activities to give it much thought.

Hermann was agreeable during these years – agreeable and distant. He never had time to accompany me to hear music or see plays. When I bought chromolithographs of the other three paintings of Cole's *The Voyage of Life* and hung them on the wall opposite our bed, he did not even notice. One night as we prepared for bed, I decided to tease him. "That picture in the middle is a little crooked, do you see? Would you mind straightening it?" I asked.

"*Ja, Ja*! There it is. Better?"

I couldn't muffle my laughter, and he asked me its cause. When I told him, he said, "You are a silly woman! What do I care about your frivolous purchases!" and blew out the lamp.

My involvement in the anti-slavery movement was curtailed however, as that same month, to my great surprise and pleasure, I discovered that I was pregnant. I was thirty-seven years old, quite past the time to have children. I told Anna before I told Hermann, as she dropped by unexpectedly one afternoon at our Astor House apartment. She found me disheveled, my hair in disarray, my apron soiled; but she was a good friend, and I didn't mind. She saw past my disorder, "Frida, something is on your mind. Is everything all right?"

Her compassion and sensitivity opened my heart. I clutched at her hand, and began to sob.

"What is this?" she said, drawing me into her embrace.

"They are good tears," I managed between cries, and with that my wails turned to laughter, and my streaked face, glimpsed in the mirror above her shoulder, was both blotched and radiant.

"Frida, you're pregnant, aren't you?"

We both started to laugh and to sway. When Otto, age 15, walked in a few minutes later, he found us dancing uproariously in our stocking feet under the solemn gaze of our ancestors' portraits.

"*Wie geht es Ihnen, Frau Spies*?" he asked, but I knew he was really asking me, "What on earth is going on? Have you gone mad?"

"Later, Otto, I'll tell you later. Just forget these two foolish ladies."

Chapter 14

A week passed before I told Hermann the news. We had a rare night out with friends at Niblo's to drink some beer and hear music. We hadn't been out together in a long time, and I was looking forward to it. But I wasn't feeling well and I became nauseous from the smell of spilled beer. I begged Hermann to take me home early. He was tired that night and didn't argue with me, but suggested we walk home. It was cold and clear; the streets were relatively quiet, and the occasional gaslights gave us enough light. I took Hermann's arm, and we matched our strides as though we were skating together on the pond back home. We were quite breathless and rosy when we entered the Astor House; on the way up the stairs Hermann put his arm around my waist, as he had years earlier. I was always thrilled by his touch and wished I could encourage more open affection from him. Impulsively, I turned on the landing and kissed him. "*Schwartzi*! What's this? *Ich kann dich nicht verstehen!*"

And that's where I told him that I was pregnant – right on the landing of the Astor House, in full view and hearing of the night manager. I don't know who was more surprised; possibly it was me at letting the news burst out in a public place. But it was Hermann's reaction that I'll never forget. He kept his arms around me, but dropped down one step and laid his head on my chest. When he lifted his face he was smiling and crying, a sight I'd never seen before and thought that I would never see again.

"*Liebchen, Liebchen*!" What great news this is! What a wife I have, what a wonderful wife! It will be a girl, I know it, as sweet and smart as Adolph and Anna's girls."

Hermann had always loved Clara and Duda. When they were little girls, he would let them sit on his knees, styling his hair and beard with their combs. It was such an unusual gentle sight, so unlike Hermann, that none of us ever talked of it for fear of making him self-conscious with them. Now that they were teenagers, he brought them gifts of ribbons and fabrics that he got from various suppliers; in turn they kissed and hugged him. I too thought this baby would be a girl, and I thought Hermann would be a good father to her.

After a few months, I noticed Otto and Fritz whispering together one Sunday morning after breakfast. When I asked what their secret was, Otto blurted out, "We think you're getting fat, *Mutter*! You'd better come to the gymnasium with us this afternoon!"

I told Hermann about their suspicion; he suggested we take them on an outing later in the afternoon to celebrate the news of the upcoming baby. We took a carriage down to The Battery and carried with us an evening picnic of cold meats, cheeses, and fruit that the Astor House kitchen packed for us. Ships and boats of all sizes and descriptions were in the harbor: sailing ships, steam ships, rowboats, punts. We were all reminded of the moment we entered the harbor almost seven years earlier. It wasn't quite warm enough to sit for long on a bench, so we walked about, Hermann carrying the picnic basket.

"You tell them," I nudged Hermann.

He spread our picnic rug on the grass. "Otto, Fritz, come here. Sit with us."

They had been kicking a ball back and forth, and both were flushed and radiant with warmth. For a scant moment I wished that this new baby would be another boy.

When they'd settled down, Hermann opened the basket. He reached in for a wrapped package of something, then hesitated and closed the basket. "Boys, you're going to have a baby. I mean a sister. Or brother."

"Your father is trying to tell you that I am pregnant. I am going to have a baby next summer. You will be its big brothers. It will be fun for you."

Otto looked at Fritz, "Do you want to play some more?"

They ran off with their ball, embarrassed more than anything else at the idea of a pregnant mother, and neither mentioned my condition again.

My previous pregnancies had gone well, and this one did too, with the exception of some mild queasiness and a lot of heartburn. When my pregnancy began to show, I stopped going out in the evening, but continued working at Assembly House and attended as many afternoon lectures as I could on the abolitionist movement. I had the chance to meet Reverend Samuel Eli Cornish of Emmanuel Church, as well as several other free black men and women. When I wrote home to my parents about them and the movement, they were astonished and wrote back with many questions about Negroes and slavery in America. "What does their hair and skin feel like? Do they smell as we do? What language do they speak?" asked my mother.

Hermann was worried about my interest in the movement, as the newspapers often called the members seditious and fanatical, but as the newspapers reported the United States government moving to nationalize slavery, I saw it as another way to help people, a logical extension of our interests back in Prussia and my work at Assembly House. I remembered a long-ago conversation with my husband when he envied the choices that the Prussian immigrants from the east had and bemoaned his own tie to his family's business. Freedom from slavery was about freedom of choice; to my thinking, it was the opposite of sedition. It was obedience to the laws of democracy.

Chapter 15

I was dressing one morning to go out to hear the great William Lloyd Garrison speak when my bag of waters broke. As Hermann and the boys had left for work and school, I called downstairs and asked that the hotel send for the midwife. By the time she arrived, my first contractions had subsided, but she stayed with me, and I was glad she did. More powerful contractions began again at midday, and by the time Otto and Fritz came home at four o'clock, their baby sister was swaddled and lying by my side in our big bed. I could sense their relief at seeing a baby instead of a pregnant mother, and both clamored to hold her.

Hermann got in late the evening she was born, after dinner with some business associates. I heard him remove his boots in the parlor, so as not to wake me. I had kept a candle lit by the bed, and he tiptoed forward and met his daughter by candlelight. To my amazement, Hermann was shy with her and reluctant to hold her. "I've forgotten how to be a father to a baby, Frida," he said. We had talked for months about names, determining to call a baby boy Walter. We had not been able to settle on a girl's name, although we had a short list of favored family names. This baby was small, but strong, and she reminded me of my grandmother whom I had loved as a girl. "Can we name her after *grossmutter*?" I suggested.

"Yes, you're right. She will be Lily. Lily Frida Reinhardt."

Those sweet sons of mine never lost interest in their baby sister. Even when she crawled into their room and crumpled their papers or pulled their noses, both were patient and playful. And when she was ten months old and sick with scarlet fever crying piteously day and night from the discomfort and fever, the boys helped me bathe her with cool water and distract her from scratching the ugly rash on her face.

I stayed in bed for a week after Lily was born. A nurse came daily to help care for me and the baby. It was August and hot; I got restless toward the end of the week and wrote letters home to my parents, to Hermann's family, and to Hermann's cousin, Antonia, telling them our happy news. Three months later, in the same post, we received return letters from both my mother and from Antonia. The sad news in one completely mitigated the good news of the other.

My mother wrote:

> By this letter I kiss you and your dear new baby. Your letter came on a day that your father was feeling tired. He read and reread your news, rejoicing, as I did. He was very happy that you had honored his mother by using her name.
>
> He lay down to take a nap after our midday meal, and when I went to check on him two hours later, I found him slumped on the floor next to our bed. Apparently he had tried to get up, but had fallen. I believe that he died quickly and painlessly, as there was no sign of a struggle.
>
> For some time he had been a little weak on his right side. We had not wanted to tell you for fear of worrying you; also, we thought that he was getting stronger. He had experienced a loss of consciousness a few months earlier, during which he was awake, but unable to remember your name or where you lived. He repeatedly asked me about you, but a moment later could not remember my reply. Later that same day, his memory returned and he felt well, so he did not see the doctor.

She described the funeral, with all our friends in Gelsenkirchen there. She told me neighbors were coming over every day, bringing *Suppen, Torten und Kuchens.* I picked up my baby, loveable and damp from sleep, and sobbed into her warm neck until I scared her into joining my cries. Even though I knew I would not see my parents again when we said good-bye seven years earlier, I always knew they were there, worrying about my family and me and somehow watching over us from across the vast ocean. I couldn't bear the reality that my father and I would never again embrace, and that he would never meet his granddaughter, named for his mother. I longed for one more walk with him through the lanes of Gelsenkirchen, one more talk about books or neighbors or crops, and one more laugh over the antics of our rooster. In my childhood, when my mother would scold me for dirtying my skirts or coming in late for a meal, my father would give me a wink and one corner of his mouth would twitch toward a smile. Who would give me a wink now? Who would give one to my daughter? The breadth of my sorrow had no limit, and with the distance and time between my father's death and my knowledge of it, I had no comfort from the rituals of home. Hermann, Otto, and Fritz didn't know how to console me. They were quiet around me, as though I were sick. They didn't ask me about my father or my sorrow, and I kept it all inside of me so as not to burden them. Only Lily listened to my aching heart, as my sobs became her daily lullaby.

The second letter that came that day was from Hermann's cousin, Antonia, and its good news got lost in the grief that overwhelmed me. When Hermann found her letter under the cushion of a chair in the parlor, he reminded me of its contents.

Antonia and her family were coming to New York. Like us seven years ago, they had decided that their life would be better here; and they determined to make the change before their oldest children left home to begin their own lives. They would arrive before Christmas; could we find lodging for them?

I had felt such solidarity with Antonia during my early years in New York through our correspondence. Greetings and news and love had flowed between us in slow, intimate voices in letters sent uncertainly across the sea. As long as I had Antonia and my parents, my strong cord to Prussia could not be cut. After rejoicing over the news that they would come to New York, I became quite touchy and short-tempered with the boys. I wasn't absolutely sure I wanted them to come to New York, but I couldn't express my ambivalence. All I knew was a deep sense of loss; another connection to home would unravel.

There was much to be done to welcome them. With Lily in my arms I combed the streets of the city looking for an apartment large enough and safe enough for Antonia, Erich, their two boys, Jacob and Georg – Otto and Fritz's old friends - and their two younger daughters, born after we had left Prussia. I found a place just behind Columbia College with a view of the river. It was only four blocks from Astor House; I remembered my early days in New York, and I knew Antonia would like being near me.

Meanwhile, Lewis Pease, a minister in Cow Bay - that unfortunate neighborhood of Five Points - had hired Hermann's police force to clean up the groggeries and underground gaming rooms around Worth and Baxter Streets. Hermann and Adolph had gone with the men on a Saturday night in early December 1848. I will be forever thankful that Otto did not go with them, even though he begged to be included. Anna and I waved off our husbands and twenty-five other members of the force as they left for Cow Bay, expecting only to twirl their symbols of authority. I was proud of how they looked, but I didn't understand, and they didn't either, that the gangs had nothing to lose and everything to gain. Another fight, another broken nose, another monotonous wait in a courtroom for another gloomy magistrate – these young toughs had seen it all. Most were recent immigrants, unfamiliar with and indifferent to the local regulations. They'd seen the law avert its eyes before when cards were played and liquor flowed; a well-placed bribe or quick fist would clear the air.

This time was different, according to the report that they put together several days later. The Buckoos from the waterfront, the True Blue Americans from the Bowery, and the Shirt Tails protecting their home turf, were all out with their girls, promenading on the narrow brick sidewalks on the unusually warm winter evening. They found trouble when the girlfriend of one of the Shirt Tails was accused of being a thieving *bludget,* by one of the Buckoos. Dressed in their finest stovepipe hats and silk vests, the gangs went after each other and Hermann's policemen went after them. The True Blues also came into it against the police, and in the mud and decaying garbage of Orange Street, with only clubs to defend themselves, Hermann, Adolph and their troops were split up and ignominiously chased from the neighborhood. Hermann's cheek was cut by a thrown pipe or brick, and Adolph fell into the street where someone's boot crushed his fingers against a paving stone.

I heard Hermann come up the staircase to our rooms and ran to the door. He was covered with blood and reeked of sweat. He wouldn't allow me to minister to him or even to embrace him. I sat on a chair, terrified for him, as he washed himself at the basin. He blurted out the story: "Every one of us was hurt, not just me. The air was full of flying objects – bricks, stones, even bones from the slaughterhouse. I had to drag one of the younger men out of a liming pit where he'd been thrown. Another of our men was tossed down a privy. Not a person came to our defense – not a neighbor or shopkeeper; I looked around me at the filthy cowsheds that the people called home. There were coarse faces in the patched and broken windows, all of them laughing and cheering the fight. That neighborhood can go to hell; it's nothing but saloons, breweries, and fences anyway. The hell with them!"

At that time the New York State Legislature had authorized a professional police force for New York City, and after this defeat at Cow Bay, many of Hermann's men quit to join the professionals. Hermann, Kees, and Adolph, disheartened, dissolved their force.

In spite of his success in business, Hermann's immense pride was deeply wounded by the failure of the police work and he became unusually restless. I was reminded by his mood at that time of our voyage on *Maria*, when Hermann had a new business idea every day. So in 1848 when Mr. Hammacher's eldest son joined the business and proposed to buy Hermann out at a very good price, I was not surprised that Hermann took it as a sign that this was the time to begin thinking seriously of leaving New York City for a new opportunity.

Almost every day the headlines of the *New York Express* and *Herald* trumpted the discovery of gold in California. "GOLD RUSH FEVER," read one, and it was like a fever. It swept through the hearts and hopes of men and women like influenza in a tenement. One article reprinted a letter sent to James Buchanan, Secretary of State in Washington, which said in part: "I have to report… one of the most astonishing excitement now in our country… on the American Fork of the Sacramento and Feather rivers… a vast track of land containing gold…" Another predicted, "A Peruvian harvest of precious metals."

I could not be out on the streets without seeing bills advertising ships like *Hartford* and *Red Jacket* that would take hopeful miners around Cape Horn to California. Others promoted travel companies that would assist New Yorkers wanting to travel overland to the gold fields. I could not sit down to dinner with my family without hearing the news that this man or that one was planning to go. Several long-time employees of Reinhardt, Hammacher were giving their notice.

Hermann was among the many struck with gold fever, the same way he had been struck in Giessen with America fever. He spoke about it in identical terms: "Our future is there, not here; we'll go directly to the Feather River," I heard him tell the boys one day. And when my enthusiasm didn't equal theirs, he said those familiar words to me, "Frida, you're not trying hard enough."

Hermann, Carl Kramer and his neighbors, and Robert Aulich and a few members of the newly-organized German's Men's Choir began meeting to explore how to exploit the riches waiting in California. Because Hermann had been first to adopt the idea, these men chose him as their leader. None of them knew what lay ahead, but they had faith that Hermann would figure it out by dint of his gargantuan enthusiasm.

My enthusiasm and desire were solely for stability for our family and myself. I had already had as much adventure and displacement in my life as I wanted. My husband's aspiration was for wealth and position, but mostly for change and the stimulation of new endeavors. I knew that he would take the boys with him. Both were clamoring to go, wild for the adventure and determined to be the equal of the men. The only way I could keep us all together was to go too.

Chapter 16

We met Antonia and Erich's boat on an icy December day. Antonia was standing near the bow as the *Freiheit* neared the dock. Her cheeks were as pink as I remembered them, and her hair escaped its cap as always. We threw kisses across the narrowing strip of New York harbor. None of us recognized Erich and the boys in their rude country clothes until they came down the gangplank moments later. Otto, Fritz and their cousins were awkward with each other, and I realized how far we had come and how much we had changed. None of them spoke a word of English, and we stayed close to them for the next several weeks as they settled themselves in their apartment, and we all celebrated Christmas in our rooms at Astor House.

"Frida, can't you do something about their clothes and boots?" Hermann said to me one morning. "They embarrass me when they come here to visit us."

"How we have changed in seven years, Hermann! We are now citizens of America, speak English, have many friends, know our way around the city, and are prosperous. Give them time; we were awkward and inept when we came too. You remember?"

"No, Frida. I was not."

Jacob and Georg went with Otto and Fritz when they returned to school in early January. I knew they would be fine and would feel at home here quickly, as my boys had. Antonia and her girls, Mathilde and Marie, spent most of the winter with Lily and me. The girls were seven and eight then; I thought they should be in school too, but Antonia was reluctant to have them leave her sight in this boisterous city.

Erich's country ways embarrassed Hermann; he showed no interest in introducing him to business acquaintances. It was through a connection of mine at Assembly House that Erich found a job driving a beer wagon in Brooklyn. Erich hated that job. He hated having to cross the river each morning and evening by ferry; he hated the heavy lifting of the big barrels; and he missed his farm back home. When Hermann, Carl Kramer, and the other men began talking about California, Erich told them immediately that he too wanted to go.

We were at their apartment for dinner one night when Erich told Antonia of his plans.

"This is your fault, Hermann!" she cried. "You have always had a *wanderlust*, and now we are swept up into your grand folly. I can't move again. I won't!" Antonia had risen from her chair and was standing with arms raised in front of her as if to stop a wild horse. Her legs were apart and firmly planted on the floor. "Erich, I beg you…"

"*Ruhig*, Antonia! Quiet!" yelled Hermann, his spittle flying across the table. "You women, leave us. Go to the kitchen; take the girls! I've told Frida, stay out of men's affairs, and I tell you too. Frida, take Antonia out of here." He made an angry gesture with his right hand, still brandishing his dinner knife.

Antonia knocked over her chair as she turned, scaring Lily, who started to howl. Marie and Mathilde were both whimpering, being unused to yelling. I put my arm around Antonia's waist and guided her out of the dining room.

I am not sure if she ever spoke directly to Hermann again.

Chapter 17

When preparations for our westward trek began in earnest, I was personally fortified by the knowledge that Antonia was going too. She and I had agonized about going with the men. When I tried to talk to Hermann about my concerns, he replied, “Do what you want. The boys and I will go anyway.” The truth was, neither Antonia nor I could imagine being left behind in New York while our husbands and sons left for California on an adventure that had a beginning but no known end. We would not know of their welfare for months at a time; nor would we know when, or if, they would return.

Hermann and the other men had met many nights in our New York parlor making their plans and eventually forming a company. They named it the German New York Company. They agreed that the company would comprise eight wagons, each with four adults. Our family would be one wagon; Erich and Antonia’s family would be another. The rest would be combinations of single men and fathers and sons, as no other women would be making the trip with us. Expenses would be equally shared, with adults owing a full share and children under age fourteen owing a half share. Our family would pay four and one-half shares, which equaled fifteen percent of the total. In California, we would reap the rewards in that same proportion.

The men didn’t have much to guide them in their preparations. Our New York newspapers headlined the gold fields, not the passage there. For the most part, their meetings consisted of drinking beer and spilling it on my tables and eating pretzels and grinding the crumbs into my carpets. The men mostly speculated about the end of the trip: “To the gold ditches!” they would toast; “…to the inexhaustible riches!”

While I could not envisage the trip itself, I could imagine Antonia and me working together to devise meals along the way for our families, to wash clothes in rivers, and to succor each other when necessary.

When one of the New York newspapers began a series called “Travel in the Far West,” and I read about the Great Plains, I began to long for summer days walking near riverbanks, away from the smells and noises of New York City. I could imagine Fritz and Otto with their shirts off in the warm sun, Lily splashing her little feet in a stream, and my hair unpinned and blowing in the wind.

I had a dream one night of Antonia's daughters weaving daisies together into garlands for themselves and Lily. I told Hermann about my dream. He snorted, characteristically, but then he put his arm around me and pulled me snuggly to him. "I can't wait to see the grasses, Frida. I have read that they ripple and surge like the ocean itself. We'll see pheasants and grouse and buffalo! Won't it be amazing to see buffalo herds and to show such a wondrous thing to our children!"

"There are trees there that grow cotton," I told him. "You don't even have to pick it because it floats to the ground in the early summer and you just gather it up. Maybe I can experiment with spinning it into thread; then it will be the next great product for Mr. Hammacher! We will sell him the idea and become even richer."

Hermann laughed until his face was red and blotchy. "No, no, no, no, Frida Cottonhead! *Nicht baumwolle*! A cottonwood tree does not make cotton! You had better experiment with spinning gold into thread; then we will get rich" *Frida Cottonhead* became his playful nickname for me; he only used it when we were alone, and even then, not often.

Chapter 18

Antonia remained hardened against her cousin Hermann for convincing her husband, Erich to uproot her and their family once again. She would not come over to our rooms if she knew he was there. But her reluctance to be left behind goaded her preparations for this trip.

She finally enrolled the girls in school, and, after picking them up one afternoon, she dropped by our rooms. While they tiptoed into Lily's room to wake her from her nap, Antonia began to cry. She leaned her upraised arm against the doorframe and hid her face in the folds of her sleeve, and her whole body convulsed with the sobs that she tried to quiet. I took her free hand in both of mine, and she looked at me with sad wet eyes. For a long moment neither of us spoke. "Frida, how can you do this again?"

"This time we will be together. We will share the chores. We will cook and wash in each other's company. We'll breathe in fresh air and see new things. We'll remember home together. We'll speak German and sing the old songs. If the men go too fast, we will just refuse to cook for them, and they will slow down. It is your company that will give me strength."

The three girls burst into the parlor, not noticing Antonia's wet face. They had draped themselves in sheets, even little Lily, and tied scarves around their heads. They entreated us to sit and watch them perform a fairy dance. Marie loudly hummed a tune that might have been by Mozart, I couldn't quite tell, and they sprang about the room, weaving themselves around the furniture and each other. There was a lot of jumping and toe-pointing, little Lily always two steps behind. At the end, they took our hands, dragged us off our chairs and bade us join them in a circle, which then spun around until all of us landed in a pile of petticoats and laughter in the middle of the carpet.

When we sorted ourselves out, Antonia and I left the girls in the parlor with dolls and books. She and I went into my bedroom

"Antonia, dearest friend, this trip is going to happen, and we need each other. Right now I need you to help me sort through my clothes." I sat her at the foot of the bed, and began hauling trunks and bringing clothes out of the closet.

"We'll make three piles," I said. "The first pile will go to California with us; Hermann tells me not to take too much. The second will be packed away in trunks and stored here at the hotel for our return. The third will be donations for Assembly House."

She had stopped crying and was getting her breath after our frantic fairy dance. She smiled at me warmly. I think we both knew that physical preparations were good antidotes to the dread we both felt about leaving New York on this dubious adventure to California. Already we had made lists of things we would take. Antonia would assemble a collection of cooking pots; no need to take two sets. I would gather medicines and bandage material into a kit for both our families. We couldn't decide how much line to take for drying clothes, so had purchased two lengths of 100 feet each. We didn't know yet whether to take soap or if we would have time to make it along the way, but we would take a little just to be sure. Antonia was a better seamstress than I was, and she volunteered to bring sewing supplies; I promised to go through our large library and bring suitable books for our children's continuing education. We had put off thinking about clothes; today seemed the right time to start.

I flung open my oldest trunk. It had been my mother's when she was a bride. On the top, crushed by the lid, were two straw bonnets with faded ribbons for tying under the chin. I put on one; Antonia the other. She grabbed an apricot-colored silk shawl from a chair back and wrapped it around the waist of her chestnut and plum striped dress like a country apron. Next in the trunk were my old wooden garden clogs. I put them on. Giggling, we threw open the door and performed a flat-footed farmers' dance for the dumbfounded girls. My clogs made so much noise that Lily began to cry. But Marie and Mathilde got the joke, and their laughter settled the little one down. Now they all wanted to be part of the game, so the five of us crowded into the bedroom to begin the choosing process.

"You might need those clogs, Frida," said Antonia with a twinkle in her eye.

"Surely not!" I piled them with the hats on the floor by the door. "They go to Assembly House."

Next out of the trunk were two shawls, homespun, several pairs of cotton stockings, and three shapeless cotton dresses I had worn during my first two pregnancies.

"To Assembly House," cried Marie.

"To Assembly House," we all replied, and I dumped them onto the pile on the floor.

At the bottom of the trunk, carefully wrapped in paper was my mother's wedding gown. I unpacked it carefully, surprised at how brown with age it had become. I buried my nose into its bodice, imagining my mother as a bride and remembering my wedding to Hermann. Antonia's girls became quiet, understanding something about the solemn moment, but Lily tugged at the skirt, wanting to see the whole dress. I shook it free and held it up to myself. My entire audience clapped hands, and I took a few slow waltz steps around the bedroom

"Someday, Lily, you might wear this. It will stay here, safely waiting for that day."

Lily wrinkled her nose at me: "No!" We all laughed, and I handed the gown over to Antonia who folded it lovingly, stuffing the sleeves with rags to hold their shape.

I couldn't bear to leave behind the scarlet silk shawl given me by Hermann's family when we left home and rationalized that I might make use of it during our journey. I had heard that orchestras and dramatic companies had formed in cities like Cincinnati and St. Louis. "This goes to California!" I started another pile.

"Let's be practical; I'll start with shoes." The girls all groaned and left us to go back to their games in the parlor. I lined up my shoes.

"Not the silk slippers," said Antonia.

"Not even one pair?" I moved both my pairs of leather boots to the California pile, then snuck one pair of blue silk slippers next to them.

"Oh, Frida! I suppose you'll take the matching blue gown and robe that you just bought."

"Good idea!" I added them to the pile. The rest of my gowns went into the trunk that would stay behind. "I'm only going to take dark dresses; they won't show the dirt so much. Five should be enough." I picked out dresses that would clean easily.

"Take that brown one," said Antonia.

"*Ach*! I've always hated it. The sleeves are too loose and the dress is old-fashioned. It has never fit right. Look! I spilled coffee on it once and you can still see the stain."

"There will be rainy days, Frida. Take it."

I added new petticoats and chemises, put in a few sachets to keep them smelling sweetly. From hooks in the closet, I gathered two light woolen shawls and one heavy one and added them to the pile.

On the shelf was my jewelry case. I carried it out, shrugging my shoulders at Antonia: "What about this?"

You can't chance losing it. Better to leave it here in storage. We've heard about savages, after all."

I turned away from her to set it into the trunk. "And, Antonia, I don't know what to do about monthly problems. It was complicated enough crossing the ocean; at least I could find some privacy there. Have you thought about it?"

I'd embarrassed her, but she answered frankly: "I'm making up some pads to take, and I'll pack extra cotton to make more if necessary. What will we do to wash and dry them? I can't imagine." Nor could I.

We heard wailing in the parlor. Mathilde and Marie were arguing over the rules of a game they were inventing, and Lily had stood on a chair to reach something and had fallen on her bottom.

"Time to go home!" Antonia gathered up her girls and left me with a sobbing child, a messy parlor, and a riotous mess in the bedroom. Hermann and the boys would be home soon. I distracted Lily with a song, straightened up the parlor, packed the storage trunk and pushed it back into the closet. As I was sorting out the rest, Hermann came in.

"What's going on here, Frida?"

I explained the pile of clothes for California and the one by the door for distribution to the poor at Assembly House.

"And the trunk in the closet?" he asked.

"I'll store it here at Astor House with our other things. It has my wedding dress, my jewelry case, and other things. They will be safe here.

"It's not easy making these decisions, Hermann. I still worry that Lily, not yet three years old, will be sick. She is not a strong child. I agonize that Otto and Fritz will find sweethearts and vocations in California and stay behind when we return, just as I separated from my mother and father."

"Hush, Frida. We are going. It is decided. Lily will be well once she is outside of this pestilent city."

"I hope you're right." I tried to get him to look into my eyes.

"Your worrying will be over as soon as we're on our way. The boys will be distracted by the adventure and the sights, and you and I will have more time together."

"We haven't had much lately, have we Hermann?" I remembered our evening at Niblo's three years earlier.

"Bring some books of poetry. We'll have time along the way. Imagine evenings reading by a campfire! I've got everything organized, the trip will be smooth as that silk shawl!" He picked up the scarlet shawl and rubbed the silk between his thumb and fingers. "Then in California we'll strike it rich and spend all our evenings in the concert halls."

It was clear to me that Hermann's fever for gold was hotter than any fever the baby could ever have. I wondered: was my jewelry going to be safer than my family?

Chapter 19

We waited, in our rain-damp garments, under Astor House's marble portico for the stage and cart to take our belongings and us overnight to Philadelphia. Even the boys were subdued. The last weeks had been frantic. We had packed our belongings, said our good-byes, obtained letters of credit and introduction to a bank in St. Louis. Now, with our first step just before us, we all waited, as if with our breaths held. Surrounding us were our carefully-chosen belongings: five trunks, one large bundle of bedding, and four smaller packages of gear, books, letter writing materials, etc. Fritz held Lily on his knee and played a little finger game with her, humming a nursery tune. Even Lily was quiet; she kept looking up from Fritz's game, taking note that all of us were still together. She made up a quiet singsong: "*Mutter, Vater,* Otto, Fritz, Baby; *Mutter, Vater,* Otto, Fritz, Baby." She never referred to herself as "Baby." *How vulnerable she must feel!*

Hermann paced; back and forth he walked, blowing on his bare hands to warm them. Each time he turned, he looked up and down the street. Then his head would fall heavily and he would concentrate on each footfall.

Suddenly Erich appeared, running up the steps of the portico, two at a time. He was disheveled and had wrapped himself in a ragged horse blanket against the drizzle and cold. I had understood that we would drive by their apartment and go all night in a convoy. "Erich, *wie gehts*?"

"We've been up all night," he stammered. "This morning we got the doctor. She's burning up, then cold; and the diarrhea and vomiting are terrible. The doctor suspects cholera!" He buried his face in his hands and stepped off the portico into the muddy street.

"Wait! Erich! Who?"

"It's Mathilde, my baby, my darling child. I must go back. We are all in quarantine; I've slipped away to tell you we cannot go with you tonight. We'll catch up with you in Pittsburgh or Cincinnati or St. Louis. I know your intended route. Mathi will get strong again, and the rest of us will be careful. *Auf Wiedersehen*!" And Erich was gone, out of sight, lost to us in the dusk's gloom.

Our stage coach and cart arrived around the corner from Vesey Street, and without the opportunity to see my darling friend, to comfort little Mathi and the rest of the family, or to consider any alternatives, Hermann hustled the children and me up the coach's step and gave the driver his instructions.

I twisted around on my seat and with my glove cleaned off the small back window, hoping to see Erich, Antonia, and their family.

"It can't be true! It can't be true!" I repeated over and over again. "We can't leave today. Hermann!"

"It is arranged, Frida. Our entire group is expecting to meet us tomorrow in Philadelphia. Calm yourself. If Erich says they will come later, then they will."

"You don't understand, Hermann. You don't understand anything!"

Our trip to the wharf was fast, and, as the ferry was about to leave, we quickly got aboard. The boys were subdued and did not go out on deck as we crossed the Hudson; but their father did, turning his back to New York and his eyes to the west.

It was cool on the river even in the cabin where a small stove was providing more smoke than heat. Lily buried herself in my lap. She looked up at me with big eyes and purposely put her thumb in her mouth. I hadn't seen her suck her thumb in more than a year. I held her tight with one arm, and with the other I unwrapped the bread and sausage that the cooks as Astor House had provided for our supper. I could not eat a single bite myself, but my boys broke off pieces for themselves. I wondered out loud about little Mathilde and where and when and how we would all be together again.

"What about Georg and Jacob? Couldn't they come with us? Their parents could catch up when Mathi is well," said Otto, as he and Fritz ate a bit of the supper.

"I don't know, Otto, but it is too late now. We are on our way to Philadelphia; they are back in New York. Can you imagine your father turning around?"

In Hoboken we got back on the stage. I was reminded of my overnights with my parents on the carriage ride to Giessen – particularly during the night. That uncomfortable, bumpy trip separated me from all I had known until then, but I was under the protection of my dear father and mother. Now I was the adult. Hermann and I were the parents, and with our children we were leaving everything familiar. I despaired for the children and myself, and I longed for Antonia, little Mathilde, and the rest of her family, but I turned my face to the window and pretended to sleep.

By ten the next morning we were in Philadelphia. Mr. Gruber, an agent of the transportation company that had arranged our travel accommodations all the way to St. Louis, met us and took us to a small inn for breakfast. There we were greeted by a few familiar faces from New York – Albert Brantlach, his cousin Kristof, Robert Aulich, Hans-Jürgen Topp, Carl Kramer – and the news that part of the track of the Philadelphia and Reading Railroad had washed out in the violent rainstorms of the past week. We would be delayed at least a day.

The men were seized with gold fever; this rendezvous in Philadelphia at the start of our overland passage was their evidence that we would all make it and that they would strike it rich in California. The inn was full of men gathering for the trip, all waiting to begin the first leg of the journey - the train trip to Columbia, Pennsylvania, on the Susquehanna River. Some like us had arranged for passage all the way to St. Louis where we would contract for oxen or mules, wagons, and supplies. Others had brought their wagons, pack animals, cooking stoves, blankets and all other equipment with them and would be loading them onto the train. I wondered how we would know what to buy. The inn was already crowded; a small, unheated room under the roof was found for us, which the five of us shared with the Brantlach cousins. I had never shared a room with anyone but my family before. In this little attic space Otto and Fritz shared one mattress, the Brantlachs shared another, and Hermann, Lily, and I crowded into a third. I went to sleep in my clothes, only removing my shoes, but late in the night I awoke and privately loosened my laces. When I awakened in the morning, I was glad to see Albrecht and his cousin were already awake and gone, as both my dress and hair were disheveled. When we went downstairs, I saw that every settee, table, and floor was covered with sleeping adventurers.

We waited that day and night for word that we could board the train. The atmosphere at the inn was like the arrival party on the *Maria.* It seemed that visions of sacks of gold were dancing in everyone's heads. Beer flowed morning, afternoon, and evening, and strangers became friends. Peter Franken, who had been a sober, industrious Customs Official in New York, got so drunk that his grown son, Peter Junior, had to lay him out behind the piano so that he wouldn't get trampled. Another man whom I didn't know lost his team of oxen in a dice game to someone in Philadelphia who wasn't even leaving on the train. The floor of the inn became sticky with spilled beer; I walked outside with Lily for a change of scenery.

"Pig, pig, pig, pig," we heard and ran to the waterfront just in time to see a group of men chase a fat sow over the end of the dock and into the water. Then all dove in after her, fully clothed, whooping and hollering. To our delight, no one drowned, and the men and the scared, clean pig climbed back onto shore.

Even though I wanted to see the city, we were warned not to leave, since repair work on the track was progressing successfully, and the train could go at any time. My only memory of Philadelphia is of soot-stained buildings, scum-filled streets, leafless trees, and the flushed faces of the men.

Otto and Fritz and the three other young ones in our German New York group, started a ball game. Hermann was aglow with dreams of his own, and gave me a wink as he moved between clusters of travelers, giving advice and helping with minor repairs.

I too was not entirely free from anticipation, and I found myself wondering what I should do with all the money, which most assuredly would come into my pocket. I envisioned a house in New York on one of the newer streets with a front room just for books. That made me remember my piano, books and other things stored in New York. It was easy, sitting in the sun outside the inn in Philadelphia, to close my eyes and to picture myself standing in a doorway of my own house. The door surround would be ornately carved with opulent fruit, and there would be lace curtains in all the windows. I would be waiting in the doorway for my carriage to take me to a concert. My fur wrap would match my muff, and inside it I would carry a slim book of poems to share with a friend over tea after the afternoon performance. I imagined myself in a pale pink dress, complimenting my smooth cheeks and rosy lips.

Just as I conjured a handsome concertmaster conducting a Liszt symphony, the boys' ball landed in my lap and woke me from my foolish daydream.

I went to bed early that night, in order to be asleep under the covers before the others came up. I fell asleep to the sound of singing and jesting from below.

We were awakened early, given some hard-crusted bread, and herded onto the crowded train. Because of the emergency, the railroad had added extra trains with no passenger cars. Some rude boxes had been fastened to the floor of a car designed to carry cattle. These acted as seats, without backs. There was a heavy curtain across one corner of the car, and behind it was one large bucket for slops. Hermann was enraged; he was not the only one. We had paid for passage in advance; this was not what we had expected. But Mr. Gruber had disappeared, and there was no representative of the Philadelphia and Reading Railroad. The men could only grumble to each other.

After a sleepless, uncomfortable twenty-four hours, we reached Columbia, where together with our baggage, we were packed so tightly into a canal boat that I despaired of living through a single night in such a condition. In fact, we were aboard four nights and an equal number of days, and even Hermann's optimism for this trip waned. It was Lily's antics and good humor that saw us through. She charmed everyone as she crawled about on baggage and climbed indiscriminately onto laps. Then, when she was tired, she made herself a little nest atop our bundles and slept, curled in a ball around her rag doll.

I thought my own spirit was failing the test of this trip, and we were not even past the Allegheny Mountains. I wondered how I could take care of my family under these circumstances. There was only one other woman aboard, and she was very young, more interested in Otto than in me. I knew that it was rare for women to join their men on this exploit. But I looked forward to Antonia being with me soon, and so I did not overly concern myself about it. As I surveyed that melancholy pile of men and boys, ordinarily crazy with optimism but this day stricken down with discouragement. I realized my matronly skills would be required beyond my family, and I wondered once again if I had the strength or the stamina.

We had bought some oranges at great expense before leaving New York, as well as some *bratwurst* and smoked eel, and we ate them all, sharing bits with other travelers on the canal boat who had brought nothing. We had expected meals to be served; and were horrified to find that was not the case. Only water and coffee were available, and we had to pay for both. To make matters worse, the water barrels brought on board the third morning leaked, and by that evening, the supply was gone.

"I heard this was the easy part of the trip," I overheard one man tell his companion.

"I have a cousin who is already there," said the other. "He's been a lucky striker, though, so I can put up with anything!"

We had another train trip, then another passage on a packet barge even smaller than the first. As crowded as it was, it was one of the most interesting stages of our trip. The small packet boats were floated onto railroad cars, then the cars were hauled by cables over rollers between the rails. In this way, our barge reached the top of a pass in the Allegheny Mountains. On the western side of the pass a second set of cables, attached to a second engine, lowered us safely down the other side.

I noticed some of our fellow passengers giving me a curious eye, expecting, I think, to see me cringe with fear. But I wasn't frightened; rather, I was despondent over the living conditions; the boys, although fascinated by the trip, were hungry and forlorn; Lily was whiney; and we were all filthy and crawling with lice. Hermann's spirit, however, had rebounded, as it always seemed to when our conditions changed. He was once again resolute and firm.

"We had some hard moments; I agree with that. But only a few. That business with the cattle cars and the water barrels – that was outrageous. But we persevered. We'll be all right. Soon we'll be at the Ohio River and on the *Enterprise*; it will be like *Maria*, you'll see. Just a little further, Frida. Keep trying."

"Hermann, we need a rest. Please, Husband, can we spend a few days in Pittsburgh? We need to bathe and to clean our clothes; we even must delouse! Then we will get some good food and sleep in real beds, with sheets! Lily doesn't understand what is happening. She is no longer sweet tempered. Give her a respite, Hermann."

"Frida! Stop it. Enough. It is you, not Lily, who is no longer sweet. You are not trying hard enough. This is only the beginning." He leapt off the canal boat before our final dockage and joined some of the men walking along the path. Overhearing their conversation, I was reminded of Hermann aboard *Maria*, always scheming, dreaming, and planning with others; always ignoring our needs. I was sick of hearing him tell me that I was not trying hard enough, when it was not true. I wanted to scream at him. I wanted to remind him that he had taken us from our comfortable life in New York, he had subjected us to this brutal trip, and that we were under his protection. But I didn't; instead, I swallowed my own feelings, once again, in order to present a picture of familial harmony to our fellow travelers.

Lily was clinging to my dirty skirts, sniffling, "I want to go home!"

"Oh, Baby, I know you're tired. *Mutti* is too. We'll keep going, Lily; we'll keep going all the way to California. Can you say 'California?' Try it! Say 'Ca-li-for-ni-a!'"

Instead she climbed onto my lap, put her thumb in her mouth, and reached up to stroke my ear.

Chapter 20

On a balmy evening on the first of April we arrived in Pittsburgh, the city of smoke. In ten days we had shuffled through the outskirts of a nightmare, enduring cramped spaces, sleeplessness, lice, thirst, hunger, and anxiety. We had left New York's slush-filled streets in a flurry of activity, which partially distracted us from the sadness of separation and the dread of the unknown perils ahead of us. We had departed in the chill of winter and had arrived in the first warmth of spring in city clothes, now filthy, torn.

The city sounds of beer wagons, peddlers' cries, and church bells had been left behind; in their place were the loud utterances and complaints of strangers in unfamiliar accents. Similarly, the stench of the East River was replaced by the fetidness of too many people in close proximity.

I was exhausted. I had lost weight and my dirty garments hung from my thin shoulders. Lily was subdued, whimpery, not at all like the playful child who had danced with her cousins on the carpet in our rooms in New York.

Hermann, uncharacteristically, looked tired too, but he revered this city as a great example of American industrialism and wanted to spend some time visiting the cotton and glass mills, blast furnaces, and various factories that had clustered where two great rivers came together..

"Otto! Fritz! Come with me, we'll inspect this industrious city while your mother gets cleaned up."

Hermann had spent little time with me on this trip so far, although he tarried with others lending a hand when needed or giving advice whether requested or not. He dealt with the baby and me with the same dispatch that he managed the loading and unloading of our baggage. Our conversations were mostly a series of commands: "Wait there! Come here! Find my hat! Wife, stop your moping!" As our companions on trains and riverboats changed with each arrival and departure, I knew no one with whom to share my anxieties or my excitements. I missed Antonia's companionship, and hoped I might look up to see her rosy, smiling face approaching us along the river's bank.

I thought often of Mathilde and worried that her sickness would delay the family so long that they would not be able to catch up with us. I could not bring myself to consider the worst possibility.

The boys were eager to go exploring. Their limbs and brains had been cramped almost to the point of atrophy for more than a week. But they saw nothing more than the river and the waterfront, for soon another representative of our travel company met us. He hurried us onto the *Enterprise*, which would carry us down the Ohio River to St. Louis.

As the *Enterprise's* side wheels began to turn, and the lines to shore were thrown off, a horseman galloped up and hallo'd the captain. "Urgent mail," he hollered and flung a canvas sack onto the deck. As we were being shown to our two side-by-side cabins, the captain's boy came up to Hermann and tipped his cap. "Letter for your missus, sir."

There was not room in our small compartment to sit among our trunks and bundles, and I took the letter to the rail. Hermann and the children followed. I recognized Antonia's girlish hand, with its rounded letters and carefully aligned words. Tearing the letter open, I read aloud:

> *Lieblinge,*
>
> First, the news is good. Little Mathilde is well.
>
> As I have felt the highest anxiety for you and Hermann and the children, I know that your concern for us has been equal or even deeper.
>
> Mathi was delirious with fever for several days after you left. When awake, the poor darling cried from the pain of her cramps. The doctor came and told us that we must do two things. First we must not let Mathi become parched. Day and night we sat with her, taking turns dripping water and broth into her mouth. In four day's time she was well enough to drink and eat on her own. As I write, she sits on the floor with her sister playing a game with a spindle. Second, we must quarantine ourselves and keep clean and well nourished. And this we did.
>
> "We learn here from the newspapers that great numbers have set out for California, and that many

> are getting tired on the journey. We have even read of cholera in St. Louis, caused by the crowded and dirty conditions there. We hope every day that you are healthy, strong, and still enthusiastic for your trip. But we know we cannot leave New York and subject our darling daughter to this long and arduous trip. We have great fears for her health and believe we must do everything to protect her.
>
> "I will write to you, *liebe* Frida, as I did from home, and we will all follow your progress as best we can. With these words, I embrace you."

Fritz rested his head on my shoulder. Hermann gave my arm a squeeze. "We'll be all right, *Frida Cottonhead.* But we will have to refigure our shares." He took Lily's hand and walked her over near the paddle wheel so she could feel the spray on her cheek. Otto offered to try to sort out our baggage and put things away as best he could.

"You still have us, *Mutter*," said Fritz.

I felt my eyes begin to fill, but the healing image of little Mathi's head on the pillow with her family by her side overwhelmed my sad feelings about our setting out on this journey without them all. I was too tired to cry, too tired to think ahead to all the things that Antonia and I were to do together that now I would have to do alone.

"*Mutter*, *Tante* Antonia is right. There are great numbers leaving for California. Since we have stood here, I have counted fifty-seven steamers tied at the docks taking on people, animals and supplies. Do you think there will be any gold left for us?"

"*Ja, ja*, Fritz." I said, but I was thinking more practically, wondering if we would be able to secure clothes and food and shelter given the competition from so many emigrants. I worried about our own readiness and stamina as I looked around me on the decks of the *Enterprise.* Our steamer was filled with emigrants and their belongings. Most were strong men and boys, gathered here at Pittsburgh from the farms and villages of New York, Pennsylvania, Delaware, and New England. Their baggage included rope, axes, India-rubber wading boots, tents, medicine, and gold testing devices. Ours consisted mostly of city clothes. We even had Hermann's top hat with us, as well as my beautiful silk shawl and Lily's rabbit-fur muff. I observed some of the women of Pittsburgh going about in quite simple dresses of cotton or skirts with shirtwaists. Most were not even corseted. A few lifted their skirts against the spring mud and revealed rubber boots. Those clothes were more suitable for the western life than mine were.

Suddenly I remembered that the sewing kit and case of medicines were back in New York in Erich and Antonia's bundles. It felt as though we were moving backwards not forwards in our readiness.

We had made it to Pittsburgh, and the trip had toughened me. I resolved to be the equal of my husband and sons. With Antonia's letter shading my eyes from the afternoon sun, I looked to the west. There would be no more tears.

Chapter 21

Our tiny cabins on the *Enterprise* were luxurious sanctuaries compared to our previous accommodations on the way to the Ohio River. Lily and I slept in a lower berth with Hermann above, and the boys had a small cabin adjacent to ours. We had just room enough to stand for dressing or washing up in the basin provided. I was relieved to have privacy from other travelers.

The first night I slept twelve hours, not even awakening when Hermann took Lily from my bed early in the morning. When I roused myself and hurriedly dressed, I found my family at the rail entranced by the scene along the riverbank of prosperous farms and charming small villages. As we were relaxed with no immediate duties on board, we could see the scene before us as tranquil and romantic.

Hermann, of course, appeared to already know every person aboard and was engaged in boastful conversation with the men near him about the superiority of traveling to California overland rather than by sea. "This way, we will see the country on our way to California. Then we will decide where to settle with our riches. All those New Yorkers who will travel the Cape Horn route will go 18,000 miles and see nothing but water!"

He had promised me we would return to New York; I meant to hold him to that promise. But now was not the time. Now was the time to learn from the other emigrants and to get ourselves organized before setting off from St. Louis.

Hermann continued, "And, equally important, this trip will toughen us for the hard work in California. Those seekers who have gone by sea will be soft and lazy when they reach the gold fields."

I agreed with him. We would be as tough and strong as was possible – if we made it.

Otto and Fritz could not wait to show me the steamer. We had only to turn around to begin the tour. There behind us were oxen and mules in close files tied between the stacks, with persons camping between and almost beneath them. Some had hung a blanket or two for privacy, but most just rolled out their bedding beside their animals.

Otto also knew quite a few of our fellow voyagers and he introduced me to a boy his age. Billy was tall and thin but strong; I could see hard muscles in his arms beneath his rolled up shirtsleeves.

His jaw was distinctive, as though determinedly set. He was shy too, but he removed his cap and greeted me cordially, "Good morning, m'am."

"Are you here with your family, Billy?" I asked him.

"No, m'am. I'm going for my family. My father and my uncles have sent me to the goldfields as their representative."

"Surely you're not going by yourself! How old are you?"

"I was eighteen the day I left home, m'am. We are a family of mostly girls – I have six younger sisters, and of my twelve cousins, only two are boys – little boys. We need to buy more land to provide for everyone."

"*Du meine Güte*! Goodness, Billy! Where are you coming from and how will you manage?"

"I'm from Onondaga County in New York, from a little town – Delphi Falls. When I left, the whole town came down to the Meeting House to see me off. I'm going to prove to them that they sent the right man!

"I'll be fine. I have my mules, Tulip and Pansy, with me. We're old partners!"

"But won't you be scared, Billy?" I asked him.

"No, m'am. What would I be scared of? I have a gun and two well-broken mules. I've slept out many nights with my friends and even alone. I'm just impatient to get underway. I'll be able to move quickly, being alone."

Fritz and Otto stood with me during this conversation, and when I glanced over at Fritz, my smooth-faced sixteen-year-old, he seemed to set his jaw like Billy's and stand a little taller.

He then told me he had $400 to outfit himself for the trip and to live for his first six months in California. "Then I'll rake in the dust and come back home," he said.

He was writing a letter when we interrupted him. "I promised I would write something every day so that my mother and father and everyone else in Delphi Falls could see America through my letters."

Billy was using a book on his knee as a writing desk, and I asked to see it. It was a cheaply-bound guidebook which gave advice to gold seekers on what equipment and food they should purchase, whether oxen or mules made the best teams, and where to look out for aggressive Indians. It also gave geological information about mileages, river crossings, landmarks, and where to find water for the teams. I asked Billy if my husband could see it later in the day, and he graciously agreed.

Otto and Fritz stayed to talk with Billy for a few more minutes. I watched the river, smooth and oily on this calm morning. The current was strong and carried small branches and leaves with it. The water was muddy and brown; I couldn't see into it as I could in the salty clear Atlantic ten years earlier. We had never camped out. We didn't have a gun. We had not purchased animals yet, nor did we know much about them. Our German New York Company was made up of city dwellers; although one or two had been farmers years earlier at home. I held onto Lily's small hand and felt a flood of overwhelming unease in my heart. Just as I was beginning to feel the excitement of our trip, just as I felt my own inner strength, I began to anguish anew over our capabilities. When the breeze freshened in the afternoon, I heard my boys laughing, "You win, Billy. Yours is the highest!" I looked aft to the commotion and saw the three tall boys flying hand-made kites behind the boat, like the little boys they used to be.

Later in the afternoon Billy loaned me his guidebook. I read most of it, relishing the practical information it contained. There were many pages of recommended stores and supplies, giving quantities and sometimes even manufacturers. I thought how helpful this book would have been to Antonia and me as we made our plans back in New York. It would have taken the guesswork out of our packing, and we would have packed fewer pans and other kitchen utensils but more items like salt which we would find expensive to buy in St. Louis. There were even a few pages about clothes, and one paragraph recommended that women purchase trousers for the trip. Another chapter was about firearms and said that some women carried pocket pistols. If only I had known these things! I took the book to Hermann, who was gazing at the scenery along the river's banks. He riffled through the pages, acknowledging the maps with a grunt.

"This is worthless. Our planning was done in New York, Frida; you know that. This is useless to us.

"Billy! Come get your book, boy. I hope it is a worthy companion to you!" He called Billy over and thrust the book at him, smirking.

"You're wrong, Hermann, and stubborn," I shouted at him, but he had turned around and pretended not to hear me.

Many times thereafter I wished I had taken notes directly from those pages.

Chapter 22

Our trip on the Ohio was a welcome respite from our earlier inconveniences. The scene along the river's banks was serene and romantic. Earlier travelers had come this way and stayed to prosper by means of their own labor. While some of the land was thickly wooded, most was cleared and farmed – the tilled rows as straight as the teeth on my comb. The houses and barns were of wood, neatly framed. Each house was set in a grove of trees and most had gardens, often surrounded by spring flowers. Sometimes we could hear children's voices, and once we saw a passel of girls with their skirts tucked up, cartwheeling across a meadow.

"See, Frida, look at how man is capable of taming nature for his own profit. Isn't it thrilling!"

"It certainly is orderly." I agreed with Hermann. "I admire the discipline and diligence of the settlers. And I'm very curious about these communities. I wonder how they're organized, don't you?" I wondered, briefly, if I should advise him to give up his dreams of California gold and to settle in one of these charming villages, which reminded me a bit of Giessen.

"I wonder if they have tamed this beautiful wilderness too much. Do you remember a phrase of Wordsworth's?

'…Nature never did betray the heart that loved her.'"

"*Ja*, Frida. I remember." He seemed uncharacteristically wistful.

But I held to my dream of our return to New York, a house of our own there, and my grown children settled into their own lives close by.

Our traveling companions on the *Enterprise* were universally optimistic about their future. I heard one man tell another that his neighbor had received a letter from the gold fields. It was from a young man who had been an apprentice carpenter. He wrote that he had dug more gold than a mule could pack. His companion laughed in agreement, and quoted President's Polk's December message to Congress, "…(such) abundance of gold in that territory… of such extraordinary character as would scarcely command belief were they not corroborated by the Army."

During the day, the men would swap ideas about routes and supplies and even items to trade along the way. Hermann seemed always to be in the center of the crowd, plotting, planning, telling the occasional joke. The men liked him. A traveler from Salem, Massachusetts, had a well-worn copy of Dr. Gordak's pamphlet, *Jelly of Pomegrante and Peruvian Pills Unrivaled for Purifying the Blood.* I was glad to borrow it and to take some notes about treatment for catarrh, dysentery and cholera.

Someone had a copy of *What I Saw in California,* published only two years earlier, and it was read and quoted by everyone. Its maps were traced, and planned routes overlaid. Another passenger had Frémont's *Report of the Exploring Expedition to the Rocky Mountains in the Year 1842 and to Oregon and North California in the Years 1843-'44*. Both these books told of the perils along the way, and when our steamer's Captain Jamieson gathered the passengers together one night to show them the firearms, medicines, and other things he had for sale, there were many takers.

"Captain! I'll have a Yager for myself. I know this gun. It is Prussian and well made."

"Actually, Mr. Reinhardt, it is made here by Mr. Whitney, Mr. Eli Whitney. I would recommend something better for you, something more rugged for hunting. Perhaps a Colt revolving rifle."

"Well, fine. But I'll have Yagers for my sons." I could tell Hermann was embarrassed at his gaffe over the Yager.

"And you'll want ammunition. I recommend twenty-five pounds of lead, five pounds of powder, and a bullet mold, as a minimum."

My husband bought the Colt and Yagers for both boys, as well as the recommended ammunition. The total cost was almost $100, which Hermann paid for out of the purse that was always buckled around his waist.

Hermann urged me to read certain sections of Frémont's book as well as Billy's guidebook so as to know about the diseases of the prairie, mountains, and desert.

"But you, Hermann, didn't even spend a minute with Billy's guidebook, yet you consider me unprepared!" He ignored me and didn't answer, bending over the firearms and scrutinizing their marks.

I had packed a chest of bandages and medicines in New York. It contained laudanum, Dr. True's Elixir for coughs, chocolate for stomachaches, clean cloths for making bandages, and much more. But none of it would do us any good as we had packed it with Antonia and Erich's belongings, and therefore it languished in New York. I bought what the captain offered: something with an alcohol base made by H. Swartz in Boston for cleaning cuts, Magic Pain Extractor in a small glass jar, and Captain Paynter's Egyptian Cure for Asiatic Cholera, as we had heard again about the cholera epidemic in at St. Louis. I packed these bottles carefully in a trunk right next to Everett & Barrows Shoe Dressing - all of them carefully wrapped in flannel against breakage. In St. Louis I would put together a full chest of necessaries.

When the *Enterprise* was out of sight of farms, the men and boys practiced loading and firing, aiming at anything that showed itself: trees, rocks, even snags in the river itself. It was obvious to me that ours was not the first steamship full of gold seekers that had bolstered their hopes, like soldiers off to war, by firing their weapons at the bullet-scarred white oak and walnut trees along the banks. Once we saw a rotted hull of an old riverboat, half sunk in the river, its sides pocked with similar blemishes.

I watched proudly as my sons practiced with their rifles, often hitting their stated target. "Look, *Mutter*! See that twisted tree trunk. Watch me hit it!"

They resembled each other more as they grew up, both tall with dark hair, high foreheads, and sharp shoulders, inherited from my family. Otto had grown a sparse mustache, which he fondled absentmindedly. It gave him a rakish look, especially as his hair usually fell seductively over his forehead. He wouldn't let me muss his hair any longer, as I could with his younger brother. Fritz's cheeks were still fuzzy and rounded. He had high color, *like Antonia*, I realized.

"Do you want to try your luck?" Fritz asked me.

"No, no! I don't like guns. It's what they represent. I've always been scared of them. I couldn't shoot!"

"You've never tried; this is the perfect time. Take my rifle! Father, pick a target for Mother, let's see what she can do."

How could I resist my son?

Hermann pointed out a snag at the side of the river. It was big and so well ensnared in the roots of a riverside tree that it was quite stationary. "Just shoot, Frida! Why not, indeed?" Hermann said, "but make sure you don't close your eyes at the last minute like girls do!" He lifted his rifle to his shoulder; I raised Fritz's, surprised by the weight. The kick back put me quite off balance, but still I could hear the cheering: "She did it! Look at that! You both hit the mark!"

I slumped to my knees. The gun clattered to the ground. Otto retrieved it. Fritz took my trembling hands and helped me to my feet. "I felt that way too the first time I tried it. It hurt my shoulder, and the noise scared me. The next time will be easier."

He turned to Hermann, "She's as good as you are, Father!"

Later, when I saw Captain Jamieson by himself, I approached him. "Should I carry a gun, Captain? One of the guidebooks recommends it. Do the other women?"

"Yes, most do. It makes them feel safe to have a way to protect themselves."

"Do you have a gun that I might carry?" I inquired.

He suggested a Colt pistol and showed me one. "This will do the job, Missus, and it's only $50."

Hermann would never consider such a purchase.

"Have you any others?"

I have a pepperbox made by Ethan Allen. It was my wife's, and she was a good shot with it. It'll fit in your pocket; and I'll sell it to you for $8."

I agreed and took advantage of a moment when Otto, Fritz, and several of our friends surrounded Hermann to ask him for the money.

"It will be too heavy for your pocket," Hermann said. He was right; I bought it anyway.

Chapter 23

Some evenings Hermann organized songfests, urging Robert Aulrich, our concertmaster, to lead us. Robert would start with American songs so that anyone who wished to could join in. Usually Hermann would insist on finishing with German lieder in order, I believed, to show off his own voice more fully.

Other evenings the men would sit on bundles and chests and share stories of their homes and families. More than one had borrowed the money for the trip against his farm or business. Some were sponsored by their families or neighbors, like Billy. One man had seen an Archimedes Gold Washing Machine exhibited by a traveling salesman, and that tipped his decision to get in on the adventure. There were two other groups, similar to ours - organized companies wherein the members would pay equal amounts to provide for wagons, teams, and provisions. One had come from Ithaca, another from Pittsburgh, and both had elaborate Rules of Regulation that forbid swearing, drinking and violation of the Sabbath. One of these groups had actually elected officers and given them military titles. One member bore the title: Captain of Gold Finding.

The German New York Company had elected Hermann as its leader, but other than that, there had been no formal organization. The next morning, after hearing about the Rules of the two other companies, Hermann stayed in our small cabin. When he emerged, he called our group together at the stern of the *Enterprise* and told them he had written our Rules, and he would read them to everyone assembled. He encouraged the group to add to the list. Since none of us was worried about our behavior on Sundays, and we did not have heavy drinkers or swearers in our midst, Hermann's rules concentrated on efficiency.

"Rule number one:" he said, "Each wagon will break trail for no more than two hours, then it will fall to the rear of the convoy, and the wagon in second place will become first.

"Number two: Two men on horseback will scout before our group so that no time is lost finding the trail. Those two will also hunt for our evening's dinner.

"Number three: Two men will keep watch throughout each night, in two-hour shifts.

"Number four: Each wagon will be packed and ready to travel by eight in the morning. We will break at noon for a half hour's rest and repast for the animals and ourselves. We will make camp each night at six. With nine and a half hours of travel each day, we should easily make thirty miles a day and be at the diggings in August.

"Number five: We will avoid the savages as best we can. In no instance will we initiate contact.

"Number six: In the event of an illness or mishap, the group will continue on, and the burdened wagon will catch up when it can.

"And, finally, number seven: No one will ride in the wagons unless sick."

I could not hold my tongue. "Hermann, do you mean that Lily and I will walk the whole way to California? And do you mean that we will abandon Hans-Jürgen , Robert, Carl or any others of our friends if they are in need? Surely not!"

I was sitting on a coil of rope behind Hermann's left shoulder. He did not turn to look at me or even to answer me, but continued,

"What do you think, Boys? Anything else?"

I saw Robert and Carl catch each other's eye.

"I think we should conserve fuel by having no more than two cooking fires each night," said Rolf Smit. I liked him and his rambunctious thirteen-year-old twins, Anton and Tom. "Also," he went on, " I don't think the cooks should have to stand watch at night."

Robert made a gesture to get Hermann's attention, but Hermann ignored him.

"Good!" said Hermann. "That's it then!"

That night, after singing Lily to sleep, I got into my nightclothes thinking to read a little by the lantern's light. Hermann threw open the door to our small cabin, catching me on the shin. He shoved me into the lower bunk, "Yes, Frida, you'll walk," he hissed at me. "Remember who is the leader!" He barged out again before I could respond, slamming the door behind him.

I lay next to Lily, frozen by surprise and hurt, trying to quiet my fury. I heard Hermann out on the deck drinking beer with the other men, telling a boastful story about his New York police force. After a while I heard Otto and Fritz go into their cabin, but it was two hours or more before Hermann came to our cabin. Even though the lantern was still lit, he did not speak to me, but climbed to the upper berth where I heard him belching and burbling, content to lie in the embrace of fool hope.

Chapter 24

We passed through Cincinnati, known as the Queen of the West. Many Germans had settled in Cincinnati, brewers and meatpackers especially, but also journalists and musicians. The city had quite a cosmopolitan reputation. There was a splendid steamer tied up at the wharves. She was the *Hibernia*, said to be one of the fastest of them all. She was an ornament to the Ohio River that day, decorated in swags of red, white, and blue. There was a band playing, and a large banner was strung between poles: "Success to the Cincinnati Boys on the Pacific Shores." We would like to have stopped and joined the crowd waving her off, but the Captain pressed on, promising us a break the next day.

Hibernia overtook us that evening, and when we got to Louisville, she was already tied up at the dock. We stopped at Louisville for a few hours to take on water, which gave us an opportunity to inspect the city. I had barely spoken to Hermann, and he now went with some men to find a local newspaper. I watched him strut down the street. His back was stiff, his neck thick and red. He swung his arms as he walked as if to clear a space around him. At that moment I could not recall what had once drawn me to him. I could not even picture his smile.

The children and I walked in the other direction around this compact city. I was surprised at dirty, soot-stained buildings, but Fritz remembered reading an account by Mr. Dickens of his trip through Louisville, "I remember that he wrote that it didn't seem so bad to an Englishman, since he was used to the ravages of bituminous coal!"

We went into a few shops, and I found the prices of commodities to be quite low – a dozen eggs for five cents! I hoped that would be the case in St. Louis too where I would need to provision for our wagon trip.

We found a park near the river and bought some candy from a woman. Lily wanted her favorite, rock candy, but the boys and I tried something new – peanuts cooked up with molasses. Another family bought candy at the same time, and soon Lily and their little girl were playing with their dolls, using a nearby bench as a dollhouse.

"This trip to California will be easy one for Lily," commented Otto. "She will always have her rag doll and us, and she doesn't need much more."

"And you, Otto, what do you need?" I asked.

"Me! I am the lucky one, Mother! 'America is the land of the future,' as father likes to quote. Fritz and I are marching into our future, right Fritz?"

He picked up a stick and put it on his shoulder like a gun, and marched to the west, shielding his eyes from the afternoon sun. Fritz laughed, picked up a stick of his own, and got in step behind his brother. I watched my boys from the back thinking how manly they had become. Suddenly Otto pretended to trip, and his brother fell over him. They rolled around on the ground as they had as little boys, wrestling and laughing, each trying to pin the other's shoulders. Lily leapt up and ran to join them, flinging herself on the heap of brothers. I couldn't resist, the strain of my encounter with Hermann and its chilly aftermath left me, and soon there were four of us rolling down the slight hill toward the river. Lily squealed with delight. The boys and I laughed until we could not get our breaths. Lily dropped her doll; I kicked off my shoes; and the boys lost their caps. At the bottom we stood up, suddenly aware that the other family and the candy seller were watching us in shock and dismay. We brushed ourselves off, grabbed hands, and marched to the top of the rise, singing Lily's favorite song: "Yankee Doodle." We picked up our scattered belongings and kept marching right back to the *Enterprise* and across the gangplank.

We flung ourselves on the bundles stacked on the foredeck, flushed, breathless, and still laughing.

"Look at yourself, Frida!"

Hermann came up the gangplank with others of our company. I tried to stifle my laughing, and covered my mouth with one hand and tucked up the stray wisps of my hair with the other. "Hello, Hermann" was all that I managed, and then the laughing began again. To my immense relief, the Captain rang the bell at that moment, a few final stragglers came aboard, and Hermann left to help bring the gangplank aboard.

On the eighth of April we reached the confluence of the Ohio and the Mississippi at Cairo and turned north up the free-flowing

'Father of Waters.' Its swiftness was felt immediately, slowing the *Enterprise's* progress north toward St. Louis against the river's southerly flow. "Sometimes its six knots against us," the Captain told us. The scenery changed abruptly. Gone were the neat farms along the orderly banks of the Ohio, replaced by broad flood plains. And the river itself was thick and muddy, like creamed soup. I thought to myself that I would be able to walk across it and not get my shoes wet.

The Captain announced that we would be three more days on board; that news caused a flurry of organizing activity for Hermann and the rest of our company.

Hermann conferred with everyone, even me, making up teams to determine our needs and to purchase our animals, wagons, tools, and provisions.

Robert Aulich, who had been a farmer as well as a choirmaster in Prussia, was put in charge of animal purchase. Peter Franken would assist him, along with his son, Peter Junior. We would have seven wagons, necessitating forty-two oxen. We would also have four horses, two for the scouts and two held in reserve for emergencies. We would take cows with us for fresh milk, and if we were unable to find meat, we would slaughter one or more as needed. I argued that we take a pig too, but Robert Aulich said that it could not walk fast enough to keep up and would be too heavy to add to the wagonloads.

"Surely we can take chickens, Robert!" I suggested.

"You will have to carry them in cages on your own wagon," he replied

I went to talk to Albrecht Brantlach, assigned along with his brother Christof to purchase our wagons. "You have seen how many trunks and parcels we have with us. Plus, there is so much more to buy: food provisions, tools, tents, and I'm not even sure what else. Will I have room in one wagon for everything?"

"The captain has explained to us that we should buy small wagons, so as to get over the mountain passes. He says we cannot hope to carry more than 1600 pounds in each one. That must include everything, *Frau* Reinhardt, your trunks from New York, all your food and bedding, and everything you need at the gold fields."

Hans-Jürgen Topp joined our conversation. Even though his wife, Kalli, had been a treasured friend of mine in New York, I had never known Hans-Jürgen well. I thought he was a shy man – at least a quiet one. That had always appealed to me, and I had often wished to know him better. His looks at caught my eye as well. He was clean-shaven and had a ready smile with which he punctuated his wife's remarks. In spite of a large frame, he carried himself gently. Here he usually carried a book with him, and while the others would be telling stories, Hans-Jürgen would often be just outside the group, calmly reading. He was a childhood friend from Leipzig of both Carl Kramer and the Brantlach brothers and had studied philosophy at the University there.

He approached me kindly, recognizing that I was confused, having no idea what 1600 pounds could consist of.

"For instance, *Frau* Reinhardt, if you determine to take 100 pounds each of bacon, flour, lard and dried fruit, you have just filled your wagon to one quarter of its capacity."

"If you think you or your daughter want to ride for some of the trip, then your weight must be subtracted from that amount."

I nearly swooned as I thought of the baggage we had with us, "Oh, *Herr* Topp, surely not!"

"As we are to travel a long way together, do you not think you could call me by my first name – Hans-Jürgen?"

I agreed and urged him to use my given name. I remembered the afternoons in New York going through our clothes and other belongings with Antonia, attempting to choose what would be appropriate for the trip.

"Hans-Jürgen, I believe I have a dozen lace collars and cuffs that came across the Atlantic with me and are now packed carefully for wearing in California! It is ridiculous, isn't it?" I also remembered packing petticoats embroidered long ago by my mother's own quick hand. "I even have several embroidery projects with me to keep my own hands busy."

"None of us knew then what we know now, Frida." He smiled at Robert and me, but it was an expression of understanding rather than humor.

Anna and Adolph Spies had given us wonderful gifts for our trip – heavy overcoats with wide collars that could fold up around our heads in bad weather. These too were packed in our trunks. For Hermann and the boys I had brought many shirts, wool and linen, as well as dress pants and heavy work pants. They had many changes of underwear and socks. I had not been able to abandon Lily's dresses and coats, knowing she would outgrow them before we returned to New York, and so an entire trunk was filled with her pretties.

One bundle was made up entirely of games and toys. Included was a small sled that had been hand-painted for Lily by Clara Spies.

Another bundle was packed with those books that we did not think we could do without: Fritz's copy of the abridged journals of Lewis and Clark, poems of Tennyson, the libretto of *Der Fliegende Holländer*, many issues of the *Dial*, two of Mr. Dickens's novels, and others. Also in that bundle was a small, collapsible writing desk made of fine fruitwoods that Hermann had not been able to resist buying before we left New York. On its lid were his initials, inlaid in gold: HBR. Packed with it were various sizes of paper as well as pens and different color inks. Sketchpads were included so that we could capture the beauty of our trip.

While Antonia and I had relegated our bundle of medicines to their pile of luggage, we had assigned cooking gear to ours. As we had lived for so many years in a hotel, almost all that I had here with me on the *Enterprise* actually belonged to Antonia. I did have the spoons given me by my father's family, stamped with the mark of the silversmith in Gelsenkirchen. Also I had cooking pots that Antonia had brought from Giessen and others she had purchased in New York: large iron pans, five long-handled pots in varying sizes, a large stew pot, and a roasting pan. I had a colander, a flour sieve, some glass vials of spices and extracts. I had a rolling pin and pans for baking pies and cakes. I even had an apple corer. And I had two tablecloths, a dark wine-colored damask and a white cutwork cotton, each with a dozen matching napkins.

I started making an inventory. From memory I listed every thing in each of our trunks and bundles. The list was many pages long, and its very length caused me to almost faint with helplessness. At the bottom I listed: "five large trunks." I remembered the porters at the Astor House bringing our old trunks down from the attic and putting them in our parlor, stacked in front of the fireplace. Otto and Fritz had distributed them to the bedrooms: two to their room, two to my room, and one to the small room adjacent to mine that we added to our suite when Lily was born. The empty trunks were heavy, even for my strong boys. When they were packed with our goods, the hotel porters had to bring small carts to carry them out. I couldn't imagine how much each one weighed, but certainly much more than 100 pounds

Now, less than three weeks after leaving our comfortable city life, I knew that more than half of what I had carefully chosen to bring was useless and frivolous. Somehow I would have to choose again, and I began checking off the essential items.

As the *Enterprise* chugged up the mighty Mississippi, past occasional small settlements, I had the boys haul the trunks out to the foredeck, one by one, and I began the arduous and sad job of setting things aside. Lily wanted to help me, and we started with my own trunk. Onto one pile I set two pairs of boots, cotton stockings, and two cotton petticoats. I handed Lily two aprons, and she folded them carefully, as I had the petticoats, and added them to the pile. I chose two skirts and four shirtwaists, they were wrinkled and mussed, but I put them onto the growing pile. I gave Lily a shawl, and she laid it on the deck and carefully folded it into a small square, "I'm helping, *Mutti*!" Lastly, I put a straw bonnet atop the small mound.

Lily saw the scarlet silk shawl that had been my going-away present from Hermann's family. While I packed everything else back into the trunk, she swaddled her rag doll in it, cradling it on her lap, the shawl's fringe all tangled in the dolls arms and legs. I heard her crooning, "Oh, Baby, I know you're tired. Lily is tired too. We'll keep going, Baby; we'll keep going all the way to California. Can you say "California? Try it! Say Ca-li-for-ni-a!"

I felt a wave of nostalgia rise through my body, but I took my clue from Lily's game, and kept going, sorting through our belongings.

Next I went through Hermann's trunk, then Otto's, Fritz's and Lily's. When I was done, I had four trunks repacked with silk dresses of mine, silk vests of Hermann's, dainty dresses of Lily's, fancy jackets of my sons. And I had one trunk packed with the clothes for all of us that I had chosen to take across the plains and all the way to California.

Next I went through our books and writing materials. I chose to take the Lewis and Clark Journal and a small amount of writing paper and two pens, nothing more. I slipped these into the trunk that we would take with us.

"How much do you think this weighs?" I asked Otto when he and Fritz came to help me put it back in our cabin.

"Maybe 200 pounds? I'm not sure, *Mutter*. But what will you do with the others?" asked Otto.

"I hope we can find a place to store them in St. Louis. Perhaps there is a hotel with a box room in the attic similar to the Astor House. We can pick them up on our way back to New York."

"You mean when we're rich! We will have so much money that we'll want to buy everything new. And, Lily's things won't fit her then; and I will have grown taller than Otto by then," said Fritz.

I knew he was right, but these clothes, along with Hermann's writing desk, Lily's little hand-painted sled, my silver spoons, and other things, stored in St. Louis, would assure our return.

Chapter 25

On a bright morning - April 11 - the *Enterprise* rounded a bend in the river. The Captain gave one long blast of the ship's whistle and announced that St. Louis was in sight. All the passengers crowded to the rail, and I felt the same breathless excitement I had felt when we approached New York ten years earlier.

The group from Pittsburgh began a song I'd never heard before. Everyone joined in on the last line, and I did too,

Aa-way, you rolling river!

After many verses, another song was started. I didn't understand a single word, but caught onto the chorus,

Chinger ringer, ring ching, ching!

Billy climbed up onto the roof of the *Enterprise's* cabin and took off his hat and began "My Country 'Tis of Thee." We all knew that one and joined hands and sang along,

...sweet land of liberty...

The captain came out of the wheelhouse and suggested we sing a German song. Hermann and our whole group turned to me for guidance, the men being too self conscious to begin a song alone. I felt my cheeks go quite pink, and all I could think of was Schubert's *Morgengruss,* which I knew everyone would know. I started it off, and soon was joined by the beautiful men's voices of the German New York Company,

Guten Morgen, schöne Müllerin!
Wo Steckst du gleich das Köpfchen hin,
Als wär' dir was geschehen?

It seemed an appropriate morning greeting, and no one but the German speakers knew it was really about a flirtation with a miller girl. We received a long ovation, then the captain blew the whistle again.

Hermann put his hand on my arm. It was his manner of apology. I knew it was the most I could hope for.

One of the men raced into his cabin and brought out his rifle and shot it into the air. That started a stampede, as all the men and boys got their guns and commenced firing. "Lily! Come here to *Mutter*!" I called, scared that someone might misaim or a gun might misfire. I grabbed her into my arms and fled to our cabin, slamming the door behind us.

Our travel arrangements, made with the travel company in New York, ended here. Now, disembarking on a St. Louis pier, we were on our own.

Our first impression was of boats and hundreds of people, completely obscuring the city itself. Fritz counted fifty steamers lying along the stone wharves as the *Enterprise* approached. Most of them were discharging freight and passengers en route to the gold fields, and all would be making a quick turn around, returning to Pittsburgh or stops along the way to bring more hopeful journeymen west. The wharves were crowded with flour barrels, bales of cotton, travelers' trunks, mules, oxen, odd-shaped parcels, drays, and people speaking every known language. Vendors moved among them, "Candy: rock candy. Candy: rock candy," called one, loud enough for us to hear before we had even tied at the dock. "Ducks, ducks, ducks, fresh ducks, ducks, ducks," cried another, carrying a wooden crate of scared quackers on his shoulder.

By great luck, a man approached us on the dock offering rooms at the Missouri Hotel for only $1 a day. We were pleasantly surprised by the price and availability and immediately agreed. The man had a handcart with him; it took him six trips to transfer all our trunks and parcels to the hotel, which was next to a fur warehouse. We were assigned one commodious room, and while it was being made clean for us, we had coffee in the downstairs parlor.

Otto and Fritz couldn't sit still for long and went to explore the hotel. In less than a minute they were both back. "You won't believe it! We saw a broadside, and this afternoon there is to be a slave auction here in St. Louis, right down the street at the courthouse."

"No! Impossible! You're right: I can't believe it." I clutched at Lily as if to protect her from the horror. "I never thought we would encounter such a monstrous thing!"

Of course we knew that Missouri was a slaveholding state, but none of us had thought much about it as we had approached, being absorbed in our own plans and dreams. On our short walk to the hotel, we had seen Negro laborers, but no more than we would have observed in New York.

Hermann went to the desk and bought a newspaper. There on the front page was an advertisement, which he read aloud:

> Four Negroes for Sale:
> Woman, twenty years old
> Girl, approximately sixteen years old
> Girl, twelve years old
> Boy, twelve years old
> All black and just from the country, sound and fully warranted.
> Also a good workhorse, cheap.
> All can be viewed at 104 Locust Street.
> Sale at Courthouse at four o'clock. Cash only.

Nothing in our experience prepared us for this. Otto and Fritz turned to us for our reactions, but we were both speechless. "Like Dolly!" said Lily comparing her brown-faced rag doll to the sketches in the advertisement.

"No, Lily, not like Dolly. These are real people. Good people! Friends, maybe!" said Hermann.

"But with dark skin like Dolly, Darling," I said. "Otherwise, just like us."

Our room was ready, and I asked Fritz to take his sister upstairs. "What can we do?" I implored Hermann.

"Nothing, Frida; we can do nothing. The law here allows this. We can only move west as quickly as we can." Hermann's hands were trembling; I'm not sure that I had ever before seen him so shaken. "I'm going to the auction at four o'clock. I want you to come, Otto. Some things are important to see, to bear witness.

"I'll come too, Hermann. We can't argue effectively against slavery unless we observe its workings with our own eyes. I'll ask Fritz to stay with Lily. I agree: Otto should see it too."

Chapter 26

We left our baggage in our room, ate a quick lunch, and went out to see the city and to begin pricing the articles that we would need.

It was obvious that this city was growing quickly in large part because of the dollars being spent by the thousands of people pouring through on their way to California. Placards advertising all varieties of outfitters, miracle gold-finding machines, individuals wanting to join companies, and trading companies willing to take clothing, jewelry, and household goods in exchange for supplies vied for the attention of the Californians. One sign nailed to a post showed a sketch of a small child, with the single word: "Lost."

I pointed that pitiful sign out to Hermann. "Could the parents have gone off without their son or daughter, and abandoned the child; or, do you think the child was lost in the hotchpotch of activity, and the family could not move on without him? We must protect Lily!"

"There, Frida, is a harnessmaker. Follow me!"

The man listened to Hermann's request. He measured Lily by eye, and no more than ten minutes later he had made a small harness for her, with a length of leather for one of us to hold onto. Lily thought it was a fine thing, and immediately pretended to be a pony, pawing her small foot against the ground and making little snorting noises. The harnessmaker smiled at her.

"Shall we have one made for you too, Frida?" asked Hermann, his eyes crinkling in laughter.

I did not see the joke.

The harnessmaker became quite grave, "You be careful now! It's not just kidnappers to worry you. Blacklegs, swindlers, and pickpockets are as thick as the locusts of Egypt. Keep your hands on your purses at all times. Many a green'un's been relieved of his money and had to return home, forgoing his golden dreams. And, the cholera's in town; keep clean, and don't go into the dirty, congested parts of the city. Get your business done, and be gone!" He said it kindly, but his serious intent was clear. He took fifty cents for Lily's harness.

Hans-Jürgen Topp joined us, and we walked around St. Louis, staying quite close together, and taking turns holding tightly to Lily's leash. The new part of the city was well organized, and we found it easy to find our way about, but the old part was confusing with odd little shops and drinking houses on crooked lanes. We found the markets and shops to be abundantly supplied and prices were to our liking. Bacon was $4.50 for one hundred pounds, wagons were less than $100, and mules cost as little as $50 each.

Many Germans had settled here, and we were all pleasantly surprised to find our dear mother tongue spoken everywhere. Further, there were several German newspapers, and in one of them we read about the abolitionist sentiment of the St. Louis German population.

In the same edition we saw an article about a company, similar in size to ours, that had left St. Louis by steamship. Its plan was to provision in Independence instead of St. Louis. Since the 360-mile passage westward up the Missouri to Independence was only $2.50 per person, Hermann and Hans-Jürgen walked to the waterfront to inquire about passage.

The boys, Lily and I continued wandering around the city. I had hoped to find a concert hall with a program we would all enjoy. Fritz thought there might be a *Turnverein* here in this city with so many Germans. He was feeling cramped after so much time in close quarters and thought an afternoon of gymnastics would be first-rate. Otto seemed content to look at the pretty girls of St. Louis. Walking in front of the Centrum, he nearly fell over a pile of construction debris, swiveling his head after a pair of young girls, who had greeted him in unison, *"Wilkommen!"* Fritz couldn't resist spending most of the rest of the afternoon reenacting Otto's near accident in pantomime.

I made mental note of the shops I might want to revisit, and we returned to the hotel to meet Hermann.

Just before four o'clock Hermann, Otto, and I walked to the Courthouse, leaving Lily with Fritz. A crowd was forming, acquaintances waving to each other gaily. Someone had wheeled in a small cart and was selling sausages and beer. Someone else had a hurdy-gurdy in a barrow. He set down a square of wood and tapped his wooden shoes loudly in time to the music as he cranked the handle. Two redheaded boys juggled horseshoes back and forth, then looked to the crowd for reward. Two men carried poles; strung between them was a sign painted on canvas:

St. Louis Spring Carnival
Fair Grounds – Saturday
Lions, Tigers, Bears, Reptiles
Wild Man of Borneo and Other Freaks
Food, Music, Dancing, Games of Chance

We saw Peter Franken and his son standing quietly with Hans-Jürgen Topp below the Courthouse steps, and we joined them.

A fleshy woman brought in the four Negroes, all loosely roped together, the twenty-year old in the lead. Apparently they were to be sold as one group. Children, all of them, even the young woman. She stopped them close to us, close enough that we could easily hear the whimpering of the youngest two. The oldest stood with her thin arms crossed beneath her thin shift, holding up her too large skirt. She was keening and swaying like a willow in the wind.

The sixteen-year old girl called out to the crowd, "Don' buy Sally! Po' Sally walk de long road, but e never gon' serve new massa! Sally sperrit droop to de groun'. E beg see m' baby des once. E don' even take hol' a he. He roll e po' haid over an' cry, an' cry. Don' buy me!"

"What does she say, *Mutti*? I can't understand her."

"I can hardly understand her myself. She has had a baby, Otto, and the poor little thing has been taken from her, before she could even hold him. Her poor heart is broken, and she says she won't work for a new master. She's strong and determined."

"Gott in Himmel!" said Otto, and he moved closer to me. His face was contorted with anguish. I put my arm around his waist and felt his body's tension.

The slave peddler called out, "Quiet!" and hit the girl on her buttocks with a stick. "Quiet!" he said again, and raised his stick against the two crying children.

"Start the bidding!" cried out the man standing next to Hermann. We had overheard him earlier speaking in German with his companion; now we realized that the two intended to buy the four Negroes.

"Speak to him, Hermann; distract him!" I prodded.

But Hermann had already engaged him. His right hand was clamped on the stranger's shoulder, forcing him to turn toward Hermann away from the auction that was about to start. "*Da werden Sie aber nichts gutes tun, mein Herr*! What can you be thinking of!"

"It's all right, just watch and wait," said the man quietly and in German. He explained that he and his younger friend were abolitionists. "My friend has come to St. Louis to help the cause here. He and his brother have a farm in Champaign County, Illinois. He came before, six months ago, and bought five Negro men and a young boy. He has freed them all. The men now work for him for wages. The boy goes to school with his own children. He will do the same for these four."

I felt the tension go out of Otto.

The auctioneer started the sale, and a man across from us started the bidding at $25. "Half the price of a mule for four humans!" Otto whispered. It was clear the man already had a few beers, and he was holding another in one hand. Back and forth it went, up $10 each time. Back and forth. The two youngest were crying again, and the girl was wailing, "Don' buy Sally!" The man with the beer bottle held up his hand and called out, "Master Trader! A moment, please!" He walked over to the Negroes, and licentiously, with the neck of his beer bottle, he lifted the short shift of the young woman, purposely spilling a few drops on her breast. The crowd went wild. "The girl too, the girl too," they cried.

"Enough!" roared the auctioneer. "On with the sale."

The man from Illinois whispered to his companion that he would soon have to give it up as he was nearly out of money. His friend gave him $10. I nudged Hermann and shot a glance at Peter Franken and Hans-Jürgen Topp. Hermann reached into his pocket and gave him $10. Peter and Hans-Jürgen did the same. Back and forth three times more, and he won the bid! Hermann took my hand and squeezed it; we both put our arms around Otto, Hans-Jürgen, and the Frankens. I felt weak in my legs and sobbed quietly, slumped against Hermann; Peter Junior and Otto wept openly. We broke from our embrace and turned to our companions, "*Danke, danke,* thank you!" we all cried. At that moment the losing bidder lofted his nearly empty beer bottle into the air; it landed just in front of the four Negroes, spewing its remaining contents and glass shards all over them. Spontaneously the crowd dispersed.

We turned to go back to the hotel. "Wait, *Mutti!*" Otto dashed over to the four Negroes on the pavement. Their new owners removed the ropes, and the two youngest stood and began rubbing their wrists and wiping the tears from each other's cheeks. Otto reached into his pocket and passed something to the girl called Sally. It was his monogrammed linen handkerchief, all he had to give.

"No concert tonight, Frida. I've set a meeting in the beer hall across the street for eight o'clock for our whole company," said Hermann when we returned to the hotel.

I couldn't wait to leave this city and had forgotten about the concert anyway. All I wanted was to shield my children from the horror and outrage of this slave state and to make our visit to St. Louis as short as possible.

At the meeting that night Hermann announced that he had booked passage on the side-wheeler *Amelia* to Independence, leaving in two days.

"I hear that oxen, wagons, rope and everything we need is available in Independence. It will put us a little closer. We'll use these two days to buy canvas and poles for tents and to provision ourselves for the three-day steamboat trip, as there will be no meals served. Any questions?"

The men cheered. There was such a commotion of gold seekers in St. Louis that every one of us had caught the gold fever again, and even I was anxious to keep moving.

As we walked back to our hotel, Randolf Settlemeyer and his son, David, had an interesting story to tell us. They had been at the edge of town when a company of Germans from Baltimore straggled back into St. Louis from the west. They had left ten days earlier with 40 cows, which they intended as pack animals! "These poor brutes could not meet their obligations, and by the second day they had lost their first cow. On the third day four died, and it went on like that, until they realized this was not the way to get to California!" Randolf stopped for a moment to wipe the tears of laughter from his eyes. "Can you imagine such *Dummkopfs!*"

Randolf made us all laugh, but privately I wasn't so sure what was so funny. Maybe cows could be pack animals. And, you could milk them when you needed to too. I kept that thought to myself.

I had observed several other families like ours getting ready for the trip; I was so relieved to see other women. One woman had twin babies as well as another little one Lily's age. Another woman seemed to be in her 60s or even her 70s.

I saw two young women in a shop trying on trousers. "All these buttons!" I heard one exclaim as I passed by. I looked in, trying not to stare, and saw that the women looked very strange in trousers but surprisingly not immodest, as they also had on long shirts hanging to their knees. They saw me watching and called me in, "Try it yourself!" called one. "Thank you," I stammered, "not now, maybe later. I have sons, maybe I'll try their trousers on." They laughed at my obvious reluctance. "But, I'm glad I saw you two dressed thusly; I will try it!"

The next morning while I was tidying up our room and was by myself, I tried on an extra pair of Fritz's trousers along with Hermann's rubber boots. The trousers felt very strange – scratchy on my thighs. I stood on one of the beds to see in the glass, and lost my balance at the sight. There was this strange creature looking back at me, a Minotaur almost, but half man and half woman not half man and half bull – trousers and boots on the lower half, a ruffled-front shirtwaist in pale lavender on the upper half, and a straw hat with flowers crowning it all. Terrified that my family would come back in, I jumped down from the bed and dropped my skirts, and at that very moment Hermann walked in.

"I'm off to buy canvas, lacings, and poles for a tent," he said. "I hear the same merchant sells boots, so I thought I'd try mine on one more time. Do you know where they are?"

He hadn't noticed that I'd spun around, presenting my back to him, pretending to pin up my hair. "I'm not sure," I stammered.

My raised arms had hiked up my skirts. "Frida! What are you wearing? Those are my boots, are they not?" Hermann was aghast at my appearance, and I knew he had only glimpsed the boots from the ankles down.

"Hermann, *Lieb*," I started, not knowing at all what I was going to say. I started again, "Hermann, *Lieb*, I will need rubber boots too. And that's not all." I raised my skirts to my knees, "If I'm to be a partner on this trip, I'll need trousers too. These are Fritz's; they're too big for me."

Hermann didn't hear my words. He stared at this half-and-half creature in front of him. His chin started to tremble and his eyes to crinkle. He felt behind him for the other bed and fell backward onto it with arms and legs outstretched. The bed springs creaked beneath him. "Yes, yes, yes! You shall have them! But, Frida, for now, don't tell the others!" He grabbed the hem of my skirt and pulled me onto the bed next to him. I cannot imagine what the people on the floor beneath our room must have thought, but I do know that the bedbugs were sufficiently agitated to make their presence known to us that night.

It was a good idea to move on to Independence by steamship, especially since it would give me a chance to try out my cooking skills underway, and in that way resolve what equipment and stores to buy or abandon in Independence. And I'd heard that there was an opera company in Independence, and I hoped that we would attend.

I spent the next day and a half buying potatoes, bacon, sausages, eggs, bread, and beer, and packing it all away. I also went with Hermann, and we both bought new boots as well as tent supplies. I asked Hermann to stay with Lily while she took her nap, and I returned to the store and bought a pair of boy's trousers made of lightweight brown twill; the salesman was not as surprised as I expected he would be. "You're not the first, Missus! Many women and girls have come in for trousers. If I may be so bold to suggest one other thing – these will be more comfortable if you buy a pair of boy's drawers to wear underneath."

And, so I did.

Chapter 27

I awoke on the fifteenth of April enthusiastic about leaving St. Louis that day for Independence. We would be traveling relatively lightly compared with past voyages, and I would be testing my skills as a pioneer, cooking under-way. All we had to do before the ship's noon sailing was to pack a few last minute items and to oversee the storage of those trunks and bundles that would be left in St. Louis. Hermann reminded me at breakfast that we might have mail waiting us in Independence, as we had left the Post Office there as a forwarding address. I was anxious to get going.

Anticipating several days of crowded quarters on *Amelia,* I took Lily for a walk in the park near our hotel directly after breakfast. We bought sweets from a candy seller, and Lily gave a coin to a monkey who danced at the end of a tether while his master played a fiddle.

When we returned at ten o'clock, I saw to my horror that all our belongings had been tossed helter-skelter onto the street in front of the Missouri Hotel. Rolf Smit and Carl Kramer were holding Hermann and the hotel manager apart. Hermann broke free and flung himself on the manager just as Lily and I rounded the corner. They both fell to the ground, and I heard a terrible exhalation, *ein Föhn*, from Hermann, as if Aeolus himself had sucked the breath from his lungs.

Lily yanked her harness line from my hand and squirmed through the gathered crowd to her father, sobbing "*Vati, Vati*!" At the sight of his daughter, Hermann let go of his foe, who had fallen atop him. Rolf was able to pull the manager to his feet; he stood gasping before hollering at Hermann, "Get your stinking things out of here – now!" He stamped up the steps and into the hotel, slamming the heavy door behind him.

Except for Hermann's heavy breathing and Lily's piteous sobs, it was suddenly unnaturally quiet on the street. Fritz helped his father to sit up and then stepped back. When he began to get his breath, he got to his hands and knees, then he stood unaided. He had an ugly bleeding cut on his cheekbone and one sleeve of his coat was hanging by threads. He put one hand out to steady himself, and I shrank back. So did his three children. None of us had seen Hermann like this before – wild-eyed, filthy, smelling of street dung. His breathing was labored and hoarse, and his eyes were bloodshot and unfocused. He shook his head, as though clearing the vapors within, and sat heavily on the step. *Who is he*? I wondered. *He's not the husband who teased me only last night. He's not the leader to take us across to California.*

He raised his arm slowly and pointed one finger directly at me, "He won't store your abominable trunks, Frida! This is your fault, bringing bonnets and silk dresses and trunks full of useless possessions. What was I thinking bringing you on this trip! These goods will be your dower, I swear! These cursed, damnable belongings you hold so dear hold us here. I blame you completely for this.

"But, I vow to you, I will be on the noon boat, with or without. That's a promise!"

He went to the public pump at the corner and splashed water on his head, combing his fingers through his hair. No one went near him. No one spoke. Without a word, he went down the street toward the wharf where the *Amelia* was waiting.

Too often Hermann had blamed me for his problems. Too often he had insulted me in front of my children or in public. Too often I had cowered under his wrath, half believing his accusations. This time I resolved to stand strong, no matter the consequences.

Otto and Fritz came to me and put their arms around my shoulders. Lily was crying into my skirts. "What shall we do?" said the boys.

"Stay here with your sister!"

I followed the manager into the hotel. He was sitting in a chair in the lobby, getting his breath and holding a handkerchief to his nose. "Sir," I began, "is it true that you will not or cannot store our belongings?" I would not apologize for my husband's behavior.

"Madam, I cannot. My storeroom is completely full of idiotic belongings dragged this far by travelers as foolish as you are. Because my trouble is with your husband and not with you, I will give you this information. There's a widow in New Washington just up the river, name of Owens. She'll store your things, and she's honest.

"Madam, when you come through here again, do not come to my hotel! I do not wish to see your husband ever again."

I thanked him for the information and went back outside. I told the boys that we must send our belongings on to New Washington. Otto hailed a man with a horse and cart.

"Will you haul some things to New Washington for us?" he asked him.

"I've taken things out of town for others just like you and been in trouble for it. Some of youse don't send the payments, and I'll not be signing contracts. You best come along, boy," answered the carter.

Otto and I looked at each other.

"If I leave for New Washington with him now, *Mutter*, I can negotiate with Mrs. Owens and join you on the *Amelia* when she stops there. If I miss you there, I'll take the next steamer. It's the best thing to do, and I can do it."

"I cannot split up our family, Otto. You can see that!"

"You and Fritz can take Lily and our California baggage with you right now down to the wharf. You'll be there just in time. I'll see you tonight; I'm sure of it."

What choice did I have? It was unthinkable to abandon our bundles and trunks. They were more than just baggage, they were my anchor, my safe harbor, and my surety that we would return. I had no time to think of another plan, and I knew that Hermann, in the temper he was in, would depart for Independence, abandoning us here in St. Louis. I gave Otto some money from my purse and hugged him to me.

Fritz hired a boy with a handcart, and he, Lily, and I left for the wharf.

Chapter 28

It was easy to find *Amelia.* She was a small side-wheeler with a newly-painted red stack, from which smoke already puffed. All our friends were standing at her rail, and when they spied us hurrying along the wharf, they hailed us, and several came down the gangway to help with our baggage. I was grateful for their solicitude. It was obvious they had been worried that we might not make it before the departure time. Hermann, however, was not among them. Rudolf, with his cap in his hand, pointed out a door. "That's your cabin, Missus. I'm afraid there's only one for all of you."

Without knocking, I opened the door. Hermann was lying on the only bed. "Get out!" I said quietly and firmly. I took his hat, coat, shoes and leather carrying case and put them outside. "Now!"

"Frida…" he began, wheedling.

"Now!" I looked at the tiny airless stateroom. "You will sleep on the deck. Fritz, Lily and I will sleep in this bed."

"Let me explain. That scoundrel, that cheat, that unreasonable man…"

"Stop. I don't want to hear your excuses. Out!"

I had left the door open; both Hermann and I could see many of the members of our company loitering just outside listening surreptitiously to our words, wondering about the outcome.

His pride was on display for all to see, but so was mine.

"Frida, we will talk first." He stood up, filling the space available, and cleared his throat as though to take charge.

I stood tall and straight. "Hermann. We will not talk first. I have had to leave Otto behind to arrange storage for our things. You, the fine strategist of our group, failed to make arrangements in advance. You, the fine leader and role model of our group, made a fool of yourself on the streets of St. Louis. You, the fine father and protector of our family, has split us apart for the first time in our lives. If anything happens to Otto, I will be finished with you. When he is back with us, I may speak to you then, but not before. Now, give me room."

This news of Otto's absence caught him off guard, and he sat back on the bed, diminished.

"Go, Hermann, give me this cabin!"

In his stockings, with his shirt awry and his hair uncombed, he struggled to his feet and lurched for the door. I turned my back on his sorry sight, trembling within, and shut the door firmly when he passed. Through the small window I heard him mutter to the crowd, "Frida needs rest. She's distraught. I'll give her the cabin to pull herself together. Who will join me for a beer?"

Fritz opened the door and quietly slid in with Lily. "I'm scared, *Mutti.* I'm scared for Otto and for us."

"I am too." We sat side-by-side on the bed, there being no other space. *If Otto can be so easily separated from us in a civilized place like St. Louis, what is to become of us when we embark across the western wilderness?*

Lily explored the little cabin, bounced about on its bed for a few moments, then settled down with her doll. Soon she was asleep, legs and arms spread wide, claiming more than half of the bed.

With great tenderness Fritz covered her with my shawl. "I have read Nicholas Biddle's report of the Lewis and Clark journey. I've practically memorized it. He quotes from first-hand accounts of expedition members, telling of an entire winter spent preparing for their trip. Each man was assigned a task and was prepared for it. We haven't even decided what our final embarkation point will be – one minute it is St. Louis and then it is Independence. Now my brother is one place, and we take off for another! Is it too late to turn back? If you and Lily and I got off at New Washington, *Mutti,* we could meet Otto and retrace our steps to St. Louis and then back to New York. Otto and I could get jobs; we're old enough. We'd be with our friends, and you would be with *Tante* Antonia; Lily would grow up with her cousins."

I turned to Fritz and asked for his handkerchief. I wiped my eyes and blew my nose, and sat up straight.

"Take my hand, Fritz. Do you see this ring that I wear? We used to call this *Dutch* gold, this rich, rosy metal. When I was a girl in Gelsenkirchen, my grandmother's wedding ring was made of similar gold. She told me that its pinkish hue reflected what she felt in her heart. My grandfather had been dead since before my birth, and it was hard for me to understand that she still loved someone who did not even exist. She told me stories about my grandfather when they were both young. He had been a farmer; but he had loved acting in local plays and tableaux. He was a prankster too who surprised his neighbors on feast days with little gifts tied to trees.

Once he tied a small bag of sunflower seeds to the tail of a horse belonging to an old neighbor lady who had admired the flowers along his fencerow. My grandmother could still laugh about that prank fifty years later."

"I wish he were here now, *Mutter*. We could both benefit from a joke."

"When I was a teenager, my mother told me how this grandfather had died. He froze to death one night coming home from the village. He was so drunk that his body still smelled of alcohol when neighbors found him the next day. He had a lady friend in the village, and she had his child a few months later."

"I don't understand..."

"The point is, my darling Fritz, that my grandmother remembered happier days. She was determined to love her husband, and so she did. She wore the ring he had given her, and she was buried with it on her finger."

"I've never seen you take your ring off, *Mutter*, even when Lily has begged to try it on."

"Your father is stubborn and proud. He can be vain, conceited, and selfish. Don't you think I know these things? He blusters with big ideas, like solving the law and order problems of New York City or striking it rich in California, but he can be lackadaisical when it comes to execution.

"But we are a pair, a brace. I have threatened him today, but he knows, and I know, that I will not leave him."

"Why not? This trip is folly!"

"Partly because of memory. He has made me laugh too, like my grandfather did for my grandmother. And because of our history together. We have traveled far in each other's company, and we are raising you three children. I have learned to love your father, and I am determined to continue doing so.

"Yes, he exasperates me at times, and he embarrasses me; sometimes he hurts me. Yes, this time is the worst. He has separated our family, by not doing what needed to be done in St. Louis.

"Back in New York I thought this was just his pursuit – crossing the whole country in search of gold. Now I feel differently. It is an adventure and a noble enterprise for all of us. You and Otto and your sister will never forget this trip."

"Father couldn't make this journey without you, *Mutter*! I see how he depends on you. Otto and I talk about it sometimes. It is as though he knows that you will keep him from going too far."

"Yes, Fritz. You and Otto are right about that. It is one element of our partnership.

"I had a dream last night, our final night in St. Louis. I was swimming in the ocean. It's funny isn't it – I can't even swim! I was carrying a huge weight, and could hardly keep my head above the waves. I twisted my head around and it was your father. It was though he was drowning, and I must save him. I kept swimming, my legs scissoring through the water, and gasping for my own breath. The next time I looked around, I realized you and Otto and Lily were depending from my shoulders as well. That thought gave me added strength, and I continued toward a far shore through the relentless chop of the sea.

"I hear the gangplank being raised. Let's leave Lily to her rest and go on deck and watch the passing scenery. I'm sure Otto will join us tonight in New Washington."

Chapter 29

The *Amelia* was crowded to overflowing with one hundred passengers and all their belongings. We heard accents we'd never heard before, and met people who called themselves Wolverines, Buckeyes and Hoosiers. Every inch was covered with bales and boxes, sacks and kettles; even mules and horses. There were several tents erected on the deck itself. Fritz, with great ingenuity, found a small area at the stern where I could prepare our meals. I put a coarse blanket on a crate full of ducks and sat there, watching the shore, hoping to see Otto and the cart with our things.

I sent Fritz for a bag of walnuts from our stores. He furiously cracked them for me, filling my skirt. As I watched the pleasant but desolate shore, my fingers found the nutmeats among the shell pieces. They went methodically into my apron pocket with a small dry rustle, and the shells went back into the bag. Our anxiety was assuaged by the comfort and the familiarity of this simple, routine task.

When Lily awoke, Fritz went off with David Settlemeyer, and I sat brooding, watching the shore.

"Are you Mrs. Reinhardt?" I heard behind me.

"I am." I saw a woman slightly younger than myself also dressed in city clothes. She had a small child about Lily's age as well as a smiling baby in her arms.

"Your husband pointed you out to me. He said you might like some company."

"Did he! Well, he is right. I had been thinking that there was no one at all on this long trip like me. I am very glad for companionship." I made room on the crate. "Please, join me on my settee." We both laughed.

She introduced herself as Florence Potter, and her two children as John and Baby James. They were also from New York City, both she and her husband had grown up in the Parish of St. Luke's on Hudson Street. I thought her uncommonly handsome. Her face was lean and her eyes wide apart; her eyebrows were dark and straight, as was her hair, which was pulled back behind her ears becomingly.

I gave John and Lily some of the nutmeats from my pockets; soon they were happily sitting at our feet, sharing their treat in equal measure with Lily's doll.

Before we had a chance to converse, we were all startled by shots being fired from the bow. We looked up, expecting to see Indians, but instead saw three deer standing on a high bluff. They were curious about us, as we were about them; but it was apparent that we were the intruders. The shots did not arouse their fears or arouse them from their repose. The shooting continued though, and within a few moments, to our surprise, the *Amelia* pulled over to the riverbank and one man got off to retrieve a fat turkey that he had killed.

"This is not New York, is it Mrs. Reinhardt?" laughed Mrs. Potter.

By the time we stopped in early afternoon at the small German settlement of Schluersburg to take on good water, Mrs. Potter and I were fine friends. We got off together with our three small children and strolled around the village. The *Frauen* took advantage of the steamers' passing up the river. Many sold foodstuffs directly from their kitchen doors. I bought some dark rye bread, and she bought some sausage; we determined to fix an evening meal jointly for our families. Back on board, I made a *Brotsuppe* with some onions and apples bought in St. Louis. She introduced me to her husband, Clarence Potter, and I introduced Hermann.

I had told her of my anxiety at leaving Otto behind and my presumption of meeting with him at New Washington. When we came around the bend at dusk and saw New Washington ahead, I was quite sure we would find Otto waiting for us on the dock.

"May I leave my Lily with you? She and John seem quite happy together. I want to go to the front of the vessel in order to see my son."

By now, we were calling each other by first names. "Of course, Frida," said Florence.

I went to the bow; there was Fritz, as anxious as I was. "I don't see him, *Mutter.*"

"Wait a moment, I'm sure he'll be waiting for us."

"Did you see him or the cart along the river?"

Now I realized that I had not, and as we got closer to the dock, it was clear that Otto was not among the men catching *Amelia's* lines.

"I hate father!" cried Fritz. He turned to me with a ferocious look on his face. "I will always hate him."

"Shh. *Stille.*"

He buried his face in my neck, too old to cry. "What is to become of us?"

I wondered the same myself. *What is to become of us? Where is Otto?*

"Frida, where is Otto?" It was Hermann.

"Yes, where?" At that moment I hated him too.

Chapter 30

I heard a tap on the door at dawn but thinking it was Hermann, I ignored it. A while later, I heard it again. "Frida! It is Florence. Are you awake?" My dear new friend had made hot chocolate for Fritz, Lily and me, and she had wrapped some bread with butter in a cloth for us. "Send Lily to me if you want time to yourself," she whispered.

That day was a frustrating one. Fritz and I stood at the rail most of the day hoping to see Otto. Hermann kept clear of us but appeared to have his eye on the road by the riverbank as well.

We were delayed by going aground at the mouth of the Osage River. The captain blamed it on our heavy lading. We floated free when the men shifted the weight from one side of our vessel to the other. At Jefferson City, many passengers went ashore to view the capitol building, but I stayed aboard, fearful of missing Otto if he should catch up with us here. Hermann stayed on *Amelia* too. He was playing poker with some men; I noticed he sat so as to keep an eye on the wharf.

I slept some that night, in exhaustion borne of worry.

The next day was Sunday and one of the passengers, the Reverend Duden, offered services in the saloon. Florence urged me to attend with her. "Frida, come with me. If you don't want to listen to the prayers, you can distract Lily and John for me. There will be singing – Fritz will like it. It will divert both your minds from your terrible worry."

I agreed, and at eleven o'clock we crowded into the saloon with the entire company of passengers, except Hermann. Men that I had observed as rowdy and dirty stood quietly in clean shirts with hair slicked back and beards combed. Florence and I were the only women, and someone dragged a trunk to the front for us to sit on. The Methodist service was solemn, and the congregation listened seriously. Even the hymns, which everyone seemed to know, were sober. Several times Reverend Duden mentioned those left behind in his prayers. When he did, I heard sniffling behind me, proof that these rough adventurers deeply felt the ties to family that were now asunder, just as I did.

The Reverend read a warning to the assembled from Ecclesiastes:

> "Then I saw that all toil and all skill in work come from a man's envy of his neighbor. This also is vanity and a striving after wind."

Fritz gave me a nudge. I turned to him and saw mature understanding in his look. He gestured toward the window of the saloon. I could see the rim of Hermann's hat. So, he was listening to the service too!

I knew he was not indifferent to Otto's absence or to my chilliness towards him. It saddened me that we could not comfort each other, but I was still angry and resolute.

That whole day the wind built until by early afternoon it was howling. Unable to make headway against the bluster, the captain drove us ashore, and the men and boys loaded wood to pass the time. All were happy with the chance for exercise, but I was discouraged by our slow progress toward Independence, where I hoped we might find Otto, or at least have word from him.

The next day, when I thought we would reach our destination, we went aground again – this time on a sandbar, and it was clear we would not get to Independence before night. The captain suggested we lighten load by walking, and most of the passengers got off on the small barge provided to ferry them ashore. I joined the crowd, and urged Florence to come too, "Any progress is better than none." The little ones picked dandelions, and we walked arm-in-arm together, taking turns carrying sweet little James.

"I'm so glad you're with me," she said.

"I too."

Chapter 31

We arrived at the Lower Independence Landing at eight o'clock the next evening and lay there all night unable to unload until the next morning. Otto was not on the dock to meet us.

I missed him with all my heart. I also missed my oldest friend, Antonia, and wrote to her, back in New York, by lantern light:

> My dearest friend,
>
> I need your comfort more than ever. We left Otto behind in St. Louis to complete some business there. The rest of us have continued on to Independence where I write this note. We have had no word from him or about him.
>
> I have endured so much change in my life that it begins to feel normal. As long as my family was near and complete, I could tolerate it, occasionally even relish the newness. Now, again, I know this journey was too risky for me to undertake. In New York we would be safe, together, and near to you and Erich and your dear children.
>
> Here we are drowning in an ocean of gold prospectors. Every one is in a hurry and is concentrated solely on his own purpose. That includes Hermann and the rest of the New York German Company. I am overburdened with the worry of Otto's whereabouts. I know not how to find him or help him; I am uneasy about his status and situation; overall, I am vexed at being here.
>
> I pour my heart to you over these miles because I am so wretched with misery; even knowing that by the time you get this letter, my darling boy will hopefully be back with us. When that joyous moment is upon us, I will write again.

In the morning I hurried off the *Amelia* and found the Independence post office, hoping to find mail from Antonia and possibly a note from Otto. There was nothing.

When I returned to the wharf, Hermann and Fritz were standing by our belongings. Lily was on top of our largest trunk whimpering pitifully. When she saw me she let out a wail that put voice to my own misery.

"Her Dolly is lost," said Fritz. "I accidentally knocked it overboard as I carried Lily down the gangplank. In a moment it was out of sight in the muddy river. She won't let me comfort her. I feel so badly. Tell her, *Mutti*."

I took Lily in my arms. Her little body was heaving with sobs and she could not get her breath. There was no comfort here for either Lily or myself. I carried her away from Hermann and Fritz and found a low wall to sit on. There was no space to be alone in this busy place, but we found privacy in a crowd of strangers. Lily lay crying in my lap like a small baby, and I bowed my head and wept with her. A passerby would have seen a mother comforting a sick child. In fact, we were a mother and child helpless with loss and unable to give or take comfort.

Florence tapped my shoulder, "Frida, Clarence has found a carter who will take our things to a field where we can camp. He is talking with Hermann now, trying to convince him to come with us so that we may be near each other."

I let her lead me back to the steamboat landing. I gestured to Hermann to load our things onto the cart. We followed the man to the outskirts of the town, and there, amidst the sprawl of tents and wagons, we found a muddy gap big enough for our two tents.

We were there until mid May – a busy four weeks.

Chapter 32

In Independence I began a daily journal. I wished I had kept one from that first night crossing the Hudson River on our way to Philadelphia, but I had not. It was better to start in Independence than not to start at all. I began that first day with a description of our tent, since it was raining heavily, and Lily and I saw little else but the inside of the tent all day.

> This tent, our home, is as small as my living room rug in New York. The floor and the walls are dark brown canvas, and there is no window. The hapless light from a candle's flame is consumed by the shadows as though heavy-laden. My own breath seems diminished too and does not come easily to me.

Lily pulled at my skirt, leaving muddy fingerprints. "Play with me, *Mutti!*" I put down my journal and gave her some scraps of paper and a pen. We played a little drawing game: I would begin a picture, Lily would add to it, then my turn again. Then we'd take turns telling the story of the picture. After a while she drifted to the floor to sit by my feet just inside the tent flap and watch the occasional stranger pass by, her thumb in her mouth and her free hand picking clods of dirt from her skirt. I continued writing:

> Hermann has attempted to fold up the edges of the tent floor so that rain cannot come in, but in some places that small dike has collapsed and rivulets flow through, bringing foul-smelling mud. From the two tent poles he has strung a line from which we may hang our clothes and other belongings. From the same poles hangs a canvas hammock for Lily to sleep in. For furniture we have our trunk and bundles. At night, Hermann will put planks across them, and thus he and Fritz and I will sleep above the

> wet floor. Florence and her family are next to us; sometimes I hear the baby crying. We have tried to converse tent-to-tent, but the rain is too loud. Only by lifting the tent flap is there enough light to write by.
>
> Lily is cranky and listless. She wants only to be in my lap or playing with me. Hermann and Fritz have put on their boots and gone to find the town, there to buy the planks for our bed and the broom that I have requested.

When they returned they were soaked but full of news.

"Frida, before I tell you of the town, let me tell you that someone has seen Otto!" cried Hermann. "Not here, but back in New Washington. This man said he had a conversation with Otto and remembers that he was going to leave by the next available steamship to join us here in Independence. He was a no-nonsense type. I believe him. Frida, my dear, we will be together again, as I knew we would."

Something in Hermann's tone made this announcement sound as though he was responsible for the good news.

"I hope so, Husband. I have used up most of my hopefulness." I found it hard to meet his eye. "I can imagine the joy you and Fritz felt when you heard. It is wonderful news."

"Look at me, Frida. I make this promise to you: we will not leave Independence without Otto. Do not forget that he is my son too; I miss him and worry as you do. We will cross America together, as we did the Atlantic Ocean. Or, we will turn back."

I could hear John and baby James next door. "Fritz, I want to talk to your father alone. Will you take Lily and go to the Potters' tent. Take this little sack; it's the last of our walnuts."

Hermann let the tent flap down, and we sat next to each other, not touching, on an uncomfortable trunk in the damp gloom.

"It does no good for me to be mad at you," I said. "I have to know that we are partners. There has never been such a fragile time for us, and our family will shatter like a dropped Dresden tea cup if we are not solidly of the same mind. Please, Hermann, tell me how you feel right here, right now. And tell me what you think we will do next."

He answered, "Well, what do you think? I'm excited, of course. What else. Let me describe to you what Fritz and I saw. To begin with we asked directions to the beginning of the trail. There we observed a sea of mud, crisscrossed with wheel ruts from those few who foolishly tried to leave between the spring rains. The little grass we saw was yet too sparse to feed any animals.

"Next we walked into town. We made our small purchases - noting the high prices, by the way, and came back here, skirting the mounds of dung from the mules and oxen that are everywhere tied to the sides of wagons. Emigrants by the thousands were idle on the streets, waiting their time to move west.

"Even Fritz, our optimistic Fritz, was discouraged. But, not me!""

"And, so, Hermann, what did that tell you? What next?"

"What next? Well, Frida, what can we do? We must wait here in Independence for Otto; this is where he will look for us. And, we will purchase what we need, continue our plan, and make the best of it."

"No! That is not enough for me. I have made the best of it too many times. I made the best of it leaving my parents and crossing the Atlantic. I made the best of it leaving my friends and my life in New York. I have made the best of it enduring this uncomfortable trip. And now my son is missing, my baby is distraught, my husband and I barely speak, and I am stuck in a dark tent in an ocean of mud. I am through making the best of it! I do not even know where to go to relieve myself!

My hair had come loose, and I stood to tuck it back and to brush the caked mud off my skirt. In the paltry light, I turned to face Hermann. "You have changed your habits toward me, Husband, and I don't like it. I sometimes feel as though I am making this trip alone, and it is a journey that I did not choose."

I kept my voice quiet. I knew if I did not, everyone camped in the field would hear us, and then Hermann would become defensive. He slumped forward, resting his elbows on his knees and holding his head. I wasn't sure he was going to answer.

"I remember what good partners we were before, Frida. Do you? Do you remember the group we began back home to help German-speakers from the east immigrate to America? We did that together. Do you remember the night you helped me when I started my import business in New York with Mr. Hammacher?"

"I remember. And more."

"Yes, more. Fritz has been reminding me.

"I could not make this trip without your help." Hermann exhaled and then drew in a large breath as though to begin with fresh air. "Don't you see, Frida, how I depend on you?"

"Depend on me! No. I don't see that. I see that you treat me as though I were frail, incompetent, and not very smart. In front of the others you either ignore me or insult me. When you first suggested this adventure, I wondered to myself if I was strong enough. I had left my family, endured a sometimes-difficult Atlantic crossing, learned a new language, and found my way in a complicated new city. Then I had a new baby, and immediately you wanted to uproot us all. So, I wondered if I could make it. I knew there would be rough times, but I counted on your assistance to get through them.

"Now we've journeyed more than a thousand miles, and it has been more arduous than either of us anticipated. Haven't I proved myself to you? You have simply not been fair to me!"

He slowly turned his head toward me and looked deeply into my eyes. Then he closed his eyes and took another large breath. "You have proved yourself, *Schwartzi.*"

I had not heard that sweet nickname in years, but I recognized that Hermann did not smile as he said it, though his tense features were somewhat more relaxed. He continued, "You have endured the rigors of this trip as well as any one of us."

"Then, what is going on, Hermann?"

"Nothing is going on! Why would anything be going on? I am the elected leader of our group. I make the decisions. It's the load I bear, don't you understand? I don't think about being fair; I'm too burdened by schedules, plans, worries."

I dipped my head in acknowledgment. "I need to know that you will not make decisions about our family without talking with me first. That is the fair way."

He sighed. "Yes. Fair. I will try, Frida. I will try."

He stood up, hunching his shoulders and shifting his feet restlessly. "I am not so good at taking advice."

With one large hand he brushed some mud off my sleeve, which I knew he meant as a kind of apology.

"Enough, Frida, *meine Frau*, my wife. The rain has stopped. Let us go locate a privy for you."

He found my boots, bought in St. Louis, and helped me to put them on. He unpacked my heavy gray wool shawl. He took my hand and with unusual tenderness lead me around the other tents and wagons, across makeshift planked walkways, to the woods at the edge of the field. There we found several outhouses. Hermann waited outside and then took my hand again. Together we found our way back. We called at the door to the Potter's tent and were invited in for coffee. Florence had a lantern lit and Clarence had rigged board benches along two sides of their tent. An empty trunk would serve as their baby's bed; at the moment Clarence held him, while Lily and John played in the trunk pretending to be puppies, yipping and growling playfully. Fritz was helping Florence make sweet bread, and both had flour on their faces and the front of their clothes. A bowl with raisins and walnuts was on a trunk top next to Florence's Dutch oven.

"Sit down! I'm making bread for both of us, using your walnuts; thank you kindly!"

Fritz gave me a small smile, and I gave him one back.

Chapter 33

"Mutti?" Fritz interrupted my conversation with Florence. "I have been talking with Mr. Potter, and he has a good idea. We could draw up some handbills with Otto's name and our location so that he can find us when he gets to Independence. I can go to town tomorrow and distribute them."

"But, what is our location – Mud Street?" Hermann interjected sardonically.

"It's a good idea, Fritz; before the rain starts again, let us go out and see if we can make sense of this place; Florence, may I leave Lily with you? She is half asleep– it's just a matter of minutes before she slips into her nap."

Fritz, Hermann, and I lifted the Potter's tent flap and walked out. It was daylight, but barely, since no sun could penetrate the misty gloom. There were figures moving about, taking advantage of the lull in the rain. A woman nearby was actually hanging a few pitiful rags out to dry on a line run between a wagon and a small tent. "They're diapers!" I whispered to Fritz, "at least we don't have that to worry about."

Our neighbors had been creative, stretching lines everywhere to hold tarpaulins up over belongings stacked next to tents or wagons. Planks criss-crossed the alleys between tents, allowing for passage above the mud. It was tedious to have to keep to the boardwalks instead of walking where we wanted. In the middle of our campground was a roped-off area for animals. Oxen, mules and horses mingled forlornly, churning up the mud and the stink, "like a mixture between an open grave and a sewer," commented Hermann, with his handkerchief over both nose and mouth.

On the other side of the animal common was a hand-painted sign high in the one remaining tree. It read: "Swillwallow, Incorporated 1849."

"Ha!" cried Fritz. "So, that's where we now live!"

I got the joke, but could not find the humor in it. "Let's keep exploring, I need to find a water pump. And I want to see where our friends have camped."

We kept walking, passing many families and hundreds of single men. Every time we passed a woman, she would put down whatever she was doing and come forward to introduce herself to me. "Tomorrow, come for coffee!" I heard over and over. In this way, I met May, Caroline, Bess, Edith, Johanna, and a few others. At the same time, Hermann and Fritz met some of the men, come to this place to wait for agreeable weather, just like us. One Dutchman, Gerd Pannekoek, traveling with his son, Jan, offered to take Hermann and Fritz the next day to meet Hiram Young. They explained that Hiram was a free black who purchased his own freedom making axe handles and ox yokes, and that now he was making wagons. "They're good value," I heard Gerd say to Hermann.

We crossed over a stile into another field, which was also churned to mud. There we read another hand-made sign, painted on canvas: "Swampville."

I guessed that all of the overlanders were camping out in conditions as rough as our own. Here we found Albert Brantlach, his cousin Kristof, the Frankens, and Rolf Smit all sharing one large tent, and next to them in a small one were Randolf Settlemeyer and his son. They pointed behind them, indicating that there we would find Robert Aulich, Hans-Jürgen Topp, and all of the others.

"We will move our things over here, Frida. We will be near our friends. Anyway, you have not unpacked yet; it will not be so difficult. There is a man with a cart, right over there. I'll hail him."

Our friends all cheered his suggestion, offering to move their tents a bit to make room.

"I cannot believe this, Hermann!" I said, loud enough for all to hear. "You have just told me that we will talk things over together, and now you revert to your authoritarian ways!"

"What do you mean? Here are our friends."

"Consult with me! Please! I want to stay in Swillwallow next to Clarence and Florence. We will see our good friends every day for months as we head west. They know I mean them no disrespect, and we are only a two-minute walk away."

Hermann turned his back to me and hesitated. "Gentlemen, thank you for your hospitable offer. We will stay where we are already settled. Frida would prefer it."

"Thank you, Husband."

He made plans with Albert and Kristof to go with him to Hiram Young's the next day, then took my arm to continue our perambulation, but laughed when he realized there was not room on the plank walk for two to go abreast.

Chapter 34

The next day while the men went to see about wagons, I tied the tent flap open for some light and spent the morning bringing some order to our belongings. A man passed by selling logs for firewood.

"It's too green to burn," I chastened him. "This must have been cut yesterday; come back in two years when it is dry and sell it to me at that price!"

"Yes, Missus, you're right. I cut it yesterday, but you'll not find anything dryer anywhere in Independence. You'll have to dry it yourself, a few pieces at a time, by the fire."

He saw my frustration, and offered two pieces of dry wood from under the load in his barrow. "These I was taking to my own wife."

I bought the two and the green wood beside. Using the green logs as supports, I shifted our sleeping platform down to ground level, organized our trunk and bundles for storage and workspace. The larger logs, cut in half, would do as stools. We would need something for a table. I found stones from a tumbled wall, and made a fire circle outside the tent, unpacked my pots, and stacked them on the large stump that the wood seller had given me for free.

Florence had gone to town with her family, and so I took Lily for a walk across the plank walks. May and Caroline hailed us and invited us into their tent for coffee. They were sisters, married to brothers, all farmers from New Jersey. We traded stories of the trip thus far. One had received a letter from an acquaintance in St. Louis telling of a cholera outbreak in that city the day after we left. "We have prayed our thanks to God that we left when we did. Perhaps you would like to pray with us?"

I didn't want to offend, and changed the subject to Otto, suddenly realizing that he may have been in St. Louis when the outbreak occurred.

"Today Otto's brother is posting notices all over town so that he will know how to find us when he gets to Independence."

Caroline patted my hand. "We will pray for Otto. I think today you will have good news."

Lily and I returned to the tent at the same time that Hermann and Fritz arrived.

"Next time we go to Hiram Young's, you must come with us, Frida. He is quite amazing. Did I tell you he is a Negro? He makes the best yokes in Independence and has built up quite a thriving business. With his profit, he has bought three other slaves, and now they work for wages building wagons with him. Hiram and the two young men are the woodworkers; the older man, his name is Nehemiah, is a tailor and a rigger. He sews and installs the wagon covers. He also makes some clothes on the side, and will make a divided skirt for you and a small one for Lily if you would like. His prices are reasonable.

"We also went to another wagon maker, Robert Weston, but the Brantlachs thought that Hiram's work was better. Tomorrow we will go back with money to place an order. Will you come?"

I agreed. "But tell me if you had any news of Otto?" I told him what I'd heard of the cholera in St. Louis.

"Nothing new. We heard that awful news too. But I am very hopeful about Otto; it has only been a few days, and there are many legitimate delays. He might have had trouble finding this lady who might store our things. Or she may not have had room, and he had to locate another place. He might easily have missed the next few boats up the river. I say that it is too early to worry.

"Fritz put up all the broadsides that he made last night. There were similar notices in numerous shop windows and posted on many walls throughout the city. They are so sad to see. We thought some had been posted for a long time, as they were water-streaked, faded and nearly illegible. Each one represents an anguished family."

I was surprised that Hermann was so openly sympathetic but decided to keep still about it. I showed him the improvements I had made to our living space. He promised to make us a table, one that would fold so that we could carry it in the wagon and use along the route to California.

After a meal of crackers and sausage, Fritz and Jan went back into Independence to buy planks for a table. Lily and Hermann and I settled down for a nap. It was our first time to relax since arriving in Independence; while there was much to be done, I knew we needed this quiet time together. Hermann settled Lily into her hammock, gently rocking her and humming a tune. I lay on our makeshift bed and suddenly recognized what he was singing. "I like hearing you sing! That's *Die Zufriedenheit*, isn't it? I haven't heard you sing in such a long, long time."

He lay down next to me, with his head propped on a lumpy folded-over jacket, and sang the words softly. When he came to the line about birdsong, we heard a strange noise outside. "It's the geese. They're flying north – a sure sign of spring," he said.

"I learned that song in Köln. Do you remember the singing club there? It was when we met. I haven't thought about it in years."

"You haven't thought about singing at all in years. You've been too preoccupied. And you haven't been in the right disposition; you haven't been *gemütlich.* One needs a generous spirit to sing. I am glad to see that you are good-humored now."

"I'm not a good-humored man, am I? I may never be. But I do wish to have a tolerant nature." He turned on his side, facing me, "Our group has made me the leader of this venture, and I am bound to make a success of it, Frida. I will need strength of character. There will be times that I will have to make difficult choices, and I will appear contrary. You will disagree with me; perhaps all of them will disagree with me. But I take this challenge seriously."

"Does it frighten you – this trip and all the responsibility?"

He answered without pause, "Of course not!"

Chapter 35

"Mutti!" Lily's call woke both Hermann and me. "What is that noise? I thought I heard Otto!"

"Maybe it's Fritz come back with the wood." I too heard a commotion. I got up and lifted Lily out of the hammock. "Yes, I hear Fritz. He must be having fun with Jan."

"But he's speaking German, Frida. Jan doesn't speak German; he speaks English and Dutch," said Hermann.

"Anybody home?" hollered Fritz just outside the tent flap.

"We're here. Come in!" I called back.

"I can't. My hands are full. Open up!"

Hermann opened the flap, and there stood our two sons, arms around each other's shoulders, grinning like sons of *Teufel* himself. I grabbed Otto and hugged him to my breast. Hermann embraced us both, and Lily squirmed between our legs and hung on too. Both Otto and Fritz were whooping loudly, and we all joined the hullabaloo until all our neighbors came out to cheer; one thrust a bottle of beer into Hermann's hands. Florence and Clarence arrived home at that moment with their little boys, and joined the excitement, knowing immediately what was going on.

After a moment, I quietly left the celebration and went into our tent and sat by myself on the trunk. Tears were flowing down my cheeks, and my whole body shuddered and trembled. I felt quite faint and put my head down between my knees, dabbing at my cheeks with my apron. Although my hands were cold, my face was hot, as if warmed by the sun. I had the thought that I was basking in the warmth of my oldest boy; I closed my eyes and saw his smooth cheeks and bright smile. *Had I seen a little trouble in his eye? Maybe not.*

"*Mutter*? Are you all right?" It was Otto. "You're shaking." He sat next to me and put his arm around my back. "I'm home. I'm well. Don't worry any more." I couldn't answer him, and we sat thusly for a moment. He sensed that my emotion was more than happiness.

"You were frightened that I would not catch up to you, weren't you?"

I nodded my head.

"I didn't realize. I'm so sorry, *Mutter*; I was thoughtless. I never once thought that you would be suffering over my absence. I just knew that I would meet you here in plenty of time to move on. I've had some adventures – well, one in particular – I'll tell you when we're all together tonight. I say again: I'm sorry."

I dried my eyes and hugged him to me again. "Otto, you'll never know how bereft I have been over your absence. I am your mother and used to having you near, used to caring for you. When I awoke each morning and saw Fritz, Lily and your father, all I thought of was the empty space where you should have been. All day I worried over you and anguished that I could not see you, touch you, ask you questions, laugh with you. Seeing you now, seeing that you need a haircut, that your shirt wants a button, that you're taller than I remembered, I am overwhelmed with both the joy of having you back with me and the remembrance of missing you so intensely."

I was embarrassing him, but he stayed next to me and took something wrapped in waxed paper from his pocket. "I've brought you a small present! It's a goat cheese, mixed with cider. A new friend of mine made it. It's delicious on crackers; you'll like it, *Mutti!*"

I kissed him on his cheek and bade him join the hubbub outside our tent. Even though I wanted nothing more than to lay down alone and savor his return, I dragged myself outside too, and joined the merry group standing in the drizzle in a muddy Missouri field.

We had much to tell Otto about our trip on the *Amelia* and what we had learned so far in Independence. Lily would not leave him alone and spent the whole evening sitting on his lap, stroking his mustache and tickling behind his ears. When she told him about her Dolly falling into the river, she started to cry all over again. "Poor, Dolly, where do you think she is, Otto?"

He glanced at Fritz. "Fritz told me he thought he saw a magic boat that evening. He said it was just Dolly's size. What did it look like, Fritz?"

"Well, you know, I wasn't sure I saw anything; it was just a glimmer out of the corner of my eye, but it was pink and had candles all around it. The captain was a duck; he was green all over, and he gestured to Dolly to jump aboard. Right at that moment, it sailed up into the night sky."

"Didn't you tell me there were lots of baby duck on it too?" said Otto.

"Right. Five baby ducks."

Lily slid off his lap and went over to Fritz and climbed onto his lap and put her arms around his neck and gave him a kiss.

When we had finished telling all our stories, I asked Otto to tell us about our trunks and of his adventure.

"The trunks are safe in New Washington with Widow Owens. She has a shed that is weatherproof and has a lock. Our belongings are inside, along with those of a few other travelers. I have paid her for one year, and I have her address so that we can write letters.

"You would like her, *Mutter*. She is about the same age as you are, and she is good-humored and able. Her husband died in a blizzard. He was trying to bring their stock in out of the storm. She has a daughter."

"Aha!" croaked Fritz. "A daughter!"

Otto went quite red, but he continued, "Her name is Jennetta. She is seventeen, one year younger than me."

"Well, what else?" said Hermann.

"She's pretty."

"What else?"

"She and her mother run the farm; they're as good as it as two men would be. She likes to dance and play piano. And she's a free thinker – you ought to hear her on the subject of women's suffrage! And she's clever. We played draughts – she calls it checkers – and she beat me more times than not."

"It sounds like she beat you 'round the head and heart too, brother!"

"I stayed at their house for four nights, but then I left to catch up with you. It was not so easy to say good-bye."

We made room for one more on our sleeping platform. I lay awake happy to hear the measured breathing of Otto by my side. *Another milestone.* I thought of all the surprises I'd encountered as a grown-up married woman – the sorrows, scares, adventures, and joys. I had expected to be a mother and had thought about being the parent of small children. Not until this moment had I thought seriously that they would fall in love, move on, and have lives of their own. I thought about expectations, and before I fell asleep, I concluded that they were nearly useless.

Chapter 36

We all slept later than usual the next morning, not even the daily bustle outside our tent disturbed us. I was awake and dressed when I heard Florence whispering my name outside our tent flap.

"It's a fine day, Frida! Shall I put up a picnic and we'll celebrate Otto's homecoming with a walk in the hills?"

The rest of the family was slow to get dressed, and we had a leisurely time over our breakfast. Hermann had made plans to visit with a German company from Philadelphia, and Otto and Fritz wanted to go off together to explore all the tent camps. I was feeling such delicious relief that I thought a day away from mud and relentless planning would be welcome. Together Florence and I cobbled together a little picnic.

"I'm going to try something I've seen other women do." Florence told me. She lay little James on a square of cotton and wrapped him up snugly; then, with my help, she hoisted the bundle onto her back, and held it in place with a large green fringed shawl, brought over one shoulder and knotted at her chest. James fussed over this arrangement, wanting to get his little arms free. But Florence took John by the hand, and we started walking, letting the little ones set the pace. In no more than a moment, the baby was asleep.

We walked south, where we could see some low hills. As soon as we got away from the tent camps, we realized they were much too far away for a day's outing. "Let's keep going anyway. We need a change." I agreed wholeheartedly.

We passed a few farms, but saw no people. In the near distance was a small church, its steeple the tallest thing nearby. "Let's go there; the churchyard will make a good picnic spot," I suggested. As we got closer we saw that the churchyard was crowded with neighbors.

"Is it Sunday?" I asked Florence.

"No, Saturday. I think it's a wedding."

We stopped at a respectful distance and watched the bride and groom come down the steps to greet their guests. Lily strained at my hand, anxious to get a better look at a real bride.

"How fortunate for them that they have this beautiful day. It will bring them good luck!" said Florence.

"Certainly it will give them a good start. Isn't it amazing how our bodies and minds are influenced by the weather?" I said.

We found a place to sit in the nearby meadow, partially concealed by tall grasses. I laid out a blanket. Florence carefully shifted sleeping James to it. John and Lily played wedding – Lily directing their actions! We two mothers took off our bonnets and lay on either side of the baby, happy to be relaxing together in the weak sun.

Florence began at once to talk, "I had not intended to marry the first man who asked me. I was going to wait, consider all choices, and in the meantime educate myself by reading all the great literatures. I would learn French and possibly Italian. Also, I wanted to learn to swim. No husband would allow that!

"Then I met Clarence. Actually we had known each other as children, as his father had been the sexton at St. Luke's Chapel, my church. But it wasn't until we were both nineteen years old that we said our first words to each other. And that was on the chapel steps where he was shoveling snow. I slipped and fell on the ice and broke my arm."

"Did you fall into his arms, then?"

"Oh, Frida! I did not! But I must have fallen into his heart. I can't remember one single thing about the broken arm or the pain, but I do remember that even then he had a smart look to his face. We shared our opinions about ice and snow and slippery city streets and by the time we had exhausted that topic, we were sitting in his kitchen and his mother had fetched the doctor, who set my arm and bound it to my side. 'Take care of her, Clarence,' the doctor said as he washed up. 'I intend to, Sir,' he answered. Isn't it funny, the things we remember?"

"I know. It's true. I remember Hermann at the opera with my father and me. He would concentrate fiercely on the music, then turn to smile at me during favorite passages. I had not had other suitors in my small town. When Hermann asked my father for my hand, I was not surprised, and I thought then that we were a good match."

"But, Frida, did you love him?"

"Love him? Then? I'm not sure. I had not thought much about love. He called me *Schwartzi,* and I liked the playfulness of that nickname."

"I thought of little else!" said Florence. "I wanted to educate myself, but I wanted romance as well. I would dream of meeting a tall and blond man wearing a cape. He would ride an enormous black horse, and he would find me one day on a bench by his bridle path and sweep me onto his saddle and gallop over the fields with me in his arms.

"Other times, usually when I was visiting one of my older married sisters, I would see the other side of love: the more practical, difficult, interesting side.

"I thought I could successfully combine both sides – the romantic and the practical - but here I am walking a trail as willed by my husband, with one small child and a babe on my back. At least, with so little privacy, I think I will not be pregnant soon again, and that is a relief."

I turned on my side, facing her. Her smooth girlish face was furrowed with wrinkles, and her eyes were squinted shut. I stroked her arm, and she opened her eyes and relaxed her features.

"I know. I know. It is scandalous!" I said. "The world's expectations for women are not of our own devising. I have often thought that if I had been born a man, my life would have been very different. It would have belonged solely to me. Unlike Hermann, I would work for social reform instead of just talking about it. And I would make sure that my marriage was a partnership between agreeable partners, so that if one wanted to go to California and the other did not, they would talk about it until they could reach a compromise."

We continued lying together in companionable silence. Then Florence spoke again, "Marriage is not what I expected, Frida." She spoke so softly I could barely hear her. "I've never said that to anyone before. Clarence is a good husband and father. But he is dull. He hardly ever talks, and when he does, it is only to comment on something at hand, not to converse on a subject. If I begin to talk to him about the book that I am reading, he will listen politely, and then he will tell me that he is going to fetch water for the animals. If I mention a worry that I have about one of our boys or that I am exhausted, he'll tell me that he knows that I can take care of it. I have had more conversations with you in the few days that we have known each other than I have had with Clarence in the seven years that we have been married!"

I sat up and took Florence's hands in mine. I expected to see tears in her eyes, but there were none. *There are worse things than being bored.* She sat up too, and we put our arms around each other awkwardly with baby James between us. He stirred and pursed up his face as if to cry. Florence picked him up and gently unwrapped him from the cotton swaddling, "I can't change what is, but I'm determined to raise these boys differently than their father was."

Lily and John called out for their lunch, and as I set it out, I thought again about expectations, and realized they were not only useless but also deceiving.

Chapter 37

Our four weeks in Independence went quickly, as there was much to do, and everyone around us was caught up in the self same frenzied activity.

Lily and I went to the wainwright's – Hiram Young's – with Hermann and some of the men. Kristof Brantlach was our expert on wagon construction and had many sensible questions about the kinds of wood being used for the wagons themselves and for their axles and tongues. He asked about brake levers and blocks and about iron tires and felly rims. He told Hiram that we wanted watertight wagon beds with high sides for fording streams and, likewise, rainproof bonnets to protect our goods. Hiram recommended that we buy wagons all of the same design, so that eventual repairs would be easier. He claimed that his wagons were easy to dismantle for maintenance or parts. He also suggested we take certain tools and some spares. Albert Brantlach recommended that each wagon be capable of carrying twice its designated load, in the event of an emergency. They all agreed on points of construction and on price and ordered seven identical wagons, as well as spare axles and tongues. They also discussed the wheels and ordered fourteen extras, seven of the large back wheels and seven of the smaller front ones. All would have iron tires to protect the wooden rims. Each wagon would measure 12 feet by 4 feet, with a 12-foot tongue and yoke. Hiram promised all seven wagons in two weeks.

He had one wagon of the kind he would build for us outside his shop, and Lily and I climbed the fold-up back step and went inside. It was exactly one quarter the size of our tent. Somehow I had hoped we could sleep in the wagon at night in the event of wet weather. Now it was obvious that our possessions would overfill the space, and we would need to stay dry in our tent. I wondered how I could organize this wagon to access our gear readily along the route. At least it was high enough to stand in, and its pale brown homespun cover allowed some light inside.

Lily wanted to play in this snug place, and since we were waiting for the men to finish their transactions I agreed.

"*Mutti,* let's play Otto Comes Home! You be Otto; I'll be the Mother. I'll be here in the house asleep, and you will wake me up!"

She lay on the rough floor of the wagon. I cleared my throat in a mannish way, "Anybody home?" I called.

"We're here. Come in!" called Lily, sitting up in her make-believe bed, yawning theatrically, and stretching her arms wide.

"I can't. My hands are full. Open up!" I answered in my low voice.

Lily opened an imaginary tent flap, and I strode in, smiling. She threw her little arms around me and began to cry. "I was frightened that you would not catch up with us," she said, in her role as the mother.

At that moment we were both startled by a real mannish throat-clearing at the rear opening of the wagon. "Is everything all right, Missus? I heard crying."

"You must be Nehemiah," I said. "My husband told me about you." I was not prepared for the look and size of Nehemiah, and Lily shrunk back behind me. He was so tall that he had to crouch to see into the back of the wagon, and his shoulders filled the opening. His skin, hair and eyes seemed equally black, only relieved by a very pink mouth. His clothes were also black; with so little to catch the light, it was hard to read his expression. "Lily and I were just playing a game, but I was also inspecting the wagon, wondering how best to organize it."

"You finish your game; I'll set over here a bit. We'll pass some ideas when you're through." I saw he had some fabric in his hand, and a palm thummel exactly like Johann had on the *Maria* many years earlier. I watched him methodically push his needle through one side and out the other, then turn the work and push it through again. Lily poked her head from behind me and watched too. Nehemiah was sitting on a low bench humming a quiet song, and, with his long legs folded, he didn't seem so large and frightening to Lily. I sat on the wagon's back step; Lily crowded next to me. Nehemiah began to tell me some ideas he had for improving the wagon bonnets. He thought he could sew large pockets onto the cover, sewing along the same seams, so as not to jeopardize the weatherproofing of the doubled-over cotton homespun. He suggested pockets on the inside to hold clothes, guns and ammunition, books, and other things that must be protected from the weather. He also envisioned pockets on the outside, with sewn-in drain holes, to store cooking supplies, tools, gold mining equipment, and such. I suggested that the pockets on the outside might be made with large flaps that could be buckled shut against the weather or casual thievery.

Nehemiah took a pointed stick and drew a design in the dust. He included my ideas along with his own. When the men came out of Hiram's shop, I urged Hermann and the Brantlachs to consider his clever option for the wagon covers.

"We'll talk about this later, Frida! I am going to meet Robert now to look at livestock."

"Hermann! A moment please! You go talk with Robert, but Kristof and Albert and I will stay here and decide with Nehemiah about the wagon bonnets."

Hermann took a deep breath. "Yes. All right." He shook Nehemiah's hand and clapped the Brantlach brothers on their shoulders, then strode off without another word.

My word, I thought, but turned and explained Nehemiah's ideas. They sold themselves, and the Brantlachs ordered all the covers with pockets. They also talked with him about the bows; he assured them they would be soaked until pliable before being bent into shape and attached. Nehemiah also had an ingenious idea for storing the spare wheels, two under each wagon, one large and one small. The Brantlachs agreed and went back into the wainwright's to modify their order to accommodate his idea.

I asked Nehemiah how he learned to draw and to sew.

"In Virginia I worked with my Master. He was an architect in Richmond and designed plantation buildings. We worked close. It was he that taught me to read and to talk properly and to draw. My Mama taught me to sew, and to pray. Together they taught me to think."

Nehemiah showed me the project he was working on. It was a divided skirt for another woman waiting in Independence as we were. "I would like to make one for you and your daughter, Missus. There would be no charge except for the material. It would be my thank you to you for trying my new ideas."

I thought to argue with him. I had already determined that such skirts would be useful at times for Lily and me. I did not like the idea of not paying for his work. One look at his face, however, revealed his pride. "I would be most appreciative, Nehemiah. Will you recommend a type of material and direct me to a merchant?"

He suggested blue denim and said he had some that had been sent from a merchant in Boston. He said it was comfortable, substantial, and would wash easily. I agreed, and he gave me a tape to take my measurements and Lily's. "You come back in three days, Missus, your skirts be ready."

When Hermann and my sons saw our skirts several days later, they all determined to order pants from Nehemiah of the same blue denim and with the identical multitude of pockets.

Robert Aulich and Hermann visited several stockyards to look over animals. Robert did not like what he saw and decided to wait a week, hoping more animals would be brought up the river. It was a good plan, and during our second week he identified and paid for – out of our common treasury – forty-two oxen at $30 each, four riding horses at $75 each, and a milk cow for $60. The stockman agreed to keep the animals in his paddocks until we needed them and arranged a contract for us to pay for their food.

Hans-Jürgen Topp along with Rolf Smit and his twins took on the task of buying repair material. They conferred with two of the families that had started prematurely and returned to Independence, as well as to several groups that had driven their own wagons this far across the country. They put together a list, and went from merchant to merchant buying iron bolts, linchpins, skeins, nails, hoop iron, and a jack. They also bought a shovel, an axe, and feed troughs for the livestock, one for each wagon.

Hans-Jürgen came over to our tent one day to talk with me. "I heard that parts of the trail are so bumpy that one could put milk in a churn in the morning and have butter by the evening. I wonder what you think of that idea."

"Are you asking me, Hans-Jürgen, because you think I'll be making all the butter for our group of nearly thirty people?" I had always particularly liked Hans-Jürgen. We had been near neighbors in New York; his wife had been a close friend of mine. I was sorry that she had not joined him on this trip, but had chosen to stay in New York to try to get her poetry published. He was an awkward man – a little too tall, but kind and generous of spirit. I had always been attracted to his calmness and his handsome looks.

A little color rose in his gaunt cheeks, "Oh, no! Only that you have more experience than the rest of us. I have seen a churn at a supplier's for $3. If you think it's a good idea, we could take turns with it."

I laughed, "It's a good idea, Hans-Jürgen. Let's try it. And, next time you go there, I'd like to go with you. I've seen some sheet iron stoves around the campground; I'd like to get a closer look. Also, I'll need a wash tub; perhaps this supplier has tubs too."

Hans-Jürgen and I went the next day, taking Fritz and the Smit twins with us to help carry. We decided that one washtub would do for our whole group, but that we would need two stoves to cook for so many. We bought the churn, seven buckets, some soap, and 30 pounds of candles. Our purchases came to $56. We put the smaller items, including the churn, into the washtub. Hans-Jürgen and I took a handle apiece and carried the cumbersome load between us. Fritz swung one heavy stove onto his shoulders, and the twins carried the other between them. With many stops to rest along the way, we got back to our tents and added to the growing pile of necessities that would accompany us.

I had made a list of the foodstuffs with which I would begin the trip. I seemed to check and revise it every single day as I talked with Florence and some of the other women. After two weeks I thought it a good time to purchase as many provisions as possible, so that we could go at short notice when the weather broke. Florence and I were to shop together, but at the last moment her baby took sick with a deep cough, and she stayed back. Hans-Jürgen offered to accompany me, as he wanted to provision for his wagon too.

We were unused to being alone together, and both were shy in our conversation. Hans-Jürgen mentioned the day's weather once, then ducked his long chin into his shirt collar. We both exclaimed at the overcrowding at Nolan's Inn, where we had heard four hundred men slept in two hundred beds. I made small comments on the little houses we passed, remarking on messy chicken yards and diminished stacks of cordwood. I pointed out a yellowjackets' nest, "I should send my boys over to help them burn that out," I said, not wanting our silences to become too long to manage.

Hans-Jürgen spoke, surprising me, "I have never had the company of children, although Kalli and I had hoped for them. I think your children bring you great happiness. If I had boys they would be just as yours are: smart and handsome and strong. My daughter would be sweet and would sleep in my arms. None would give trouble or worry." He tucked his chin back into his collar.

I acknowledged the compliment, but thought to myself that with no children of his own, he could not imagine the responsibility, encumbrance, or worry that was bound and parceled with parenting. "I am glad for the company of my family on this journey. I imagine that it is lonely for you at times, even in the company of our friends."

He kept his face down and in that way accepted my comment, and we arrived at the provisionary.

I bought the following bulk items:

300 pounds	Flour
40 pounds	Cornmeal
100 pounds	Bacon
50 pounds	Sugar
30 pounds	Coffee
50 pounds	Dried peaches and apples
25 pounds	Rice
25 pounds	Beans

I also bought vinegar, saleratus, salt and pepper, lard, and a large crock of pickles. Onions and potatoes I would buy just before we left, along with any available fresh produce and sausage. I paid $60 for these provisions and the storekeeper agreed to deliver them the next day. Hans-Jürgen finished his order too, but as he had another errand to run in town, I walked briskly home alone, feeling that an important final chore had been accomplished.

I was calm, and I was ready to go.

Chapter 38

On a sunny day in the middle of May I sat on the south side of our tent. Families and groups had been leaving Independence for nearly a week. Others had taken their place, coming west from St. Louis and other departure points. The ground had thawed, the mud was nearly gone, and the great prairie to the west was abloom with spring. Our wait was longer than we expected, but now we were ready, our preparations complete. I had only to buy a few fresh provisions. In the morning we would strike the tent, harness the animals to the wagons that were mostly packed and already heavy laden, and join the procession of optimistic Argonauts. But that morning I had some rare time to myself. Hermann and Otto were helping the Brantlachs load their wagon. Fritz had taken Lily and little John with him to the edge of town to wave good-bye to his friend, Jan.

I brought out my small mirror and unfolded its cover. Back in New York I had accompanied my friend, Kalli Topp, Hans-Jürgen's wife, to a cabinetmaker. As she discussed a project of her own with the craftsman, I admired his sales models. These were miniature prototypes of desks, chairs, and other things that he offered for sale. A small folding mirror caught my eye. The glass was framed in cherry wood, simply incised with the merest suggestion of three rounded columns. Its maker had ingeniously hinged a cover to it so that the glass could be protected when closed and thus carried easily and safely by its owner. The cover could be folded open to act as a stand, or the whole apparatus could be hung by a small brass ring, which was also its clasp. When closed, it was not much bigger than my hand. Charmed by it, I bought it without a second thought.

It had been packed in the trunk so long that it was covered with lint. I blew it clean and hung it from the tent's pole. I took the pins from my hair and let it out onto my shoulders and ran my fingers through the thick tangle and along my scalp until its whole mass was loose. I took my hairbrush and went at the snarls and tangles with vigor, brushing hard until both the brush and my scalp tingled. It was warm in the sun and I rolled up my sleeves and undid the top two buttons of my dress. When I looked in the mirror, I was surprised at what I saw. There was the girl I had been before leaving Prussia. My complexion, darkened by the spring sun, looked youthful, so did my shiny hair, now lying about my neck and shoulders. The biggest surprise were my eyes, my dark eyes. The last time I had truly examined myself in a glass, they had looked tired, sunken in their sockets, and lacking luster. This day they shone bright. I blinked and turned this way and that, thinking it was a trick of the light. But it wasn't a trick; my eyes reflected the way I felt: able and enthusiastic about our start. When we left the sheltering portals of Astor House on March 20, my mood was reflected in the cloudy dampness. This day, May 19, my disposition was equal to the sweet smell of spring, the heat of the mid-morning sun, and my own anticipation to begin the trail.

I brought out my journal, and wrote a few lines:

> There is relief in unbinding my hair, loosening my buttons, escaping confinement. Tomorrow we relinquish our hold on another place that has become a home of sorts. Although I will leave behind both friends and familiarity, I won't miss this one. I have shed many of my accustomed habits – some were left in St. Louis, others in New York, a few even in Gelsenkirchen and Giessen. Tomorrow I'll discard one more – petticoats!

Chapter 39

We woke before dawn. In a dreamlike state, I dressed Lily and myself in our new blue split skirts, made strong coffee, and cut thick slabs of bread for our breakfast. A tune was playing itself over and over in my head – one I could not recognize, even though I tilted my head trying to hear it better. I remembered the drums and trumpet that I conjured as we approached New York harbor on the *Maria.* I also remembered our old friend Adolph reminiscing about his first Atlantic crossing, and how he thought he heard music. I was able to complete my morning chores; after all, that was a routine I was used to, but my thoughts were so insubstantial and jumbled as to make no sense. I was hardly aware of the bustle around me as Hermann and the boys attempted to knock down and pack the tent. I didn't even notice as the first corner collapsed, bringing the entire tent down on Hermann who was still inside, untying lashes.

"*Gott in Himmel*!" I heard his muffled cry, and it brought me more fully to my senses in time to see Otto trip over the flailing tent pole and fall on top of his cocooned father, further pinning him in his canvas shroud. Fritz, Lily, and I grinned at each other. Hermann managed to wriggle his flushed head and arms out from under Otto's legs. He grabbed one leg, like a drowning man reaching for a raft. By now, our sleepy tent city neighbors had awakened and gathered to watch the commotion. *How would Hermann react?* Slightly stunned, he looked around, hesitated for a moment, caught my eye, and laughed.

Our plan was for all the members of the New York German Company to meet at the edge of town; we were the last to arrive. It was obvious that we needed to practice getting our tent down and our gear stowed. Florence and Clarence and their little boys arrived as we did. While not members of our group, they would travel along with us, at least in the beginning. I was grateful to share those early days with Florence.

A large company from the Albany area was just leaving.

Their group numbered nearly thirty wagons and had chosen mules to haul them. It was a noble sight to see those small, tough, earnest animals straining obediently. Each wagon flew a hand-sewn red, white, and blue striped flag, reflective of Albany's Dutch ancestry. There were several women in the group; each wore an apron similarly striped. They had made sweets from molasses, and as each wagon got into line, these candies were thrown to the crowd waving them off.

Following them came a gaudily uniformed Massachusetts company, carrying sabers with a swivel gun on each of their wagons. I wondered if they thought they were going to war.

That first hour, when we finally got going, was like a party, a celebration. Our oxen were fresh, and so were we. Many others were also getting underway, and there was much cheering and waving amongst the friends and strangers. I felt an unaccustomed sense of equilibrium. I was resolute in my desire to return eastward to New York, but I was also excited to be heading westward to California at last. We did not even stop for lunch, but instead ate some bread and dried fruit as we walked out.

Ours was the lead wagon, but only for the first hour, as it was obvious that Hermann was not yet a teamster. He began in good humor, walking alongside the lead yoke, bellowing commands: "Giddap! Gee! Haw!" Within a half hour he was hoarse, and we'd gone less than a mile. Then he tried positioning Otto and Fritz at the heads of the lead yoke of oxen with ropes to their bridles to direct them and to urge them forward. He would crack the long-handled, long-lashed whip he had bought in Independence. Each time the noise would startle the boys, distract the oxen, and our wagon and all the others behind would lumber to a halt, all piling up around each other. The prevailing mood was of such good humor, such relief to be underway at last, that the whole company indulged Hermann for the first hour. Although I did overhear two men on horseback say,

"Look at that green horn!"

"He'll not get far!"

Then Robert Aulich, who was driving the wagon behind us, offered to go first for a while. Reluctantly, Hermann gave in, and we fell to the rear. Soon we were passed by Clarence and Florence's wagon, then by a group of young men traveling by foot and pulling a sledge behind them. When a small wagon, pulled by a single yoke of oxen and driven by a woman went by, Hermann tipped his hat to her politely. But I saw his complexion turn quite red.

"Otto, Fritz, get up there with Robert and watch him drive! I think we've got the slowest, stupidest beasts of the group," ordered Hermann, knocking the closest animal on its nose with his whip handle. It started to bellow, the others stopped in their tracks. Lily, who had been skipping alongside, chattering to the oxen, became anxious and begged to be carried. I picked her up and caught up with Florence, Clarence, and their two little ones. I knew Hermann's moods, and wanted to avoid this one.

At five o'clock, Fritz fell back and walked with me. He took Lily on his shoulders, and she fell asleep, her tousled head jouncing along with his every step. "*Mutti*, I think you should be the one to drive our team! You should watch Robert – he is quiet and patient. Like you, *Mutti.* Robert carries a whip too, but he only uses the butt end to touch the shoulder of the ox next to him. He speaks to them no louder than I'm speaking to you. You know how musical he is? Sometimes he sings to them!"

"Why don't you try driving our team, Fritz?"

"Can you imagine Father letting me drive on our first day when he has had such trouble?"

I thought for a moment. "Fall back, Fritz, and tell him I need to talk with him, but that I am caring for the children and can't come to him myself."

I took Lily from him and gathered little John from his father's shoulders, strapping their baby on my own back. When Hermann caught up with me, I was perspiring from carrying the baby and entertaining John and Lily.

"What is it, Frida?"

"It's nearly six o'clock. We said we would stop each evening at six. I'm sure Robert and the others are waiting for your direction."

As he hurried forward, Fritz and our wagon caught up. "These oxen are not stupid, *Mutti*, but they are slow. It is frustrating. I can walk faster than the team. Maybe we should have bought mules. They say they're faster."

In another half hour we caught up with the rest of our company. We had been going for seven hours and had covered only ten miles, not the thirty that Hermann had set as each day's goal. Hermann was despondent, blaming the oxen, blaming the wagon wheels, complaining about the blisters on his own heels. He picked on young

David Settlemeyer who was playing a game with a ball, seeing how high he could bounce it. "David! *Junge*! Don't you have anything better to do? Come here, I'll box your ears! Randolf, you should have left this brat behind with his *Mutti.*"

A moment later I overheard him talking with Carl Kramer and Rolf Smit, "What a useless, unfortunate undertaking this is." I couldn't believe my ears, especially as I was highly stimulated by our first day. The weather had been fine and the sun's heat had brought forth the sweet and sour smells of the grasses, flowers, and earth of the prairie. The children and I had kept pace without complaining, and we had been distracted by the butterflies, damselflies, and nesting songbirds along the trail. I remembered how Antonia and I had encouraged each other back in New York by imagining walking together in the wide-open countryside. I thought it was even better than our dreams and wished she were here to see for herself.

As the boys set up our tent, I began preparations for supper. "No, Mrs. Reinhardt, tonight it is our turn." It was Peter Franken Junior. "My father and I worked out a schedule as we walked along today. We have thirty-two people, plus Lily. We thought that each night two pairs could cook for sixteen people each. This way no one will have to cook dinner more than once every eight nights. Tonight my father and I will be one pair of cooks and Kristof Brantlach and one of Rolf Smit's sons will be the other pair. You and your family can bring your plates in half an hour. We are making flapjacks, and we have honey!"

I climbed onto the wagon in relief and reached for my writing materials, close at hand in one of Nehemiah's clever pockets sewn on the inside of the wagon cover. I thought to write to Antonia and Erich or to Anna and Adolph back in New York but instead began a letter to my mother. I knew that she was fearful for us as we undertook this trip; she did not have the comfort of daily newspaper articles about the journey.

Mumie,

I begin this letter to you with kisses.

We are at the end of our first day of prairie travel. Our camp is cheerful. All around are our cattle and those of other groups,

> feeding upon the fresh spring grass. The jumble of tents and pale wagon covers resembles a small village, and as I watch, the activities remind me of home. Someone is mending a rip in a shirt, another is milking a cow; in the air is both the yeasty smell of bread rising and the faint notes of hymns being sung by a group camped behind us.
>
> Most of our group is in a carefree frame of mind, glad to be underway at last. I see several men rolling out bedrolls in the open to sleep under the stars.
>
> Hermann is repacking some of our things, as our wagon was the slowest today, and he believes that he must get the weight lower in the wagon box.
>
> Your grandsons are setting up the tent for the night; Lily tries to help them, dragging blankets through the dust. She has misplaced her hat, and her hair is in a tangle around her face. As I watch, Fritz reaches down and twists it back and secures it under her collar. Once I worried about her ability to make this trip; she was so often sick in New York. But not now! Now I worry that she has only men and boys to play with. I am her only female influence! If I were to cut off her dark curls, an observer would think she is a boy.

At that moment a horseman came by our campsite. He was riding back to Independence to buy another yoke of oxen, realizing already that the two yoke he had were not enough. "Do you need anything, Missus?" he called.

"Yes! Thank you. Will you mail a letter for me?" I quickly put my note to my mother into an envelope and gave the man some coins.

At the same moment Peter Junior called us all for supper. We were ravenous, all of us, and quickly finished the flapjacks, most of us wishing there were more. I made a mental note to plan for a very hungry crowd when it was my turn. I also wondered what Hermann would do when it was his turn to cook.

My legs were tired from walking, but I wasn't weary; it seemed as though no one else was either. Clarence and Florence came over to chat when their own supper was over. They brought with them two brothers who had staked out their mule nearby. Isaac and Reuben had no interest in the gold rush. Isaac was a barber and his younger brother was a wheelwright. Their plan was to offer their services along the trail to the overlanders. They looked so alike, I thought they were twins. "Isaac always has a white cloth over his shoulder, ready for the shoulders of his next client; that's how you can tell us apart," said Reuben.

Otto and Fritz built a fire, and Peter Franken Junior and some of the other young ones drifted over. We all sat on the prairie grass, not even needing rugs or blankets, and watched the sparks fly up to mingle with the stars in the vast night sky. The night sounds felt protective, heard by us in the sheltering shadow of our wagon. Robert came over and started everyone humming along to some careless tune of his own invention. Lily nestled in my lap and was soon asleep. I leaned against Hermann's shoulder, relaxing my usual guard against his moods, and was soon asleep myself.

Chapter 40

There is nothing but boundless prairie for one hundred and thirty miles from Independence to the Kansas River. And, each day as we inched across this expanse, I grew abler and more confident. Each night I went to sleep thinking: *Yes. This is possible!*

Our group rotated the lead wagon as dictated by Hermann, but at times the going was so easy that two or three wagons could travel abreast. Then each team's driver could converse with the others and at times, one teamster would manage two teams. Progress was slow, since the oxen set the pace. Often I would walk ahead or off to the side with Florence and the children to investigate the terrain. Lily and John quickly discovered prairie dogs and could spot their burrows before I could. They would run to the mounded entrances always a moment too late to catch the nervous little rodents. When they saw eagles or hawks circling, they waved their arms in the air and called to the little prairie dogs to run and hide.

One afternoon I overheard Lily, "You be a hawk, John!" He chased her through the high grasses of the prairie with his arms outstretched, screeching in childish imitation of a red-tail; she hopped and ran in circles in front of him, her arms curled to her chest, her teeth chattering and her nose twitching like a prairie dog. He caught her easily and to my distress pretended to eat her up. Before I could intervene, she jumped to her feet, "Now, John, I'll be the hawk!"

Lily was accustomed to a nap in the afternoon. The first few days without one, she was fretful in the evenings, and one night fell asleep before supper was even served. By the third day I approached Hermann with an idea.

"I've noticed that each morning you and the boys hitch up the same six oxen to our wagon, and that the two largest are always yoked together in the lead."

"*Ja, Ja,* and I must admit it was Fritz's idea. He thinks they will work better for us if they are in the habit of being in the same position. I think the boy is right this time. He and Otto have been experimenting with the positions. They like the big ones in the lead. You remember how stupid I thought the oxen were our first day? Well, I was right! Two of them are quite stupid, and Fritz and Otto have put them in the middle. It's working well. You should try driving them, Frida; even you could manage the team now!"

"I think I will, Hermann." I turned away, hiding my smile, and decided to save my idea until later.

I waited until Hermann and Otto had gone hunting for prairie chickens or grouse for dinner. It was early afternoon, and I was carrying Lily on my back.

"Fritz! Would you teach me to drive?"

"It is easy, *Mutti.* Give me Lily and take the whip." He swung Lily up onto the broad back of the docile ox next to him. "Here you are, Silvester; you won't even feel the load."

Lily lay her head down on his muscular neck and stretched her arms as far around as they would go. She smiled sleepily at Fritz and me.

I laughed, "Silvester!"

"Yes, I've named them all. Silvester and Nikolaus are in the lead; the daydreamers come next - Violet and Pansy. Do you see how bluish their coats are? The smallest and youngest are in the rear – Geld and Check."

"And, I suppose they come when you call them?"

"Well, almost. Silvester knows that he's the boss. When I get him in the morning, the rest will follow him. Nikolaus doesn't like the yoke, but he'll submit to it when I scratch him behind his ears."

"Look at Lily, the motion is rocking her to sleep. Can we slide a blanket under her and put a strap over her legs so that she can nap here? It is what I was hoping for."

Fritz and I walked along companionably while Lily slept. He showed me how to keep the oxen moving forward as well as how to turn them. "The main thing that I have learned, *Mutti,* is that they can be steered but never driven. They pace themselves. When Lily wakes up, I'll show you how to stop them."

We ascended a long hill. At its top our eyes rested on the broad expanse of rolling prairie; one vast carpet of grasses stretching as far as we could see until it met the sky in the farthest distance. In vain our eyes endeavored to catch a glimpse of something manmade, a cultivated field, a house or shed, but except for the slow-moving train of wagons before us, there was no sign of civilization.

"What do you think of this country?" I asked Fritz.

"I love it! There is so much to see – grasses, birds, snakes. I've never seen such animals: badgers and gophers – imagine! I love the long views from the hilltops. It's not like New York!

"I remember when Otto was missing. Remember? I was so frightened! I remember that I wanted to turn around and go home, to be where things were familiar and safe. I didn't believe that we would ever be prepared for this trip. I had no faith in Father and not much in myself. You called this an adventure – do you remember? You said I'd never forget it in all my life. Well, you were right. I believe I will remember every single minute of this trip. Sometimes I'm so excited by it all that my blood seems to heat up. It makes me glow! I love this bountiful prairie! And, I wouldn't have believed that so many people would be following the same dream."

He continued, "And I love the evenings when we slow down, choose our campsite, and feed the animals. I like it when the light fades and I see other campfires and hear the murmur of others' voices. I feel safe within our own fire-lit circle. Our campsite seems like home."

"Is it what you expected, Fritz?"

"Not at all. I knew that I would see places and things that would be new to me. But, I didn't know that I would meet people from all over the country sharing the same vision. I walked this morning with a wild-looking old man from eastern Canada. He had come by foot all the way to Ohio to find his brother, hoping he would go with him to California to get gold. When he couldn't find him, he decided to go alone. He's seventy! Not only that, he has no fingers on either hand. He lost them all to frostbite fishing off the coast of Newfoundland. With only his two thumbs, he packs up his mule by himself. After a while he told me I was too slow and he had to make time, so we waved good-bye to each other."

He continued, "Behind us are two families, traveling together. They want to meet you, in fact. They have ten children between them – all girls! I never guessed we would be part of such a huge migration!"

We heard a commotion and saw Hermann and Otto coming our way.

"One other thing, *Mutti*, before they join us. I wanted to ask you something. I think this would be a great adventure even without the possibility of a gold strike at the end. Do you agree?"

I gave his arm a squeeze just as Hermann arrived.

He didn't notice that I was driving the oxen or that Lily was sleeping astride Silvester.

"Frida! It is my turn to cook tonight and Otto and I have been to the butcher's shop! Look here!"

He dumped the contents of his burlap bag at my feet.

I gasped and tears sprang to my eyes. I signaled to Fritz to keep the team moving forward. They had shot at least fifteen prairie dogs. One of them was still twitching. Hermann noticed and with a quick movement crushed its head with the heel of his heavy boot.

I recoiled from the scene, clutching my stomach. "How could you?" was all that I could say. Otto seemed to shrink behind his father as though hiding from me; Hermann dismissed me with a wave of his hand and a derisive exhalation.

That night Lily and I took some sausage and crackers and asked Florence if we could join her family at dinnertime. Lily and John resumed their favorite game, pretending to be prairie dogs, chasing each other around the campfire, then coming together to rub noses in homely reunion.

When I returned, our tent was set up, and I put Lily in her little nest of blankets and told her the sad story of *Hans Guck in die Luft*, the little boy who was so absentminded and distracted that he walked right off the end of a wharf and drowned. Otto and Fritz had loved that story when they were little. They would squirm in their beds, glad that they were not so forgetful and were safe in their familiar quilts. Lily listened quietly then blinked up at me, "*Mutti,* was Hans a bad boy? Was he being punished?"

"Hush, sweet baby. It's just a story; it didn't really happen."

I slid into my own covers and wriggled about to get comfortable on the hard ground. I thought about all the ancient children's stories from my own youth as a way of distracting myself from the insensitive scene of Hermann with the prairie dogs. When he came in, I was still awake. "That was a cruel thing to do, Hermann; what if Lily had been awake and had seen the results of your hunt. She thinks of prairie dogs almost as pets. Haven't you heard her naming them – *Spotty* and *Blackie* and *Pointy Ears*? I think she believes that there are only a few of them and the same ones keep popping up out of different burrows!"

"For God's sake, Frida! You are sounding like a child. We are on the frontier here. It is my job to provide food, to lead our group, to protect us from the Indians. I can't be aware every minute of how thin-skinned you are. Lily must grow up fast, and you must help her do that."

"Hermann! She's not even three!"

"Yes, she's not even three. And we're not even half way to California. We're not in the city now. It's going to get harder and harder. Now is the time to get tough, before the summer gets hot and we reach the mountains. If you think this is a lark, you are mistaken. Are you with me or not?"

"I am with you. And I am tough and I ask for no special treatment for myself. But I expect you to consider Lily's needs. You are not the only one on this trip."

"Hush," he hissed at me as the boys came into the tent for the night. As he climbed under our blankets, he flung out his arm, catching me with his elbow across my breast. I yelped in pain, but my call was met with silence.

The next morning Otto told me that they had made a stew, adding potatoes and onions to the meat. "Father and I may be good hunters, but we're not good cooks, *Mutter*! Our friends tasted the meal, but very few finished their bowls. I don't think it smelled quite right. *Ach*! It was an experiment – now we know not to try prairie dogs again."

"Otto," I said, "Do you remember that you and Fritz would play at being sea captains when we first came to New York? Your imaginations would carry you out on the piazza and across the blue seas. You would pretend to swing in the rigging like pirates and would order each other to give over the gold or walk the plank. Do you remember?"

"Of course, but I was a boy then. Why do you mention it now?"

"You pretended to be sailors because that is what you knew then. Lily plays at being a prairie dog. She can mimic all their antics, poses, and barks, and she and John run together jumping and yipping just like the little animals. I worried at first that they would step in a prairie dog burrow and twist a leg in the hole, but I see that they are careful. It is pretending and fun for them, just as it was pretending and fun for you and Fritz to shout orders at each other."

"Those terrible burrows! I worry about the oxen stepping in them too. Along the trail, where it's packed down, it's not so bad, but sometimes we go off to the side to pass another wagon, and I curse the prairie dogs and their holes."

"But Lily doesn't curse them Otto. She loves to chase after them, chirping and chattering as they do. It was thoughtless of you and your father to kill them and to think that we would eat them."

"Father told me it is my duty to find meat for our group."

"Not prairie dogs!"

Chapter 41

I met the families with the ten girls the next day. Medorum Crawford and his wife Prudence were traveling with her brother Amos Smith and his second wife Bess. Bess was eighteen, the same age as Otto, but was expected to be the mother to Amos's five girls who ranged in age from Mary, who was fifteen, to the youngest who was seven.

I tried to be friends with Prudence. It was obvious that she carried the burden of caring for both families and that she needed a friend. But I had trouble being near her. Prudence didn't seem to have time for her own personal hygiene, and she smelled as bad as my old dog back home after rolling in the pig's pen. She kept their two wagons swept clean and seemed always to be busy kneading dough or plaiting someone's hair. She even knitted or mended as she walked by the side of the wagon. But, as for her own body, I always knew she was approaching before she even came into sight.

Bess was a sweet thing, but she hadn't acquired the skills of cooking, cleaning, mending, or minding children. She and the oldest girl, Mary, liked fussing with each other's hair, and when they could, they caught up with Otto and Fritz and teased them about their city ways. That left all the work for Prudence, and she never let up, not wanting to disappoint her husband and her brother. She had a nervous habit of winding one or two hairs around her finger, then pulling them right out of her head. Consequently, she had scant hair on either side of her thin face.

Prudence was extremely fearful of the savages that we would meet along our trek, and she wondered aloud how to protect her girls, all the while pulling long brown hairs from her head. One day when we stopped by a stand of tall trees to have our midday break, I told her that I was going to bathe Lily and myself in the small creek there. "Would you like to join us, Prudence, and bring your girls?" I inquired. "My friend Florence and her little ones are going to come too."

"No! I will tell Bess and Mary, but I shouldn't dare be out of sight of Medorum and Amos. What if the savages should come and find us naked?"

We hadn't seen any Indians, except a few back on the streets of Independence and St. Louis. "Prudence, I don't think we have to worry about that here, but I could ask one of my boys to keep watch on the other side of the trees."

"I've heard there are wild ones near the Kansas River – they're Pottawatomies. They're the Fire Nation. I don't want to be caught by no fire starters!" she answered. "If I was you, I wouldn't go into the trees; I certainly wouldn't get myself naked!"

I wondered if she was going all the way to California without a bath, but I knew it was none of my business and changed the subject. "I've never been a knitter. Will you show me what you're making?" She had been knitting as we walked along, the needles clicking as grayish wool snaked out of the bag carried around her neck. "I'm impressed that you never seem to look down at your work!" She held up the almost-finished project – to my surprise it was a man's undergarment.

"Oh!" I could feel the color rise in my cheeks. *What could I talk to this woman about?* I was relieved by the distraction of Lily running to me with a small cut on her finger that needed attention. Her straw bonnet had gone missing once again, one shoe had come loose, and her split skirt was twisted part way round. I was reminded of Hermann's admonition: for Lily this trip was a lark.

"She's a pretty little thing," said Prudence. "How ever do you keep her so clean!"

Chapter 42

I begged for an extra half hour at our midday rest to bathe in a sweet water stream and asked Otto and Fritz to stand as watchmen while the women bathed – Lily and I, Florence and her little ones, and Bess and Mary Smith. I thought it best to give my sons a job rather than to leave them to poke their curious noses through the bushes. I had observed them watching Bess and Mary. They were pretty girls, buxom and ruddy; I could understand when I overheard Otto, pretending to peek through the tangle of trees and underbrush that sheltered the river from the trail.

He gave a long, low whistle, "Well, well! Look at that – pink and pretty! Better turn around, Brother; I think Mary's trying to catch your eye. Look at those legs!" He whistled again.

"He's just pretending," I whispered to the girls.

I suggested that everyone scrub first, "Then I'll check your heads for ticks." Fritz had told me that he read in the Lewis and Clark Journals that they were plagued with ticks. We were plagued with them ourselves, and every night shook out our clothes and checked each other's heads.

Just then I heard the boys again.

"She's probably got ticks," said Otto.

"Who cares?" Fritz answered with a laugh.

Then the men took over the stream. I could imagine the pile of dirty, dusty clothes by the bank of the river: breeches, shirts, vests, underclothes, socks, probably a couple of blankets from 'round men's shoulders.

The men claimed they didn't need a watchman, but I stayed near, drying my hair and Lily's, just in case. We heard Fritz jump in first with a proud holler. Anton, Tom and Peter Franken Junior must have been right behind him, and those four would have nearly filled up the little pool in the stream. We could hear them splashing and laughing. It sounded as though they were all going to drown each other. Lily wanted to join the fun; I tried to explain that it was the boys' turn. Then we heard David Settlemeyer swing out on the rope swing, left by earlier travelers, roaring like a wild jungle beast, and landing with a loud splash, shrieking when he hit the cold water.

That night when I was in the tent putting Lily to bed, I overheard Fritz talking to Otto.

"Had you ever seen Father naked before?"

"Not 'till today."

"I looked up from the water and saw him with some of the other men, walking gingerly down the embankment and realized I'd never seen him naked before. That's odd, isn't it?"

"I noticed how big and hairy he is," Otto said.

Fritz continued, "I saw him pick his way around some sharp rocks, and I noticed how small and pink his feet are, round like the rest of him, but hairless. Even though he was only one of the naked men, he seemed to dominate. He reached out his hand to old Felix Mittler, to steady him, an intimacy that surprised me. You know what I mean."

He continued, "It wasn't just his size that was so overwhelming, but that he was the head of our family - the father. I was looking up at him, the way I did when I was a little boy, and he seemed very important and very weak at the same time. He covered himself with one hand but couldn't cover his large belly and buttocks; both sagged and jiggled as he picked his way down. He looked disgusting, especially since all the other men were slim and muscular. His face was dark with suntan, but the rest of him was so white that he seemed bluish and cool in the trees' shadow. When he stepped into the sunshine at the edge of the stream, I saw how strong he was around his shoulders and arms, and was reminded of how scared of him I used to be. He launched his bulk through the air and into the center of the small pool, scattering the rest of us.

"I didn't want to play in the pool anymore, not with him there. I quickly washed myself and dressed. I thought how vulnerable we are. He wouldn't be able to protect us if the savages came."

"So, now you've seen him naked," said Otto. "So what?"

"So nothing. I still don't understand him."

Chapter 43

One afternoon Hermann, Fritz, and I were walking, ahead of our group, scouting for a place to camp for the night and idly talking about local Indians. Otto was driving the oxen, and Lily was walking along with him. She had found the leather halter made for her by the harness maker in St. Louis and was playing a game in which she was the lead ox, and Otto had to drive her as well as the team. The game had kept her busy for hours. As it didn't require much participation from Otto, besides an occasional gentle nudge with the whip handle, he was a willing accomplice.

We stopped for a moment as I had seen a clump of pink flowering late spring cives and thought to gather them for our larder.

A cry rolled down the line of wagons: "Kansas River in sight!"

"We will continue on the trail a bit later than usual," said Hermann. "We'll settle our camp down by the river. I'll have a chance to see how the crossing is, and in the morning it will be easier for all of us."

Fritz and I agreed. We continued our conversation about the Pottawatomies as we continued along the trail. Fritz had heard their Thunder tribe lived nearby. Someone had told him that they had once been fierce warriors and skilled horsemen.

I shuddered and repeated Prudence's concerns. "Have they bothered any travelers ahead of us? Should we put Lily in our wagon and get our guns out?"

"Leave it to the men, Frida!" said Hermann, scowling at me.

"It is not in my character to be fearful of people; you know that, Hermann. It's just that we have not had our first encounter with a full tribe yet; I want to be prepared and to protect our family."

Fritz pointed ahead of us, "Someone's approaching. Look!" We stopped, awaiting their arrival.

Galloping toward us were eight Indians, men and women. This would be our first encounter. They all rode astride, even the women, and the men had painted their faces red and blue. In front of us they reined in their ponies, and two leaped to the ground and approached us.

Instinctively I grabbed Fritz and attempted to put him behind me, as though he were still my young boy. He stood his ground, merely taking my hand in his. Hermann took a step forward toward the Indian draped in a red blanket. He put his hand in the air, as a signal to stop them. I couldn't stifle a small cry, but it went unheard in the commotion of the horses' restless hooves. The Indian crossed one arm over his chest and began a long speech, which I took to be a welcome. It gave me a chance to stare at him, unabashedly and raptly. He had beads of fanciful colors around his wrists and ankles, and more beads decorated his moccasins and deerskin pants. Both he and the woman standing next to him wore western shirts, undoubtedly given them by other overlanders. And while he was wrapped in a red blanket, she wore a blue jacket that must have once looked fashionable on Broadway. They carried with them an earthy smell, like mushrooms.

The Indian's eyes were very dark and they never left Hermann's face, continuously and subtly moving from his left eye to his right. He had a thin scar along his cheek, and the lower part of one ear was missing; in spite of that, he was gentle looking. Surprisingly, I felt the mood around him to be calm. The guidebooks that we had seen gave little information about relationships with Indians except to suggest that their horses were superior and could occasionally be traded for. I glanced at their horses. They were well cared for, and all had beads around their necks, like their riders.

He put his hand to his side, signaling that he was finished. His companion attempted a translation.

"Cheef!" she exclaimed, indicating the man in the red blanket.

"Chief," Hermann repeated.

"Cheef Nah-nim-nuk-skuk!" she declared.

"Chief Nanuksuk," Hermann repeated.

"Nah-nim-nuk-skuk!" she said, louder this time.

"Chief Nanuksuk," he said, louder too.

"Father. May I try?" asked Fritz.

Hermann nodded without turning his head.

"Chief Nah-nim-nuk-skuk."

She nodded and smiled for the first time, displaying irregular and yellowed teeth.

She continued with her translation, "Watty, beeg watty," she swept one arm to the West. Cheef Nah-nim-nuk-skuk carry."

Hermann and Fritz looked at each other and shook their heads.

"We don't understand," said Hermann.

"Watty, watty, watty!" She made a gesture like scooping water for drinking.

"I get it!" said Fritz. "Water! I think they're telling us that the river is near."

"Well! We already know that," said Hermann. "This conversation is exasperating, and it's wasting my time!"

By now our friends had all caught up and stopped, keeping a safe distance. Other groups had arrived earlier and had stopped for the night; I could see their campfires in the distance. I was anxious to set up camp too.

"It's getting late," I pointed out.

"Watty. Carry." The Indian woman came quite close to me. She held her arms as though cradling a baby. "Watty. Carry."

"Hermann," I said. "I think I understand. They have come out to convince us to hire them to ferry us across the water! It sounds quite biblical to me. Maybe they can part the water!" I felt the tenseness leave my body.

The Indian in the red blanket put out his hand to Hermann. I saw Hermann hesitate then meet his eyes and take his hand.

Chief Nah-nim-nuk-skuk and his female translator mounted their horses and all galloped back toward the riverbank.

"I'm not sure what I've just agreed to," said Hermann.

Chapter 44

It was nearly dark that night when we finally made camp. Our designated cooks for the night kindly provided a quick, cold supper of crackers, cheese, and sauerkraut. Most of the men went with Hermann to scout the river crossing. Jan Volker, Fritz Mittler, and Kristof Brantlach stayed behind.

"*Ente! Ente!* Duck! That's what sauerkraut reminds me of!" said *Herr* Mittler, with a satisfied sigh. My wife would prepare duck *Nürnberger art* – Nuremberg style. First she would rub it with lemon. Then stuff the cavity with onions. She'd cook the sauerkraut in a little beer while the duck roasted. Then it would all go on a worn old blue platter: the duck, the sauerkraut, maybe some mashed potatoes, all sprinkled over the top with sliced grapes! Now, that was a dinner!"

Kristof had been lying on the ground on his back with his straw hat over his face. He pushed himself up onto his elbows, "My mother would cook her *Kraut* with onion and apple and serve it with smoked pork. There would be bowls of *Salzkartoffeln*, turnips, carrots, and pitchers of apple wine."

"Where is your mother now?" I asked.

"At home, in Sachsenhausen, across the river from Frankfurt. Albert and I left for New York when we were fourteen and sixteen. I don't remember much about home, but I remember my mother's cooking. Did you ever hear of *Zwetschgenknödel*, *Frau* Reinhardt?"

"Plum dumplings! Did your mother use the blue plums?"

"*Ja, Ja.*" He lay back again but did not put his hat over his face.

"Do you write your mother?" I asked.

"No, 'mam, I cannot write in German; neither can Albert. He could write some words when we first came to America, but now he's lost the knack. I wonder what she would think of this adventure that we are on."

"Kristof, we have known each other a long time; please call me Frida. I can write in German. If you and Albert would like to dictate a letter to your mother, I could write down the words for you; then you could sign it."

"Your mother would like that, Kristof," said Fritz Mittler. "I have two sons. They came to New York as young boys with my wife and me. But as young men that city became too crowded for their liking. After four years they went together to Argentina. When their letters come to me now it is like a holiday! Their handwriting on an envelope makes my old heart beat fast with longing for them. They have also lost the ability to write in German. We write to each other in English; once in a while they even have to use a Spanish word!"

"I wish I had family to write to," said Jan Volker. "I came alone to America after both my father and mother died the same winter. In New York I have no one either." He bowed his head over the patch he had been sewing on his hat; I noticed, though, that the needle was still.

Our little group fell silent. I had been sitting on the ground, leaning against a wheel of our wagon. Lily slept on my lap. She stirred and coughed in her sleep.

"I'd better get this little one to bed."

Chapter 45

In the night a storm came across the prairie from the west. Hermann and Otto got up twice to refasten the tent to its stakes. Still, rain came in under the sides, soaking our bedding. The wind tore at the tent flap, and the thunder woke Lily; I brought her close to me, snuggling her head and shoulders onto my chest and out of the dampness. I got little sleep through that night, worrying about our wagon and our friends, and I was aware too of Hermann's restlessness.

We were all glad for the light of morning to assess the chaos and to check on the animals, even though a light rain continued. But when I pushed open the tent flap, Chief Nah-nim-nuk-skuk was the first thing I saw. For all I could tell, he may have been standing there all night. He indicated with gestures that we should load the tents into the wagons quickly. I looked about me, and realized that the river was directly below us, perhaps a quarter mile across. I had neither seen nor heard it in the night. Now I saw that it was swift and swollen with spring rains.

The Chief waved to several Indians; they came over and signaled that they would pull our wagon to the landing and onto a ferry. The ferry landing was just below our campsite. There were two boats tied there, and as I watched, a large wagon, twice the size of ours, was loaded on one ferry that had the advertisement "Fish Bros. Ferry" gaily painted on the side in shiny red paint. Three burly redheaded white men were operating that ferry. The Fish Brothers, I guessed.

All around me our group was breaking camp, foregoing breakfast, rapidly securing all belongings onto the wagons. "Frida, close Nehemiah's pockets, quickly!" called Hermann. I tied them all shut, fumbling with the wet laces, and then gathered Lily into my arms and followed the wagon to the landing.

At that moment Fish's Ferry took off. Two of the redheads were aboard, steering it with long poles, but the only propulsion was the river current itself. The ferry left the river's side slowly, then quickly gained speed. I watched as it was swept downriver, spinning once in a whirlpool. The large wagon on the ferry lurched to one side, then the other. As it approached the middle of the river, the ferry tipped perilously, and one man was swept overboard. The other couldn't control the ferry, and as it tilted sideways, the entire wagon rolled over into the muddy river water and floated on its side out of my sight around the bend.

I could see several people on both sides of the river running downstream apparently wanting to help. Two men clamored onto a small log raft, and with only their hands for paddles, entered the fast-moving stream. In a moment they too were around the bend. More people ran to the river, calling to others with the tragic news.

"Hermann!" I screamed. "Look!" But he was handing $5 to the Chief and didn't see. "Hermann! Stop!"

"Quiet, Frida!"

"No, listen to me! Tie our wagon to the ferry! Strap it down! Listen to me!"

Otto and Fritz and the Brantlachs had seen the disaster too and ran through the rain and mud onto the landing.

"Father, *Mutti* is right! Tie the wagon down. Secure it." Fritz implored him.

The Chief was paying no attention, and his men were dragging our wagon onto the ferry. Another Indian was standing by ready to undo the lines.

Albert Brantlach grabbed Hermann's arm. "Do it, Hermann!" He pointed out to the middle of the river. "That last ferry, it tipped the wagon into the river! Do it, Hermann."

Hermann shook his head as though just awakening. He took his handkerchief and wiped the rain from his face. "All right, Albert, if you say so. Otto, Fritz, find strong ropes; tie it down."

He went to the Indian who was soon to untie the ferry. "No!" he said loudly, and pushed him away, standing guard by the bollard himself.

I suddenly realized that Lily was missing. "Lily!" I shrieked.

"She's here, Frida, up here!" It was Hans-Jürgen, Hans-Jürgen Topp. He was holding my darling girl in his strong arms, and she was smiling up at him, holding her fingers out in front of her face. I knew they had been playing a counting game.

Tears of relief sprang to my eyes. I turned to see Otto and Fritz jump off the ferry. Two Indians with long poles took their places, and Hermann untied the line. I watched in horror, hardly daring to draw my breath, as all we owned swept down river. Our Indian pole men were skillful; the ferry missed the maelstrom. In just a few minutes it was in calm water at the other side, and in a few moments more it was tied to a landing there and another group was unlashing our wagon and pulling it up the embankment.

"What about us, Hermann?" I asked. The rain was now only a drizzle, but we were all wet and hungry.

"We'll go last; after all the wagons are across, the ferry will come back and take us."

"And the animals?"

"You'll see."

It took all morning for our seven wagons to go over. Each was secured to the ferry with ropes, and all crossed without incident. As the ferry returned for us, I saw some of the men herd our livestock down to the water's edge. Robert Aulich was astride one of the horses, with a line to the three others and another to our cow. He urged the horse into the river. At the same time, Fritz mounted Silvester.

"No!" I cried out, but it was too late. He urged Silvester into the river and the rest of our oxen followed behind. Six other men did the same, jumping on the backs of their lead ox. I lost sight of Fritz's head in the frenzy of anxious, muddled animals, all churning up the river as they fought to keep their heads above water. When I glanced down the river away from this frenzied scene, there was Fritz already standing on the bank, waving his hat at me. I also saw the large wagon that had been capsized off the raft being manhandled up the other side of the river. Somehow it had been rescued and apparently would continue the trip.

Otto led me down to the waiting ferry. I clung to his hand, "Otto, how many more river crossings will we have?"

"I don't know, *Mutti;* a lot, I think.

Chapter 46

"Do you think we'll have mail waiting at Fort Kearney, *Mutti*?"

"Otto! Are you hoping for a letter from New Washington, from Jennetta Owens?"

"I haven't heard from her, you know. Back in Independence I thought I'd have a letter."

"Did you write her from there, letting her know that you'd come back to us safely?

"Yes. More than once."

"If you think she has forgotten you because she has not written, you might be wrong. She might be neglectful about writing because of many reasons. Maybe she doesn't trust the mail service or maybe her mother is keeping her busy. It's possible that she is timid."

We walked along quietly for a while. I thought to myself that I had more time on the trail to talk with my sons than ever before. Of course there were distractions, and we all had chores, but the largest part of the day was spent just walking. This section from the Kansas River towards Fort Kearney was easy going. The meadows flowed up and down small hills, and we were fit. Grass and water were plentiful and our equipment was in good condition. It was a fine place for walking and talking.

We pointed out wildflowers to each other, trying to remember their names: carpets of bluebells, foxglove, little spiderworts, and something red with sticky sap for trapping insects that we couldn't name.

Lily had begun coughing the night we were soaked in our tents by the banks of the Kansas River, but her spirits and energy were not dampened. As Otto and I walked and talked, she was sleeping on Silvester's broad back.

"I have seen Bess and Mary flirting with you and Fritz. I wondered if Jenetta was still your sweetheart." Walking along the rutted trail made it easy to talk openly with Otto, as we both watched our footfalls and did not need to look into each other's eyes.

"Bess is married to Mr. Smith; you know that, and I know that. She is pretty, I'll admit, but headstrong. She's my age – eighteen - much too young to be his wife and the mother to all those girls."

"Did she tell you that?"

"Well, in a way. The other night Fritz and Peter Franken Junior organized some foot races. I think you were milking the cow then.

All of us got into the relays, even the little Smith and Crawford girls." I noticed Otto sneak a look at me out of the corner of his eye.

"Go on, Otto. Then what."

"Bess pretended to trip on a log and fell into my arms. She made a noise, sort of a moan. 'Oh, my ankle, my ankle,' she said. But I noticed that she was giggling. Then she whispered in my ear, 'I wish you were my sweetheart.'"

"That must have been a surprise. What did you answer?"

"Answer? I was too shocked to answer! I just disentangled myself and ran back to the starting line."

Poor Bess, I thought. "It can't be easy for her, can it?"

"Or for me!" Then he pointedly changed the subject. "*Mutti,* are you making butter?"

I was making butter. We had finished the supply I had brought from Independence, and I was trying out the scheme that Hans-Jürgen Topp had suggested; that is, I had put milk into our churn that morning and was hoping that as the wagon jounced along the trail, sweet butter was forming. "I am, Otto. Shall we have Johnnycakes with dinner? It's my night to cook."

"You have it too easy!"

"Otto; sometimes you sound just like your father!"

Chapter 47

Fritz helped me with dinner that night. I had soaked some dried beans all afternoon, and when we made camp, the beans were soft enough to cook. I set Fritz the task of chopping onions and scraps of jerky into small pieces. I mixed flour, saleratus, salt, butter and milk for Johnnycakes. While I rolled out the dough, he put the beans in our biggest iron pot and when they were boiling, he added the onions and meat.

The day before I had seen some wild spring parsnips along the trail, and had pulled one to taste. It was bitter, more so than domesticated parsnips, but good. I got Lily to help, and we pulled many more until my apron was full of parsnips, rich earth clinging to each.

"What do you think, Fritz, shall I wash these parsnips and add them to our bean pot or serve them separately?"

"I don't like parsnips! Don't you remember? Serve them separately, definitely!" he said.

"I was thinking, *Mutti*. I might take my plate tonight and eat it over with the Smiths and Crawfords. They're going to take a day off tomorrow to fix something on one of their wagons and to let a lame ox rest for a day. We might not see them again."

"Are you such friends with the Smiths and Crawfords, Fritz?"

"The little girls like to play with me. I taught a few of them some cat's cradles that they didn't know."

"All the little girls?"

"Well, the older ones. One."

"Ones? One?"

"Well, Mary. She knew how to make the cradle, but not the manger or candles or cat's eye."

"Tell me about Mary, Son."

"I like her a lot. Did you ever notice how her nose turns up at the end? But I know she's mischievous. It's like entering the lion's den being with her! I never know what she'll do next."

"What do you mean?"

"She knows I grew up in New York, so sometimes she pretends to be a demure city girl. Then she brushes her hair back dramatically with her hand, holds her head at an angle, and walks on the balls of her feet, like a dancer. Other times, especially when she's with Bess, she's a bit… rough and ready; she'll tickle me and flirt. When

Bess's not around, and she is with the little girls, she's playful and fun. She tells them stories that she makes up in her head. Sometimes she acts out the different characters. And, can you believe it – she can run as fast as I can!"

"Maybe she's trying to figure out who she is, or who she will be when she gets a little older."

"She misses her real mother. She told me so. She died only a year ago."

"How confusing for her now that Bess is married to her father."

I'd neglected the pot while conversing with Fritz. We both smelled something burning at the same moment.

"Oh, no, the beans!" The bottom layer was burned to a crust; we transferred the rest into another pot, and I got to work frying extra Johnnycakes. The butter was sweet and my traveling companions liked the cakes. We stretched the beans as best we could, and I was glad to have parsnips too to serve to the hungry men.

Burnt beans! As I lay in my blankets that night, I thought this day had been especially pleasant; my only worry was burnt beans… and Otto and Mary and Fritz and Bess.

Chapter 48

We arrived on the southern bank of the Republican River in warm sunshine. In two days we would reach Fort Kearney. It was so fine that Otto and Fritz and some of the younger men went for a swim while I laid out our midday meal. Many other travelers had chosen this same place for a break, and as we stopped our wagons, others we had met along the trail waved greetings to us. Clarence and Florence were among them; they had gotten ahead of us a few days earlier. Clarence went with Hermann to help take our oxen out of harness for watering at the river's edge. Lily ran to play with little John. Others stood fishing on the bank of the river, and there was boisterous cheering every time a fish was landed. Carl Kramer and Rolf Smit would be cooking for us that night; I was happy to see them join the crowd of fishermen.

I called to Florence, "Come and help me with lunch!"

"Frida, I don't like that cough of Lily's. How long has she had it? She gets quite red in the face when she can't get her breath."

I glanced over where Lily and John were climbing onto the wheel of our wagon, then daring each other to jump off. They had kicked up the dust of the dry trail, and Lily was coughing.

"It's not usually so bad, Florence. I think it's the dust."

"But she was coughing the last time we were together; wasn't that four or five days ago? Lily! Come hear, let me have a look at you."

Lily obediently came over to Florence and curtsied, "Hello, Mrs. Potter."

"Sit with me a minute, Lily dear; I want to see if you stop coughing when you are quiet."

Lily fidgeted, and John called her to come back to play with him.

Florence beckoned to her son, "Come and sit with us; Johnny. I have a story to tell you. Do you know why this river is called the Republican River?"

Both children shook their heads.

"There are lots of Indians who live near here. They're called the Republican Pawnees, and the river is named after them. Once upon a time they had a chief named White Wolf. He didn't like that white men were coming here because he thought that this place was for his tribe."

"Is he mad at us, Mother?" asked John, his little brow furrowed.

"No, sweet child. This story happened a long time ago, now he is gone and the Pawnee Indians get along with the white people. But a long time ago there was almost a terrible fight near here, and White Wolf was the Indian leader. The white people had a leader too. His name was Mr. Pike. Mr. Pike told White Wolf that he had to hang the American flag at his village. He told him Mr. Jefferson, the President of the United States, ordered it. White Wolf had to do what he was told.

"How many Indians?" asked John.

"There were four hundred Indians, and only about twenty white men with Mr. Pike. The Indians wore buffalo robes and breechcloths, and painted themselves with white, yellow, blue, and black paint. The white men were frightened of them."

"Did they have a fight?" asked Lily.

"No. That's the interesting part. They listened to Mr. Pike and they agreed to hang the American flag and to be part of the United States."

"That's not a good story! No fighting! Come on, Lily, let's play Indians and white men!"

"In a minute, Johnny." Florence put her ear to Lily's chest.

"She's not coughing now, Frida, but listen to her breathing. Do you hear a little rustle, a windy sound?"

I put my head to my dear child's chest, and I did hear a bit of what Florence described. I felt Lily's forehead. It wasn't warm, but it was damp.

I met Florence's eye. "I think it's nothing, but I'll watch her carefully.

"Lily, John – no running around now. Ask Mrs. Potter for another story, while I lay out our lunch."

By the time we finished our midday meal, black clouds could be seen in the west. By the time we cleaned up, the clouds shrouded our view, reaching as they did from a point seemingly as high as the sun, all the way down to the earth. The storm set up whirlwinds, and zephyrs picked up the dust and swirled it around us. Lightning leapt within the gray and black mass of moving, gyrating clouds, and the sound of its thunder frightened me. The animals were restless; all four horses were wild-eyed and yanked at their harness ropes, tied to the backs of various wagons.

"Otto, Fritz! Quick, harness the oxen. Let's get across! The river is shallow; we'll have no trouble; let's beat this storm," called Hermann. "Frida! We'll want robes or blankets to cover ourselves. And, quickly, close up the wagon."

I had heard that a tornado's funnel could suck six oxen and a wagon into the clouds as though they were a handful of feathers. "Hermann, we can wait. The storm will pass. We'll be soaked in the rain. Lily has a cough. Please. Have common sense!" I pleaded.

"Do what I tell you, Frida!" He grabbed my arm, and shoved me toward the wagon.

I felt the familiar fear that I had felt before. We would go forward on nothing more than my husband's foolish confidence. "No! Hermann!" I rubbed my arm.

"Yes, Frida!" he pushed me again and snatched Lily up and thrust her into my arms. He turned to help the boys. "Fritz, get a towrope too. We'll get across the Republican, beating the storm. We'll shelter over there on the other side under those trees." Common sense would never trespass on Hermann's stubborn belief that he would prevail, no matter the probability.

But Hermann could not prevail against storms and could not win me to his side of an argument by bluster and shoving. I couldn't push back, weighing no more than half his two hundred pounds, but with each incident I set my resolve more firmly to protect Lily at all costs and to hold our family together.

Chapter 49

Before I could gather the boys, Hermann grabbed the towrope from Fritz and sent Otto across the river by horseback with one end, instructing him to fasten one end to a strong tree. He fastened the other end to the stump of a tree on our side of the shallow river.

He called to the other men. “Harness your oxen quickly!”

Hans-Jürgen was reluctant to go, but the rest didn’t argue. *Why didn’t they question him*, I wondered. Hermann had a way of just wearing people out. “Hans-Jürgen, I’m sure I saw a funnel forming in the clouds! You go first. Lead your oxen across, keeping one hand on the guideline that Otto has strung. Go, Hans-Jürgen! Go now!” urged Hermann.

By now the rain was coming down in full force. I never saw it rain harder. It was so loud that Hermann had to put his mouth to Hans-Jürgen ’s ear so that he could hear him. “We’ll rest on the other side, beneath the trees, while the trail dries out,” he yelled at him, patting his shoulder and urging him forward as Hans-Jürgen took his team down the incline.

I wrapped a blanket around Lily and myself. I knew we should wait; I wanted to wait, but I could see that was impossible in Hermann’s present state. Hermann told me to stand in the lee of the wagon, to take refuge from the wind that buffeted us harder with each passing minute. Suddenly we heard the first rifle crack of thunder, reverberating from ground to sky and within our very heads. The wagon gave scant protection from the wind and none from the rain and noise. Lily clung to me, trembling.

I watched Hermann send one wagon after another into the river after Hans-Jürgen. Two men were at the heads of the lead oxen in each yoke, one holding the guide rope with one hand. I saw Hans-Jürgen Topp’s team make it across, then the storm released its full fury, and the scene was obliterated from my view by curtains of rain, blown sideways in the attendant winds accompanying the storm’s front.

From a distance the clouds had looked layered - as though put down by a paintbrush - murky and thick, in varying shades of gray, from nearly black to greenish. Now, inside the storm, the clouds became menacing, dark and yellowish, with nearly solid water lashing sideways. The wind came in furious gusts, shaking the wagons and tearing the grasses from the ground and the leaves from the trees. Lily was crying in fear. I couldn't hear her over the rumble and roar of the rain, wind, and thunder, but I could feel her sobs against my chest. My ears popped just as I heard a ripping sound and turned in time to see our carefully designed wagon bonnet tear from one side to the other.

Hermann approached me, although I neither saw nor heard him come, and yelled directly in my ear. "You will go across with Carl and Rolf."

"What? I can't hear you? What did you mean – Carl and Rolf?"

He put an arm around my shoulder and pushed Lily and me against the wind towards the riverbank. The corner of Lily's blanket came loose and flapped wildly behind us. Hermann saw Lily, nearly buried in my chest, sobbing, coughing, and clutching at me with white, wet hands, her eyes tightly shut. All he did was grab the errant wet blanket with one hand, and wrap it tightly about her, without comment. We were soaked through and any uncovered skin was crimson from the pelt of the rain. The noise overwhelmed our senses; there could be no conversation, no argument against his madness.

Carl was waiting for us at the edge of the river, apparently by prior agreement. Hermann nodded to him, he snatched Lily from me, wrapped her quickly in a piece of rough canvas, covering even her face, and plunged into the river, holding Lily in one arm and the guide rope in the other. I cried out for her, but at that moment Rolf picked me up and entered the river. I struggled to get loose and hit him on his back with my fists. He realized my fury and put me down. Then he placed one arm firmly around my waist, and with his free hand grabbed the rope. We stepped into the angry, rising, rushing river.

I lost my blanket immediately and even though my hat ribbons were tied under my chin, I lost it too. I was drenched by the rain and muddied by the churned river water. There was so much water, I could scarcely breathe, and only knew whether my head was in the rainwater or the river itself by the degree of muddiness. The storm had swollen the river, and bushes and other debris came down on us. At one point a log caught my hip and I lost my footing. Without Rolf and the rope, I would have been taken down the river.

I was gasping for breath when a rogue gust caught us in mid-stream. We stopped, turning our backs to it. When we were able to continue, a blinding lightning strike hit nearby. I was able to see Carl in front of us also stopped in mid-stream, with a bundle held tight against his chest. Hailstones pelted us like rocks. In a moment after the first hail fell, the air was literally filled with balls of ice – some small as a grape and others big as a goose's egg. Over the roar and clatter of the storm, I could hear the beasts bellowing their pain and anguish over this punishment. We had no way to protect our heads and faces. Anyway, my only thought was to get to the north side and get my baby back in my arms, and I dragged Rolf forward.

Suddenly Otto appeared out of the storm directly in front of me. He grabbed my hand and hauled me onto the land. "Lily? Where's Lily?" I hollered into his face.

"Here, *Mutti*. Here she is."

She was white and cold and coughing piteously. I took her from Carl and indicated to Otto that we had to have shelter. He half-dragged me to a wagon, and gestured that we should crawl underneath. There in the mud, I soothed Lily, hugging her close and singing one of her favorites, "Oh! Susanna," over and over, remembering how I had sung to Fritz on *Maria* many, many years earlier, crossing the Atlantic to New York, caught in a different sort of storm and scared then too. Otto brought me a dry blanket from somewhere, and I wrapped her in it. In time her coughing stopped, and in exhaustion she fell asleep wrapped in a borrowed blanket under a wagon in a sea of mud. I raised myself on one elbow and turned to the river. The storm was still furious but its wrath was spent and the sky was becoming lighter.

I could see across the river just as Hermann and our wagon began to cross. Robert Aulich was there to help him. I watched them fasten one loop of a rope around the guide rope and another around Nikolaus's neck. I saw Hermann raise a stick and lash Silvester over and over, until he took the first step into the river, pulling Nikolaus, and the team and our wagon into the river. The wagon floated, but its weight immediately pulled the rear pair of oxen off their feet. As they lost their footing on the bottom, they pulled the middle pair along with them, and, as I watched, the rope broke, and Hermann, the wagon and the team were swept downstream.

Chapter 50

The storm passed and left in its wake a steady, choking drizzle and the heat of midsummer.

I was the only one who had seen Hermann, Robert Aulich, and our wagon upturn and wash down the river. I heard someone call out, "Where's Hermann?" and for a moment I lay silent, exhausted, and absolutely and completely indifferent to the outcome of his folly. Slowly I raised myself and pointed to the east.

Several men ran through the mud in the direction I indicated. Before they had gone far, we all saw Hermann and Robert walking toward us, as though they had parted the huge gray storm curtain and stepped into our world. Robert was holding his arm awkwardly, as though it was broken and I could see that one side of his face was badly abraded. I watched as they approached. Hermann had his arm around Robert's shoulders, helping him; but I had the thought that he was using Robert's obvious distress as a distraction so as not to have to meet my eye or explain to us his outrageous decision to cross the river at that time. In a way I was sorry that it was not Hermann who had been injured, as I felt he deserved it. In my imagination I could see his face bloodied and scraped like Robert's. I knew I would not comfort him. I wondered to myself what we would do if he were hurt and unable to continue. An actual shiver of relief passed over me as I closed my eyes and imagined taking him to Fort Kearney, leaving him there to recuperate, and returning to New York with Lily and the boys.

Of course, that was not to be.

He told us they had washed up on a shallow bar downstream, and he called to Otto and Fritz and some of the others to help him, mentioning in passing that Pansy, one of our middle team, had broken his leg, and that he would shoot him and leave his carcass in the river.

Thankfully most of our belongings had been tied securely into the wagon and were safe but wet. Nehemiah's ingenious pockets stayed closed, even though the entire bonnet had ripped from one side to the other. Everything was saturated with the river's muddy water: letters, papers, books, clothes, even our bedding.

Our provisions were either lost or drenched. The flour, sugar, beans and other dry goods were soaked, and I threw them away. Our onions, potatoes, and beets were swept downstream in their basket. The bacon, sausage and cheese were saved, and I was able to scrape the mud off them.

My sewing kit survived, but my needles had already begun to rust. I scoured one with river sand and patched our wagon's bonnet. The doubled-over homespun had torn jaggedly, as though a lightning strike had etched thereon its own image. As I worked my needle back and forth through the rough, wet cloth, I could not rid my thoughts of leaving Hermann and turning back, and I actually conjured an image of following the well-defined track eastward, with the warm afternoon sun at our backs. I pictured us with just the four horses, one packing the bare necessities; Fritz, Otto, Lily and I sleeping under the stars; giving advice to the westward bound Argonauts; and arriving back in New York in early autumn into the warm embraces of dear friends.

If only I could have fixed Lily's fretfulness as easily as I mended the cloth bonnet cover. She couldn't calm herself. She continued to cling to me even after a few days had passed, begging to be carried, whining, sniffling and crying. She screamed piteously whenever she saw Carl or one of the other men. She wouldn't go near her father, and even her brothers could not soothe her.

"Poor Pansy," she would keen, giving a name to her fear and misery, even though Pansy was an ornery animal and not Lily's favorite. When I held her, which was almost all the time, I could feel her little body quivering and trembling. In addition, her cough got worse. I began giving her a few drops of laudanum in the evening as a palliative to ease her restlessness and to help her sleep.

We arrived at Fort Kearney on June 22 – I remember, because it was my birthday, my fortieth birthday. We were behind schedule and in disarray. We had left Independence several days late, various problems had caused us further delay, but the main reason was that Hermann had simply miscalculated our daily mileage.

We would not have made it to the fort without the help and support of our friends. Several of the men gave us dry clothes and some doubled up in order to lend us their bedding until ours could dry. Hans-Jürgen Topp was often at my side, taking my arm to steady me when needed. We seldom talked, but he would whistle or hum as we walked along. I was glad for his company.

The hot, damp weather brought out the mosquitoes in great numbers; by the time we ascended the northernmost sand hill and looked down onto the flat grassy valley of the Platte, we were red and swollen with bites.

Fritz Mittler, the Brantlach brothers and some of the other men asked for a meeting of our whole party. Hermann refused, "Not now!" He and Otto and Fritz yoked our milk cow in place of Pansy. This necessitated padding the heavy wooden yoke so that it could ride on the neck and shoulders of the smaller beast. "Can't you see we're trying something new here. No time for meetings!"

I overheard someone grumble, "Hermann! You are acting like Napoleon! You must confer with us."

"Fritz! Back that stinking cow in here!" growled Hermann, pretending not to hear.

I wondered why they had accepted his leadership so long; perhaps they were scared of his rage if they replaced him. Possibly no one else wanted the job. I wondered why I gave into him. Was I afraid of his anger, was I frightened of being alone with the children so far from the familiarity of home, or was I simply exhausted? Every communication we had now was focused on our journey. We spoke of maintenance projects, like tightening the iron rings on the wagon wheels; we talked about ways to go faster, schemes to shorten our rest periods, routing short-cuts, and the potential for Indian raids or wild animal attacks. We never spoke of our past in Prussia or New York, never recalled family or friends, did not read or discuss books and ideas. I might have been traveling with a stranger, except that this person was both my husband and the leader of our group, and as such made continuous demands on me. When I drove the oxen, he scolded me to hit them frequently so they would go more quickly. If I suggested sleeping out in the open to enjoy the immense sky and bright moon of a summer's night, he would insist on my assembling the tent. Every single day he argued with me about Lily napping on Silvester's back. The only relief I had was at night, as he had taken to sleeping by the tent's flap. I was thankful not to have intimate demands made of me, as his very body would have revolted me.

Our trail met with the trail from Omaha, the Old Fort Kearney Road, and others. We stopped for a moment on a bluff to take in the sight before us. The valley was teeming with life. The whole view, up and down the muddy Platte, was of long trains of wagons, mules, oxen, horses, and men in motion or encamped on the grassy bottomland. We could see the fort itself, some distance in front of us, built of dried bricks. All around were tents, wagons, and piles of belongings apparently left behind by other travelers.

Fritz turned to me, "Well, *Mutti*! Didn't you think we were in the wilds? This looks like civilization!"

I was as surprised as he was.

Friends we met along the way hallooed to us as we approached, as did strangers. I should have been joyful at seeing familiar faces, but our condition and my worry had made me despondent. While Fritz was driving the team down the long gradual slope toward the fort, I crept into the wagon and under the bonnet so as not to have to be sociable.

Lily had seen the river. She wrapped her little arms around my neck and head and put her face quite close to mine. "I don't want to cross that river!" she said, very seriously. "You tell my father!"

"I promise, my sweetheart, my little *Budlein*, we will not cross that big river. We will stop here at the fort. We'll set up our tent. I'm sure there will be children to play with. Maybe John will catch up to us there and you two can pretend to be prairie dogs again." I rocked her in my arms. She relaxed against my bosom and with one hand stroked her own cheek and with the other stroked mine.

While my sons set up our tent and put the cattle to grazing, Hermann went into the fort and directly to the commander's office. He introduced himself as the leader of our group and told him of our troubles, minimizing their consequences. He asked him for some bread to satisfy our longing. That accommodating and courteous man gave him an order on the quartermaster's department, and when Hermann returned, he had fifteen pounds of fresh bread with him. He went to help the boys, and I unwrapped the bread from its clean white cloth. Its aroma brought Lily to full wakefulness. "Oh, my sweet girl! Smell that! They've put corn meal in with the wheat, potato water, and even a little molasses, I think. It smells like the bread I made in Giessen; the only thing missing is currants!" I took the nearest warm loaf in my hands and turned it. "See, the baker has cooked it before an open fire rather than in an oven; it's nearly burned on this one side." Lily took another loaf as lovingly as I had, and put its crusty rough side against her cheek. She looked up at me dreamily. "*Mutti*, how does it taste?"

I laughed out loud. "Of course! We'll have a piece!" Without bothering with a knife, I broke off chunks for each of us. It was lovely brown inside, from the molasses of course, and it was moist, salty, and slightly chewy. Neither of us could speak, our mouths full, but we shared a smile as I broke off another piece for each.

I celebrated my fortieth birthday with Lily and with that good bread.

Chapter 51

Fort Kearney had only recently been renamed to honor a brave general of the Mexican wars. Its old name, Fort Childs, was still chiseled overhead on the wooden entryway. I went into the fort under that signboard the next morning with Hans-Jürgen Topp and a few others, while Hermann inspected our wheels and greased the hubs. The fort was being enlarged in order to give assistance to the unexpected hundreds of wagons passing by. A large sawmill took up the middle of the property, designed one day to be the parade ground. There were provisionaries around the inside walls of the fort, and outside as well, selling almost everything to the travelers – food stuffs, used and new harnesses, tools, gold-mining equipment, Indian beadwork, and every manner of goods left on the side of the trail by over-burdened westerners.

Hans-Jürgen offered to accompany me on a shopping expedition. He knew I had my hands full with Lily, and offered to carry my parcels. I was able to buy coffee, flour, saleratus, sugar, beans, and, surprisingly, some fresh greens.

A man just outside the gate of the fort was selling books from a cart. He had rummaged through all the left-behind belongings of other travelers. Hans-Jürgen and I lingered to finger the soft leather covers of his books and savor a moment of leisure, reading a poem or a passage aloud to each other. When he and Lily went behind the cart to look at a few nature books that the man indicated might interest children, I felt a hand on my shoulder, and when I turned, there were the smiling, sun burnt and mosquito-bitten faces of May and Caroline, the sisters, married to brothers, I had met in Swillwallow back in Independence.

We three embraced fondly. Meeting these old friends – acquaintances really, who had become friends through shared travails – was like a tonic for me. We stood with our arms about each other's waists and quickly exchanged our news. They had a tale to tell, and stumbled over each other's sentences in the telling.

"Have you seen Indians, Frida?" asked May.

"Yes, but not many." I described Chief Nah-nim-nuk-skuk and his role in helping us across the Kansas River.

"We know why you haven't seen many!" said May "The Sioux are at war with the Pawnees; they're too busy to bother our wagon trains."

"Well, not entirely!" interrupted Caroline. "On the evening of the nineteenth, eighty Sioux warriors galloped at full speed into our camp."

May continued: "Each had a weapon – either a gun, or a bow with arrows, or a lance or tomahawk. Many had shields."

"We were terrified!" added Caroline, and both visibly shivered.

"They came two by two on their ponies, galloping, like Caroline said. We didn't know what their intentions were. Our husbands and some of the other men motioned them back, but they continued forward."

"Some were shouting," interrupted Caroline. "Don't forget that part!"

"On a signal, they all jumped off their ponies and sat down on the ground in a line. Their chief beckoned to Roy, Caroline's husband, to come forward. He did, and I thought he was very brave. Tell what happened next, Sister."

Caroline picked up the story. "The chief stood up and grasped Roy by the hand and shook it as a token of friendship. Every warrior in succession then stood up and shook his hand in turn. Then they beckoned to the other men in our party, and in two lines they passed by each other shaking hands."

"It was a most amazing sight!" said May.

"They showed the men scalps of Pawnees they had captured in reprisal for stealing some of their ponies during the previous winter, and they inquired about a Pawnee warrior they had wounded a few days earlier," said Caroline.

"In fact," continued May, "we have a doctor traveling with us – Tuttle is his name – and only the day before he had treated a young Pawnee warrior who had been shot four times in one leg. Roy and Simon, lied and told them we had seen no such person."

"But we knew that the warrior, who could not yet gather the strength to walk, had been hidden by a kind traveler in the bed of his wagon, and was probably not far behind us and coming our way."

"Sister and I watched all this from behind our wagon," said May, "and about then we fell onto our knees and raised a prayer to our Lord to protect the young Indian from certain scalping."

"We had a fire going, and the Sioux asked to use it to cook their buffalo meat. They begged a little bread from us too. All the while they were cooking and eating, we were looking eastward, hoping that the wagon with the injured warrior would not come into sight. To our immense relief, the Indians finished their meal and galloped away before the wagon arrived." Caroline finished the story.

All the while during the telling of this frightening story, Hans-Jürgen was kneeling by Lily's side showing her the drawings in a book he had found about snakes and lizards. It seemed he was the only one of the men she felt comfortable with, including her father.

"Is this your husband, Frida?" asked May.

"No, no," I stammered, feeling the color rise in my cheeks. I realized they had never met Hermann in Independence. I looked down at Hans-Jürgen, calmly soothing my anxious daughter. "Please, may I introduce you to my friend – one of our group – Hans-Jürgen Topp; he's a friend of my husband's, and of mine. A friend of both of ours."

As Hans-Jürgen stood to shake hands, I saw color in his cheeks too. Lily put her arms around his neck, and he stood holding her in his left arm while he shook hands with the two sisters.

I inquired of May and Caroline where their encampment was. "My Lily has had a cough for many days. Do you think your Dr. Tuttle would be willing to take a look at her?"

Their tents were on the other side of the fort from ours. After supper, I walked over with Lily. Fritz wanted to come too. He had a cruel blister on his heel caused by the unraveling of some stitches in his boot. I had tried to clean it, but it was festering and giving him considerable pain.

"There's to be a dance tonight, *Mutti.* If this doctor is any good, he'll fix my dancing feet! If you don't need me tonight, I'll be going. There's a girl here who plays violin and she's promised to play *Money Musk, Zip Coon*, and other favorites of mine. We'll have a bonfire."

We found May and Caroline and their husbands. They indicated Dr. Tuttle's tent to us, and we called out asking for his assistance.

He gave us time and help, and asked for no recompense. But we paid with our time. Dr. Tuttle was short of stature and long of conversation. By the time we'd spent an hour with him, we knew all there was to hear about his first wife and her drinking problem, his second wife and her sickly mother, most of his neighbors, including one with a prized hog and another with a hole in his cheek, and quite a lot about his childhood in a family with sixteen children, all of them boys. But he was also a kindly man, with a gentle touch. He distracted Fritz with a long story about his two baby brothers getting stuck in a well, and lanced the blister before Fritz could holler.

He relit his pipe and then turned his attention to me. He told me about his mother and how he missed her. "She never laid a hand on any of us," he said, "she was that kind and patient. My father – now, that's a different story. I think this long trail makes a mean man meaner. If he were on this trip, he'd be whippin' us all as hard as he'd be whippin' the cattle!"

He asked me about Lily, and while I told him about her current cough and some of her childhood diseases, he laid a gentle hand on her back. Lily flinched, and I told him about her experience on the river and how it had made her mistrustful of men.

He left off talking to me and turned his attention directly to Lily, speaking to her in the same tone as he had to me and to Fritz. "I'm a doctor, Lily. Your mother tells me that you have a bad cough. Is that right?"

She nodded her head, not meeting his eyes.

"I want to listen to your chest so I can hear what your breathing sounds like inside your body. I'll do it by asking you to lie down on your mother's lap. I'll put my ear to your chest. Then I'll ask you turn over; I'll put my ear to your back. Then I'll tell you and your mother what I hear. Go ahead, lie down on your mother's lap."

Lily lay down, clutching my hand, but allowing Dr. Tuttle to listen.

He muttered a bit, and then said, "Geese! I meant to tell you about the geese we had. The big one was as tough and ornery as our old bull. If you came near any of his wives, he'd hiss at you and flap his big wings. He bit me once – on my nose!"

Lily giggled. The doctor felt her forehead and the glands in her neck. He turned her over and listened carefully at her back. Then he sat her up and asked her to cough and to spit onto a flat piece of glass.

"Now pay attention to me, and I'll tell you what I heard. When I listen to your breathing it reminds me of that old goose: hiss, hiss, hiss. It should sound like a small drum: thum, tum; thum, tum; thum, tum. Are you a strong girl?"

Lily nodded and this time she met his eye.

"Are you strong enough to ride in a bouncy wagon?"

She nodded again.

"I want you to ride in the wagon and to stay dry. Also, I want your mother to heat some water whenever she can, and make a little tent over the kettle so that you can breathe the hot, wet air. Can you do that?"

"No," said Lily in a small voice. "My father doesn't let me ride in the wagon." She continued to look into his face.

"Send you father to me. I'll ask him to let you ride for a few days. Now go on home and ask your mother to boil up some water, then right to bed, Lily!"

Dr Tuttle pulled out a small notebook. Her wrote down Lily's name and the date. As I gathered Lily into my arms, I saw him write one word with a question mark after it: "Pneumonia?"

I sent Hermann to meet Dr. Tuttle; he came back after dark, smelling of pipe smoke, and silently slid into the bed next to me. "Frida, are you awake? Lily can ride in the wagon. We'll leave something else behind, some of the tools perhaps or the butter churn. She'll be better soon."

"What did the doctor tell you, Hermann?" I whispered.

"He thinks Lily has pneumonia. He says it can go into pox or whooping cough."

I caught my breath; Hermann put his arm around my waist and pulled me to him. We lay close and quiet. After a moment he continued, "Dr. Tuttle seems competent, Frida. He told me that Lily would be all right but that you should watch her carefully. She should drink water, more than usual – you'll have to boil it first. Also, you must make sure she doesn't overdo and that she rests. I trust that doctor. Did you know that he speaks German? It seems his mother came from Marburg, just up river from Giessen – such a fortuitous coincidence! Lily will be all right. Just do what this German doctor orders."

I thought of the recent storm and river crossing, of Lily's soaking clothes, of her fear and misery. I wanted to lash out at Hermann. I wanted to lay the blame for my darling daughter's sickness directly at his feet. *How could he have put us all in such peril?* But, more importantly, I needed him on my side helping Lily, not working against me.

"Hermann? You can't possibly doubt that I will do whatever the doctor suggests for my precious child! But, you, what will you do for her?"

"Me? I said she could ride in the wagon. She clings so to you, only you; what can I do?"

"I didn't know that you had noticed," I said. "You can talk to her. She is scared of the rivers. Can you promise her that there will be no repeat of that last crossing?"

Hermann was quiet, but I detected that he nodded his head. After a while his breathing slowed, and I knew he was asleep. Soon I was too. We woke in the morning in the same position – Hermann's arm thrown over my waist - my muscles cramped.

Chapter 52

The next part of our journey would be 340 miles to Fort Laramie. Dr. Tuttle had set Robert's arm and wanted to check it one more time, and so we delayed our leaving an extra day. I needed that day to catch my breath; so did we all.

Florence and her family caught up with us, and she offered to have Lily play with John, and, to my great relief, Lily was willing. With a whole morning to myself, I sat down to write letters. I was able to dry some paper from my writing box, and just as I was settling down, Otto ran up to me. "*Mutter*! Mail has just been delivered at the fort and we have two letters – one for you and one for me!" Otto was trying hard to be nonchalant about receiving a letter, but he kept shifting from one foot to the other, anxious to go off on his own to read his letter.

"Thank you, son; why don't you sit in the shade of the tent to read your letter."

I opened the envelope addressed to me, addressed in the hand I knew as well as my own – my mother's – as distinct as the arrangement of features on her face. She had always leaned heavily on her pen, scratch marks were not for her; and she favored capital letters for exclamations. She had always watered her ink in order to moderate her heavy strokes with a lighter color. This envelope was creased and dirty and even had a small rip on one corner, but her handwriting sang out to me as freshly as birdsong on a spring morning. It had come a long distance, but it had found me. It began with warm expressions of love and familial concern for Hermann, the children, and me.

Her letter continued with comments about the mild winter they had experienced in Gelsenkirchen. She said the last rose in her garden was still blooming on Christmas day. She related news of our neighbors and friends. As I had not lived there in almost twenty years, some of the names were unknown to me, and I was mildly surprised that my mother wrote as though I should know that the *Bürgermeister's* young wife was a flirt or that the Müller's second grandchild had been born with a clubfoot.

When I read her closing line, I gasped: "Your father sends you a kiss." My father's death had coincided with his receipt of my letter announcing Lily's birth, nearly three years earlier. I checked the date at the top of my mother's letter one more time. It had been written on February 16, 1849 - four months ago. I could not imagine my dear, capable mother descending into forgetfulness, nor could I fathom her making such a grievous error. Her good memory was an inspiration to me as a child. She would play a new piece on the piano, going over each bar slowly and carefully. Then she would set the music aside and play it from then on by memory. But her mother, my *Oma* Anna, had suffered a deranged incoherency for the last several years of her life. Often my grandfather would have to lock her into a room in order to get some sleep or complete a task.

I closed my eyes and remembered my father and mother standing in the doorway waving good-bye to us when we left for New York, both trying not to cry. Then, my mother's hair was lightly streaked with gray, but her skin was smooth, and her posture youthful. She had an old green and black shawl of mine thrown over her shoulders, and there were smudges of flour on her dark skirt. I wondered how she looked now and if her fingers could still nimbly braid hair and embroider. I remembered the slight intake of breath that always signaled she was about to say something that I should listen to attentively. I felt my eyes well up with tears of helplessness, and I reached for pen and ink.

> *Liebe Mutter*,
>
> I have your letter telling me of the last rose of winter. It has reached me half way across America. Here in the warm summer I am surrounded by wild flowers of every color, and I am reminded of childhood picnics in the hills with you and my father. I collect the flowers and tie them with a ribbon, wishing I could bring them to you.

I told of the prairie dogs, and of the immense night sky, the games and dances that the boys attended. To calm my own anxiety, I wrote about commonplace things. I described some calico that I had seen and told her that I would try to buy some and would send her a sample. I told her about wild berries I had picked and how I would try mixing them with batter the next time I had a basketful of them. I boasted about the boys and what good horseback riders they had become and told her that Lily sometimes rode on the back of an ox.

I ended my letter without telling her anything of our travails or about my worry over Lily:

> Our family geography is so far extended, *Mutti*, I long for your letters, which transport me to a place closer to you. I am uneasy about your health, as you grow older, and I am not there to see for myself. Perhaps I am only imagining things that this terrible separation intensifies. I wish that you would have our doctor write to me directly to tell me about your health.
>
> Do not forget that this daughter loves you and worries as mothers and daughters have worried about each other through all the ages of mankind.
>
> With tears of love in my eyes, I write this.

As I finished this letter and was about to start another to Antonia back in New York, I saw Otto out of the corner of my eye. He looked happy and somehow manlier; he raised his letter to his lips before folding it and putting it gently back in its envelope and into his shirt pocket.

At that same moment a young lad about Otto's height approached me with his hat in his hand. He had wet his hair and smoothed it back, but that did little to disguise the distress in his eyes.

"Missus, I met a boy with the name of Kristof. He told me that you are a good writer and might be willing to write a letter for me. I wouldn't ask, except it's important." He stood expectantly, then blurted out, "My name's Daniel; they call me Dan. It's about my father. He's dying."

I quickly agreed and reached for another piece of paper that had dried in the sun.

"Dan, why don't you speak slowly, and I'll write down what you say. If you go too fast, I'll ask you to go more slowly. I'll read it to you when you're done, then you can sign it."

Dan sat on the ground, but turned his body so I couldn't see his face. He didn't begin right away, but seemed to compose himself as he shifted his limbs into a sitting position. I had a chance to observe him and guessed him to be no more than fifteen years old. He was so thin that his shoulders, chest and hips all seemed the same dimension around, and his bare ankles poked out from his pants. His shirt was overly big, and its sleeves hung below his hands. He didn't seem a hungry boy, rather one whose physique was inherited. The skin of his neck and arms was pink and blistered; I thought that it would never accommodate to the sun. *His mother would insist he wear a hat*, I thought to myself.

I wrote down what he dictated:

> Dear Mother, Jane, Emily, Charlotte, and Aunt Margaret,
>
> Father has for the last week been exceedingly ill. He cries out in the night and calls your names. The ache in his head is fearful and he is sick in his stomach. He had a hardy constitution when we left home, but now he is weak, and I do all the work. His traveling days are about ended.
>
> What shall I do when he dies?
>
> Your son and brother and nephew,

I read it back to him slowly, looking up after every sentence to see that I'd got it right. I asked Dan where he had traveled from and he told me from a farm in southern New Jersey. He told me his family depended on the gold that he and his father were to bring back. They were traveling light – just the two of them with two mules. They had been traveling quickly and had not made many acquaintances along the trail. He told me that he would wait at Fort Kearny for an answer from his mother, since he didn't expect his father to last more than another day or two. I asked him his age.

"Fourteen, m'am," he answered.

"You speak so well, Dan. I am surprised that you can't write a letter."

He told me that his father was educated and read to him his whole life. Then he showed me that both his hands were twisted with deformities. "He thought I'd have trouble with a pen."

What would become of him? I thought. *What will become of my mother, of me, of Lily?*

I had no spare energy to help this boy. Awkwardly I put both my arms around his scrawny shoulders and patted his back, "Dan, the commander of the fort is a good man; make him your friend." It was the only advice I could offer.

Chapter 53

I was not the only family member writing letters. To my surprise, Hermann asked for some paper from my supply.

"I want to tell my parents and brothers what they are missing!"

When he had finished, he asked me to read what he had written and to add my greetings to the letter if I wished,

Dear and Respected Family,

You think I have forgotten you because I have not written for so long, but you are mistaken. I think of you often as I walk across this glorious landscape, and old reminiscences crowd my memory. I am not discomforted with letter writing, only busy with the details of leadership. I wish now to tell you of our westward adventure and to send my warmest greetings to all the family, hoping the receipt of this letter coincides with robust health for you all.

The early part of our trip from New York to Independence was accomplished mostly with the assistance of public conveyance. Our group, of which I am the leader, took this leisurely time to plan for the long trip across the prairies and the mountains. We met many interesting people along the way; most shared our own dream. I do not wish to brag, but often I was able to assist them with their own preparations.

At Independence – in the fine state of Missouri - we bought wagons, oxen and provisions, and on May 20 we left that city in joyous spirits. Since then we have followed the well-worn trail of those that have gone before us, which traces the courses of the little streams and rivers that refresh our beasts and ourselves. At night we encamp near other travelers and spend the evenings maintaining our wagons and other gear. We have met Indians;

and I give them credit for their grace on horseback and for their ingenuity.

We have lost one ox, but our remaining cattle are strong. I am always thinking of ways to make this journey go more quickly. Today I am of the opinion that the high bonnets of our wagons are a fault of design. There is too much windage; the force of the wind against the surface makes the labor much harder for our cattle. I will reduce the dimensions and overhaul our provisions. I am also planning for ways to shorten our rest stops.

I cannot begin to describe the beauty we encounter. The soil is rich, the timber bountiful, and the rolling hills are covered in grasses and wildflowers. When I lift the glass to my eye, I see more of the same in endless waves, as well as the occasional antelope, elk, prairie wolf, or plover. As we approach they give leg-bail, but other game is plentiful; we have fresh meat most nights. One night it was raccoon, roasted over our campfire. Taken with coffee, it provides a feast fit for the gods. I look forward to bringing down my first buffalo, but so far we have seen none.

There is always the temptation to stop and to explore and, perhaps, to give up the objective – gold – in order to make our lives in this wide-open, bountiful countryside. But the greater riches are to found at the end of this trip, and we will persevere. Until that goal is reached, we rejoice in this journey.

Please send my good wishes to all my nieces and nephews and friends in the *Zollverein* and receive warmest regards from your son and brother,

Hermann stood in front of me with feet wide apart and arms folded across his chest while I read his letter. I turned over the single sheet, expecting to find more. There was no more, and I looked up at him. “Add your own greetings, if you like,” he said, and then turned and strode off to join a group that was repairing a wagon wheel.

Are we on the same journey! I wondered. There was no mention of our river crossings, no acknowledgement of Fritz and Otto's accomplishments, not a word about mosquitoes, heat, dust, storms, fearfulness, and nothing at all about Lily's health.

Hermann's family had become my family during our years in Giessen. They had celebrated the births of our sons and had helped us through the mishaps of early childhood. When one-year old Otto tottered too close to a firebox, it was his dear *Grossmutter* who had put salve on his burned palm and soothed away his tears. It was also *Grossmutter* who had taught both boys the little finger games that they passed along to Lily. Their friends had become my friends. I missed them as I did my own mother in Gelsenkirchen, and I longed to hear their news and to share the yearnings of my own heart. Involuntarily I stretched out my arms as if to clasp his parents to my bosom, but no answering look of affection or fond embrace met me in return, only the single page of Hermann's letter.

I took up the pen:

> By the time you receive this letter, our journey will be finished, and, if all goes well, we will be in California. It is my fervent wish that there we will find a letter from you, sent to the address Hermann provided you by letter from New York. I fall asleep most nights with your dear faces before me, wondering about your health and happiness. I wonder if young Oskar won the hand of his sweetheart and if Sofi's twins are now walking.
>
> You can see by Hermann's letter that his enthusiasm remains as high as always. I can only say that he is right when he describes the lush and beautiful countryside that we travel through.
>
> You would be proud of Otto, Fritz, and Lily, who join me in sending kisses to all,

As I wrote the children's names, my eyes welled with tears, and I knew I could not begin to tell Hermann's family all that was in my heart. Thus I finished the letter to Giessen.

Chapter 54

Hermann announced that he would take over the scouting and delegated the droving from Fort Kearney to Fort Laramie to Otto. He expected that portion of the trail to take twenty days. "Can you do this, Son?" he asked Otto. "Of course, Father. I'm eighteen – not a boy anymore!" He looked to me as though he was hoping for a challenge – a storm or a river to cross – to prove himself to his father.

Teamster work is hard work. Otto asked Fritz for help with the harnessing, and he let both Fritz and me know that he would expect us to do our fair share of the driving. "In the afternoons if I'm tired, I'll have you take over," he said to me gravely.

The men had new tasks to learn – caring for the beasts, scouting the trail, maintaining the equipment, while I did my usual chores: caring for Lily, laundry, mending, and cooking. They sometimes acted as though I was lucky, having some relief from cooking when others prepared the evening meal. They forgot who set up the tent in the evening and took it down in the morning, or who got up before everyone else to start a fire for coffee, bacon, or to warm leftover beans before they even left their bedrolls. Some mornings I even baked bread. Usually it was too much trouble to set up the big stove, and I cooked on the ground over an open fire, swinging the pots and kettles from a pole set between forked sticks driven into the ground. More than once the coffee kettle fell into the fire putting it out. Another time one of the sticks fell over and emptied all the beans into the fire. I scraped off most of the ashes and served them anyway.

Fritz liked scouting. He had fun being out with the younger group. I wasn't surprised when he called out shortly after we left Fort Kearney, "Otto, ask Mother to drive! Let's ride out into the hills!"

"No Fritz. You go yourself! I have a responsibility."

I had taken a holey old sock of Otto's and stuffed it with grasses as a doll for Lily. I sewed cross-stitches for eyes and a mouth, and puckered up a bit of it for a mouth. Some of the grasses stuck through the wool like hair. It didn't look much like a doll. But Lily, astride Silvester, cooed to as though it were a baby, ignoring its obvious beard, "Sweetheart, I promise, no more rivers! If we come to a river, we'll just stop and take off our boots and play in the water. I'll protect you, Baby."

I walked along with Otto. To my surprise, he told me about the letter he had received from Jennetta. "I'm not sure if she is being playful or serious. I don't have a lot of experience with letters from girls."

"Hmmmm," I replied, afraid that saying more would cause him to quit this conversation.

"She reminded me of talks we had with her mother at dinnertime back in New Washington - discussions about slavery and women's suffrage. She told me about some lectures she had attended. She also recalled all the things we had done together – playing checkers in the evening, dancing in her mother's barn one afternoon, riding together on her mother's plow horse."

"Hmmmm. Where did you ride to?"

"Just to some nearby woods where we discovered the last remnants of snow in a secluded shady hollow. I wrote our names in the snow with a stick."

"What did she do?" I asked.

"She drew a heart around them."

I couldn't help but smile at Otto. "What else did she say in her letter?"

"This is the confusing part. She told me that she received a letter from me on her eighteenth birthday. 'Did you mean it as a present, Otto?' she wrote. 'Or did you mean it as a promise that you would come back to St. Louis for my nineteenth birthday, when I will be an old spinster?' I don't know what she was getting at; does she want to marry me? I'm only eighteen!"

"Hmmmm." I shrugged in his direction.

"I've been wondering how Jennetta would like this westward journey if she were here with us. Would she join our nighttime ball-plays? I know she would like the music and dancing. Would she help you with the household chores and me with the droving? Do you remember Bess Smith; she and Jennetta are the same age? Bess didn't help Prudence Crawford, her own sister-in-law, with caring for the young ones, cooking, or anything. But Jennetta's nothing like Bess, that flirt!"

"Why don't you describe Jennetta to me. Pretend she is walking along next to us, just as dusty as we are. What do you suppose she would have on?"

Otto closed his eyes for a minute, "She would have on a blue linen dress, the same color as the spiderwort blooming around us. It would have no sleeves."

He closed his eyes again, and I guessed he was imagining her nakedness through the sleeve openings as she swung her arms.

He cleared his throat and spoke some more. "I think her skin would be smooth and white as the moon. She would carry a straw hat. If she dropped it, and the oxen trampled it into the dirt, she'd just wave her hand in the air, and we'd both laugh."

Otto licked his lips and suddenly his cheeks went scarlet. He turned his gaze westward along the trail, "I wonder where Fritz is?"

Lily wanted to get down from her perch on Silvester.

"I want to put you in your harness," I said to her.

"What do you mean, *Mutter*? She's safe!" said Otto.

"I heard a story earlier today, Otto, a terrible story. A little girl, almost Lily's age, was jostled out of a wagon ahead of us and run over by the team and wagon close behind."

"Did she die, *Mutter*?"

I nodded my head and took a hold of Lily's little foot, while she was still on the ox's back.

"*Mutter*, you remind me of something from the earliest years of my life. Father used to put me astride a large farm horse and would lead it in a circle all the while laughing and telling me that he would soon make the horse rear and buck. I would clutch the horse's mane in fear. I would stare at the door of our house hoping you would come out, ready to cry, but more scared of my father's reaction than of the horse itself. Suddenly you appeared through the door and walked quickly to the side of the horse. You took my foot in your hand and smiled up at me. I don't remember how long you walked next to me and the horse nor how or when I got down to firm land."

I answered, "I remember, Otto, for a long time after you would keep your tiny hand twisted in my skirts wherever I went."

Chapter 55

We moved along next to the muddy Platte without mishap. Hermann roved in front and behind, always talking with other travelers, always returning at night with a new idea.

On the third evening he told us that the next morning we must lighten our load in order to float our wagon across the south branch of the Platte. He had made a list of our belongings that we could do without. All were household goods, and I protested when he said our stove, washboard, butter churn, and all but one pan and pot must be left at the side of the road.

"There will be no quarrel, Frida. After this crossing we have a steep hill to climb; we have to save our animals for the mountains ahead. All in our group must do the same," he said, giving me no chance to further my arguments.

Otto picked up his argument, "*Mutter*! Do the sensible thing! And I notice that you wear your split skirt or trousers every day; why don't you leave your dresses behind too?"

I ignored his remark, wondering if he was suddenly punishing me for having heard too much about his sweetheart.

"Have you talked to Lily about the crossing," I called after Hermann in frustration as he walked away.

"You talk to her," came his answer, flung over his shoulder.

Lily had heard this conversation and was whimpering.

Otto softened and assured us both, "We've had almost no rain for several weeks now. The river will be low."

"Otto! Look at it. It is as wide as the Kansas, and the current is at least as bad. And it's muddy and full of debris!"

"But, we're not crossing here. Just wait."

In another mile the Platte split, and Otto was right. We had only to cross the southernmost, smaller branch. Otto organized our group to help each other, furnishing relays of oxen that steadied the wagons from ahead and behind as each wagon was pulled across. Once I glanced Hermann helping some strangers during their passage across, but he left it to Otto and Fritz to get our belongings and ourselves to the other side. Otto told me to wait on the embankment with Lily. He and Fritz would get the wagon across then would come back for us on horseback.

It took all afternoon and much labor to reach the other side. The water came up to the body of the wagon, but it was calm and did not threaten our provisions. Otto did a man's work that day. Lily and I had plenty of time to watch wagon after wagon go smoothly from one bank to the other. We heard the voices of the men and boys taking the wagons across: "…push it off now…let her swing…you there on the left, you rogue, pitch it ashore…get away from Smoke, he's a mean beast…" Then we saw a man playfully toss his son into the river, among howls of laughter. By the time Otto came back for us with a horse, Lily was calm. With Lily between us, and me clutching his waist, Otto probably remembered his ride with Jennetta.

Chapter 56

I was grateful that the crossing of the south branch of the Platte went without mishap. I was proud of my sons. They worked well together, and cooperatively they helped others. And I was thankful on Lily's behalf, as she appeared calmed.

Someone had discovered a fine spring of good water, the first sweet water we had found in many days. Mostly we had taken water from seep wells dug by ourselves or others before us. Some members had experienced stomach cramps from the seeps. We filled all available containers from the spring.

Hermann rejoined us at our campsite under a stand of cottonwoods on the north bank of the river. He was subdued and didn't comment on the river crossing.

It was someone else's turn to cook the evening meal. When it was over, Hermann called our party together. "Carl and I have ridden ahead. Tomorrow we have a long climb up California Hill. I want us to get an early start. I'll wake everyone an hour earlier than usual. The next day we'll traverse the highland between the two branches of the Platte. Then we have a long and very steep descent down Windlass Hill. I want everyone tonight to check your wheels and harnesses. Get your ropes out and put them somewhere convenient; we'll need to use them to brake the wagons on the downhill slope." He paused and looked at each member of our party. "Do you agree?"

Everyone nodded in agreement. As the group dispersed, Carl came forward and shook Hermann's hand.

We were not able to cross the highland in only one day as Hermann had hoped. In fact it was more than fifty miles from the South Platte to the North Platte, and it took us three and a half days. We had good water and grass along the trail, and firewood was plentiful. Lily was coughing less, and I let her walk with me. Together we collected dead wood and stuck it into the back of the wagon for a future campfire. We also found black currants and gooseberries and gathered them in our aprons. We saw plump plums and wished that they were ripe. Antelope and deer were abundant and comparatively docile, and Fritz proved himself to be an expert hunter.

Here we saw our first buffaloes. The herd – perhaps a thousand beasts - appeared as small figures on a nearby hill. We estimated that it was a herd of a thousand or more. My boys reached for their guns and took off after them, but it is a futile undertaking to chase after them on foot. They are huge and heavily built but are swift runners. I am sure it would take an Indian's fast pony to catch one.

Later I saw three buffaloes and a calf behind a bluff that we approached. They were no more than three hundred feet away, and I could inspect them at short range. As soon as the cow caught sight of me, she stared at me with fiery eyes. If I believed in the devil, I would have thought it dwelled in that angry beast. I took to flight, grabbing Lily into my arms. But the animals also started to run, and I saw that we had a mutual dislike for each other's society. I stopped running and watched them gallop off. It would never have occurred to me to kill such a robust member of the animal kingdom, but I heard a shot ring out, and the calf fell dead. It was Peter Franken Junior who brought it down. He butchered it quickly and gave us all meat, instructing us to hang it inside our wagons to dry in the clear air.

Lily would not enter the wagon with the buffalo meat hanging there. For her afternoon nap I put her back in her favorite spot – astride Silvester.

Suddenly there seemed to be buffalo herds everywhere. One stray herd came running into our cattle, which was already pegged close together for the evening. Albrecht Brantlach took aim to scare them away and accidentally and unhappily brought down one of our milk cows, leaving us with only three. As Robert Aulich had taken upon himself the job of milking, I believe he was secretly glad to have one less animal to milk each morning and evening. But I had noticed that the cows were letting down less and less milk as we forced them to walk in the hot sun so much of the day, and I was angry at Albrecht and worried that we would not have enough to meet our needs.

As we approached Windlass Hill, our party became quiet; I believe that no one spoke for the last two miles. We had learned from others that the three hundred foot slope was very steep - twenty-five degrees, and that many wagons before us had overrun their pack animals and raced down the hill to crash at the bottom. Otto conferred with Hermann, then elected our wagon to go first. He harnessed only two oxen, leaving the remaining three at the top of the hill, facing away from the hill. He rigged a stout line from the harness of the three oxen to a tree, so that if they lost their footing, there would be a secondary brake to the whole apparatus. With a series of ropes and pulleys, Hermann managed the braking line to the three at the top, while Otto walked beside the two beasts on the down slope. They also rough-locked the wagon wheels, so that the pulling oxen were dragging the wagon along the well-packed trail. I watched from the top, along with everyone else in our party. My concern was for Otto, and I truly did not think about our belongings until a loud cheer went up, and I realized that our wagon was safely on the flat and disappearing into the high grasses there.

Hermann and Fritz stayed at the top to help the others. Lily and I half skipped, half rolled down the hill. There we found Otto setting up our camp beneath ash and dwarf cedars, many names and dates carved into their bark. Clearly this was a favorite campsite as we saw the remains of many cooking fires and there was a complete absence of kindling and of all herbage. I was glad I had collected firewood the day before.

It was a long afternoon for the men and boys bringing all our wagons and beasts down the steep hill. They completed their task without a single misfortune. It was my turn to cook; and as I had most of the afternoon to work at it, I produced a fine meal of venison, wild cives, warm bread, and gooseberry pie. After dinner Hermann suggested that Robert Aulich lead us in some songs; he chose the first one *Die schöne Müllerin* , a sentimental song he learned at the singing club in Köln. I was stirred by his rich voice and thankful that we had successfully undertaken a difficult part of the trail, that Hermann's mood was more settled than usual, and that Lily's cough was waning.

Chapter 57

When I allow my mind to ravel backwards over our long journey from New York, I wonder how I kept my wits about me. The disappointments, misfortunes and discomforts were numerous: saying our good-byes to Anna and Adolph, the Hammachers, and other friends in New York; little Mathilde's terrifying bout with cholera and Antonia and her family's decision not to come with us; and my endless packing and repacking of our trunks, each time making the sorrowful decision to leave behind things that reminded me of Gelsenkirchen or Giessen or New York.

I can still almost smell the stale air and perspiring bodies on the overcrowded cattle car on the train trip from Philadelphia to Columbia, Pennsylvania. I recall the horror of the slave auction in St. Louis and can close my eyes and nearly choke over the stench of the muddy tent city where we camped in Independence. I will never forget the time separated from Otto – the worst memory of all. The tight feeling in my back and shoulders is reminder of Hermann's ever-increasing bullheadedness and the several times that he shoved me in his anger and frustration. I recall the frightening and dangerous river crossings. And above all, I bear in mind my mounting concern over the frailty of my baby girl.

Besides those major hardships were the minor ones of leg cramps after all-day walking, tired back from stooping over a ground fire, chapped lips and face due to the ever-present dry wind, and constant concern about available water, fuel and grazing for the cattle. Further, there were the mosquitoes and flies, the worry about Indians, and the flash storms that came across the prairie, leaving the trail a river of mud and us slogging heavily through it.

But occasionally circumstances conspire to open my mind again to the opportunities that await us in California and to revel in the beauty and majesty of the trip itself. It is then that I remember our days walking between the two forks of the Platte River on our way to Fort Laramie. It was our most pleasant time; each day brought a new discovery.

One night in early July we camped near two fellow travelers, newly met: Sam Bates and Green Russell.

Mr. Bates told us he had spied alluvial gravel along the banks of the North Platte a few days earlier. "I dug with a pick and shovel and found a conglomerate of rock. I called over to Green who panned and washed it, and to our surprise and pleasure we found a few cents worth of gold. Don't you know, we were surprised!"

Mr. Russell continued, "We camped there a few days, while dozens, maybe hundreds, of other wagons passed by, paying us no heed. Together we made a hand rocker out of a cottonwood log, and in two days we cleaned out the vein!"

They estimated their diggings to be worth $200! Mr. Russell kept it in a leather pouch tied around his neck, but he poured some of it into my hand, making sure that any spillage would land in my apron and not be lost. I had never touched unworked gold before. It was silky to the touch, even though the edges of the small pieces were jagged. I held it out to the waning sun. The rays reflected a deep rosy color, not unlike my grandmother's old wedding ring. It gave me strength.

All the members of our German New York Company came to see it.

"Our fortunes are made," called out Carl Kramer, laughing. "Let's dig along the Platte!"

"*Freundin, vorwörts*! Onward!" shouted Hermann. "In California we'll find gold by the barrelful. Do we want to stop or make haste?"

A cry went up from the whole group. "To California! Onward!"

The next day was our best yet, fueled by the group's enthusiasm – twenty miles, with only a short midday stop to graze and water the cattle, still short of the thirty that Hermann had allocated for each day's journey, but good progress nevertheless.

When we were about 115 miles from Fort Laramie, we camped a half-mile off the trail under some trees. We were exhausted and hot and our entire company was glad to lay about, thankful for the shade. Two horsemen galloped fearlessly into our midst in such a cloud of dust, we could only see them clearly when they were in our circle and had leaped nimbly from their strong horses. They were two slender young Indians, their limbs delicate. I marveled at their grace and wondered how their small hands and wrists could draw the strong sinew of their bows, which were strung over their shoulders. They were bare, except for woolen blankets wound round their hips and beaded leather moccasins on their feet. One gestured to the southwest, and we all saw a band of Indians approaching us. Counting women and children, it numbered more than one hundred persons. The chief arrived first and handed Felix Mittler, our oldest member, a document signed by the commander of Fort Laramie, stating that this tribe of Sioux were not hostile, but most friendly, and that every traveler should avoid insulting them.

We soon learned that they had come to barter for some of our provisions, but as we were not abundantly provided, we could give them very little. The chief and his squaw and three children, along with a few other adults, camped immediately next to us, and as I was curious to learn something of their customs, I filled my pot with coffee and baked two large pancakes in my pan. I had some extra milk from our cows, and so I prepared a supper for the Indians near us. Others from the band approached, all wanting to partake of the meal, but the chief thought that he had more rights than the others, and cried, "*Womeski*!" a command that scattered the rest.

After the meal most of my guests left with many expressions of gratitude.

The chief and his squaw remained, and we sat together for a while. Hermann and the chief smoked. I thought the chief quite dignified as he puffed and let the smoke out gradually through his nostrils. Our conversation consisted of silence and occasional signs. After a few minutes, the chief's wife left our circle. When she returned she brought me a pair of deerskin shoes, finely embroidered with pearls. I wondered what to give her in return, and thought of my little folding mirror. I had not had it out since leaving Independence; in fact, I was not sure it had survived the river dunking. I opened our trunk and foraged among our clothes, thinking I had placed it within the folds of a dress. I had no success there and next tried the pocket in our wagon's bonnet that held our book and writing implements. Finally, I found it in another inside pocket. Thankfully it was unharmed, though covered with river silt. I cleaned it gently with the corner of my apron and paused to look at my own countenance before returning to our fire circle. My sun burnt skin was as dark as the Indian woman's, but not as smooth, as I had scars from old mosquito bites and swellings from recent ones. But what particularly caught my eye was my mouth – dry and chapped, of course, but with deep lines running down at each corner, and my lips themselves set in a thin straight line, the muscles taut. It reminded me of my ancestors' portraits hanging in the front room of my parents' house in Gelsenkirchen, those likenesses that I had shrunk from as a child.

I continued to stare at my own visage, purposefully pursing my lips outward then gently rubbing my upper lip against the lower to bring some color there. I ventured a smile and found that action caused cracks to open in the corners of my mouth. *Had it been so long since my last smile*?

I folded the mirror and returned to our dying fire. Fritz gave me a quizzical look, as though I appeared different to him. I sent a wink his way, and ventured another smile. Lily was watching me curiously. She jumped up and joined Fritz as he sprang to his feet and led me back to the fire circle.

I gestured to the Indian woman to make room for me next to her on the ground. Lily crawled into my lap to see what was going on. I indicated my folded mirror and Lily reached out and gently opened the cover revealing the mirror. Lily held it in front of her own face, then turned it so that it caught the reflection of the flames before us and sent the brightness to Fritz's eye. She giggled. Fritz shielded his eyes. The Indian wife sat quietly but alertly, and when I handed her the mirror, she opened it and looked at her own face. It was obvious to me that she had seen mirrors before, as her hand went to her forehead and swept a stray hair behind her ear. Then she touched her mouth lightly with the tip of one finger, pursed her lips, rubbed them against each other, and smiled at her own reflection.

She handed it back to me, and I hesitated, meaning to make her a gift of it. I remembered buying it in New York. I thought of all the times I had repacked our belongings during our trip, always discarding items, but always choosing to keep my little mirror. I took it back into my hands, slipped it into my apron pocket, then reached up and let my hair down, handing both my tortoiseshell combs to my Indian friend. She smiled for the second time, revealing many missing teeth, and swept her beautiful black hair up onto her head and awkwardly fastened it there. Lily rescued the mirror from my pocket and held it up to her, and we three laughed together with girlish pleasure.

One morning a herd of buffalo came in our direction like a threatening black cloud. We could feel the earth tremble with the pounding of their hooves, and our cattle became agitated with the unexpected and horrifying noise of their wild snorts. I have no idea how many there were, but they seemed to be innumerable and the noise they made was deafening and terrible. Our wagons were directly in their path. We gathered all seven close together, tied the horses and cows behind them, and the men loaded their guns. At the last possible moment, the buffalo shied away, the enormous herd missing us by mere arm lengths. We could smell their rank sweat and the stink of their matted coats and hear their individual breaths as they thundered by us. I felt both terrified and thrilled by them, and although Lily reached up to me to be held, she too seemed in awe of their power and magnificence. She reached one hand toward the galloping swarm; I snatched it back in horror.

Some of our hunters' sportsman-like ardor was aroused, and two beasts were shot. They were cows, and, in consequence, the meat was particularly tender and flavorful. That night we ate their humps and tongues, roasted over a fire of dried buffalo chips. Otto thought to throw the large hind leg bone into the hot coals of the fire and in an hour we tasted the baked marrow. I have never tasted anything so rich and delicious.

We learned to burn buffalo chips along this stretch of the trail, where there was scant firewood. We carried empty bags as we walked ever westward, and each pedestrian picked up dried chips for the evening's fire.

I had looked forward to some of the landmarks along the trail, the way I had anticipated our initial land sighting after crossing the Atlantic. In quick succession we came upon some of them: Courthouse Rock, the narrow spire of Chimney Rock, and then the looming bulk of Scotts Bluff.

At Courthouse Rock, which people say resembles the courthouse in St. Louis, Otto put the oxen in my charge, and with the wonderful energy of youth, he and Fritz climbed its sheer sides and carved their initials in its soft sandstone. "You'll never guess, *Mutti*, what is at the top!" exclaimed Fritz when they descended. "A miniature windmill made of sticks and dried leaves, whirring in the breeze!"

I thought that it was truly marvelous, the ingenuity and energy of our fellow travelers.

Chimney Rock appeared like an upside down funnel. Otto went off by himself to investigate it. When he came back he told us he had chiseled Jennetta's name on the southeast corner of the rock. "You've never seen such a place! I could hardly find room among the initials, hearts, names and dates. My favorite inscription was 'T. Rooks and Woman!'" he said.

Towering Scotts Bluff itself was the largest, most imposing, of the rock formations rising from the flat plains that we had been crossing. We had to keep the wagons moving, as the trail was narrow here, and there were others before and behind us, but Lily and I wandered off to the base of the high bluff. There in the hot sun we saw a lizard warming himself on a dark rock. As he took no notice of us, we walked on and soon saw several turtles doing the same. Now we were both excited and continued our investigation. Around the next bend we saw black-tailed prairie dogs, and to our amazement, we watched small owls descend into their burrows! We hurried back to tell Fritz and Otto, and on the way heard the unmistakable soft dry whirr of a rattlesnake. How relieved I was that he announced himself so clearly.

At Scotts Bluff someone before us had fashioned a crude sign and nailed it to the side of the ramshackle little trading post there:

Scotts Bluff.
One third of the trail behind.
Two-thirds left to go.

The next morning we passed a lone tree; something queer was caught in its branches. I was told it was a dead Indian, laid to rest in the branches and wrapped in a buffalo robe. We had heard from others along the trail that Indians molested the graves of the Californians in order to steal clothing and that sometimes they contracted cholera from those clothes, adding to their distrust of us. Perhaps this savage had died of the cholera.

A single Indian idled under the tree. Intending to respect his grief and keep ourselves far from contagion, we gave wide berth, but he approached us indicating that we should give him food. He held a note in his hand; we expected it to be a letter of commendation, like the one we had already seen from the commander of Fort Laramie. Instead it read as follows:

"This Indian stole from me. Give him hell!"

That night we circled our wagons and kept our livestock inside the circle. Until now it had been the practice of the man designated as night watchman to spend the night dozing on a wagon bench. This night for the first time, two guards were posted, each to make sure the other stayed awake.

The next day we would arrive at Fort Laramie, where we would rest and provision for our trip over the mountains.

Chapter 58

At Fort Laramie Hermann announced that our progress was too slow. He had done some figuring and had calculated that our animals, in spite of constant urging, moved at no more than two miles an hour. Our daily average, with allowances for stream crossings, clearing the path, and other contingencies was no better than 15 miles, even though the oxen were in the yokes nine or ten hours a day. He told me he was frustrated that we were always waiting for this one or helping that one or arguing, talking, meeting! He was infuriated seeing the parties with mules moving past us, and he determined to increase our daily runs to twenty miles.

He gave me some money for provisions, left the minor repairs and care of the animals to the boys, and spent his time in conversation with the officers at the fort and the few travelers who had been over the South Pass already and had returned eastward. He was sure he could discover a more direct route.

South Pass was the key to our whole trip, he told me. "It is the demarcation line, Frida. Rain that falls on its east side flows to the Atlantic; rain on its west side empties into the Pacific." I knew that, of course; travelers had been discussing South Pass ever since Independence.

People who had seen the Pass described it as resembling an easy broad valley; I heard one man, who had returned from there, say he didn't even know he was there until someone pointed out a wayside sign. Hermann was anxious to have it behind us. I was too, since we expected our trip to ease after South Pass, even knew that we still had the high Sierras to cross. Everyone warned not to get caught in those western Mountains when the snows began in the middle of October. Hermann estimated that we would need sixty days of travel to reach the western side of the Sierras – sixty days from July 22. I thought we would make it with time to spare, and I agreed with Hermann that we had to increase our pace.

Hermann was frustrated by the caliber of the officers and their men at Fort Laramie. "There is a maddening absence of industry and civility," he grumbled. "I expected the army would have an efficient ferry across the North Platte here, but now they tell me their boats are either lost or in disrepair, and it's obvious that the soldiers demonstrate insufficient zeal in replacing or repairing them. A few, I believe, have even taken Indian wives." He told me he had observed half-breed children taking dinner with the soldiers.

"I heard stories told by the soldiers of overlanders building their own rafts and then scuttling them after their own crossings so as to deprive those of us coming after them and therefore to prevent trail congestion on the north side! Imagine that!" Hermann was outraged. "Furthermore, I heard that several of the unscrupulous soldiers were silent partners in a ferry upriver and had every reason to delay the repair of the army ferries and to urge the overlanders along the south bank to cross at that place, where they demand the shameful price of two dollars for each wagon. I've made up my mind to ford the river right behind the fort where it's broad and shallow."

He said he had attempted to make the acquaintance of the fort's commander, Winslow Sanderson, for the purpose of finding information about the trail on the Platte's north side, but he was rebuffed by that intemperate man who, Hermann said, seemed to be living exceedingly well at this remote outpost. "Finally, he begged me to take a glass of beer with him, but I snubbed him."

"It's impossible to tell fact from fiction," Hermann said. "One officer claimed there was an impassable mountain directly along the route on the north bank, which necessitated a detour of 160 miles. Another quoted Sanderson, 'A mountain goat can't go up the north side of the river.' I heard that supposed quote again and again, and did not believe it even the first time. These Fort Laramie men sadly deceive travelers. Despite their pronouncements, I am determined to cross the Platte and travel on the north bank. I believe we will save several days by that route."

He argued that the westward trail on the south side was overcrowded with travelers. "We will have to herd the animals a mile or more off the trail each midday and evening just to find forage, and we'll lose precious hours in the process. We will not be able to move at the pace I want, as the roadway will be so crowded with other travelers, most not caring about the urgency to get over the mountains before the first snows. We will follow the river, although on the opposite side of everyone else. Rivers run through level land, not up and down mountain paths!"

I thought out loud, "I wish I could talk with the Indian chief who supped with us days earlier. He and his men would know about the trail on the north side."

Hermann agreed, "He was an impressive fellow, even though his intellectual faculties were probably meager, and his language seemed to consist of a limited vocabulary. But I observed that his men respected him and that he exercised his position as head of the family. Did you notice that when his daughter threw a rope of beads around Fritz's neck, the Chief spoke one word to her, and she retreated beyond the light of the fire? Fritz is a strong, manly boy, but I am sure he did not guess at the thoughts running through the girl's head. But I recognized her admiring glances and was impressed when her father banished her from the group. I should like to have questioned him and perhaps employed him as my guide."

I thought to myself that Fritz knew precisely what the pretty Indian girl was suggesting.

Hermann spoke with a great many emigrants encamped around the fort. He reported that some were abandoning their wagons and oxen and dispensing with most of their goods in order to continue their travels with one mule or even with nothing but a two-wheeled cart.

"That's not for us, Hermann!" I exclaimed, frightened that he would follow that example.

"*Nein. Nein.* Not for us."

He said he poked through piles of trunks, clothes, boots and shoes, pikes, picks, shovels, piglead by the hundred, even rifles and mounds of foodstuff – bacon and hard bread moldering in the sun. "It is pitiful!" he said. "How could those people have been such poor planners!"

His mood while we were at Fort Laramie made swift journey from arrogance to pig-headedness to frustration and back again.

On our second day Hans-Jürgen Topp and I went to the post trader's store to provision. The prices were tremendously inflated, but I had to buy basics for this next leg of our journey, as I did not expect to come to another resupply point until California. I bought one hundred pounds of flour for $11, twenty pounds of sugar for $20, ten pounds of coffee for $5, a quart of molasses for $1, and ten pounds of bacon at $5. That left only $8 for a few eggs, a small bag of hard potatoes, and a few handfuls of wilting vegetables from the $50 that Hermann had given me. I needed salt pork and Hans-Jürgen bought a slice as big as my hand for $1. That pork was an experience. When Hans-Jürgen and I got back to our encampment, I put the pan over the fire and into it put the innocent looking piece of pork. It sizzled, frothed, sputtered, crackled, and fairly danced in the pan. When finally subdued, it was the size of a dollar. My pork had vanished into smoke.

Hermann appeared as Hans-Jürgen and I were laughing over this deception. I wiped my damp face with my apron and attempted to explain the joke.

"Give me my change, Frida!" he interrupted.

"I've spent it all, Hermann. The prices here are outrageous! I had nothing extra for rice or dried beans or even a sweet for Lily."

"You stupid woman!" he spat out, "Can't you even shop without my help? You've been skinned! Skinned of my money!"

Hans-Jürgen retreated to his own wagon. Lily clung whimpering to my skirt. "Then take it all back, Hermann, and see if you can do better!"

"You'll see how I do; you'll see. Just wait!"

The next day I discovered what he would do when he announced to me, in front of our entire group that we would strike out on our own. We would cross the North Platte here at Fort Laramie, leaving in the morning. He offered scant reason. He gave me no warning, sought not my counsel, nor his sons'.
"No, Father! You don't mean it!" gasped Fritz.

"We'll see them at the diggings, *Mein Junge*, and we'll be there first!" He turned abruptly and left us all, calling out over is shoulder, "Why don't you appoint Carl as your new leader!"

Otto took a few steps toward his father, turned to look at Fritz and me, then left our circle, joining his father.

Our group fell quiet. No one spoke a word - not Robert Aulich, the Frankens, Hans-Jürgen, Albrecht, Kristof, Carl Kramer, or any of the others. Then I heard little David Settlemeyer whisper to his father, "He's crazy, Father. We should stop him!"

"Of course we should, if it is possible. What do the rest of you think? Shall we stop him?" asked Randolf.

"Randolf, you know there's no persuading Hermann of anything, even if it is to save his skin!" answered Rolf Smit. "I suggest you hoard your argumentative energy for a time when its expenditure will bring you benefit!"

Then Hans-Jürgen stood and raised one arm, "Hermann has suggested that we nominate Carl Kramer to be our leader henceforth, and I agree."

Everyone nodded silently in agreement. "And now," continued Hans-Jürgen, "let us leave Frida with her family to digest this news." He came close to me and put his hand gently on my shoulder. "After supper, Frida, I'll come over and we'll go for a walk together. All right?"

I nodded in stunned astonishment.

"*Mutter*! We must do something! Father is mad. I've heard the rumors about the north side. You have too. There is a good reason that everyone takes the trail on the south side. How can we make him see that this is wrong, dangerous?" asked Fritz. "If he won't listen to us, he can go off on his own!"

I could barely think, let alone speak. I looked into his troubled eyes, noted his clenched fists and tense jaw. "We can't be separated from each other, Fritz," I whispered, my breath coming in gasps. "All I've got is the family. All you've got is the family. We cannot be separated from each other."

"We can! Otto and I can do everything that Father can do. We'll let him take a horse and go the northern route by himself. We'll continue with our friends. We'll see him at the gold fields. We'll follow Carl Kramer's directions; we know he'll be reasonable, more reasonable than Father. And he'll help us if we need it." Fritz's saliva was flying out of his mouth as he formed his plan. He grabbed my forearm in an iron grip, "It's settled!"

"No, Fritz. It isn't settled. I agree with you about his unreasonableness, and I agree that you and your brother are as able as he is. But, Lily is weak. I have to know that we are all together and that our number one objective is to get her, and all of us, safely to the end of this journey. Many times I have acquiesced to his demands when I didn't agree with them – you've seen me. It is not because I am weak or pathetic, but because I know that more important than our staying dry, or collecting buffalo chips, or finding grass for the animals – even more important than finding gold in California – is keeping our family together. If I have to say good-bye to someone close to me one more time in my life, Fritz, I will die."

I took his fingers from my arm and clutched them in both my hands. "I need your help now as never before. Help me with Lily and help me with your father's moods and demands."

Fritz let out a groan and closed his eyes.

"Fritz, maybe you are right. Maybe your father should go alone; maybe you and Otto could lead the rest of us over the mountains to California. Probably it would be more peaceful. But, how do we know we would find him again? How can we be sure he wouldn't have an accident and need us, or that we might encounter an emergency and need him? Keep your good humor even as you work twice as hard as before. Do it for me and for your little sister." He pulled his hand out from mine and nodded that he heard me and that he would do as I told. I put out my arms to him, but he rebuffed me, turning to walk back to our tent site where Otto was helping Hermann lighten our load by leaving our extra wagon wheels and axle by the side of the trail.

That night our family ate the last supper that we would eat with our friends. It was a rabbit stew made with bits of bacon, cives and laurel leaves, ably cooked by *Herr* Mittler with help from Robert Aulich. Hermann indicated that I was to eat with him in the shade of our wagon. He cleared his throat and set his mouth in a special way that I had come to recognize as a signal that his words would say one thing and his tone another. "Frida, I have made this decision because it is the right one. No more easy days of prittle-prattle along the trail. We will go swiftly with no extra baggage – no old men holding us back, no long evenings of children playing games, and no extra paraphernalia to weigh us down. But I swear to you, we will be triumphant.

We will be at the gold fields first and find the choicest location. And when we're there we'll buy new clothes, find the opera house, and live like princes."

"And, what about our friends, our friendships? What about Florence and Clarence who are supposed to catch up to us? And Dr. Tuttle – don't we want to stay near the doctor? Hermann, what about New York? What about returning to New York? I don't care about living like princes, you know that!"

He set his mouth tighter. "*Ja, Ja.* We'll all go back to New York. I promise."

In the drear light of evening, heralding a storm, I helped with the after-supper chores; I wanted to be with our friends. Otto and Fritz went off with Peter Franken Junior and the other younger members of the group. I saw Hermann sitting with Carl Kramer, waving his finger in Carl's face, probably telling him how to be a leader.

Hans-Jürgen took Lily up in his arms and walked a little ways off with her, humming a tune that she liked. I finished the washing up and went to join them. We walked around the square fort to the other side, waving occasionally at acquaintances. We saw abandoned wagons for sale, some with faded signs: For Sale - $10. "Look, Frida, another dream discarded."

I nodded at him, looking up at his gaunt sun burnt cheeks, which had become dear to me. "Yes, Hans-Jürgen, another dream – my dream – lost. How can I make this trip alone with Hermann? I need the rest of you to lighten my load. He thinks it will be easier and faster, but he's wrong. Wrong again. I wonder if I will see you again, Hans-Jürgen?" I knew then that I could not bear to separate from Hans-Jürgen. My chest tightened, and my eyes welled with tears.

We both turned to watch Lily, poking the toe of her boot through the spilled belongings of someone's trunk left behind. She leaned down to tug at a straw hat garlanded with faded yellow and orange silk flowers, and at that moment Hans-Jürgen took my shoulder and turned me to him. "I am wretched, Frida, wretched and so sad. Don't go! You lighten my load too, and more; I don't want you to leave me," and he kissed me softly, sweetly on my mouth. I couldn't help myself and leaned into him, clutching at the back of his shirt. He pressed himself against me, then in the continuous movement of turning me toward him, he turned himself away, and when Lily set the hat on her head and turned laughing for our approval, we were standing side by side, my hand still twisted in his shirt. I knew I would remember this moment for the rest of my life – remember the excitement of his kiss and the quiver of my longing body.

Chapter 59

I awoke early to find every member of the German New York Company up and ready to wave us off. I could see the concern on each face, but I could not help wondering if many weren't glad to have Hermann out of their lives.

Hans-Jürgen came over to our site, "Where are you going to cross?"

Hermann had already hitched our five oxen and one cow to the wagon.

"Right here! Right at Fort Laramie. The river is wide, but it's shallow. We'll ford right here."

"I've heard there's quicksand," said Hans-Jürgen, speaking to Hermann but looking at me. I thought he looked as though he had no sleep all night. I could hardly keep myself from touching him, and stuffed my hands into my pockets.

"I've heard that too. We'll keep the team moving."

Robert and Carl joined us. "Hermann," said Carl, "Let's get you and your family across safely. We'll hitch all the teams to your wagon. If one or two yokes get stalled in the quicksand, the rest will pull them out."

I fixed a hurried breakfast, coffee, bread and cold sausage, unable to calm my breathing, and then packed up our tent and belongings. By the time I was ready, forty-one oxen and one cow were hitched to our wagon. There were men on either side of the string to keep them moving.

Old Felix Mittler kept me company as I finished my chores. "Mrs. Reinhardt, I'll be sorry to see you go."

"I know." It wasn't the best time for me to have this conversation, distracted by packing the wagon and distraught as I was by this up-coming separation.

"Why does your husband insist on this absurd idea – is he crazy?"

Crazy! I met *Herr* Mittler's eye, as Hermann thrust himself between us, "This time you can ride with Lily," he said, as though bestowing a gift. I had no chance to answer *Herr* Mittler. I merely took his extended hand and squeezed it as Hermann herded Lily and me to the river's bank.

In that way, Lily and I, jostling along on the wagon seat, reached the north side of the North Platte, without incident. Our friends quickly unhitched their oxen and waved good-bye. We turned westward again, this time alone, and they drove their teams back across the river.

I saw Hans-Jürgen; last to drive his team down the river's embankment, lift his hand as if to wipe a speck from his eye.

That day and the next we plodded westward. The odd yellow gray light of the night before had heralded rain, and it began that morning and continued lightly but steadily for five days.

I loved the rain as a child. I loved the way it changed the smell of things. Apple blossoms became both sweeter and slightly sour. The shaggy coat of my old dog, which seemed to have no smell when dry, took on the same odor as our attic. My mother would let me go outside in a summer rainstorm and stand, head uptilt, feeling it on my face. I marveled that our ordinary days were transformed by light that seemed to be reflected from a gray pearl. People grew closer, conspiring in a congenial way against the weather. When I would abandon the rain and go back inside to be toweled off by one of my parents, the indoors would seem snugger, cozier, and the day perfectly suited for a game of cards or another chapter of a favorite book.

This rain brought no pleasure. We were soaked all the time. We slid in the trail's mud, often falling to our hands and knees in the combined muck of wet dirt and animal dung. Our clothes were filthy, our boots leaked, and we were chilled much of the time. I knew, however, that even summer's brightest day would not cheer me or keep me from missing Hans-Jürgen's kind, undemanding companionship or our one passionate kiss.

Hermann had been right. There was plenty of forage for the animals on the north side of the Platte, and we made good time, in spite of the muddy conditions. None of us felt like exploring. We spent the days walking silently, brushing away the mosquitoes, lost in our own thoughts, with raindrops dripping from the brims of our hats. This endless drizzle did not remind me of the rain of my childhood, and there was no common, warm shelter from it.

At night I cooked in the rain, sometimes only beans with molasses and some bread. Bread would only last a day or two, then would turn spongy and quickly grow mold. Somehow I would start a fire with a bit of dry kindling or grasses kept in the wagon. We would sit for our supper in the rain. Our clothes were drenched, as was our bedding. We slept in the dank tent, which was also beginning to grow mildew. It smelled musty and sour, but was our only protection against the rain. I tried to keep Lily dry, which was nearly impossible, and her cough returned, waking her often in the night, as she gasped for breath.

We heard wolves day and night; I feared they were drawing nearer, sensing our inability to protect ourselves. The first nights I did not dare to close my eyes for fear that hunger had rendered them bolder and that they were circling our insubstantial tent. Many times I fell into half-sleep, jerking awake with the imagined sight of hundreds of them slinking closer to our campsite.

We saw Indians one afternoon. They were mounted on ponies high on a ridge in the distance and did not approach. We also saw a few travelers, all of them single men, hurrying with only a mule or a handcart towards the goldfields. I retain no memory of the countryside around us, only of the gray, relentless rain.

On the third day out of Fort Laramie we came by a grave marker. It read:

Two Children Killed by a Stampede

There were neither names nor date, although the carving in the pine board looked fresh.

"What's that?" Lily asked me.

"It's a monument, a marker where people are buried," I answered. "It's for two people who must have died here."

"Were they sick?"

"I don't know, but I don't think so. I think they had an accident."

"If I die, will you make a marker like that for me?"

Hermann, on hearing this last question, turned and walked away.

"Lily, you have a bad cough, but people don't die because of a bad cough. I will take care of you until you are better. So will your father and your brothers. We will all care for you."

She seemed to accept this answer, and wiggled out of my arms. "Watch Lily, Fritz," I called and walked off the trail and behind a large boulder. There I wept the tears I would not let Lily see, then wiped my eyes and refreshed myself as best I could. But I would never forget Lily's frightening question.

The next day we passed another grave marker. The rains had washed away much of the dirt, and the grave was partially open to the weather. The stone read:

Elizabeth Day Buchanan, age 26
June 30, 1849
Not friends nor physician could save her from the grave

Otto pointed out to me that the body was wrapped in a bed comforter and wound with a few yards of a kind of string made from strips of what looked like a faded cotton dress. There was a note tacked to the wooden cross asking passersby to repair the grave if needed so as to protect the body from the wild animals.

"Hermann, stop. We must rebury this poor woman. Perhaps she is the mother of the two children whose grave we saw yesterday."

"There's no time for burying, Frida. She's just as dead above ground as in the ground."

"Wait! What if it were my body? Wouldn't you want someone to care for my body?"

"You'd be dead. It wouldn't matter."

Otto took our shovel in hand, "Keep going," he said, "I'll do what needs to be done."

I acknowledged to myself at that moment what I had suspected for some time and *Herr* Mittler had confirmed: Hermann was going mad.

The next morning, as I boiled wheat, which would suffice for both our breakfast and our midday dinner, I saw Lily cradling her little sock-doll. She was singing, "Nearer, my God to Thee." I didn't even know she knew the anthem. She had the words nearly right, and had made up a slow tune to go with them. She wrapped her doll tightly in a cloth, then dug a shallow hole with a pointed stick and laid it in the depression. She commenced to cry, wiping her eyes, but still singing that mournful dirge. She performed that little ritual over and over, reburying her little doll, until it was time to leave.

After the five days of rain, we had one good day and then the light rain began again for another day. When the sun finally came out, I said to Hermann at breakfast, "We need a break. All our belongings are becoming mildewed, we have no dry clothes, and I've discovered weevils in our flour."

He met my eye for the first time in a long time, and I noticed how bulging his eyes had become. "Frida, no stopping! Don't even ask. We must get to South Pass quickly and through the mountains before the early winter snows. And we must do it before the crowd that took the slow route on the south side of the river."

"How then, Husband, can I air out our provisions and wash our clothes?"

"I don't care."

I put my hand on his shoulder, "I have reminded you before and I'll do it again. We are on this difficult venture together, and it will fail if we do not work together!"

He swung away from me, twisting my wrist in the motion.

I called out in pain.

"Hermann!"

"Figure it out yourself," he said.

Fritz had heard this exchange. "I have an idea," he said. While I packed our tent, he folded the wagon's bonnet forward until about two-thirds of the wagon's bed was open to the sun. We took turns that day airing out our provisions, picking weevils out of the flour, and hanging our bedding from the bows as though they were clothes lines.

That night, camped by the river, I asked Fritz to prepare our supper, and while he fried bacon and boiled beans, I washed my clothes, Lily's and his in the icy river water. Lily helped me with the rinsing. Hermann and Otto sat by the fire, drawing maps in the dust at their feet. The next day we hung the laundry from the bows. "We look like tinkers," Fritz joked.

That night Otto asked me if I would wash some things of his. “I’ll help with the wringing,” he said. I reached out and mussed his unbarbered hair, “Of course.”

As I lay in our foul-smelling tent, listening to the rain on the leaves, and seeing the tent’s seams weep, I thought about Hermann and wondered about his feelings toward me. I thought that the people you love have two sides to them. One side loves you back, and the other is the thoughtless side that ignores, defiles, stings, sometimes abuses, and generally vents worries and frustrations against you. I believed he loved me still, even though this trip had rendered him incapable of showing it. Further, I believed the strain of the trip and the over-arching need to beat the snow in the mountains had temporarily made him crazy. I thought that arrival at our California destination would be the antidote to his behavior. But, we had a long way to go.

Chapter 60

We traveled through an enormous valley with the Black Hills and Bighorn Mountains far to the north and the Laramie Mountains seemingly as far to the south. Moving along by ourselves afforded more time to observe the country we passed through, as there were fewer social distractions. The higher mountains were surprisingly brown on top. When the sun finally came out, it glinted on high waterfalls, and often, using the glass, we could see mountain sheep on the slopes.

The trail usually followed the bank of the river, although sometimes it detoured away around canyons and gorges. It was rough and rocky, more difficult than the open prairie and we had to watch our footfalls. In the rain, the mud was slick and slippery, and puddles were everywhere. When it was dry, the ruts left by wagon wheels and hoof prints were unexpectedly deep and sometimes treacherous.

Even though there were few travelers on this side of the river, I saw piles of goods at the side of the trail, as people before us had reduced their loads. On a flat rock by the trail was a small pile of pins and needles, a string of glass beads, a jewsharp, some buttons, and two small hawksbells. All together they could not have weighed more than two pounds, yet some poor soul had felt the necessity of lightening his load one more time. Further along, stuck in the crotch of a tree, were three boiled shirts and a fine set of pearl buttons. Seeing them reminded me of my own packing back in our rooms at Astor House.

Once when we were immediately next to the river, we looked across and saw Dr. Tuttle and his wagon. He was so far away as to be not more than a speck, but I recognized his wagon by the brown stretcher that he hung on the side of his wagon's white bonnet. He saw us too, and took off his hat and waved it to us. I waved back as did little Lily. I had the idea that he was signaling us.

We crossed tributaries flowing from the high mountain streams many times each day, usually merely driving the animals across, occasionally having to raise the bed of the wagon on blocks to keep our belongings above the splashing streams. The fresh water was luxurious; even on rainy days, while one or another of us drove the team, the others bathed themselves luxuriously, rushing willingly to catch up to the wagon. The grass was abundant, and thanks to the rain, it was healthy and green. Clover and vetch were everywhere, as well as phlox in every imaginable color. Hermann was sure our going was easier than that of those transporting themselves along the very well-worn route on the south side of the Platte.

I thought we encountered more graves along this route than we had before. Some were marked with just a plank scratched with initials and a date, others by a crude cross. We passed one that read:

Mr. Billow
Killed by an Indian Arrow
This is that fatal Arrow

Tied to the board were the two pieces of a broken arrow.

Something else had changed when we crossed the river to travel its north bank by ourselves. Otto was spending more and more of his time with Hermann. Together they would harness the team in the morning while Fritz helped me pack our tent and prepare for the day's trip. Then, often without explaining themselves, they would range ahead on foot, scouting for game or reconnoitering the trail. After passing Mr. Billow's grave, I became frightened – all the more so with Hermann and Otto absenting themselves for so much of the day. I began carrying my little pepperbox pistol in my apron pocket, hoping I would never have to use it, since I wasn't sure that I would have the nerve.

Fritz and I talked about the possibility of an encounter with hostile Indians.

"Would you shoot an Indian, *Mutti*?"

"I don't think so. But I don't know for sure. I might if it was to protect Lily or you. I think I would take out my gun as if I were going to shoot someone, that would scare him away."

"What if it didn't?"

"Then I'd shoot it in the air. That would stop him!"

"Back at Fort Laramie I heard a boy tell a story of Indians grabbing a gun from a man and shooting the fellow with his own gun."

"*Gott in Himmel*, Fritz! What should we do?"

"We should get back on the main trail as soon as we can. There's safety in numbers, they say.

"You know what worries me more than Indian raids, *Mutti* – breakdowns. Father has left behind our spare wheels and spare tongue. I understand he wanted to lighten our load, but now we find ourselves on a much less traveled trail with no one to help us if we break down. Father doesn't know how to make a new tongue or repair a wheel; neither does Otto, neither do I. If we were on the main trail and we had an axle break, for instance, we could probably find a replacement on an abandoned wagon by the side of the trail."

"Yes, Fritz," I answered, "You're right. We have to convince your father to get back on the main trail. We are safer when we're with friends, or even with strangers. And, of course, there's Lily. She's coughing less, but only because she's riding in the wagon all the time. What if she gets sicker? Who will help?"

Lily was a little stronger on this leg of our trip, in spite of the frequent rainfall, as generally the climate was fresher, cooler. Overall she was quieter, with no other children to divert her. And, since we traveled alone, we weren't always breathing the dust of the wagons before us. Still, her breathing remained shallow, and I continued to be concerned. Now we slept under blankets at night, all of us getting restorative sleep, once we were used to the howling of wolves.

Chapter 61

Hermann treated me like a stranger during this lonely drive on the north trail. Or maybe it is more accurate to say that he treated me like a business acquaintance. He never conversed about anything except the challenges at hand, and then it was mostly to make demands: "Pack up the tent, Frida," or "Gather wood along the path." He and Otto rarely talked about what they saw on their excursions; at least they were able to keep us well supplied with fowl, rabbits, and once a wild sheep.

He answered my questions, but rarely began a conversation.

Every evening I would ask if he had seen any other overlanders.

"Yes," he might answer. "I saw three."

I would have to inquire of their nature.

"I saw three men traveling together with a string of mules."

"How many mules?"

"Many dozen. They aim to set up a sawmill in California and are carrying the blades, belts, and other equipment to set themselves up in business."

"What do you think of that endeavor, Hermann?"

"Stupid."

Then, perhaps, he would refill his coffee mug and call to Otto to help him check on the animals.

I would set up the tent, put Lily to bed, and by the fire's light Fritz and I would reread sections of *The Journals of Lewis and Clark*, the only book that we carried. Fritz was amazed by how little they knew about things that we knew so much about, for instance they thought prairie dogs were ground hogs. He was equally surprised at the similarities, even though their trip was more than forty years earlier. They saw badgers and elk, and so had we. They too shared gifts and provisions and even cooking fires with Indians they met along the way. Fritz read that they met a band of Indians who were all naked, except for bright paint in many colors. "I would have given them pants!" laughed Fritz.

I was grateful for the company of my youngest son. He had always had an easier temperament than his brother. Back home in Giessen when visitors came and knocked on the door, Fritz would be first to greet them. He was comfortable with strangers, trustful. He was also obedient; as a little boy he would be the one who put his boots on the mat instead of kicking them into the middle of the room. He liked bedtime since it meant reading stories together. His was an accommodating, facile nature, willing to explore new things. Otto had been unyielding, wanting the same routine and crying if it varied. When they made up little childish games, pretending to be cavemen or pirates or knights, Otto was the one who made up the rules, and Fritz went along with them willingly. When I would walk them both into town to the market, Otto would be impatient to get there as quickly as possible and then to get home immediately. Fritz would want me to stop and identify flowers along the way or check the progress in a bird's nest or stop to climb an old apple tree.

In New York it was Otto who wanted to join Hermann's police force, with its rigid rules of conduct. Fritz was more interested in trying various athletic games, following the serials in the newspapers, and making up games either with his friends or alone with his lead soldiers.

Now they were young men, and their personalities were developing differently, as they no long had to be together under my watchful eye. Otto naturally gravitated to Hermann's inflexible way of doing things. Fritz was more thoughtful about things, always considering of alternatives and wondering what was around the next corner.

"You know, *Mutti*, for father, going west is instinctive, as natural as swimming upstream is to a salmon," he said to me one day as we walked beside the plodding oxen.

Chapter 62

On August 2, nine days west of Fort Laramie, we camped on a bluff overlooking the northerly bend of the North Platte. Many weeks earlier we had seen advertisements along the route for the Mormon Ferry at this spot. Now from our overlook it was just below us, and we had a clear view of both sides of the river. On the heavily-traveled south side we observed mountains of discarded personal possessions given up by the emigrants to lessen their loads for the river crossing. Using Hermann's glass, we saw the usual detritus: trunks by the hundreds, barrels and kegs of provisions, leather harnesses, extra wagon wheels, tools, stoves, washtubs, churns, gold digging and washing equipment, a piano, and every conceivable jimcrack hauled from eastern cities, all sacrificed with undoubted anguish by people at their third or fourth wagon-lightening.

Besides the abandoned goods and chattels, both banks of the river were swarming with travelers and their beasts. Tents were being set up, animals driven into the river. Men at the river's edge were bent double washing clothes, amidst piles of unwashed linen. I imagined I could see their hands, red and swollen from using the harsh soap in the cold river water. As I watched, one man lost his grip on something red – a shirt, perhaps – and it joined the debris swirling down the river. One fellow had a sign on his back and was beating a drum. Otto speculated that he was advertising his own ferry. We could hear the din from our elevated post all the way across the river.

The river was too deep at this place to be crossed by fording; every Argonaut had to cross by ferry, whether he had a wagon with a team of ten oxen or was traveling with nothing more than a pack on his back. The Mormons had set up the ferrying operation the previous year. They did it, I had heard, to help the emigrants but also to raise money in support of their study of latter-day saints. "They have a gold mine here, fleecing one and all. It's as good as a California mine!" sneered Hermann after watching for a while. He often expressed disgust at other men's successes, especially if they were making money at his expense.

The Mormon Ferry was a large one; it could take two or even three wagons, depending on their size. It was well organized, and a long line of wagons waited to cross on it. We were impressed with the orderly fashion with which the Mormons loaded the rafts, tied down the wagons, attached lead ropes from the cattle or mules' harnesses to the back of the raft, and rowed across. Each load took no more than two hours from the time the ferry passengers paid their fare to the time the ferry returned to the south side of the river for the next load.

Many, though, refused to wait in the line; all along the bank there were men making their own smaller rafts out of felled cottonwood trees, and a few rafts were being hired out by enterprising Californians, making some money off the backs of fellow travelers.

"Look at the mess we would have been in if we'd waited to cross here!" Hermann pointed out to us boastfully, sweeping his arms toward the crowded south bank. "Now what do you think of my plan to leave the others behind and make haste on the north side?"

Before I could answer, Fritz called out, "Look!" We all turned in time to see three wagons tied together, front to back, like three train cars, but with their wheels removed. With lines fore and aft to both shores, men began skidding the train down the gentle embankment. On the other side, oxen began to pull, urged on by drovers. The contraption floated, but not far. As the first riffles of the river hit the sides, the wagons began to list. The men on the south side were not strong enough to haul them back, and before they reached the full force of the middle of the Platte, all three wagons turned over – first on their sides, then upside down, and then disappeared from sight altogether.

Lily looked up into my face, her brow knitted in concern, "I'm scared of rivers."

A moment later one of the smaller rafts started across. We could see four large men on each corner with long sweeps and in the middle was a wagon lashed to the raft. They got to the middle of the river where the current was strongest and lost control of their forward motion. The raft began a slow spin and one corner tipped in the air. Three of the men threw their weight onto the high side, which steadied the raft. But the fourth man lost his footing and fell overboard. The three continued rowing and made it to the north side of the river. We watched until the sun went down, but the fourth man never surfaced.

"No wonder there's a line of travelers waiting for the Mormons," said Fritz solemnly. "They're fair-priced no matter what their charge."

As the light left the sky, we saw teamsters driving one more group of oxen and mules into the icy water, yelling at one another and the beasts, the cattle thrashing and lowing. It did not seem to me that all the animals had got across, but in the twilight I could not be sure.

That night the sky's colors were as spectacular as anything we had seen before, as though celebrating the end of the rain. Intense orange, red, yellow and blue radiated from the west and were reflected as a dappled quilt in the river. Each color appeared to command a section of the sky, but in a blink of an eye, would trade positions with another as though partners in a dance. At times the blue and red would combine, throwing off an ethereal violet. I automatically turned to point it out to Hermann, forgetting the ugliness of his behavior in the beauty of the moment He was examining the contents of our wagon's jockey box where tools and extra iron bolts, linchpins, and the like were carried. I could tell by his posture that he would brook no interruption. I watched with foreboding as he sorted through the items, setting at the side of the trail our jack, crowbar, and mallet.

Then I thought of Hans-Jürgen and, wishing he were here to enjoy the sunset with me, I closed my eyes and conjured his image. He wore a green shirt, dark like the needles of a pine, with rolled sleeves, and I saw him thrust his tanned hands into his trousers' pockets. I boldly reached out my hand and took his arm, feeling its warmth. He turned his eyes away from the sunset and gazed at me, while taking my hand in his and sliding both back into his pocket. I felt my cheeks flush.

In the morning as Hermann and Otto hitched the animals, Fritz scouted for the safest route down off the bluff.

The most direct route seemed to be immediately in front of us, although it was steep, rocky, and twisted. Fritz approached us up the path, panting with the effort, "Father, this is a tortuous trail! But I've found another. There is a more gentle way down about 200 yards back. We missed it last night as a large boulder hides its entry, but it's easy to get around, and the way down is gradual. I can see that others have gone there before."

"Never mind!" said Hermann. "I won't go back. We'll be fine here; the wagon is lighter now and it's downhill – easy for the animals."

"My way might even save us time, Father!"

Hermann didn't give Fritz the courtesy of a reply, just took his place at the lead ox's head, thrashed him on his rump, and urged the team forward.

Fritz spoke to me, loud enough for his father to hear him, "Father's obstinacy will be death of us!"

I agreed, of course.

In that moment, at the very first turn the children and I heard a sharp snap, and the team came to a halt. I saw Hermann grab the hat off his own head and fling it to the ground. He picked it up and whipped it across Silvester's nose, setting up a bawling that rivaled Hermann's loud cursing. Otto ran forward then came back to tell us that the wagon's tongue had snapped in two pieces due to the team being forced around the sharp turn. "We don't have a spare, and Father is in a rage."

The animals were stranded, still in harness, on a perilously narrow trail, on one side of which was a steep long drop-off. Hermann regained charge, spitting out orders: "Otto, run down to the encampment, see if you can find a spare tongue. Try to get one from an abandoned wagon, no cost to us! Fritz, get large rocks to brace the wagon wheels. Frida, get the first two animals out of harness and onto flat ground. Hurry! Then, come back for the next pair!"

I recognized the emergency and the need for speed. "Here, Hermann, take Lily; I won't take her in front of the animals and the wagon on this precarious course."

Lily shrunk from her father, winding her arms around my neck. "No," she cried. "Don't make me!" It occurred to me that Hermann had rarely held Lily in his arms since we left New York.

"Take her. She won't get hurt, Frida! Go!"

"No, Hermann. Go yourself! I will not put her in danger. Do it yourself!"

He grabbed Lily out of my arms, swung himself in front of the lead pair, and set her by herself on the muddy uphill embankment.

"Do what I say!" He took his place again by Silvester's head and began unfastening his harness.

"No!"

I heard Lily scream; then, like a nightmare, I saw Hermann's free hand fly into the air. For a fleeting moment, with every hair's follicle clear before my eyes, I could not imagine the reason. Next I felt his slap on my cheek, fueled by the full extent of his fury and delivered with the force of his considerable weight and advantage, as he stood slightly uphill of me. My whole body spun to the right, twisting my head and neck, and I fell to the ground, catching myself on the palms of my hands in the gravel and dislodging rocks that dropped noisily off the side of the trail. I stopped my forward motion before falling off the edge myself and lay for a moment covering my face with my hands. He grabbed my arm and yanked me to my feet, pushing me up the hill after Lily. "Then get out of my way," he spat after me.

Fritz came back with rocks to wedge the wheels. Otto returned with a spare tongue. Somehow they rerigged the wagon; somehow the animals were hitched up again and pulled the wagon down the hill with no further incident. I lay on my side with my back to the activity, curled around Lily, too stunned and too furious to even cry. When the trail was clear, I took Lily's hand and we walked down to the busy gathering of wagons, mules, oxen, and travelers. "*Mutti*, you've got a bruise on your arm," Lily said. "Poor *Mutti*!"

I asked her to look at my face too. "Do I have a bruise on my cheek too?"

She reached out her fingers and stroked the left side of my face, then leaned forward and gave it a gentle kiss. "Your face is red, and it looks all dirty and purple around your eye. Lily will kiss it again."

Some enterprising Mormons had set up a small variety store on the north side of the Platte, and we walked over near it. They were selling sundries, provisions, and whiskey. Even though I could use more beans, rice, and flour, I could not bring myself to enter the store. I saw Hermann go in, however, and come out a moment later with four pints of whiskey. He shouldered past me, not acknowledging my presence.

Our wagon was stopped near the store, and Lily and I waited in its shade, as swarms of other travelers milled about. I couldn't find Otto or Fritz; probably they were taking advantage of this short break to mingle with other itinerants, telling and sharing experiences. In spite of the noisy crowds, I felt lonely and helpless. A large wolf's head and pelt were nailed on the store's end wall. He was a ferocious looking animal with an enormous head and long fangs. I presumed he had just been shot. I noticed that Lily refrained from looking in his direction, but I concentrated my attention on his fearsome looks as a distraction from my personal troubles.

I heard a noise behind me, and turned to see the large Dutch group from Albany just pulling out; it seemed they had less than half the number of mules with which they left Independence, and this time the women were not waving, and there were no red, white, and blue flags decorating their wagons. They looked as forlorn as the rest of us.

Bits of conversation swirled around me:

"A man was found in the river, face down, with a bullet hole in his head and $87 in his pocket. No one knows his name."

"…drowned, herself and all seven children by the sinking of a boat."

"This morning a lady from Missouri was safely delivered of twin boys!"

A loud cheer went up as a large train of mule wagons from Boston all got across safely.

Hermann had hailed a man he knew and went to talk with him. "The rest of our groups is far behind us. They wouldn't listen to me when I told them that the north side of the river would be less crowded and the thoroughfare gentler. Yes, we've had an easy time of it!" he boasted.

Then I saw a young woman I remembered from St. Louis. She and her friend had inspired me to have trousers sewn for myself. I was glad for a familiar face and approached her with Lily in my arms. She remembered me and poured cups of weak coffee for both of us, inviting me to sit in the shade of her wagon. She looked curiously at my face, but didn't immediately comment. I asked her if she knew the whereabouts of the German New York Company, Dr. Tuttle, or Florence and her family. I felt so lonely, and I missed Hans-Jürgen. At night I lay awake wondering how he would react if he knew that Hermann had struck me, fantasizing that he would confront my rude and violent husband, forcing him to leave us and to continue to California alone. Then he would comfort me, holding me quietly, gently in his arms.

"There was a doctor at our campsite on the south side just two nights ago; I can't for the moment remember his name. He read the Words when we buried my friend. Do you remember Camilla? She was with me buying trousers when we spoke in St. Louis."

She began to shake, this young woman whose name I did not know. I took her into my arms, and she collapsed sobbing and gasping for breath onto my lap. I stroked her hair and caressed her bony shoulders and slim back through her thin blouse, colorless after many washings. Lily sat next to me and gently patted her arm, crooning to her as I had seen her do with her doll. In a while Lily shifted position and patted my arm with her other hand. We sat thusly, quietly for many minutes, perhaps a half hour. At one point Otto walked near us – his eyes registering disbelief when he saw my eye - but I indicated with a jerk of my head that he should leave us, and he did.

In time her body wore out from her wracking sobs, and she quieted and sat up, wiping her face with a cloth. "May I tell you what happened? I've had no one who would listen to me!"

"Of course. I want to hear."

She began to tell a confused story of Indians stealing their blankets, a broken wagon wheel, and her friend's fall while scouting for the trail along a dry streambed. She blended into her tale names of people I didn't know: Mordecai, Jacob, Millard, and Nathaniel. She spoke these names angrily, fairly spitting out the syllables.

I listened, knowing it did not matter that I understood her account, only that I witnessed it with her. The longer she spoke, the calmer she became. Lilly wandered off and joined Fritz who was examining a crate of chickens and apparently negotiating for some eggs.

"Can you tell me more about her fall? Was she injured?"

"I was with her. Mordecai had ordered us to go ahead and find the trail, as we had somehow lost our way. It had happened before, and Camilla and I had found it before. We slid down an embankment in order to cross a dry stream. The rocks and boulders were smooth, but all jumbled up, and we had difficulty walking across them. Camilla slipped several times, each time catching herself with her hands; but once she couldn't catch herself and her ankle twisted and she went down on a sharp branch caught in the rubble of the streambed. She cut her underarm from wrist to elbow. Her blood was everywhere! I tore off my sleeve and tried to wrap it around her arm."

"What about her ankle?"

"It was twisted bad, but she could walk with my help. I got her up the embankment, back the way we'd come, and we limped back to the men and our wagon. By then her clothing was soaked with blood and she was quite faint."

She continued, "I cleaned her cut as best I could, trying to pick out the little pieces of dirt and splinters of wood, then I bandaged it with clean cloths. We didn't have anything medicinal with which to clean it; now I wish I had asked to borrow something from another group. I feel guilty about that! Millard, her husband, strapped up her ankle, and then two of the others went off to scout while we rested. In an hour, we were back on the trail, and Camilla managed to keep up, even though she was weak, leaning on me most of the rest of that day."

"So her ankle wasn't broken?" I asked.

"No; in fact by the next day she could walk without help, just limping a little. It was her arm that was troubling her. It was hot and swollen. At our midday break, I took off the bandages and could see how red it was and puffed out. I cleaned it some more, picking out more river silt and a few blood clots, then bandaged it again. That night she couldn't sleep and told me in the morning that she thought she had got the fever. I felt her neck and she was damp and hot. She showed me some swellings in her armpit and a redness running up her upper arm." She started weeping again.

"Was Camilla your sister?" I asked.

"No," she replied, wiping her nose and eyes on her sleeve. "We grew up in the same town, in houses next to each other. Both our fathers were fishermen, and both were lost at sea. Maybe that's why neither of us wanted fishermen husbands. Both of us were also the oldest daughters in our families and burdened with first-born tasks. When some older men from a town nearby – Smithtown it was – announced they were going to the gold fields, Camilla and I let them know we might be interested."

"How old are you?"

"I'm nineteen, same as Camilla. She married Millard, and I married Mordecai, and we left within a week of our weddings, stopping in Huntington to pick up their friends, Jacob and Nathaniel Ross. It's Jacob and Nathaniel who are financing the trip. Millard and Mordecai are the partners furnishing the muscle; although I think Camilla and I were brought along to provide most of that. Oh! It hasn't been easy." She started to cry again, this time quietly as though continuing a long-time habit.

"They're bad men! All of them. I could tell you stories…"

"What's your name?"

"I'm Permelia. I was Permelia Jones, now I'm Permelia Ketchum, slave to Mordecai Ketchum and his friends."

I wanted to hear her story, but I also wanted to know if she had seen Dr. Tuttle. "Tell me what happened next to Camilla."

"I put hot compresses on her arm whenever I could, morning, midday and evening, but they did no good. By the third day her arm had a bad smell and the skin around the wound was turning black. Camilla was very sick - very, very sick. She was hot to the touch, couldn't sleep, couldn't walk. The men insisted we keep going, and they made space for her in the back of the wagon, her legs hanging out the rear. By then she was bed-fast and often delirious. How she suffered traveling in this condition over a road clouded with dust! She beseeched her husband piteously to leave her by the side of the road, and I begged Mordecai to leave me with her. They paid no attention.

"On the fourth day she became unconscious, and when we finally stopped at the end of the day to camp for the night, she was dead." Permelia started to sob again, and laid her head on my lap. *She's only a year older than Otto*, I thought.

She calmed herself and continued her narrative. "I washed the dust from her face and kissed my sweetest friend good-bye. Then some other emigrants joined the men in digging a grave at the edge of the trail without even a tree to shade it. One kind soul lined it with willow brush. By the time I had cleaned her, her husband came for her and laid her in the grave with no coffin at all. The same man laid more willow brush over her body. Emigrants we had never even met came to the gravesite, and a doctor offered to read from his bible. I knew in my heart that Millard would turn away his thoughtful gesture, and I stopped forward and accepted his offer. I could see he was a kind man."

Permelia was whimpering again.

"Was he a short man? Was his name Dr. Tuttle, by any chance?" I asked.

"Yes. Tuttle. I think that might have been his name. He was short, and talkative. He is less than a day ahead of us."

"What will you do?" I asked.

"What are my choices?"

"A woman doesn't have many, does she? Perhaps you could go back to Fort Laramie and wait there for your husband's return next season," I thought out loud. It flashed through my mind that Lily and I might return there too; instantly, I recognized the futility of even considering a plan that would separate our family.

She hesitated as though pondering this idea. Then reached out her hand and lightly traced my swollen and discolored eye, "Missus, I wonder if you have been considering the same thing?"

"I suppose I have," I answered quietly.

"No. I'll go to California with these brutish men, cooking for them and being their slave! When we're there… well, I'll figure it out then. You know what my biggest worry is now? Pregnancy! That would be the end for me; my days would be numbered, I know it."

"How long do you wait here?" I asked.

"A day or two. Our wheels have shrunk and the blacksmith is supposed to tighten the iron rims."

Permelia and I stood up. I embraced her again, "I hope you catch up with us; we are leaving any minute now."

"Thank you for sitting with me and hearing my story. I hope your eye heals quickly," she said. "I don't know your name either." I told her. She smiled. "Mrs. Reinhardt, you look good in your denim trousers!" she called as I turned and walked back to my family.

I never saw Permelia again, as we left within the hour, but thought of her sore heart many times as we continued westward.

Chapter 63

As we got under way Otto and Fritz came to walk with me. "Your eye, *Mutti*! What happened?" asked Otto.

"It looks terrible," added Fritz. "Did that happen as we were sliding down the bluff?"

I thought I should not tell them what really happened; I thought it would do no good to me or anyone else for my boys to hate their father. I also knew I could not lie to them. In the moment that I hesitated before speaking, Lily blurted out, "Father hit *Mutti*! I hate him!"

Fritz took my arm and stopped me, "Is this true?"

I looked away, hoping to distract him from is question, but I couldn't stop the quiver in my chin.

"It is true."

"I'll kill him!" he spat out. "Wait here with Otto," he spun around to catch up with Hermann.

"Stop him, Otto! I don't want this!" I started to cry.

Fritz came back and put his arm around my waist. Otto took Lily onto his shoulders and put one arm around my shoulders.

"It's getting worse, isn't it?" asked Fritz. "In the beginning he was prideful and arrogant; then he became imperious and domineering; now… now he's…"

"Violent, out of control, and crazy," filled in Otto, surprising both Fritz and me. "We've got to stop him!"

"It's bad enough that he bullies our animals… now this!" said Fritz.

Lily was whimpering and holding her arms down to me. I took her from her brother, "Please, listen to me, Otto, Fritz. I will manage your father, but not now. When he is raging, he is not capable of listening or even thinking. Please, for me, do not bring this up with him now."

Fritz put his free hand on his brother's shoulder and spoke to both of us, "Now listen to me! If he hurts you, *Mutti*, one more time, I will take the whip to him harder than he puts it to the backs of our animals. We four will leave him behind and get to California on our own. I won't care if the buzzards find his body in the night!"

I couldn't help but smile, in spite of my humiliation and pain, at the picture Fritz provided us of Hermann lying besides the trail encircled by black vultures, the beady eyes in their ugly wrinkled gray heads all eying him, as he tried to bluster and boast his way out of his predicament.

"Leave it alone for now, Fritz; you too, Otto. We have bigger problems to solve, caring for each other, getting to California."

Together they nodded in agreement, but I noticed that neither went forward to take over the droving for the rest of the day.

Chapter 64

Three days of hard travel brought us to Independence Rock. The trail was diverted from the river by a difficult canyon. We had not understood the problem, and had filled our only water barrel just half full in order to keep the load light. That half-barrel was only enough for the animals for one day. We passed small pools on the second and third day. They were either alkaline or thick with mud. One was so alkaline that when our cow and two of our oxen attempted to quench their nagging thirst from it, they became sick. We doctored them by tying pieces of bacon fat to the ends of sticks and pushing it down their throats to neutralize the effect of the alkali. Hermann kept busy with the animals. Twice I tried to talk to him, to tell him how painful my face was and how disgraced and angry I was by his behavior. He made sure we were never alone.

Our pace slowed to no more than one mile an hour the last afternoon before Independence Rock as we could only use three oxen for pulling, lashing the leads of the other beasts to the rear of the wagon. As we neared the Rock, a wind storm bore down on us, driving before it the sand and gravel of the trail. It was impossible to look up, as our eyes would become immediately filled with sand. I carried Lily and tied a handkerchief over my face. The wind was so hot and dry and violent as to render respiration difficult. When we finally reached the Rock and the banks of the little Sweetwater River, our throats were dry, our lips cracked, and our eyes red and swollen. That night's supper was gritty with the wind-driven sand.

The storm blew itself away without a drop of rain falling. After supper we could see the grand Rock, rising above a broad valley, like a whale on a beach. It was covered with inscribed names of the mountain men of years past as well as nearly every traveler who had passed this point since. Otto and Fritz insisted on incising their names, but could find no place that was bare enough to do so. Finally they hit upon the idea of Fritz standing on Otto's shoulders, and in that way they reached above the thousands of names and wrote:

Reinhardt Family of 5 - August 5 '49

They called to Lily and me to come have a look, and we clapped our hands and praised their ingenuity. Lily insisted on touching our name. I lifted her up as high as I could. Fritz, still on Otto's shoulders, reached down as Otto steadied himself against the great rock itself. He lifted her up by her hands, grabbed her around her chest, and in this way Lily rubbed her hand on our name, then kissed it and looked down at me, "Now we're all safe, *Mutti*!"

But I noticed that many of the 1849 dates had been etched there in early and mid-July – many weeks earlier - and there seemed to be hundreds of them. All would beat us to the gold fields.

For the next one hundred miles we were in the valley of the Sweetwater River. It was easy going for the cattle, and Hermann, frustrated by our previous slow progress, drove them hard, often passing other groups along the way. I observed that our beasts were much fatigued, due to the short feeding they had, as well as the intense heat. Hermann urged them along nevertheless.

Here also were poisonous springs, smelling strongly of sulphur, and appearing dark and scurfy. We saw and smelled several dead oxen in the vicinity, and one just in front of us died within the hour after drinking from such a spring and was left upon the field by its owners.

Each time we encountered someone else's hardship, Hermann's reaction was the same. He would get my attention by touching my arm or catching my eye, "It's sad, Frida, but it's not our problem."

How could I disagree with him? It was sad. Trusted animals died or were abandoned; exhausted travelers took up their load or were left themselves at a wayside, often too sick or ill equipped to move forward or backward; dreams were dashed, replaced by despair.

Hermann knew that my inclination was to stop and to lend whatever assistance I could, to share a stranger's burden. His frequent reminder, "It's not our problem," was his way if dissuading me. He would prod our oxen along as though showing off the superiority of our team under his leadership.

We had problems enough of our own. I knew that. Beneath them all was my own helplessness and growing desperation.

All the westward routes came together at the Mormon Ferry; every Californian was then on this same crowded road. I yearned to see our friends and thought there was a good possibility to do so.

On the second day from Independence Rock, we caught up to Dr. Tuttle and his group. I first caught sight of his wagon in the late morning, and I approached Hermann at Silvester's head, setting myself solidly in front of him.

"Look at my face, Hermann. Look what you've done!"

He paid no attention and tried to walk around me.

"I see Dr. Tuttle's wagon ahead. I want him to examine my eye. At the end of the day I often see double and cannot even read or write. I'm going to see him whether you agree or not!"

He grunted assent.

At our midday recess, Hermann pulled the wagon close to Dr. Tuttle's. "Boys, take the animals to the river then let them graze," he ordered. He walked over to Dr. Tuttle himself, turning his back to me as he greeted him. I watched his gestures, saw the doctor turn and look at me for a moment, then laugh at something Hermann told him.

They talked for a long time, and then went to inspect something in the doctor's wagon. Obviously they had finished with me and my injuries. Hermann came back to our wagon as I finished preparing our dinner. He gestured that I should join him at Dr. Tuttle's. I took the pot off the fire, leaving it by the coals to stay warm, and went with Hermann.

"Hello, Mrs. Reinhardt! It's good to see you and your family again. Your husband tells me you stumbled into a tree in the dark of night, and I see the results! You'll have to tell us what you were looking for at night all by yourself! Well, poor Missus, that is a classic black eye if ever I saw one!

"Hello, Lily! Did you ever see such colors – blue, black, green, and an overall rosy glow? My, my, my - look at that!" It reminded him of one of his brothers, and off he went on a story of his next youngest brother and a terrible schoolyard fight he got into… with a girl. He laughed as though he'd never told the story before, and looked at us waiting for our reaction.

"Dr. Tuttle," I said, ignoring his story, "I'm having trouble with my vision. Often in the late afternoon and evening, when I'm tired, I get double vision, and I can't force my eyes to focus."

He had me sit on a log and he examined my bruise and eye. He felt the bones of my face, tenderly, and probed around the soft bruised tissue. He mumbled to himself, "That will be all right."

"Any other bruises, Mrs. Reinhardt?"

I showed him my arm.

He mumbled some more, "Bad fall!"

He asked about headache, hoarseness, or fever. I shook my head.

Then he looked into my eyes, asking me to strain my eyes to the left, the right, up, and down. He spoke to me, "Madam, your eye is bruised too. Hasn't your husband told you that the white of your eye looks bloody?"

"No, Doctor. He has not."

He fashioned a bandage with soft thick cotton and tied it firmly around my head. "I don't want you to use that eye for two or three days. Give it a rest, and drink hoarhound tea, if you have any."

For once Dr. Tuttle did not interrupt his care with a personal story. He got out his notebook, wrote down my name, the date, and his diagnosis: "Love licks." I thought that I had received more sympathy from Permelia, in spite of her worries, than I had from Dr. Tuttle and Hermann combined.

He patted my shoulder, "You'll be fine in a few days."

Chapter 65

Even though I had my worries, I had to admit that every person on America's East Coast could make this trip if it were all as easy as the section along the Sweetwater. In spite of rough peaks and ridges all around, the valley itself made for easy travel. The trail was smooth and well packed, the small river assured water, grass was plentiful, and although we were steadily climbing, the slope was gradual. Antelope were abundant, and we had fresh meat.

There was even some interesting sightseeing. While Hermann drove the cattle, the children and I walked to Devil's Gate and looked down at its four-hundred foot narrow canyon, cut through a spur of the granite hills. I thought it a freak of nature, as the rock appeared split asunder by the Sweetwater River. Cool air seemed to spill over its rim, and birds glided over and down into its depths. We saw bluebirds, swallows, eagles, and a red-breasted hawk with a mouse or vole in its talons. We four sat at the rim. Fritz hallooed loudly, anticipating a returning echo. When he got one, Otto and Lily tried too. "You try, *Mutti*!" begged Lily. All three turned my way. I opened my mouth, and the most I could manage was a sigh. But I smiled at them for I was enjoying our short break from trudging westward.

Three days later we forded the little Sweetwater and crossed to its north side, entering a gorge. It was quite different than looking down at Devil's Gate, for now we were gazing up from the bottom of a narrow, twisty canyon, with steep, rough perpendicular rock walls and a thick growth of willows on the river's banks. Twice more within the canyon the trail forded the river. And all along its banks through this gully were dead oxen and the remains of wagons left behind, probably the result of flash storms catching unwary travelers.

Fritz borrowed a fish net from someone and had luck in the Sweetwater. That night I rolled his catch in flour and cooked them in butter for a palatable supper.

The next day we diverted from the river, heading directly west, while the river meandered to the north. Immediately the landscape became dry and sandy again. This time we had brought water and grass for the animals, but we worried that it wasn't enough.

Moving through a morass, the boys thought there might be water for drinking just beneath the surface if only they could dig a hole. They took turns with our shovel a little way off the trail, and within minutes we heard shouting.

"Now what?" said Hermann.

"Come! Quick! You won't believe it!" called Fritz.

Hermann grumbled and told me to take over the driving.

In a minute he too called over, "Frida, stop the team! Bring Lily! The boys are right: you won't believe it."

It was so unusual for Hermann to stop the team for anything that I could not begin to imagine what had caught his interest: A grave? A dead animal? Some detritus left behind by someone? Gold! I tied a lead line to a large rock and went to join them.

The boys had, in fact, found water, at least a kind of water. They had dug no more than a foot through the turf when the shovel hit ice! When I got there, they broke off large pieces for each of us to suck on as we continued along this dry, hot trail. "Imagine how cold the winters here must be." I remarked.

"All the more reason to move along quickly," answered Hermann, characteristically. He turned to hurry back to start the team on its way again, but paused and turned toward me, "How is your eye, Frida? Can you take off the bandage now?"

"I'll try." As we walked along, I removed the bandage, filthy with the dust of the trail. I had no double vision at that moment. I investigated my face with my fingers and realized that the soreness had abated. "Yes, Hermann; it's better."

"*Schon Gut*, Frida. I was under duress, you understand!"

That was not the only ice we saw that day. A storm broke overhead just as we were making camp, and with it came more hailstones than we had ever seen before. I had set up the tent, but the weight of them crushed it to the ground. The combined force of the wind and hailstorms rent the wagon's bonnet, again. The only relief from their cutting edges was to be found under the wagon, where all five of us crept to wait out the storm. When it was over, and within no more than twenty minutes, all the ice had melted, and the last warm rays of the sun fairly shone through the unexpected clear air that followed the storm.

Chapter 66

While we had been usually alone during our days along the north bank of the Platte's North Fork, here we were part of a countless throng. One day before our anticipated destination of South Pass, I began counting the wagons that we passed: fifty-two! And another twenty-two passed us. Add those to the hundreds plodding along at our same pace, and the congestion made my head swim. It was impossible to be lonesome here, as the road, from morning till night was as busy as Broadway. But I was lonesome, lonesome and tired.

We did not know where our German New York Company companions were – behind or ahead. I had not seen my dearest traveling friend, Florence, or her family in weeks and worried about their condition and whereabouts. I was footsore and generally exhausted, the same condition that I observed in many of the people around us. People waved at one another, but didn't have the energy they had earlier in the trip to walk together, talking, laughing, picking flowers along the trail. I thought constantly about Hans-Jürgen, missing his tenderness.

I had a series of recurring daydreams that would steal into my thoughts unbidden as I plodded along the trail. In one, I anticipated an outing with Hans-Jürgen in New York. We would go to the theater, just the two of us. In my trance, I imagined myself standing in front of my old mirror trying on gowns and shoes that would appeal to him. Always I would settle on a dark blue dress with a low-cut bodice that I would cover with my scarlet silk shawl in order to shock him a little with my boldness and thereby elicit his shy smile. In another reverie Hans-Jürgen would surprise me as I washed my hair in a stream. Without asking, he would take the soap and finish the job, washing my neck and shoulders as well. Then he'd take my comb and untangle the snarls gently. I would imagine that we would both hear Hermann on the other side of a stand of bushes, but that Hans-Jürgen would continue anyway. I could forget my troubles in these fancies.

It was hot and dusty during the day; I had taken to leaving my stockings off and noticed that my calves were no longer rounded but stringy with muscle. Often in the night I awoke with leg cramps, sometimes so severe that I could hardly bear to stand in order to stretch and relieve the contracted muscle. Lily was often either cranky or listless. I kept a handkerchief tied across her mouth all the time to guard against the dust, but she hated it and tore it off whenever I wasn't around. I faithfully boiled her water as the doctor had recommended. Our diet was monotonous, completely lacking in fresh vegetables, and all of us were suffering with sores in our mouths and cracks around our lips and nostrils. We had not had a day of rest in three weeks.

I made bread for supper on the night of August 9. As I no longer had a bowl or pan for mixing, I was obliged to mix it directly in my one frying pan, the iron of which gave it the color, but not the taste, of rye bread. Fortunately, my family liked it, and we had it again the next morning at half past five as we prepared for the trail.

That day we gained the South Pass of the Great Rocky Mountains – a place of high anticipation to us and all emigrants. It is not a pass in the usual sense. There are no steep, rugged, or threatening rocks; in fact, the approach is so gradual as to appear flat, and the Pass itself must be twenty miles wide. If there had not been a sign, we might not have known we had reached the summit:

South Pass of the Great Rocky Mountains
elevation: 7550 feet

There a brook splashes over the rocks and makes its way to the Pacific Ocean. By its side there was a second sign:

Pacific Spring – This Way to the Pacific

Hermann thought it a fitting omen that the rest of our trip would be down hill and that most of our toil was behind us. I thought that with a little stretching I could reach my left arm out over the flowing waters of the Atlantic Ocean and my right arm over the waters of the Pacific.

I took up a cup and drank my first sip of the water of the Pacific, passing it around to Fritz and Otto. None of us made the effort to carry the cup to Hermann, but kept our small celebration to ourselves.

I thought it the best water I had ever had, even though I recognized that it flowed away from all I held dear.

Chapter 67

We moved through the exhausted crowds and made camp four miles farther west. As Hermann drove the team those few miles, Fritz swung Lily up on his shoulders and walked with me. I knew that he could only relax when his father was out of sight. Sometimes I would see him involuntarily making fists when he was near him and he never met his father's eye. Even though he had not witnessed the blow, I knew he dwelled upon the incident and wondered about our marriage.

Lily was soon asleep, jostling along on her brother's shoulders. Fritz spoke quietly, "I wanted to linger at South Pass, didn't you? I wanted to find a tree and in its bark inscribe our initials and the date, or, failing that, I wanted to erect a stone or a sign announcing that the Reinhardt family from New York City had traversed the whole of the country from Atlantic Ocean to the Rocky Mountains. We should have celebrated our accomplishment with music, dancing, and even fireworks!"

"Maybe your father would have sung. You have to admit he has a beautiful voice."

"These days my father wouldn't waste his breath on singing when he could be talking, blustering, and ordering us around."

Hermann called a halt by some low bushes, and he and Otto took the animals out of harness.

"We could celebrate with a good meal, Son," I said. "Look at all the sage hens over there; there must be a dozen."

He was glad for the diversion and left me to set up our camp, taking his gun from the wagon.

When he came back, he was laughing, "One shot scared them away, but not before I got the fattest hen of all!"

I used the hen to make a soup, using the last of our rice to thicken it. I had found some gooseberries along the trail and made a pastry pie with them. Still tired, we ate our soup in silence until I presented the surprise pie. Lily, Otto, and Fritz clapped and cheered for the tart pie. Hermann ate his piece slowly. When he finished his last bite, he cleared his throat. "Frida! This was an excellent pastry. Thank you."

We all turned in surprise to observe him, surprised by his unusual words of gratitude.

He cleared his throat again, "We have made it without incident to South Pass. Our dream will be realized; now we know it! Tomorrow we will rest our animals and ourselves, while I decide which route we will take to the gold diggings – now only eight hundred miles away. We should be there in just thirty days."

Fritz helped me with supper's clean up. "Without incident – ha!" he whispered to me.

As I put Lily to bed in the tent, I overheard Fritz ask Otto, "Is Father right? Will the rest be easy?"

Otto answered groggily, half asleep "No, of course not. We have many more passes, slopes, ravines, and rivers to cross; they won't be easy. You and I have both read about the mountains to the west of here – and we've heard the stories from a few people who have been there before. Father believes what he wants to believe; you know that. He's not only foolish, he's mad! Hoard your energy."

So, I thought to myself, Otto is as disillusioned with Hermann as the rest of us.

Chapter 68

We camped two nights by the Pacific Springs stream, four miles beyond South Pass, an essential respite for all of us.

Our cow and oxen were looking pitifully thin. I had to milk the cow only every two days, and then could expect just a small amount of milk. The oxen were gaunt and held their heavy heads low. Several had runny eyes and sores around their mouths and feet. All of them had particularly foul breath. I had some emetic in our medicine chest and gave it all up for Hermann to dose the poor animals. Fritz and Otto walked them a mile off the trail to find abundant grass and stayed with them all day. When they returned at suppertime, they had only four oxen and the cow with them.

"Where's Check?" I asked.

"Check's dead, *Mutti,*" answered Fritz, forlornly. "Poor Check! While the others ate the fresh grass we found, he just stood there. Then he collapsed onto his front knees and toppled over without even a grunt or a moan. Otto and I carried grass to him and put it right into his mouth, but he hadn't the energy to chew it, and within the hour he was dead."

Check was the youngest and smallest of our team. He was docile and followed the others without complaint. None of us could believe that exhaustion would take him first. "What can this mean for the rest of them?" I thought out loud.

"We're past the worst of it. We'll manage with four oxen. It's downhill now," said Hermann, with feigned heartiness; but I could tell he was worried.

"What about the cow?" I asked.

"I'll give her a rest from pulling and tie her lead rope to the back of the wagon."

Hermann had been checking the wagon all day, tightening the wheels' iron rims, greasing the axles, and constructing a makeshift repair to a broken bow. As it was a dry clear day I aired our bedding and washed our clothes in the cold stream nearby. I also baked enough bread for the next several days and made biscuit dough with the last of the eggs that Fritz had bought back at Mormon Crossing. In the middle of the afternoon I took out my journal. I hadn't written an entry since Independence, and I wondered how I could begin to tell of this adventure since then. Lily played in the stream. I sat on a rock with my journal on my lap and watched her making walls of stones to divert the flow along the stream's edges. She was absorbed and carefree, jumping in and out of the little stream fearlessly. Sometimes she called to me to watch her progress. Sometimes she asked for help as when she tried to move a large heavy rock into place. "Not now, Lily, I'm busy. Maybe later."

She was determined and got her little hands under the rock and lifted it and walked a few steps with it before it splashed into the stream. "Uh, oh!" I heard her say, brushing away the drops of water on her split skirt and shirtfront. Again she picked up the rock, and again it splashed. She kept at it, and finally added it to her little dyke.

I picked up my pen and began to write:

> We have persevered. Our family has held together. We are all exhausted but alive. Yesterday we crossed the backbone of the country, and Hermann says the rest will be easy. We will continue westward, together.

I set my pen down. How could I begin to describe this experience? I thought of the wildflowers, the magnificent buffalo. I remembered the dead Indian in the tree and the soft moccasins, given to me by an Indian wife, on my feet at that very moment. When I thought about parting from our friends, I felt my throat constrict, and in a moment I was weeping in loneliness.

Lily was still working as water engineer, and I concentrated my attention on her smooth strong arms and legs, brown from the sun. I continued:

> Sometimes I think everything is coming apart. Sometimes I believe we are spinning in the wind and whirling about with the dust and mosquitoes and chips of buffalo dung. I don't know where we will land. I can't imagine where Lily will grow up or if she will remember this trip or even survive it. I want to envision the future, but I can't. It is cloudy, like fog on a river that I strain to see across.

> What will become of my sons? I think my husband is going crazy. What shall I do to help him?

I felt the easy well of tears again and put away my pen and journal and went to help Lily build a barricade against the unrelenting flow of the stream.

Chapter 69

One day's rest was not enough for our animals. Our cow had a limp, and though I inspected her hoof for a cut or sore, its origin was not obvious. The oxen would need many days of rest, with good water and food, but Hermann would not hear of it. The next day – August 12 – Hermann had us on the trail at half five, with no breakfast in our stomachs.

As we walked, Hermann blustered, "While you idled yesterday afternoon with paper and pen, I drove hickory wedges between the iron tires and the felly rims." *Where does he think his fresh bread came from,* I wondered, *or his clean shirt and pants.* He continued, "Did you see the accident yesterday morning? The front wheels of that wagon traveling parallel to us had shrunk so much in the dry air that the iron tires rolled right off! I have averted such an accident for us." He looked at me as though expecting an ovation.

All I could think of were our oxen. They were not only exhausted but also skittish. With Check gone, Hermann teamed Violet with Geld, against the advice of both Fritz and Otto. "Boys, I learned one thing from my father, and you should learn it from me: The father makes decisions, and the sons do not question them!"

He continued, "Furthermore, oxen are stupid. They don't think about who they want as a pulling partner!"

The boys dropped back and walked beside Lily and me. "This day's not starting well," muttered Fritz.

We watched Hermann continuously prod Geld with the butt of his rifle. When dumb, sweet Geld stubbornly acted out his misery by tossing his head, we saw Hermann brutally attack him. Geld reared up on his back legs, knocking Hermann's gun from his shoulder. Hermann was so angry that he picked up the gun and struck him over the head with it, bending it to a fine curve and ruining it entirely. Otto and Fritz ran up to diffuse the worsening situation.

"Take over, Boys. See what you can do with this irritable beast. Look at what he's done! Not that I care about the loss, though it was a good gun and a beauty; now I'm relieved of the burden of carrying it. Anyway, I'm not going to California to hunt!"

I wasn't surprised he had hit Geld; after all, he had attacked me only days earlier.

I knew I would never forget or forgive Hermann for hitting me. How could I? Nor would I ever fail to remember Lily's scream of terror as he raised his hand against me or the look of hatred in both boys' eyes – never seen by me before – when they realized what he had done.

Chapter 70

At Big Sandy, Hermann announced that we would begin traveling at night.

"We'll leave after supper."

"After supper, Father?"

"It is desert for the next forty miles. No water. We'll travel by night."

"And what about Lily, Hermann?" I asked.

"You'll have to think of something," he said. "Do I have to solve every single little problem on this trip?"

He told us that others had advised him they would make the trip at night when the animals could be cooler and require less water; he determined to do the same.

He softened a little and said, "Of course I worry about my daughter, my little *Budlein*. But, if she can splash in the stream, she must be better."

I made up a bed for Lily on the driver's seat, the only part of the wagon with springs. This stretch of the trail was so rough, I wasn't sure she wouldn't bounce out, let alone sleep, so I rigged several straps to hold her and the bedding in place. Before supper I wrapped myself in a shawl and tried to get some rest for the upcoming night's walk, but visions of Indian raids under a moonless sky took hold of my imagination, and I could not sleep.

The boys filled our water cask and gathered as much grass as possible. Otto went hunting and shot three hares. We had an early supper of boiled hare and bread, and at six in the evening a silent signal for departure must have been given. From all quarters of the camp men began clucking to their teams and snapping their whips, and a large caravan of wagons surged westward.

The trail was dry and dusty, the late-day sun in our eyes. In less than an hour the sun went down leaving a brilliant golden yellow sky, which, as we watched it, paled to white shafts of light dividing the entire firmament into thoroughfares of radiance.

But by half seven all light was gone, and the dark lay in the ravines and valleys and seeped in to fill the spaces between wagons. We clustered together more closely than usual; no one strayed off the trail. I knew the moon was waning and wouldn't show itself for many hours, and the stars gave scant light. Lily was loathe to ride alone in the wagon, not able to see us, and she walked by my side, clutching my hand and begging to be carried. I lifted her and carried her until my arms ached, then passed her to Fritz. She fell asleep in his arms, but when he tried to transfer her to the wagon seat, the jostling woke her, and she cried to be carried. Otto took over, and carried her for another hour. Finally, as the moon began to show itself as a pale orange glow at earth's rim, she fell asleep again, and Otto was able to lay her on the wagon seat and to cover her warmly. The rest of us wrapped blankets around us, as the night was excessively cold.

There was a terrible stench along this section of dark trail. When the moon gave us enough light, we realized that we were walking through a graveyard of abandoned wagons and decaying carcasses of oxen and mules. Apparently the animals had died in this desert for want of water. We all yearned to stop to make coffee and to rest the beasts, but could not imagine lingering in this place of death. Other travelers around us, scarcely to be distinguished in the darkness, continued moving too, all of us walking quietly with no noise except the creak of wagons and occasional words of encouragement to the animals.

Night travel was something new to me and, except for the smell, strangely and surprisingly exciting. I could imagine us as an army marching upon an unsuspecting enemy, muffling our steps, or as robbers creeping upon a slumbering town. Even so, I hoped not to make many night marches in spite of its novelty. The dust was terrible, the stink of dead animals overwhelming, and fatigue so overcame me toward dawn that several times I found myself with both arms draped around the neck of an ox, more asleep than awake.

We did not stop once that night. Otto and Fritz fed the animals handfuls of grass and held a bucket of water to each as they walked. When finally the sun came up in its entire dazzling splendor, I was exhausted and begged Hermann to stop.

"We'll stop when the sun is high," was his answer.

It took two days, or rather two nights, to cross the desert and arrive at the Green River. The second half of the trip was up and down hill, and the going was very hard on our team. They were annoyed by the constant dust and sand, which hung round them and oppressed their breathing. Twice we had to let the wagon down steep ravines with a rope and pulley system, fastened to the harness of one yoke at the top of the hill, to keep it from overrunning the team and crashing at the bottom. This we accomplished at night with no moonlight. Clouds accompanied our eventual arrival at the river and with it a warm south wind, which stirred up even more dust.

I thought our poor team was nearly used up. All four were straining on the flat approach to the river and gasping for breath, even though their instinct informed them that water was near. The back two looked more dead than alive, as though we had walked them off their legs.

I was also near to collapse. Lily was moody, tired, and her cough was relentless. I could read the strain of the last two nights on the lined faces of Hermann and the boys, and I wondered how Hermann could continuously urge us along while at the same time show such signs of physical exhaustion himself.

At the Green River crossing, he told us to take the animals out of harness and drive them to the river for water, and he went to inquire about the ferry that would take us across the river.

This ferry was owned by a Frenchman who had concluded that establishing a monopoly of one ferry at this crossing would bring him more fortune than any other endeavor in California might. He charged eight dollars a load and took three or more loads on each trip. The river was too deep and wide and its current too strong to ford, and this was the only ferry across. When Hermann came back, his displeasure and exasperation were evident in his flared nostrils and scarlet complexion.

"Eight dollars! The *Französisch* – damn him! Damn him all to hell! He's a cheat and a scoundrel! He demands eight dollars to take our wagon across this stinking river, and that doesn't include the animals that must swim. That's not all. He's busy now. Damn him! He has a line of wagons waiting to cross. He thinks he can take us in four days. *Verdammt!* Four days! I will cross now!"

Hermann was clenching his teeth, and, though his face was red, he looked black as thunder. His body was stiff seemingly ready to splinter. He paced in front of us then walked to the wagon and kicked a rear wheel, knocking the spokes out of the wheel and causing the wagon to tip awkwardly to one side, spilling out our bedding and a bundle of clean clothes. Anything I said would add fuel to his raging fire; I gathered Lily into my arms and walked to the river's edge where Otto and Fritz were watering the animals. I told the boys about the problem.

"I know," said Otto. "I've been talking to some other people. Just look how many people are waiting! Over there is a government train; they must have forty wagons and hundreds of mules, and they were here before us. Someone told me the Frenchman could be bribed. Shall I tell Father?"

I urged him to wait a while, warning him of Hermann's wrath. The boys turned to look at their father and saw the wagon tipped up. "Did Father do that?" asked Fritz.

I nodded. "You see how mad he is."

"I see how mad he is, mad and crazy both. At least there are dozens of wagons all around us abandoned by poor souls. We'll find a wheel that will fit," said Fritz, always my problem solver.

The next time the ferry returned to our side, I saw Hermann confront the ferryman again, waving his arms, possibly threatening the man. He walked over to where we were still watering the animals. "I am not going to pay his prices or wait in line. We will float our wagon across. He is *ein Esel* – an ass! Get the oxen back in harness, Otto, Fritz – right now. We'll get across without him."

I couldn't stay quiet. "Hermann. We have only three wheels! Look at this river!"

He stared at me, but I don't think he saw me. "Otto, Fritz!"

"Hermann!" I handed Lily to Fritz and touched my husband's tense shoulder. "Look, Hermann!"

He turned and glanced where I was pointing, then swung back toward me, his rage still evident in his bulging eyes and clenched jaw. For a fleeting moment I thought he was going to hit me again, and I turned my body away. "What, Frida? What?"

"Watch those men there, Hermann. They're trying to drive all those mules into the river. Watch, Hermann!"

This time he really looked. The men were having frightful difficulty. They had turned the mules away from the river, brought them slightly up the embankment, then turned them again toward the river and were driving them fast toward the edge. The mules would strike across the land but would get frightened at the strong current; some entered the water but turned and swam back to shore. The men drove them several times, howling at them and making full use of their whips. As we watched, ten of the mules swam out into the current on the fourth try, the remaining twenty or more returned to shore once again. The mules in the current could not swim against it and were swept downstream.

"Hermann, our animals are not as strong as those mules, and those mules were not pulling a wagon. I beg of you, abandon that plan."

He collapsed onto a tree stump at our feet, cradling his head in his arms. "Boys, find forage for the animals," he mumbled. "Frida! You don't understand. None of you understand. We have to beat the snow." He turned his face to me. The bluster I had seen there had been replaced by anguish and despondency. This time I turned away; I couldn't comfort him for I had too much suffering within me.

Chapter 71

Grass was plentiful here, despite the crowded riverbank. It was the best grass we had since leaving the States. We were grateful for that. Otto drove the animals a short distance and found shade for our campsite and ample forage.

I took Lily to the river's edge and commenced washing clothes in its muddy waters.

Fritz found a perfect match for our broken wheel, but as Hermann had left our jack hundreds of miles behind, he had no way to replace the new wheel. Fortuitously four of the soldiers of the government train rode up on horseback and offered their assistance. Three put their backs to the tipped wagon. The third and heaviest sat his considerable weight on the high side and amusingly barked orders, "Heave-ho, me hearties!" They righted our wagon quickly, put a stout stick under the wheel-less corner, and mounted up again, all in ten minutes.

In thanks, I invited them to share a campfire supper and spent the rest of the day preparing from our dwindling stores. Fritz inquired of me if I had invited them in order to have others around to dampen his father's ire.

"It's possible!" I answered.

"I only have the two remaining hares, and there will be eight of us, plus Lily, for supper. See what you can shoot, Fritz, when you're finished with that wheel repair."

I was able to buy four eggs from another group and made dough of flour, butter, salt and eggs that I rolled out on the wagon seat, and thus made a hare pie to be served with biscuits. As I worked the crust, I wondered when I would next have the luxury of a stout kitchen table to work on, mixing bowls of various sizes, and an oven whose temperature I could trust.

Fritz returned with six plovers.

"How did you do it?" I inquired, knowing how shy plovers are.

"They all dispersed as soon as I shot one; then they'd come back to feed at the same place. I'd shoot another; they'd fly off and then come back again! Tomorrow I'll get more! But, see what else I've found at the riverside. Isn't this dock?"

He had gathered a large bunch of weeds in the front of his shirt, holding it up against his chest with one hand, carrying the birds with the other, and clutching his rifle under one arm.

"It is!" I hadn't seen it since home in Giessen, and I was amazed that he recognized it. "I'll make a soup."

Just when I had thought we were reaping nothing but a harvest of troubles, Fritz brought small relief.

Hermann had absented himself for most of the day but found us just before suppertime.

"What's going on here, Frida?" He was still flushed and breathing heavily.

"Company for supper, Hermann. I've asked some of the officers who helped Fritz repair the wagon wheel. Here they come."

He turned away from the approaching men. I watched as he closed his eyes and took a deep breath, let it out, and took another. When he turned back, he was in control and smiled at the men, extending his hand, "Welcome!"

Having guests around the campfire was a pleasant respite. They brought us a present in gratitude: ten pounds of rice; no gift could have been more sweet. Hermann found his last pint of whiskey and passed the bottle while I served our supper. I had many compliments on my banquet; not a morsel was left in pot or pan. Lily took a shine to the youngest and shiest of the four men, Corporal Bryerly, and coaxed him into a game of cat's cradle, soon settling contentedly in his lap. We sat in the light of the fire after supping, talking about the trail to the east and the challenge to the west. Hermann complained about the delay and the cost at the Green River ferry crossing. The heavyset man, Sergeant Frederick Felton, said he would talk to the Frenchman in the morning to see what he could do. Then he took a harmonica from his pocket and warmed up with a few little tunes that were unfamiliar to us.

"Will you sing if I play songs that you know?" he asked.

We agreed, even Hermann.

He started with "Jim Along, Josey." I remembered it from a play I had seen in New York with some friends and so filled in such words as I remembered. My voice surprised me – thin and quavery where once it had been bold. *Like my grandmother's*, I thought.

He went right into "Columbia, the Gem of the Ocean," which we all knew. The hearty male voices drowned out my own and thrilled me. Next came "The Long Ago" and "Old Dan Tucker." Lily asked for "Oh! Susanna," her favorite, and he played it softly. Corporal Bryerly urged her to stand up and sing, and she surprised us all by walking briskly around the campfire, swinging her arms like a soldier, and calling out the words, "Oh! Susanna, Oh don't you cry for me!"

"One more," he said and put the instrument to his lips for "God Bless our Native Land." To my utter amazement, Hermann sang the German words; and as each of us realized what he was doing we dropped out, one-by-one, until he alone finished the song.

"Thank you," he said to Sergeant Felton . "Thank you for the music. Thank you all for helping my son today with the broken wagon wheel. And above all thank you for offering to talk to the French ferryman."

By the time I had finished the clean up and gone into the tent, Hermann was asleep. I could see his face by the light of the dying fire. It was relaxed. He had no strained look, no wrinkles of worry, no flushed capillaries. I could see there the handsome young man I had met more than twenty years earlier. For the first time in months, I felt a small wave of warmth in my heart for him.

Chapter 72

Sergeant Felton approached us early the next day. I poured him coffee.

"I have argued your case with the ferryman, Mr. Reinhardt," he said. "He has agreed that you can join as part of our group. The price will be as stated: eight dollars. He is taking us across tomorrow, probably in the afternoon. We have already started getting our mules across, and it is no easy task. Of the ten that got in the river's current yesterday, three never made it, and the others straggled across far downstream. We already have two men across who spent the afternoon chasing them."

I waited for Hermann to answer; finally he raised his head, "I'm not sure my beasts can swim across."

"We have more than a hundred more mules to take across. The Frenchman will take one end of a long rope across later this morning. We will thread each mule's harness loosely to the rope. That way they will at least all end up in one place. And when our wagons are across, the animals will be settled down and ready to be harnessed right away."

"If they don't drown in the current itself."

"You do what pleases you, Mr. Reinhardt, but if you want to make use of our rope, I offer it to you in thanks for your wife's excellent supper and company last night." Sergeant Felton left without finishing his coffee.

Lily, the boys, and I were glad for another day of rest. Our oxen and cow would have at least a day and a half with good grass, plentiful water, and no wagon work. While Hermann decided how our animals would cross, Lily and I walked around the large encampment. I knew I could use a female companion and kept looking for groups with women. There weren't many, but I did see three women and a few children sitting near two tents quite far from the riverbank. I was hailed as we approached, "Good Morning! Join us!" I was glad I had worn a calico skirt that morning, as they were also in skirts.

They introduced themselves as Rachel Bieber, Susannah Witt, and Tabatha Laidler and bade me sit and take coffee with them. I was full of coffee, but empty of friendship and joined them with pleasure.

There were various children about, and a sweet-faced blond girl of about six took Lily's hand, "How old are you?" she asked. Lily held up two fingers. "She'll be three in a few days – August 15," I added. The two went off on an adventure.

"Mrs. Reinhardt!" exclaimed Mrs. Witt after they had wandered off. "August 15 was yesterday!"

I couldn't believe I had been so distracted as to forget my baby's birthday. "Oh, no!" I blurted out, feeling the heat behind my eyes, which foretold tears, "What shall I do?"

"She doesn't know what day it is, my dear; you can celebrate it any day, any day at all. We could have a little party right now, if you like."

"I couldn't do that. Lily has two brothers. We'll do something festive together." I was overcome with their kindness.

I spent all morning with these good women from Kentucky, hearing their travel stories. At midday two of their husbands returned successfully from fishing and all urged me to stay for a meal of boiled rice and fresh fish. I declined, saying that my family would be expecting me.

"Which is your camp site?" asked Mrs. Witt. "I'll send my twelve-year old, Faxon, to tell them you're staying here."

I agreed - delighted to stay, happy for the company of women, and relieved to have a change in my routine.

As Mrs. Bieber and I were cleaning the fish, her husband returned and introduced himself as Doctor Hans Bieber. He fetched himself a ladle of water and came back and sat with us.

"I've just met a fellow traveler - also from Kentucky. He claims to be a doctor himself and is offering his services by means of a sign affixed to the side of his wagon. There was quite a line of men waiting to see him; I could not resist lingering and spying a bit, wondering what was going on, as most of the men in the line looked no worse than I do myself."

"What did you learn from this doctor, Hans?" his wife asked.

"I learned that he should learn from me! He had convinced quite a crowd that their tiredness was due to bad blood accumulated along the long trail. He was nothing more than a blood-letter! He had this stylish little brass box with slotted ends, which concealed a dozen knives. It had a spring action that caused the knives to flash out to scissor the patient's flesh. He possessed a three-legged stool, which one man after another would sit on to lose his pound of blood. You should have seen the earth around that chair – slick with blood!"

"Land sakes, Hans! Did you speak to him?"

"I did. I asked him what other remedies he prescribed, and he answered: 'purging.' Apparently with similar misguided zeal, he scours the insides of patients with stomach or bowel disorders with harsh laxatives and emetics. He told me he also favors calomel, thinking that the watery saliva that it produces helps to bring up the bile! I've heard such outrageous ideas elsewhere, but this man had no modern cures at all. What he did have was a pocket full of money. He was charging each patient two dollars!"

"Dr. Bieber," I interrupted, "I have a daughter with a chronic cough. The dust, of course, makes it much worse. It weakens her, and when it is very bad, we put her in the wagon. A doctor looked at her many weeks ago and thought he heard something in her chest resembling pneumonia. What would you advise for her?"

"I would have to examine her, of course. Probably I would recommend that she should stay out of the damp of evening and that you should always keep her warm. And another thing, it is my opinion that it is more healthful to camp away from the crowds. Some doctors believe that cholera and some other diseases are contagious and are spread where people are gathered in tight proximity. One time I opened the flap of an Indian tent, expecting to find it abandoned. It was, in fact, abandoned – by the living. There were two or more corpses there, partly wrapped in blankets. It was dark, and I couldn't tell the number accurately. But I believe that Indians also believe in contagion and did not want to enter that wigwam."

I liked this man, Dr. Bieber.

When the meal was ready, we all gathered around, sitting on the ground in the shade of the wagons. Including Lily and myself, there were twelve of us, enjoying the fish, rice, and good biscuits made by Mrs. Laidler.

After lunch Dr. Bieber continued his tale about the so-called doctor he had just observed. "He claimed to have treated three hundred cases of cholera and only lost two of them. I don't think he knew the difference between cholera and diarrhea! He offered opium for all bowel ailments and claimed a cure if the patient didn't die!"

"By the way, Mrs. Reinhardt, have you noticed that we hear less about the misfortune of cholera now than we are west of South Pass?"

I admitted that I had not.

"It is my belief that the chill mountain air that we are enjoying is detrimental to the spread of cholera. Here some people might get it and not know that they have it, because their symptoms are so slight."

I heard Fritz call me and turned to see his approach. He didn't look quite right.

"*Mutti*, Father sent me to find you. He has something to tell you."

I introduced Fritz to my new friends, but I could see he was anxious to be off, so gathered Lily and said good-bye.

"What is it that your father wants to tell me, Fritz?" I asked as we walked back.

"He'll tell you." He turned his head away from me and wiped his sleeve over his eyes.

Chapter 73

I found Hermann uncharacteristically lying in the tent. He raised himself on one elbow. "We've lost the cow."

"Lost the cow? What do you mean? I just milked her this morning."

"Well, she's gone; that's all there is to say."

"No! That's not all! Tell me. What happened?"

"The army fellows rigged a line across the river. I went down to the riverbank and watched them send one mule after another across. They didn't like it! You've never heard such braying. But they got across, every one. Sergeant Felton came to me and asked if I wanted to use the rope for our animals."

"And? Did you weigh other alternatives? What did you do?"

"I didn't like the idea. Mules are different. Some people think they're better swimmers than cattle. It was against my better judgment, but there was Sergeant Felton urging me once again."

"And, so you agreed?"

"I did. Sergeant Felton forced the issue. Fritz brought the oxen and the cow. I'd already dispatched Otto over on the ferry to be there to receive them. I attempted to send Silvester over first. Fritz and I couldn't get him to go into the river. We whipped him hard, and then Felton and one of the others from last night came and prodded him with sticks. Finally he surged in, and we sent the other three and the cow immediately behind him."

"The cow drowned, didn't she Hermann? She isn't lost, she's dead, isn't she?"

"Yes, Frida. The cow didn't make it across. She fought against the rope around her neck, twisting to get back to our side of the river. I think she strangled herself."

"Did you try to save her, Hermann? Did you go into the river, along the rope? Did you make any effort at all to reach her?"

He shook his head and smirked as though my question was a joke.

I couldn't abide the thought that our cow, which had traveled more than a thousand miles with us, sometimes in harness, had died in this violent way.

"Frida, how else was she to get across?"

"I don't know, and I don't know what we'll do for milk or butter. She was a good cow, easy to milk and docile in the harness. We'll all miss her."

"The fellows from the army train said you could have some ass milk from them."

"It's not the same. It doesn't have the fat. I don't think it will make butter.

"I can't bear to tell Lily that we've lost another animal. She knows them as her family, you know." I told Hermann.

"Have Fritz tell her."

"And another thing, Hermann: we have forgotten her birthday. It was yesterday. Lily is three years old now."

"And, I feel one hundred," he answered.

Chapter 74

Dr. and Mrs. Bieber paid us a visit in the morning as we were tying our belongings onto the wagon in preparation for the river's crossing.

"I've brought something for your daughter's birthday celebration," said Mrs. Bieber. "It's peppermint oil, from my husband's medicine chest. If you add a few drops to cow's milk and let it juggle along in the back of your wagon, it will make a fair treat for the palate."

I thanked them both and told the sad story of our cow. "But I have some of her last milk, and when we are across, I'll add the peppermint oil to some of it."

"Where is your pretty little girl?" asked Dr. Bieber. "I'll examine her, if you would like."

I called to Lily and she readily succumbed to his questioning and probing. "You don't chatter as much as Dr. Tuttle. Are you really a doctor?" she asked.

"She's a smart little girl, Mrs. Reinhardt. I'm impressed with her vocabulary," said the doctor.

"She has only grown-ups to talk to most of the time; her brothers are nearly grown men. Do you think she has pneumonia, Dr. Bieber?"

"I do. I think she has pneumonia and probably has had it for quite a while. Listen to her chest yourself. You will hear how rapid her breaths are."

I put my ear to her thin chest and could feel her heart beating as though it was under nothing more than a silk shawl. "What can I do?"

"You don't want her to start wheezing. Keep her dry and warm and make sure she drinks water all day long – boiled water. That will keep the cough loose. I hate to give you this news: It will be very hard to cure her pneumonia on the trail."

"I'll find a way! I have to." I thanked them for their kindness, hoping we would meet again on the way.

As the Biebers walked away, Hermann, Fritz, and Sergeant Felton came to pull our wagon by hand down to the river's edge. Lily begged to be carried and buried her face in my neck, trembling. *She is so smart*, I thought.

I called out to Hermann, "I want to talk to you! Lily has just been examined by a doctor."

"When we get across!" he answered.

The Frenchman loaded our wagon with dispatch, taking Hermann's eight dollars without a thank you. As I stepped aboard the raft with my family, I watched a group of Missourians push their homemade pontoon raft off the embankment. It was swept a mile downstream. When we reached the river's south side, safely thanks to the Frenchman, the Missourians were attempting to cordelle it up the stream, fatiguing and laborious work. At least they were safe too.

Chapter 75

As we crossed the Green River on the Frenchman's raft, I saw Otto standing on the south side of the river. He had harnessed our oxen and on the backs of two had stacked and secured enough grass for our four remaining animals for at least one day. He was gazing west, shading his eyes from the afternoon sun and watching the wagons before us plod westward. His posture was like Hermann's, although he did not resemble him in the slightest. Even from a distance I could see that his teeth and fists were clenched and that his shoulders were tight like someone expecting a blow. He looked impatient, as his father often did.

While the Frenchman poled us across Otto turned and gestured to us to hurry; although he must have known we had no means to affect our speed.

I raised my arm to wave at him; my sleeve must have fallen away, baring my arm. Fritz reached over and gently touched the bruise left by Hermann's grip. "He could have broken your arm," he said.

I watched Fritz clench his own fists, "Sometimes at night I lie in the tent plotting my revenge against him."

"Fritz! Don't think about it. There is nothing to be done."

"I imagine concealing a flat rock in my hand and hitting him with it. Once when he stood beside me on a riverbank, I barely controlled my impulse to push him into the rapids below. I hate his meanness! He has less control than Lily! You're not frightened of him, are you? But I am," he continued. "He may hold up his pants with an old piece of rope to compensate for the weight he has lost, but he is still larger than I am and stronger and meaner. He can summon strength from a smoldering rage; I only seethe."

"Have you tried remembering an earlier, happier time with him?" I asked.

He thought for a moment. "I have such a vague memory of my early childhood before coming to America. I remember a stone house with flowers outside and a steep stairway just inside the doorway. I remember sitting on the lowest stair watching the bees in the flowers by the open front door. I remember you, *Mutti*, sitting on a step above me. I would lean against your leg. Isn't that where you cut my hair? I also remember a shaggy dog that chased the bees and snapped at them; he snored in the night, sleeping under the table in the kitchen. I remember my *Grossmutter* and *Grossvater.* She was cheerful and liked to play with Otto and me. He was tall and wore a beard that was tangled and scratchy. Didn't we once have a crowd around a large outdoor table with pitchers of apple cider and mountains of food on platters? I have no memory at all of my father back then."

He stopped and stared at me. "It's odd, isn't it, that I can't remember him in Giessen?

"Why did you come to America, *Mutti*? I mean, why did you agree to come with him? I'm sure it was all his idea, not yours. I can't imagine that Father spread out a map of America on our kitchen table in Giessen and asked you where you wanted to go! You would have wanted to go somewhere where there would be a garden, with bees.

Our ferry approached the shore. Otto stood on the makeshift dock waiting to catch the lines. His hair was in his eyes, as it always was. Fritz spoke again, "I remember one other thing. I remember how much I loved Otto when we were little boys."

Chapter 76

That night, as usual, Hermann wandered off after supper. Whenever we camped near others, he would insinuate himself into their gatherings, telling his own adventures, seldom listening to theirs. When I finished cleaning up, I left Lily with her brothers and went to find him.

Together we walked up to a bare knoll. I felt oddly awkward with him. Even though we were seldom out of sight of each other, we were rarely alone. He began telling me about the people he had met – Missourians, a father, his five sons, and one nephew.

I interrupted him. "Husband, it is Lily I want to talk about, not a family of Missourians. Dr. Bieber confirmed that she has pneumonia."

He answered, "My grandmother had pneumonia when I was a boy. I remember it clearly since the whole family was summoned to her deathbed. But she didn't die, and within the month was cooking the Christmas goose! Lily will be all right. She's a tough little girl, and she has you to care for her."

"And you too?"

"Of course. Me too."

"Dr Bieber said it would be nearly impossible to cure her along the trail."

Hermann swung around and faced me squarely, "What do you mean by that?"

"I mean we should be talking about Lily's health!"

"Go ahead. Talk!"

"Hermann! Don't you understand? Lily is sick, very sick. She has had pneumonia for more than a month. All the care I have given has not helped. I carry her much of the time – or her brothers do. Sometimes she rides in the wagon or atop Silvester. I try to keep a cloth tied over her mouth against the relentless dust, but it's no use, she pulls it down half the time anyway. The only way she will get better is to rest. We need to stop for a while – maybe ten days or two weeks. We could make camp in a nice place on a river or a stream; Lily could rest; so could the animals."

"It's impossible, Frida!"

"How will you feel if she dies, Hermann?" I asked.

"If she dies, if any of us dies, I will feel as though I have failed!"

"Failed? Is that all?"

"Listen to me, Frida." He took my hand and gestured for me to sit with him on the edge of the knoll. He took a stick and drew a map in the dust. On the right was a vertical line representing the Green River, just crossed. He continued drawing east to west, naming places as he marked them: "Here is the Bear River divide; then there's a cut-off that we might take to save time getting to the Humboldt River. From here to the end of the Humboldt, if we follow it all the way, will take us about four weeks. That's with no resting. He gave me a stern look. The mountains start about here – the Sierra Nevada." He drew jagged lines, to indicate mountains, the way a child might. "Once we're across the mountains, we're in the Sacramento Valley, and the trip is virtually behind us."

"I know today is August 17. Let us say we rest here until September third or fourth. It's still summery, warm during the days; it would be a good time for Lily's recuperation. We would get to the mountains by October first, and be in the Valley a week later. What's the problem with that?"

"The problem! You mean the problems! First of all, the mountains are like no others we have seen. They are steep, and I hear they often have snow by late September. Can you imagine climbing mountains and negotiating passes in the snow, Frida! We would never make it. Second, we don't have the provisions for an extra two weeks; and there is no place to purchase them. Third, what if we have an emergency and have to wait somewhere for repairs or something like that? You're not thinking straight!"

"What if we have an emergency? We have one now! Don't you understand?" I was shouting at him, trying to make him understand.

Hermann turned to me, a nerve twitching in his jaw. I had seen that look many times before. He grabbed me firmly by my upper arms, "Lily will be fine! Trust me! She's a little girl and tough. If my grandmother survived pneumonia, then my daughter can too."

I was too overcome by his arguments to reply immediately. I brushed his hands away. "Are we going to make it, Hermann?"

"We'll make it. I told you to trust me. I have figured it all out. But we must keep moving and get through the mountains before winter. Figure it out for yourself, Frida!"

I thought for another moment, "What if you left me here with Lily? When our friends catch up with us, I'll come along with them." I had a vision of Hans-Jürgen finding us by the trailside and putting us under his care.

"No. No, Frida, I won't allow it. We don't know that they will come this way. At the rate they were going, they could be anywhere – they might have turned tail for home, for all I know. We will stay together, moving along quickly, and Lily will get over this pneumonia. You and I will rejoice with her and the boys when we get to the diggings!"

He stood and walked away, leaving me alone. I felt a bubble of sadness and helplessness well in my chest and up to my throat. Tears sprung to my eyes, and I dabbed at them furiously with a handkerchief, wailing aloud where no one could hear me, "What can I do? What can I do? Somebody help me!" The same hallucination of Hans-Jürgen floated before me. I held my breath as though I could hold his comforting image a moment longer, as though I could feel his hand on my arm and his breath on my cheek. But there was no one there, just the dusty knoll, adorned with Hermann's hand-drawn map, already defaced by the relentless wind.

Chapter 77

Some things seemed different to me after we crossed the Green River.

First, our fellow travelers were now hardened by the journey. All had lost animals, most had lightened their loads to the barest minimum, some had buried friends and family members along the trail. The holiday mood was over. The excitement of anticipation was gone. All of us longed for only one thing: the end of this difficult trip. Meetings with others along the trail were less social and usually confined to the brief sharing of useful information.

Second, the countryside through which we traveled challenged us in new ways. The hills were steeper and necessitated back locking on our descents. For each plunge there was a corresponding climb, each being slightly higher than the last, or so it seemed. Fortunately the grass remained abundant and of the highest quality. Our animals had regained some of their strength from their enforced rest at Green River, and thanks to the good forage and ample sweet water streams for drinking, they moved along satisfactorily.

Our noon and evening campsites were the most beautifully situated of any along our route. The mountains towered above us, occasionally displaying dustings of snow in the first light of morning. Valleys spread below us through which creeks ran fringed with willows. We stopped in copses of Canada firs, taller than any trees we had seen before. Excepting some stunted cottonwoods along the Platte, I don't think we had seen a real grove of trees since leaving Independence, and these were refreshing to our eyes. One day after lunch I looked around for Otto and Fritz. Not seeing them, I called their names. I heard Fritz's laugh – clear and uninhibited - but could not locate its origin. "Look up, *Mutti*!" I heard. There they were seventy feet or more from the ground, high in the branches of the tree affording our lunchtime shade.

Hermann allowed long midday breaks. "These oxen have been used unmercifully. I will rest them as often as we can afford to get them conditioned to push over the highest passes."

I was surprised at this sensible approach but refrained from voicing my relief.

We awoke each morning before break of day to cool northwest breezes. I often had to crack through ice in our bucket to get water for our coffee. Most mornings I would have liked to linger by the warmth of the fire.

By the time the animals were harnessed and we were underway, the sun's earliest rays would create shifting shadows of the mountains and tall trees over the valleys and ravines. The air was clear as a diamond, and from the tops of the ridges we could see to the distant Eutaw Mountains.

We finished each day after sundown, building a bright grass fire in order to have light for setting up our campsite and picketing the animals.

Lily made it her job each day to collect wild flowers – Michaelmas daisies, bachelor buttons, dandelions and buttercups - which she would arrange artfully around our tent and campfire each night, her little hands stained yellow from the buttercups. "Do you like butter?" she would say to each of us, smudging buttercups under our chins in one of childhood's most endearing games.

I would forage during our midday breaks and one time found enough wild plums for a pie. While these rest periods were welcome, there was no pleasure without its drawbacks. The mosquitoes were aroused and pleased by our presence during those days. They annoyed us every minute of our four-day passage between the Green and Bear Rivers. It was impossible not to scratch their bites; every one of us had open sores. I carried a small amount of Turner's in case of burns; I found that a drop on each mosquito bite helped to take the sting away and kept us from excessive scratching.

One morning Hermann wondered out loud how we would make it over the high ridges before us. Surveying the area, he meandered off the trail into the grasses and returned with an armload of pickings. "Look here! There's flax everywhere among the grass. It reminds me of European flax, proof that this is fertile soil." He called the boys over to see it.

"See these fibers!" he peeled them away from the long stems. "These are phloem. We could ret and scutch them and make yarn and weave linen right here."

Lily looked at her father as though he had lost his mind. I couldn't help but smile; while I had often thought he was losing his mind, at that moment I realized he was truly in his element, recalling those things he had known all his life.

"Now, this region is the first I've seen that is worthy of a farmer's notice! The rest that we've been through is not worth a cent – desert land, mountains covered with boulders, and red soil that will not even nurture a tree." Hermann announced. He tipped forward onto the tips of his toes, a gesture I had not seen in years. "What do you think of it, *Schwartzl?*" I couldn't believe my ears.

On our fourth afternoon we forded the Bear River, which was wide but shallow, allowing the oxen to linger in the river to cool their feet and drink their fill. Otto shot a wild goose and four ducks.

That night we stopped within sight of a settlement of some old mountaineers and Indian traders. One man, whose age could not be guessed by his features or his posture, invited us for a visit after our supper. They had several skin lodges, tents, an ox-wagon, and some bush houses. All around lay horse trappings and Indian goods of every description – clothing, feathers, tools, bows and arrows. There were children of all ages and colors, and a mixture of women, mostly Indian, although I saw two women with light hair and blue eyes. The men were in a tent playing Monte on a skin. Apparently they had adopted the native custom of taking as many wives as they could feed. Each man had several and offered them to Hermann, Otto, and Fritz in exchange for whiskey. By the nudges between my sons, I gathered that they were tempted.

I was more attracted by their fine fat horses in the meadow on the opposite side of the trail. "Hermann," I whispered, "ask them if they would sell us a horse." I was thinking ahead that I could ride with Lily if she became weak, or we could yoke a horse with an ox if we lost any more of our team.

They agreed to sell us a horse; the price would be $300. "You'll trade your wife for a drink of whiskey but will charge me $300 for a horse!" exclaimed Hermann.

"Or," said the man, "you can play a game of Monte with us. If you win, you get our best horse."

"And if I lose?"

The man turned his attention to me. He pointed a filthy finger right at my chest and gave Hermann a broad wink.

The trail had turned north at Bear River and at noon the day after our encounter with the mountain men, our route was joined by the western terminus of the trail known as Sublette Cutoff, which had left the main track shortly after South Pass, nearly two weeks behind us. As we approached, I could see many messages fluttering in the breeze nailed to posts and trees, and I wondered idly but hopefully if there would be news of Hans-Jürgen and our friends. As we approached, we saw two easily identifiable wagons slightly off the trail – exact copies of our own.

"*Mutti*!" called Fritz. "It's them! Those two are the Brantlach and Settlemeyer wagons!"

My breath caught in my throat and my heart raced. No sight could have pleased me more. I brushed the dust off my traveling-trousers and tucked stray, dusty hairs under my sun hat. I knew Hans-Jürgen would be there since he traveled and camped with the Brantlachs; the very idea made me quiver. As we approached, I recognized Albert, his brother Kristof, Jan Volker, Randolf Settlemeyer and his son, and old Felix Mittler. *Six people – three per wagon. Usually four people accompanied each wagon. Where were the others*?

Albert was the first to see us, and he came to take the lead line of our oxen, greeting us all warmly. He shook Hermann's hand and then turned to me, and I swooned right into that good man's arms. "What's this?" he said, embarrassed.

I quickly regained my feet, "It's just that I'm so glad to see you! Excuse this tired woman's emotions!"

Jan Volker helped Otto take the oxen out of harness and put them to grazing. The others gathered around. All of us started talking at once, telling of our adventures. They had nearly caught up with us at South Pass and then had received erroneous information from other travelers that we had taken the Sublette Cutoff. With six oxen to each wagon, they drove their teams hard, hoping to catch up with us. When that failed, they realized we must have taken the other route and had waited a day at the west end of the Cutoff to see if we would pass or if they would hear word of our approach.

"Where are the rest?" I asked, hoping principally for news of Hans-Jürgen .

Randolf Settlemeyer cleared his throat, "We had some bad times several days past Fort Laramie. You remember Gerd Amsel? He liked to sleep under the stars, as you will recall. One night the wind shifted, and sparks from the fire blew onto his blankets."

"Oh, no! Say no more! Lily's here." I gasped and clapped my hands over her ears.

Randolf continued, "We buried him the next morning, marking his grave with the seat from his wagon. Felix inscribed it with his name and the date of his untimely death."

"That wasn't the end of it; our bad fortune had just begun," continued Albert. "That same night we camped in close quarters with many others. In the night we heard a commotion and were told that two people in the tent next to the Frankens' tent had died in the night of cholera. We hitched our wagons in that dark hour to escape the disease, but it was too late."

He looked at his brother, and Kristof continued, "By afternoon young Peter Franken was struck with violent diarrhea and vomiting. His father did everything for him, giving him boiled water from a spoon and drops of Dysentery Corrector every few hours. Sadly, his administrations were to no avail."

I looked over to my boys expecting to see tears. Both looked as though the joy of life had been drained out through their veins, but neither cried. *They had seen so much*!

Kristof looked at Albert, "You tell the rest."

Albert turned his back to us, "I can't," he said blowing his nose.

Felix Mittler took over. "It wasn't only young Peter with the cholera. Rolf Smit got it too."

"Who else?" I blurted.

"And Hans-Jürgen Topp."

I couldn't control myself and lurched to our wagon, slumping against the side. My tears came – unstoppable - soaking my face and my shirtwaist.

"No, no. Not Hans-Jürgen ," I whispered, between choking sobs.

And aloud, "Are you sure?"

His caring visage swam before me, and I reached involuntarily and lightly touched my lips. Hermann was baffled by my overt grief and came to my side.

"Hans-Jürgen and Rolf were our long-time friends, Frida; I will miss them too. You must write to Hans-Jürgen's wife when we get to California."

I nodded, "Let me be alone for awhile, Hermann; take Lily and the boys and comfort them. I need to be by myself."

He would never know that while I mourned for Gerd Amsel, young Peter Franken, and Rolf Smit, it was for Hans-Jürgen that I wept. I had experienced too many good-byes. Not one was as painful as this one. In that instant, I knew I must resign myself to being no more than Hermann's wife. Whatever fantasies I had and repressed were over for good. My heart truly broke. This was not at all like the dreadful grief when I learned of my father's death. That knowledge also came long after the fact of death and was accompanied by deep sadness and loneliness. I thought then of all the things I had failed to say to my father, of my sorrow that my daughter would never know him, and of my worry over my mother's remaining years alone.

Even in its earliest moments, this grief was different. I was physically weak, with stomach cramps coming in waves and severe shortness of breath that left me unable to gulp enough air. It forced me to my knees and then to my side with my legs drawn up nearly to my chin.

Felix Mittler approached me with a cup of water.

"*Danke*," I muttered, turning away from him.

I slept, deeply and dreamlessly and awoke to Hermann's shaking me. "Frida, it is three in the afternoon. We must get going. I want to make ten more miles today."

He helped me to my feet and gave me his handkerchief. "You must wash your face."

Lily was on Fritz's shoulders; Otto was at Silvester's head. When they saw me stand, they started forward. I took hold of the back of the wagon and followed, one step at a time.

Chapter 78

Along the sixty-mile journey from the western end of Sublette's to Soda Springs, Hermann got to know a professional guide, Mr. Myers, who had traveled this way before in 1843. Hermann walked along with him for two or three days, questioning him relentlessly. Mr. Myers' ultimate goal was the American River, near Sutter's; that immediately became Hermann's objective too. Mr. Myers plan was to leave the Oregon Trail by way of a 150-mile cutoff – Hudspeth's - to the so-called California Trail. Hermann determined to follow him, even though it meant we would bypass Fort Hall, one of the few places to buy provisions this far west.

I was reluctant to miss a chance to provision and told my husband.

"Borrow from the Brantlachs or Settlemeyers!" he said.

It was such an enormous relief to be in company with a few of our friends once again. I asked if they had stores to spare. They said they did. *Of course,* I thought, *they have only three to a wagon instead of the four they provisioned for.*

I was too distraught to argue with Hermann. I was getting hardly any sleep, as my uncontrollable mind drifted in wakefulness to unrealized fantasies with Hans-Jürgen. Sleep deprived, I managed the simplest of routine tasks only. Once, stirring a pot of rice, half asleep, half in my own dreams, Otto put his hand on my arm to get my attention. "*Mutti*! Are you all right? I've called you three times!" For an instant his warm hand registered against my skin as Hans-Jürgen 's touch, and I reddened and gasped.

I thought at times my heartache would lead to madness. I wondered ceaselessly and idiotically if Hans-Jürgen knew he was dead. Then I would argue with myself internally: *Yes, he knows, and he is struggling to rejoin me. No, it is not given to the dead to know anything*.

Only the regularity of one foot following the other kept me sane.

At Soda Springs I took out my journal and attempted to write of the deaths of our friends. I knew I must write to Kalli, Hans-Jürgen's wife, when we reached California. I couldn't imagine what I would say, but she had been my close companion in New York, and friendship dictated that I must send my sympathy. I thought that I might put some words down while my own grief was fresh, but I found it truly impossible to contemplate Hans-Jürgen 's death. In my memory's eye, he was still as robust as I had last seen him. My mind continually veered off, remembering his kindnesses to me, his gentleness with Lily, and the longing and passion in his kiss. Worse, I conjured images of Hans-Jürgen and me together, reading, following a bird's song, even bathing in a river.

Instead of truly writing what my heart dictated, I merely made note of a few things we had passed as we continued northwest along the Bear River: Thomas Fork Crossing, Big Hill, Soda Springs. I tried to capture the beauty of the landscape, but that too was impossible, and my notes from that day merely listed observations:

> "Bird with black glossy head and tail. Thunderstorm to our south. White and brown rocks. Hawks whistling. Day has been hot."

Soda Springs was a curiosity. Water effervesced as though it were carbonized, gurgling over the edges and leaving rusty sediment. Its taste was unpleasant, slightly acidic and distinctly metallic. Its smell was fetid - like an old swamp. The most surprising aspect was its warm temperature. Currant bushes grew around the springs, and Lily urged me to help her collect berries, I found specimens of petrifactions and lava. I wished I could show them to Hans-Jürgen or at least carry some home but knew that we could add no weight to our baggage.

Only a few miles past the Springs, we veered southwest off the Oregon Trail, following Mr. Myers' wagon train onto Hudspeth's Cutoff and had steady going, with good watering and grasses. We climbed high over the Portneuf Range, wound through several canyons, passed tall buttes, and crossed many small rivers and creeks and one large valley. Each day we saw geese flying south.

As before, we shared the preparation of the evening meal and sat congenially with our friends around the fire afterwards. Often old *Herr* Mittler would sit by me. He was lonely and liked to tell little anecdotes about his wife before she died and his two sons before they left for Argentina. "Back in New York I thought this trip would give my life some purpose; now I wonder why I am making the effort." His eyes would water and his long, thin nose would drip.

"And you, Mrs. Reinhardt? Do you sometimes wish you had elected to stay home?"

That was the exact question that I could not answer. "No," I said after a long hesitation. "I cannot say I am enjoying this trip; it is a hundred times more difficult than I expected. But I could not have stayed in New York and watched Hermann and my sons leave without me. Enduring this trip, I keep us together."

"Your husband can be difficult," he said quietly, poking at the fire with a long stick.

I shut my own eyes tightly to keep the tears back. *Did this lonely old man know how cruel and violent Hermann could be?* "Yes."

"I saw Dr. Tuttle at the place where we waited for you – by Sublette's. He said you walked into a tree in the night and had a bad bruise."

I turned to look at him. He was watching me kindly. I felt my shoulders relax and thought I would tell this man all that had happened. I took a breath but stopped, thinking that nothing would be gained by burdening him with my plight. I didn't think it would help his loneliness, and I was frightened that the truth of my humiliation and shame would spread to the others and then back to Hermann, whose temperament would be badly affected. "Yes," I answered again.

We sat in companionable silence for a while.

I cleared my throat, "*Herr* Mittler, may I ask you a question about Hans-Jürgen's death? Where is he buried?" I felt the familiar knot form in my throat. "I'll write a letter of condolence to his wife, Kalli. She was my close friend in New York. She will want to know."

"*Frau* Reinhardt," *Herr* Mittler began. "Hans-Jürgen mentioned your name to me many times. I know he valued your friendship and worried about your passage on this difficult journey. Several times when we walked together, he remarked on the sound of the wind in the grasses or an unusual pattern of clouds and then told me he wished he could point them out to you."

I could not contain my tears, which flowed freely.

Herr Mittler continued, "When he became sick, he knew it was cholera and that he was dying. Before delirium set in, he asked me to find you and care for you."

I couldn't speak. *To care for me! Yes, I needed care; Hans-Jürgen's care.*

"But, to answer the question that you asked – we made coffins of planks from abandoned wagons and buried Hans-Jürgen, Rolf, and young Peter next to each other in one large grave, marking it with the lid of Rolf's small trunk, onto which I inscribed their names. They lie just to the west of little La Prele Creek where it flows under a natural stone arch."

I swallowed and dug my fingernails into my palm, fighting for control.

"Do you keep a journal?" he asked me.

I shook my head and whispered that my journal writing was sporadic.

"I find it cathartic," he told me, as he rose to check the picketing of the animals before going to his tent. "Usually I start with remarks about nature. Sometimes that's all I write."

The next day at our nooning, I made a hurried meal of bread and cold beans, then took out my journal. I remembered *Herr* Mittler's advice as I wrote.

> Morn clear. Air fresh and cold. Water froze in the pail. Birds serenaded us in the morning - cries, quacks, and whistles - as we disturb their activities. Also songbirds – robins, bluebirds, catbirds, and others too swift for identification.
>
> Passed two Indian villages, two or three miles apart, with horses grazing near them. Mr. Myers identified them as Snake Indians and assured us they were not troublesome. At the first village, several inhabitants came out to beg from us. They were dressed in all manner of costume, several in breechcloths and nothing else. One finely dressed in a tall black hat and coat and trousers, which he must have got off emigrants. Another had a woman's skirt over his shoulders, like a cape. Squaws rode over to us with papooses hanging from their saddles. Men and women had feathers behind their ears, and many also used them to

decorate their heads. They were filthy in the extreme, nothing like the Sioux. As we passed the second village I observed women running their fingers through each other's hair extracting vermin which were then collected in a bowl, as if for the evening's meal. We did not bother with them, merely greeting them and going on.

Many abandoned oxen along the trail. A pair sank down still in the yoke and was left to die thusly by someone preceding us.

Otto shot at two ducks, but lost them when they dove in the river. He got four fine young wild geese. They were of full size, but their wing feathers had not grown enough to enable them to fly; he and Fritz drove them to a thicket where he shot them as they attempted to escape. We will have a feast tonight and soup with dumplings tomorrow.

Fierce horseflies attack the animals and us. At least the cold nights have rid us of mosquitoes.

Passed another grave marker:

Albert Douglas, aged 4 months.

I was not able to write what was in my heart, but *Herr* Mittler was correct: it was healing to focus my attention on something, and there was an abundance of interesting things to write about.

Chapter 79

On September first we got to the end of Hudspeth's Cutoff where it joined the longer California Trail, which came south from Fort Hall. It was our belief that we might see the mighty Humboldt River on that day. But on a signpost erected at the crossroads was a note that we had yet 130 miles to go. All were heartsick with disappointment, as we most earnestly desired to reach the Humboldt and to follow its course westward.

That night I fried the last of the goose for our company of eleven, adding the small pieces to some Wethersfield onions I had picked along the way. Those onions made tears come twice: first when I picked them and was reminded of old acquaintances at the market at home in Giessen, and second when I peeled them for the pot. I had rice from the bag given us by the fellows in the army train. I took pride in the good meals I provided.

After dinner Hermann apprised us of our dilemma. We had traveled 1200 miles since leaving Independence on May 20. We had been on the trail for 104 days. I could perform the arithmetic in my head: less than twelve miles per day. No wonder Hermann was worried about our progress. He told us it would take a minimum of a week to reach the Humboldt, more likely ten days, with the possibility of added time if we encountered problems. Then it would take two weeks – probably more - to reach the mountains. If we had no emergencies and the oxen were well fed, watered and rested, we would arrive at the Sierras in late September. If we encountered problems, we would arrive in October. He did not believe we could get across if there was snow. Hermann was having trouble reconciling to our setback of not yet gaining the Humboldt River. He shook his head, mumbling, "We'll never make it."

In that rare moment his vulnerability revealed itself to me and our friends.

"We have to make it, Hermann," said Albert Brantlach. "What is our choice? Do you think we should camp here until next spring! Of course not! Now the trail is well packed and there is water. We'll make the best of it."

Fritz spoke up, "I'm tired of this journey! My only pair of boots has holes in both soles; when I searched through the wagon for the leather that I was sure I had brought all the way from New York for patching them, I could not find it. Did you throw out the leather, Father, to save a few ounces?"

"Mind your manners and respect your father!" Hermann growled. "You are *eine Junge* – nothing more, Boy! Go hide behind your mother's skirts!"

Hermann was back in control at Fritz's expense.

He was wrong about Fritz; he was wrong about a lot of things. Fritz wasn't a boy anymore. His physique and character had changed. He was as tall as Otto and shaved his soft whiskers several times each week. I put my hand on his arm to quiet him. This was not the time to anger his father.

Fritz and I walked together the next morning.

"Tell me what's on your mind, Son."

"I'm not a boy anymore! Look at this hair on my chest! I'm afraid it will spread to be a thick mat on my back and shoulders like father's. Sometimes I wonder if I'm becoming him. Will my stomach bulge, my neck fatten, and pouches droop under my eyes. Will an uncontrollable rage sweep through my body?"

He didn't want my comfort and purposely walked away. I understood that he was a little frightened of growing up. I also understood that he wanted to be my protector but didn't know how.

I looked around for Otto, but didn't see him. He seemed to be absenting himself more and more from the heart of the family. He continued to do chores and to perform his share of the work with the wagon and the animals, but he was indifferent to the rest of us. Like Hermann, he simply concentrated on the task of getting to California. I knew the reason, although he never spoke of it. Often as I walked off the trail or away from our campsite I would find a heart freshly carved in a tree or drawn in the dirt with the initial "J." Otto had someone to talk to, even if the talking was in his head. It seemed to bestow sharper focus to his days and gave him his own reasons for finishing this trip.

I looked down at Lily walking beside me. Since she had learned to talk, she had been a chatterbox, running her words together so quickly as to be unintelligible at times. Now she was usually silent, her little lips chapped and cracked. Sometimes she had the energy for a little game or an exploration, but more often was content to hold onto my skirt, sometimes pressing a handkerchief to her mouth against the dust of the trail. She had grown so thin that her little shirtwaists hung loosely on her bony shoulders. Often she begged to be carried, and I hardly noticed the extra weight.

Chapter 80

By the side of the trail the next day we encountered a large sign:

CITY OF ROCKS

Immediately we entered a freak of nature: it was a jumble of rocks, caves, caverns, walls, and holes. It was chaos, as if this part of the world had been lifted to a great height and dropped with a crash. Some boulders were stacked one on top of the other and looked as though a child could push them over, sending all parts thundering below. We saw rocks resembling urns, columns, pyramids and forts. The path would only reveal itself to us at the last moment, as we would drive the oxen directly toward a wall of rock, sometimes 300 feet tall. I found it both frightening and romantic.

"What do you think of this, husband?" I asked Hermann.

"I think it better not slow us down!"

Hans-Jürgen would be awed by this, I thought. *He would want to explore with me.* "Come on, Fritz, let's go ahead." We each took one of Lily's hands, and went forward, wandering among the ledges and boulders, exclaiming over the grandeur. We discovered a small grotto – an oasis – with a little brook and a fringe of birch.

Lily wanted to show off her prowess at climbing, "Watch me, watch me!" She scampered over the granite, finding foot holds in the smallest wrinkles of the rocks, and pulling herself over ledges. She discovered a perfect slope for sliding, climbed to the top, and slid down on her bottom, scaring me in the process. "Enough, Lily, you'll put a hole in your trousers!"

"Once more, *Mutti*!" and before I could answer she climbed the slope again, exactly like a monkey, making me grin.

Hermann and Otto caught up with us, and we ascended through a narrow pass that led us to a long difficult descent to Goose Creek and its broad valley. The grass there was three or four feet high. A bit of rain at midday kept the dust down. We anticipated easy travel.

We stopped the night of September 3 by a hot spring. The water was hotter than could be borne. I thought to use it for washing clothes but could not stand the temperature on my hands and did not have the patience to wait for some to cool in a pan. Kristof Brantlach observed that it was hot enough for Thomosian immersion techniques, but all of us remarked that even a sick person could not stand immersion even in the hope of a cure.

In the night there was a flash rainstorm, and in the morning we found the trail too muddy and slippery to continue and, therefore, delayed our leaving until the sun dried the dirt. Two Shoshone Indians approached us, looking somewhat more pleasant than Snakes. Mr. Myers had no use for the Shoshone. He called them Diggers and said they would eat anything they could dig from the ground – even worms and insects. He also warned us against them; he had heard stories of raids in the night, stolen food and animals, and even water in barrels being poisoned by them. These two had three freshly killed mountain goats for sale to emigrants. Fritz touched one of the animals and pointed around, indicating that he wanted to know where to shoot one himself. One pointed to a ravine above us, "heap, heap," meaning there were many to be had. They were small, pretty animals, with interesting horns shaped like fishhooks. Lily took a stick and made some curved lines in the dust. "Look, Fritz! Goats!"

Fritz, who had become sullen around Hermann, suggested to him that we could buy some meat or that he could take his gun and try to find them in the ravine.

"I have no money for goats."

No money for goats. Up until then I had not thought much about our money. Hermann kept a purse tied round his waist and always seemed to be able to pay our fees at river crossings or to give me money for provisioning. I was about to question him when I thought I heard a commotion behind our wagon and went to investigate. There I saw a young Indian opening one of the pockets in our wagon's bonnet, with clear intent of robbery. I rushed to stop him, and in that moment he grinned at me like a demon and snatched Lily who was holding my skirt, turning quickly to run away with her.

With all my strength I threw myself upon him and with both arms tried to wrench Lily away, but his grip was tight. I reached for his hair and used my weight to swing him into the wagon's side. That stunned him but not enough. He kept a strong grip on Lily with one arm, and hit me in the face with the forearm of the other. He made no noise, nor did I, being preoccupied with my task. Suddenly I heard Lily's wail, and I began screaming too.

Hermann, Otto, and Fritz came running; the Indian fled, bleeding from his shoulder and hollering then as loudly as Lily and I.

Lily was terrified. She shook and gasped and clung to me with both arms and both legs. When I calmed her enough so that she could speak, she just repeated over and over, "I want… I want…" choking between syllables. My poor baby did not know what to hope for. She didn't even remember the comfort of a safe home anymore.

I noticed something in her mouth. "Lily, you've lost a tooth!"

"I bit him," she wailed. "I bit him so he would stop hitting you."

I stood swaying, clenching many long black hairs in my fist. Fritz took Lily from me, but she sobbed hysterically, "No, no, no. *Mutti*!" She reached her arms out, imploring me to take her back, and I did.

We had to leave that place. "Move on, Hermann. Quickly."

A mountaineer with a mule camped near us that night and joined the men for a smoke before bedding himself down under the stars. He told us that we had saved more than 120 miles by taking the Hudspeth Cutoff. Even that news could not cheer us.

Now Lily's cough returned. It was not due to the dust, since the night's rain had dampened the trail. This time I blamed it on the stress of the trail and her frightening encounter with the kidnapper.

We moved as quickly as we could, anxious to get to the Humboldt, as we had heard the Shoshone were not to be found that far west. Each day we traveled more than fifteen miles, driving our poor oxen beyond their endurance. There were hundreds of others moving along with us, all dusty, tired, and equally unwilling to banter.

Lily was always tense, unable to relax even in my arms. She awoke many times each night, trembling and sobbing. Her crying would lead into long debilitating attacks of coughing, leaving her exhausted. Her breathing became more labored than it had been, and she complained often of stomachaches and suffered diarrhea.

The afternoon sun was high in the sky when we encountered the Humboldt River on our seventh day of travel from The City of Rocks. Its location surprised us again, this time favorably, as we did not expect to reach it for another two days. We could only conclude that the signpost announcing 120 miles was in error. I felt we had gained two days and begged Hermann for a day off in reward in order to rest ourselves, our animals, and to give Lily a quiet day toward recovery.

Hermann did not agree to a day's rest, but did consent to quit in mid-afternoon.

Uncharacteristically, he sat with me. "Mr. Myers has warned me that the Sierras will test us more than any other part of the trip – more than we can imagine. But, if we find no snow in the mountains, I will give us days to rest then."

"If we make it, Hermann."

He paused, "Did I ever tell you about *Oncle* Oskar, the doctor? He wasn't a blood uncle, but was a childhood friend of my father's. My brothers and sisters and I called him *Oncle* Oskar. I don't know if he was a good doctor or not, but I remember that he always taught his patients to self diagnose, to take their own pulse readings by feeling for the beat in their necks. 'Did you take your pulse, Hermann?' he would admonish me when called to my childhood bedside."

It was so unusual for Hermann to sit with me, so unlike him to become pensive. I waited for him to continue.

"'Did you take your pulse?' became a slogan in our family's business. If we lost a client, if the flax crop was late, if we miscalculated our expenses, one of my uncles or my father would ask, 'Did you take your pulse?' He meant did we try to diagnose the problem and create the solution by ourselves, taking a moment to evaluate all circumstances.

"Here by the Humboldt River I can hear *Oncle* Oskar, 'Did you take your pulse, Hermann?'"

Hermann looked me in the eye.

"Are you taking our pulse, Hermann?" I asked.

"I am. I'm thinking of the challenge ahead at the Sierra Nevada and of other things."

"You mean Lily?"

"Yes. Lily. And more.

"We are nearly out of money. I have only a few coins left. I have a letter to a man in Sacramento, but until we are there, my purse cannot be refilled. The price of every single thing along this trail has been more than it should have been. We have been charged double for the wagons, animals, equipment, and provisions compared to what I had budgeted for. And then there's the cost of the damned river crossings – exorbitant!

"I lie awake in the tent at night while you administer to Lily. While you give her sips of water and help her to fall asleep again, I pretend to be asleep, thinking about everything.

"And I hear you cough in the night too."

I wondered if he heard me go outside of the tent to spit.

Hermann was staring at the ground, literally wringing his hands. His voice quieted, "I have an infection near my ankle. It started as a boil that I could not keep clean. Maybe if I had asked you to put a clean cloth over the spot, it would have gone away; but I didn't. Now the top of my shoe continually rubs against it."

I had noticed that Hermann often limped, turning one foot in as he walked. I'd never asked him why, being unable to offer him sympathy.

"Did you consider cutting away the top of your shoe for relief?" I asked.

"I did not want the others to know of my distress," he admitted.

He continued, "I'm remembering *Oncle* Oskar's advice. Frida, our pulse is weak.

"We have made it to the headwaters of the Humboldt. The water is clear, the grass is luxuriant, and I believe this next stretch will be easy going. But you can see that we cannot let up our pace."

Hermann reached out and took my hand, twirling the plaited ring made for me ten years earlier by the sailmaker Johann. It was loose but my knuckles were swollen and it stayed on my finger, gathering the dirt of the trail.

After dinner Felix Mittler suggested that we had been lax and must return to our previous behavior of posting a guard through each night. We were seven adults: Albert, Kristof, Randolf, Jan Volker, Felix Mittler, Hermann, and myself. And we had three boys: Otto, Fritz, and Randolf's son, David. At twelve years old, David was too young to stand watch, but Fritz and Otto could take their turns. Felix recommended that I should be excused to care for Lily. That gave us eight to stand sentry, which he divided into two teams of four watchmen. The teams would alternate each night watching over the animals and the tents. Each watchman would stay awake for two hours; therefore, each individual would only lose two hours of sleep every second night.

Hermann praised *Herr* Mittler's plan.

Chapter 81

What was there to do but to plod on, step after step, day after day.

The river sustained us with clear water, lush grasses, and even fine trout. Young David Settlemeyer caught frogs, and one night his father skewered frogs' legs and cooked them over the open fire for our supper. There were no trees, except for an occasional stunted willow; we cut wild sage for fuel. Thunderstorms passed every day. The accompanying rain would soak us to the skin; when the sun would re-emerge, our clothes would be caked in dried mud. Evenings were cold; we would build campfires with whatever fuel we could find. I wished for buffalo chips, but we had not seen those animals for weeks. Often we sat under the wet heavens at suppertime with nothing but our hat brims to keep the rain out of our food.

I was grateful for *Herr* Mittler's company; we all were. He was a good storyteller and would distract us at night with remembrances of his boyhood in Baden, where his father was a minister in the government. He had known *der Grossherzog* when he was a boy and remembered being on a small boat with him on the Rhine where servants met them at a landing and served a meal by candlelight in spite of bright sunshine. Such different circumstances than our own!

His father wanted him to stay to be part of the anticipated economic boom when Baden joined the Prussian *Zollverein*. But *Herr* Mittler was young and carefree and determined to come to America with his young wife and two sons. His stories of their passage to New York during bitter cold winter months reminded me of our own crossing ten years earlier with our own little boys; although our voyage was easy in comparison to his. When his wife died in New York and his sons left to have their own adventures in Argentina, he thought he had one more chance in life to begin again and had signed on with Hermann and the others to find his fortune in California. Now his interesting tales always ended on a sad and lonely note. At least they diverted our attention from our own discomforts.

The Humboldt was unlike any river we had encountered thus far. It did not gain in size or strength like most rivers, but remained shallow, slow, and relatively narrow. After traveling along its northern bank for several days, we noticed that it seemed murky and dark. My sons attempted to fish from its side, but neither caught nor saw a single fish. Further, its banks were barren of all but grass. The farther we went along this odd river, the less current there was and the more turbidity. Many times in the past, I had luxuriated after a day's tramp, covered with so much dust as to be unrecognizable by my own family, by going down to a river's edge, rolling down my collar, taking off my hat and sousing my head, face, and arms under the cool elements, and then righting myself again refreshed and clean. As this river became more tepid, salty, and alkaline, it brought no pleasure. In fact, we had to rely on dug holes to water the animals.

Death was all around us. One day I counted 108 carcasses of oxen and mules along the trail. I wondered, fearfully, when our remaining four beasts would join them.

We passed a wagon train from Illinois. They were stopped to reconnoiter after a mishap that had occurred several nights earlier. Their cattle had been turned out to graze in the night, and they had set no guard over them. In the morning twenty-two were missing. Some of the men started up into the mountains in pursuit, assuming that the Diggers had carried them off. They followed their trail almost thirty miles up into the high snowy mountains and finally found their oxen, some slaughtered, some hamstrung, and the rest forced to jump off a high bank into a kind of natural pen from which it was impossible to free them. The rascals could be seen dancing upon the rocks, jeering at them, but taking care to stay out of rifle shot range. I cringed on hearing their story, and at the same time was envious that they were resting at the side of the trail. I asked Fritz to clean my little pepperbox pistol and resumed carrying it in my pocket, hoping to never use it.

We were nearly suffocated and blinded by the alkaline dust kicked up by those in front of us. I fashioned a handkerchief to cover Lily's nose and mouth, and she stumbled along holding my skirt usually with her eyes closed. The dust was the color and consistency of ash, and it stuck to us like glue. Our clothes were permanently stained by it and our bedding was saturated with it. Climbing under our robes and blankets at night was like going down a prairie dog's hole. I tried every night to beat the dust out of Lily's bedding to relieve her constant cough. On nights following severe rainstorms all our bedding would be clammy; we grew to prefer the dampness to the dust.

This ashy dust also built up on our wheels; often we had to stop to scrape away the accumulation.

When Hermann observed the mask I had made for Lily, he found my last remaining petticoat and asked me if he could cut it into pieces to drape over the oxen's noses too. I thought I would never again wear such a garment and gave my consent.

During the middle of the day, the heat was unmerciful. Often we rested in the afternoon, and at night when it became a little cooler, we drove on, finding a campsite well after dark.

More than once we passed rows of wagons, empty and abandoned. In order to save as much as possible, their owners had unharnessed their cattle, packed necessities on their backs, and driven them on without the burden of a load to pull.

The land we traveled through was monotonous, even with the mountains as backdrop. All of us had seen plenty of mountains, had exclaimed over a profusion of formations by this time. Earlier in the trip I remember that I stared with awe at distant mountains, thinking they looked like the backs of elephants and conjuring myself into dark Africa on safari. Now my imagination was not up to the task.

Some days we would tramp through grasses almost waist high; other days the boys would have to wade up to their chests into the marsh areas to gather forage for the animals. In spite of the travails, we had no mishaps and covered fifteen to twenty miles each day. Evenings there were always chores and maintenance on our equipment, performed by the weak glow of a campfire. We rarely spoke, harboring our energy for our tasks, and fell exhausted into our bedrolls.

My sweet Lily found the strength to go on. She had never been a crying child, and didn't start now, though she had plenty to weep about. I could not cure her of the diarrhea, though I begged milk from the occasional traveler who had a cow and cooked rice in it for her. In the beginning she would be embarrassed by her frequent dirtying of her underclothes. "Don't tell my brothers! They will think I am a baby!" she exclaimed. Then, when it happened daily or more, she became resigned to it. I tried to keep her clean, but it was impossible under these circumstances, and she developed a sore rash.

Hermann was less difficult during our march along the Humboldt. He conferred with the other men on details of travel, he rested the oxen during the hottest hours of the day, and he frequently asked me at bedtime about my health and Lily's. I knew the infection on his foot was no better, as I smelled it in the tent at night when he removed his shoes. I never asked him about it. The circumstances of each day made me too tired to exert much compassionate effort.

Chapter 82

I did not know when I agreed to this trip that I would walk to California. I don't believe that Hermann or any of the men realized it either. If I had known, I might have argued for the sea route instead of the overland trail. But, by the time we walked along the miserable Humboldt River, I could walk with the best of them. All day, all night, over mountains, through ravines, on gravel, mud, stepping-stones across a stream, in gumboots or bare feet — I could walk. It was the one thing I could do, that all of us could do. We could walk.

Our four remaining animals could walk too. It was all that we asked of them, to walk. They too kept going, ascending, descending, while hot, parched, fly-bitten, and often hungry. Fritz had named them long ago at the beginning of this journey: Silvester, Nikolaus, Violet and Geld. With names, they acquired personalities. Silvester was the leader and a stern taskmaster, urging the others when they held back. Nikolaus, like the saint Fritz named him after, was passive and generous. When grass was scarce, it seemed that Nikolaus would eat less than his share, then move aside for the others to feed. Violet was skittish. He was the difficult one to put into harness, and he was jumpy along the trail, easily spooked by a rabbit in the grass. Geld was placid like Nikolaus, but lazy. We all thought that Geld fell asleep in the harness, even while plodding along the trail.

Even with enough grass and water along the Humboldt, Violet and Geld were failing. Nearly every day one or the other would collapse in the yoke. We would bring water and grass to the poor beast, down on his knees, then pull and prod him back onto his feet. Our companions still had six oxen each pulling their wagons, although several of theirs were also near death.

"We could pool our animals," suggested Randolf Settlemeyer one day. "If we get desperate, we can abandon one wagon, add one man's belongings to your wagon, Hermann, and divide the strong oxen among two wagons."

Hermann didn't answer immediately, but I did. "That is generous of you, Randolf. Thank you. We will remember your offer."

We camped near a large group one night, which included the Turner and Allen train. Hermann remembered this mule train as having left Independence two days before we did. They had advertised for passengers with a sign on their lead wagon "Sixty Days to the Diggings!"

Like us, they were now more than one hundred days on the trail, and they had switched their mules for oxen – two facts relished by Hermann. They had run out of provisions, and had sent Mr. Turner back all the way to Fort Laramie with an empty wagon to buy flour, crackers, bacon, coffee, and other foodstuffs. He arrived with a full wagon the night we were near them. When I saw the sacks of beans, rice, and flour, as well as baskets of apples and potatoes, I suggested to Hermann that we spend our last coins and buy a few things from them. Our larder then consisted of a small amount of fat bacon, crackers that were musty from continual wetting and drying, almost no coffee, beans or rice, and no more than ten pounds of flour. We had seen men with scurvy all along the trail. With no more pickles or vegetables of any kind, I worried that we would be stricken with it next.

"Let us at least buy some apples and potatoes!" I implored.

"I can't leave us with no money at all, Frida!"

"I trusted you Hermann! How could you let this happen?"

He looked away, ignoring my outrage.

"Could we barter something for apples?" I spoke aloud what came to my mind.

"What do we have that they would want, Frida?"

I thought about our meager belongings. This train would not be interested in my remaining two dresses. Hermann and the children had only enough clothes to change once into clean things when I washed the clothes on their backs. I thought of their warm coats, but adjudged we would need them. "What about Violet or Geld?"

"You're thinking like a crazy woman!"

"No, listen! They have switched to ox trains; apparently their mules could not take the strain. They must have at least thirty-five wagons, I'm sure they always need more oxen. They might buy them at the right price or swap for them!"

As Hermann stood staring at me as though I had lost all sensibility, a man galloped into our camping area on a fat fresh horse. He was dressed in half Indian costume, with trousers of buckskin, moccasins, and a collarless shirt. He was dark skinned, either sunburnt or dirty, and most of us initially mistook him for a French mountaineer, there being many in this part of the west. We gathered around him, and someone asked if he'd come from the California diggings.

"The diggings! Yes! The diggings! Just two weeks ago I was at Sutter's. There was gold aplenty!" He saw me standing at the edge of the gathered crowd and sent me a wink.

One man from the Turner and Allen train asked how much a man could dig in a day.

"A lazy fellow might easily get five hundred dollars in a day. Are you a lazy fellow?"

"No Sir! Thank God I've been brought up to work hard all my life."

"Then, Sir, you'll get twice that!" He swung his horse around and continued along the trail in an easterly direction.

No one could talk of anything except this mountaineer's story. Each time it was retold, the amounts grew. The members of the Turner and Allen train broke out a bottle or two of whiskey and celebrated the near approach of instant, easy wealth.

"Mutti, don't you think he resembled one of the men in that army train who supped with us several weeks back?" Otto asked.

"I'm sure it was he! They had some good horses. I think he was just scouting ahead of the group. Then, when given the chance, he had himself some fun with our neighbors."

Both boys smiled at me, "I think so too."

"And the apples and potatoes, Hermann, shall we trade our animals for them?"

"Not now. I've heard of a cutoff, a shortcut. It has a store - Lassen's Store. If he is a decent man, he'll let us work for our provisions. I want our own team for crossing the mountains. And, let us remember that if worse comes to worse, we can slaughter them for food."

I had thought of that and rejected the idea. There was no fat on those beasts. They were hide, horn, and gristle. Maybe I could make a pot of soup from each, nothing more. And could we stomach that soup? I wasn't sure.

Chapter 83

September 16 we reached Lassen's Cut-off. There was a large sign at the junction:

Short Cut to the Diggings
Feather River Mine - 120 miles
Good Water, Grass, Supplies Available

Many wagons had stopped at the fork in the road, and men were gathered, weighing the merits of this northerly shortcut against the approximately 180 miles straight on to Sutter's. There were notices posted on sticks as well as a newly painted red barrel with letters and notes left by those who had passed earlier. Some warned against, others favored Lassen's Cut-Off. The Humboldt River continued straight ahead. Off to the right were wheel tracks, proof that many had chosen the northerly route to Lassen's.

"There's a thirty-mile desert to cross," I overheard someone say. "My team can't tolerate that!"

"But there's a forty-mile desert of deep sand ahead on the straight-ahead Truckee route. I've heard that oxen get mired and die because no one can pull them out," answered his companion.

Another answered, "I'm leaving my pitiful yoke here to fend for themselves. I can walk 120 miles in a week with my food on my back!"

"If we continue along the Humboldt, we continue along with the thieving, filthy Diggers!" commented yet another.

Other people retold the melancholy story we had heard before of the Illinois Donner and Reed Group's harrowing experiences in the Sierras in 1846. No one wanted to be stuck as they had been, immobilized by the winter snows without adequate provisions. At least forty of them had died, and the survivors admitted they had been reduced to eating their flesh. That was another reason expressed by some not to go the Truckee route

Albert and his brother and the others came to confer with Hermann. "What will you do, Hermann?" asked Albert. "I don't like the sound of a thirty-mile desert; furthermore, the rest of our group will be looking for us at Sutter's."

"Herren, I'm going the short way. It's not even arguable. We'll take the easy way. I talked to a man earlier, a Captain Palmer, accompanying a government supply train. He advised taking the short cut - the Oregon Road - as far as Lassen's. He said the crossing of the Sierra Nevada by that route would be no worse than South Pass."

"We should stick together, Hermann." Said Herr Mittler.

"Then you'd better stick with us, Boys! We'll mine the Feather River, then we'll drop down and help you at Sutter's. We'll all be together again!"

I didn't know what to think and was not so quick to decide as Hermann. Of course a shorter, easier route, one that had a store along the way, tempted me. But we would be saying good-bye to friends once again, striking off alone.

"Why don't you come on the Cut-off with us?" I urged them. If it is 120 miles to the Feather River, as the sign indicates, then it is probably another 60 miles south of there to Sutter's. For you it will be 180 miles whichever way you go."

"Your logic is good, Mrs. Reinhardt, but if we have an emergency, I'd like to know that the rest of our party is coming along behind us," answered Jan Volker.

I could sympathize with his answer. "That is true for us too, Hermann."

"Frida, we're going to take the cut-off. Remember that we took Hudspeth's; that was a smart move!"

I had to admit that he was right. "We should take grass and water then, enough for a three-day crossing, just to be on the safe side," I suggested.

"Ja, Ja, Frida," he said condescendingly.

Chapter 84

But Captain Palmer had deceived Hermann. Worse, he brought utmost heartbreak to us.

As we left the Humboldt River, the first day's trip was easy. Grass was aplenty, and the route went so straight in a westerly direction that we had to shade our eyes on that first afternoon - September 16.

By the second day we came to the desert. There was a sign by the wayside: "Black Rock Desert," but we had no need for an indicator. The grass stopped immediately, as though a torch had seared the land. In fact, we had to retrace our steps a precious two miles to find grass to cut for the desert crossing, as so many overlanders before us had trampled or cut the forage next to the waste land. We thought we would be across in two days; in fact, we had to rest most of the daylight hours due to the burning heat, and only drove on at night, through choking alkaline dust. Previous travelers had dug wells; we watered our animals from them. Early one morning, before making our daytime camp, we saw a beautiful mirage to the southwest in which appeared a long lagoon of blue water with small islets all bordered with tall trees. Our animals saw it too, and picked up their pace toward it, not understanding that it was a trick of the desert.

Hermann reckoned we made seventeen miles the first twenty-four hours on the desert and the exact same on the second day, but still we found ourselves surrounded by a barren, arid landscape. Another sign by the side of the road indicated that we had thirty-three miles more before we could regard our own poor cattle as saved. Hermann wrenched the sign from the ground and dashed it to sharp splinters against the hard-packed ground. " I should never have trusted Captain Palmer or anyone who recommended this route!"

The third day the appalling salt flat that we had been crossing became sand; we had exchanged one desert for another. On that single day I counted eighty-one abandoned wagons and 1,663 oxen and mules, dead or dying.

The next morning when Otto went to bring the animals in for harnessing, he found Violet dead on the ground. It was not entirely unanticipated, as he had been falling to his knees over and again the day before. Once more Hermann insisted we lighten our load. "Empty the trunk, Frida; we'll leave it behind."

I took our belongings out and wrapped them in our canvas ground cover.

Hermann took my wash tub and stove and put them next to our trunk.

Next I heard him call to the boys, "Take the tent out of the wagon; henceforth, we'll sleep under the stars."

"And, when it rains, Hermann?" I asked, frustrated and aggravated by his uncooperative decision-making.

"We'll fold the ground cover at its middle and pull half over ourselves."

Hermann found other things: sperm candles, medicines, my mirror, and a book of Lewis and Clark's adventures. He put them on the wagon's seat. "Choose, Frida. Leave behind two of these things." I set the candles and the book on top of our old Prussian trunk at the side of the trail.

Then he harnessed the remaining three oxen awkwardly, two in a yoke in front, and Geld behind.

The weather was calm and quiet, not yet hot. I thought I could see flowers ahead in the moonlight and walked ahead to investigate. Fritz ran up to me. "*Mutti*, you'd better come. Geld is down."

The poor animal's sides were heaving, as it lay on its side, still in harness. It was beyond my help. Hermann ordered the boys to rearrange our team so that only our two strong oxen were in harness. He took my arm, "Frida, take the lead line and walk ahead. We'll catch up."

Otto spoke, "If we were by ourselves, we could do what other travelers have done before us - take our knapsacks on our backs and go on foot."

I heard Hermann's reply, "Not yet, Otto; not yet. Get your gun, Boy. There is no help for Geld."

Silvester and Nikolaus dragged on, half dead with hunger and thirst. At midday Nikolaus collapsed.

Hermann took both out of the yoke and prodded Nikolaus to his feet. He told us to stay by the wagon, and drove both oxen before him, hoping in this way to reach the haven of water sooner.

He told us later that he crested a small rise in only thirty minutes and there found bubbling springs and an acceptable grazing place. Some of the springs were hot, but others were cool and sweet.

He let the animals eat and drink their fill then returned to us, carrying a vessel of water to assuage our terrible thirst.

We had fallen into sleep as soon as Hermann left us. He woke us as he returned, "There are springs just ahead. Come on, Boys; harness the animals. While you refresh yourselves at the pools, I'm going to trade this heavy wagon for a lightweight farm cart. There are many abandoned just ahead. Also tie handkerchiefs around your noses against the unbearable effluvia; there are decaying carcasses everywhere."

Chapter 85

With only a light cart to pull, the going was easier for Silvester and Nikolaus. And, once out of the desert, the road improved. Most of our fellow travelers were now carrying their utensils and food on their backs, having left their cattle and wagons behind. The valley we crossed was covered with volcanic ash, here and there patches of greasewood and, surprisingly, many springs. Near the springs we found coarse grass and fine rushes, which satisfied our animals. While stopped at one refreshing pool, I walked a few yards to another, which was steaming. There being no other travelers near, I asked Hermann and the boys to look the other way and gave Lily and myself the rarest pleasure: a hot bath. The water was exactly the right temperature to soothe our muscles and increase our circulation. We took turns scrubbing each other's back and hair. For the first time in many weeks my sweet girl smiled and looked rosy and healthy. We both dressed in our split skirts and clean shirtwaists, and I tied back her hair with a new pink ribbon I'd saved. Thus refreshed we continued through that valley of dead animals.

The trail inexplicably turned north which concerned us. It continued blazing hot during the days, and we continued our practice of taking long breaks at midday. We could travel after dark here, as we followed the example of others and burned greasewood bushes along the trail. It was festive looking out at a long sinewy line of tall flickering flames lighting the adjacent hills.

On September 27 we passed through the gorge at High Rock Canyon at night. The moon was nearly full and it illuminated narrow ravines that ran sideways to the back hills. It was a sublime sight; we could hear singing and whooping along the trail as others enjoyed the same view. I remarked to the boys that it had been some time since we had heard singing.

"Let's try for an echo," suggested Fritz. He hallooed down a side rift and was rewarded with his words ringing along from cliff to cliff. Someone behind us fired off a rifle to hear its reverberations. That noise woke Lily, and she tried it too. Before long we heard people, and even a mule, up and down the track attempting an echo.

Chapter 86

Now wolves howled throughout the nights, and we had ice on our pail every morning. Dark clouds loomed over the mountain peaks. Winter was near.

Hermann's mood altered between day and evening. During the day when he could see the long Sierra mountain chain, covered with dark pine forests, stretching across the horizon, he was buoyant, almost joyful. He would range in front of our animals, often with Otto, then come bounding back, "Prod those two beasts! They're going well! Don't let them get lazy! When we get to the trees, we'll rest." At night, when the dark mountains would fade into the black sky and the sun's warmth would abandon the earth, he would become morose and uncommunicative, unable to conceal his worry.

By now he was limping all the time. I persuaded myself to investigate, and when I saw his ankle, I was shocked at the swollen infected carbuncle I saw there. I remembered the terrible story that Permelia told me about her friend's infection which lead directly to her untimely death along the trail, and I was sorry I had not attended to him weeks earlier. I insisted that he allow me to put hot compresses on each morning and evening and that he keep a clean cloth against it at all times. Fortunately he had not set the remains of my petticoat aside, and each day I would tear off a small square as bandage.

Lily could not ride in the new smaller wagon. I carried her almost all the time, sometimes not knowing if she was awake or asleep, attached to my back like a limpet. Her cough was now chronic, weakening her a little more each day. She had diarrhea some days, and some not. When I saw the Sierra, fringed with the dark pines, all I could hope for was that we were nearing Lassen's and that there would be a doctor there.

After eighty tiresome miles we finally reached those dark pines. The trees were tall and straight and more beautiful than any firs we had ever seen. They presaged our next obstacle - the Sierra Nevada. Hermann announced that we would have a day's rest before continuing.

Unwelcome visitors interrupted our day off. They were five California Indians, completely naked and armed with bows and arrows. They made us understand that they wanted gifts from us.

We hove nothing to give, I thought. *We don't have enough for ourselves.*

Others had warned us about these Indians; they told us that they were the poorest of all the Indians, that they wore no clothes but perhaps an animal skin in the cool of the evening. We had heard that they collected acorns and made bread from their grindings. I was using our day of rest to make bread; when a loaf was ready, I gave them one, begrudging the gift. They took it and backed off. I watched as one took a bite and spat it out, not liking its unfamiliar wheat taste. He threw the remains to the ground. After they left, I sent Fritz to pick it up.

Otto, our finest shot, brought in six sage hens. We were all pleased to have game again.

The next morning we began our climb of the first and highest peak in the Sierra chain. It seemed to our eyes to be five miles high! We did not expect to find water in the high peaks, so burdened ourselves with a half barrelful in the cart. The first half of the ascent was not too taxing. To minimize the efforts of our team of two, Hermann and the boys got behind the wagon to push, and I drove the oxen. When the trail became even steeper, we did as others around us did. We unpacked the cart entirely, and turn by turn, carried our meager belongings to the next resting place. Then we drove the oxen up, pulling only the empty wagon, and reloaded. We had five such portages, dragging our goods on our backs; finally we reached the summit and were rewarded with a beautiful view of the mountain chain extending in both directions. I made us coffee and served fresh bread at the top, thus reviving our strength for the arduous trip down the other side, slipping, sliding, and constantly worrying that the cart would overrun the oxen.

"Well, Father! You said that would be like South Pass. You were absolutely wrong!" commented Otto.

Someone overheard him, "But, we're through it, Bucko!" he hollered, clapping both Otto and Hermann on their backs. "It's mostly downhill the rest of the way. We have done it! We have got through the Sierra Nevada! Rejoice! You're through the worst pass of all!" To Hermann's amazement, the man took both his hands and swung him around several times in an awkward dance. When Hermann finally broke free, the stranger danced over to me, picked me right up off the ground and swung me twice around before depositing me back on terra firma, and going on his way.

Lily laughed, a joyous sound, "Me too, Fritz! Swing me."

We'd reached Fandango Pass.

We camped that night with the Washington City Company, whose captain had gone a two days' journey ahead to scout the route. Upon his return from the Pitt River, fifty-five miles from our present camp, he brought back the worrisome news that Lassen's Ranch in the Sacramento Valley was still three hundred miles away.

"We don't have the food, Hermann!"

"We don't have the stamina, Frida!"

Dark clouds obliterated the stars and moon and we heard geese flying south. One of the men of the Washington City Company said that was a sure sign of heavy weather. Hermann advised an early start. At daybreak thick, dense, rolling clouds enveloped the peaks around us. The night had been particularly cold, and now every mountain had snow on its flanks. Upon awakening I urged all to put on our winter underclothes and our gumboots, as I feared the bad weather. By the time we were on the trail, heavy rain started. I wound a blanket over my head and shoulders, fairly suffocating Lily tied on my back. By midday the storm passed, and our soaking clothes steamed in the sun.

In three more days, during which time our conditions remained the same - rain in the morning, hot sun by noon; very cold nights; ascents, descents, flat valleys and small streams to cross, we reached the Pitt River. We were now in California, but it was not what we had expected. When we reached the summit of the Sierras, we had expected to see the vast Sacramento Valley spread out before us. Instead we saw endless miles of mountain ridges and gorges to traverse.

We followed the Pitt for eighty miles, crossing it eleven times; with each step I reminded myself that if we had taken the Truckee route we might have reached our destination by now. At least the trail had turned west again.

I walked along with a Mr. Kelle. His company - the Western Train - called him Captain Kelle. They had nearly twenty heavily-loaded wagons, and I asked him if he had stores to spare. "Yes, Missus. We have bacon, beans, sugar, and much else. But if I give them to you, I won't have them to sell at the mines." He preferred to take it all to the gold fields, knowing that he would get the highest price there. I indicated my sick daughter riding on my back, and he undid the flap of his nearest wagon and gave me several handfuls of dried apples. He was a shrewd man; for the rest of the day my mind worried over the question of whether to hate him or not.

That night I cooked the apples and made a sauce of them. The smell of those apples brought my whole family to the campfire long before our supper was ready.

"I want to give it all to Lily," I announced. The rest of us ate stale crackers and a broth made from the bones of our last rabbit.

We went to bed earlier each night, it seemed, as we were all worn to tired sinew. But that night I asked Hermann to sit with me at the fire after the boys joined Lily under the tarpaulin.

"I don't think she is going to make it, Hermann." I started to weep.

He put his big hand on my knee, and I noticed his wrist bones sticking out under his shirtsleeve. "I don't know what to do, Frida, but I won't let her die." He meant it; I knew he meant it.

"If she dies, I will die too." I looked him straight in the eye, wiping my eyes with the palms of my dirty hands. "We need to keep her safe until we get to a doctor."

"I'll give up half my rations."

"Half your food won't help her, Hermann. She needs rest. Further, she needs to be dry and warm and out of this endless dust. That's not all. She needs my full and constant attention as well as that of a doctor."

"I can't perform a miracle! We'll be at Lassen's soon. Let us hope there is a doctor there. When she gets better, she will remember this trip all her life. I need my sleep; come to bed."

Chapter 87

We had heard that the Governor of California had sent rescue missions to save the travelers from death by starvation, although we had not actually seen one. Making a small detour in the valley of the Pitt, I saw five such wagons pass on my left and surmised the nature of their errand. I was much annoyed that they got past us, and that we had not called to them or driven directly in their direction. Their humane captain evidently saw us through his field glass and knew that we too were in need of his help. He rode over on his horse.

We must have looked a wreck through his eyes. Our oxen could barely drag our light farm wagon, my skinny boys walked on either side of the yoke, prodding and hitting them with sticks, and Hermann and I dragged our feet in the dust next to the wagon. After a brief greeting he asked how we were situated as to provisions, whereupon I showed him our stock.

"Is this all you have for four of you?" he asked.

"Five," Hermann replied, indicating the bundle on my back that the captain had not noticed.

The captain thought it would last us the fifty miles until the first settlement, where we could buy food.

Hermann scuffed the dust with his toe.

"We have no money!" I exclaimed. Hermann turned toward me and gave me a reproachful look.

"Wait here," the man said. He returned in ten minutes with seven pounds of crackers and said that if we would send one of our sons with him he would give us a good piece of beef.

Fritz clamored up behind his saddle and when he returned he had twelve pounds of beef.

"Beef!" Otto exhaled mightily with the one word. "We'll be as strong as oxen after today's meal!"

We all looked at our two remaining cattle, their bones protruding, their weak legs splayed, and their heads hanging practically to the ground. They were both caked with mud. "I'm already as strong as those oxen," answered Fritz.

Those fifty miles took five days. There was not a blade of grass along the way, and the oxen grew even weaker. We could scarcely get them to move. When we were about half way, the road led down such a steep mountain, that we could only proceed by sliding. We tied a stout rope to the back of the wagon, and all three - Hermann, Otto, and Fritz - acted as a brake so that the wagon would not slide down over the heads of the cattle and crash at the bottom. The ravine at the bottom was so narrow that there was barely room to set up our makeshift shelter for the night.

The road ahead led over a mountain, steep and covered with boulders. Here more overlanders had abandoned their wagons and cattle.

"Frida, Otto, Fritz, we'll never get the cart through this chaos and over the mountain. It's time to learn from the example of others. We have to leave the wagon here."

Grim faced, the boys unpacked the wagon. They made up packs for each ox of about sixty pounds, including our remaining food, one pot, our bedding and canvas shelter, and a bucket for carrying water. Then they fashioned packs for themselves and Hermann with our warm clothing. I took my hairbrush and mirror and a small sliver of soap and put them in my pocket. Then we climbed the mountain, pulling and prodding Silvester and Nikolaus all the way.

I fell many times, cutting my hands and bruising my knees. The oxen fell too, so did Hermann and the boys. Each time, someone ahead or behind would give encouragement or a helping hand. Our breath sometimes gave out, and we rested; we made seven miles, each of them laborious. We camped in the open, none of us having the strength to figure out how to set up our protective canvas without using the wagon itself as its back wall.

Chapter 88

I could not go on.

Lily had been restless most of the night, coughing, and sometimes delirious. Again and again I awoke and bathed her head in cool water and gave her small sips to drink. She slept with me under my blankets and was alternately feverish and shivering. More than once she fouled her underclothes.

Both my boys had the bleeding gums and open sores that indicated scurvy.

When I looked over at our oxen, they were eating the dusty gravel of the trail.

I wasn't well either. I had a severe headache behind my eyes, and often I was doubled over with cramps. There seemed to be an alarm bell noisily and insistently tolling in my head. I thought it was a cautionary bell, warning me of something, like a brass bell on a fire engine. *Should we flee its approach?* I wondered to myself. *Or, should we calmly step aside and let it rush past?*

I was seized with panic and knew only one thing: I could not go on.

"Leave me here, Hermann. Leave me here with Lily and the boys. Go on yourself; we'll follow when we can."

He looked at me as though I were entirely deranged. "Frida, don't be ridiculous."

"I can't go on. I won't go on."

Others were streaming past us on the trail, making a little detour around our group as we lay in our bedding half on, half off the path. I didn't care.

"I won't go, Hermann. Go yourself."

He stood up and started a small fire to boil water for coffee. Then he began fussing with the animals, testing their tethers, as though they were strong or willful enough to break them. I didn't stir; neither did Lily or her brothers.

"I'll go with you, Father," said Otto finally, without enthusiasm.

"I will too," said Fritz.

"No. Leave Fritz with me. You and Otto go ahead. Get fresh animals, food, and a wagon or barrow that Lily can ride in. Come back for us."

He made up a small pack with his own warm clothes. Otto did the same. They each drank some coffee directly from the pot and put some crackers in their pockets.

"Fritz, move everyone off the trail. Take care of your mother and your sister.

"I'll bring help, Frida."

"Hurry."

It was October 31 when Hermann and Otto turned their backs on us and rushed ahead to get help. They had not been gone an hour before snow began - large graceful snowflakes at first. I lay with Lily in our bedding and watched them land on our blankets and settle there for a moment before being displaced by the next one. Lily awakened for a moment and opened her mouth to catch a snowflake on her tongue. "Can I make a snowman with Fritz, *Mutti*? " she muttered.

"Soon, Darling Girl."

The snow intensified, each flake no longer distinct but part of a blanket descending upon us. Fritz dragged our belongings to the side of the narrow trail and made a kind of envelope of our canvas cloth, as a bed for Lily and me. He staked the miserable oxen closer to us, set out the remaining pot to catch snow for melting, then brought his own bedding and the rest of our belongings inside the canvas wrapper too.

In spite of the worsening conditions, pedestrians continued to pass us. I saw a woman walking with a pack on her back and a feeble boy so sunk in torpor that she was leading him with a rope. Then came a tall man, an ex-army officer by his uniform; he carried nothing but a saber. Behind him came two girls, obviously his young daughters, each with heavy packs. Neither of them had gloves and their hands were wet and red. One girl had lost a shoe, and her foot was bound in rags. I thought to call out to the man that he was asking too much of his children but could not muster the strength. A mule walked by with a man draped crosswise on his back, apparently no one in control. Soon our bed was so covered with snow that the persistent travelers couldn't see us, and several times people stumbled right into and over us.

Lily slept through most of the day. At dark the snow continued with no abatement. "Are you hungry, Fritz?" I asked him.

"Yes, but it doesn't matter."

"Are you scared?"

He didn't hesitate, "Yes."

"I have an idea. Let's imagine we are in New York, and we are going out for dinner at Adolph and Anna Spies's house to celebrate Halloween; we did that once, do you remember, and we bobbed for apples. What do you hope they will serve to us?" I tried to get his mind off our perilous circumstances.

"It doesn't matter."

"I'll bet you would want a beer to start with and some cheese. What kind?"

He faltered for only a moment, "Camembert."

"Any others?"

"Liederkranz and some Roquefort." I could hear him lick his lips and swallow.

"Oh, wait, maybe *Heringsalat* instead of cheese."

"You can have both. Now, what about soup?"

"You know I've never liked peas, but now I crave *Grüne Erbsensuppe* served with sour cream and pumpernickel bread."

"We all crave vegetables. Will you have meat for your entrée or only vegetables, *Herr* Fritz?"

He started listing some of his favorites: "Goose, *Sauerbraten,* and ham cooked in Burgundy. Then potatoes – yellow potatoes, I think. And beets and red cabbage cooked with bacon, and a huge salad made with green beans." He was quiet for a moment, "Could we make it spring time and have asparagus too?"

"Oh, yes! With hazelnut butter."

"I wonder what the Spies girls are doing now, Duda and Clara. When I was little and they were even littler, I thought they were so smart! I didn't mind playing with them, even though they were girls."

"We'll see them again when we're home, home in New York," I reassured him.

We were both silent for a moment. Then Fritz spoke, "Is Lily all right?"

She had been still for a long time, had not even coughed.

"Oh God, Fritz!"

I shook her to waken her and then shook her again, harder. "Lily!" I screamed.

Fritz pushed off the canvas and snatched her from beneath the blankets, "Lily!"

He put his ear to her chest, then lifted her over his head, gently shaking her, his arms and her limp body trembling together. "I can't make her breathe! Lily! Lily! Breathe! Breathe!"

I grabbed her from Fritz, back in my arms, her head lolling back. "Lily! Breathe! Oh my God!" I cradled her to my breast and looked at her sweet pale face, her eyes closed, her lips dry and slightly parted. She was gone from me.

A man stumbling through the blinding snow heard my wail. He tripped over our bedding, "Excuse me, 'mam."

Chapter 89

For three days I lay in that same place, recognizing neither day nor night. The clanging in my head was replaced by a low calming hum, which served to obliterate all other sounds. Fritz wrapped Lily's small body in his own shirt and then wound the last remnants of my petticoat tightly around that precious package which I held in my arms and crooned to while we waited for Hermann and Otto to return. I suppose Fritz tended to our oxen. I know he brought me water and a kind of broth made from crackers. I asked him to find one of her hair ribbons and clutched its silkiness in my fist. Several times he suggested that he dig Lily's grave and that we bury her ourselves. Each time I refused. "Your father has to bury his baby daughter. He must do that one thing."

On the morning of November 3 Fritz and I were lying under the canvas when we heard Hermann call my name. "Frida, Frida! We're back!"

Fritz threw off our meager cover and stood.

"Where's your mother?

"She's here, Father."

"Where's your sister?"

"She's here, Father."

I struggled to sit up and to hold up the bundle I had been protecting for three days.

"What do you have, Frida? A package wrapped in your old petticoat?"

"I have my daughter, Hermann."

"Oh, God! No! No! Not Lily; God, not Lily!" An ancient, primeval wail exploded from his heart, which brought Otto running. Both collapsed to their knees beside me, and together they took Lily from me and cradled the weightless bundle between them, still solid and so nearly alive.

I gestured to Fritz to tell them what had happened. In a voice husky with grief, he told them what had happened, finishing with: "Mother wouldn't let me bury her until you returned."

Hermann was gasping for breath and groping for words.

"Shh, Hermann, there are no words," I said, "Only tears."

I was lost to grief, to bitterness. I could not comfort my sons or my husband. I could not bury my baby. I reached my arms out and took her back to my bosom.

A Negro man approached me and, removing his hat, sat by my side. I had noticed him out of the corner of my eye standing just outside our family circle. He told me he had traveled back from Lassen's Ranch with Hermann and Otto and quietly introduced himself as Hamilton Coffey.

"Such a good thing, the life of a child!" he said. "It is a gift, the most generous of gifts, renewing itself endlessly, every minute of every day, every gesture."

I nodded, dry-eyed.

"A thief has come in the night and taken your most precious child. In her place, he has left a doll. That is what you cling to, Missus. This doll cannot be nursed to health and reared up to be a woman; it is just a doll."

"I know. I know that. But I don't know what to do next." I looked him full in the face for the first time. Part of his face had been mutilated and he had lost an eye; the rest was lined with memories of epochs of troubles. He had felt pain, and I believed I could trust him. "What should I do?"

"A doll can't know death. It had no life, so none can be taken from it. Why don't you give her to me; I'll work with her brothers to prepare a grave."

I passed the airy body of Lily over to this stranger, who took her so gently, that his action triggered a surge of anguish and wailing from my heart. As I fought to get my breath between sobs, this stranger, this Negro, called to Hermann, "Your wife needs you, Mr. Reinhardt."

It is sometimes easier to talk to a stranger; there's a formality but also an intimacy. He comes from nowhere and might be gone tomorrow. When Hermann came to my makeshift bed, neither of us could speak. He lay awkwardly beside me, and I curled myself into his arms. He drew me close and stroked my hair, sobbing, sniffling, and choking as I was. For a long time there were no words. The weight of his anguish wiped away my bitterness, "I should never have left you, Frida; never, never. I misjudged. How can I forgive myself?"

"I had thought that the worst had come to us, that nothing could be more terrible than the ordeal we had undertaken." I spoke breathlessly, between sobs. "Fritz felt it too; I know he did, as we lay together after you and Otto left. Then the worst really came."

I continued, "I told you that I would die if Lily died." Hermann's sobs intensified. "But I don't want to die. I want to be with you and the boys. Help me!"

I felt his nod, and after time our sobs subsided. Otto and Fritz approached and kneeled down next to us. We both struggled to sit up and embraced the boys. All of us wept, unashamed; we'd lost so much.

"We've made a grave with Mr. Coffey's help, *Mutti*. It is shallow, but we have rocks to cover it with," said Fritz.

"It's the best thing to do, Mother, Father," said Otto.

"My babies! My boys! It is the best thing." I looked at their gaunt faces, streaked with mud and tears – both looked old, tired, wholly dispirited. Otto seemed more vulnerable than I had observed in many years; he was literally trembling uncontrollably. "Come." I stood up first, so unsteady, that I had to grasp Fritz's shoulder to maintain my balance. I took Otto's hand, and urged him to his feet; Hermann and Fritz followed my example.

Mr. Coffey was standing near the steep side of the ravine, cradling the white parcel that held the mortal remains of my darling girl. Scratched into the cliffside were her initials and the dates of her birth and death and the line, *Our Only Sister*. Beside him was a shallow hole, and next to it a substantial pile of dirt and large rocks and the heavy shovel we had brought to dig for riches. Someone had lined the hole with sweet straw.

I nodded to Hermann; he took Lily and laid her on the straw. Other tired emigrants, unknown to us, stopped along the trail, not to stare but to grieve with us. I took my locket from around my neck and looked one last time at the entwined hair of my dear parents, then dropped it at Lily's feet. I reached out and took the hands of my sons; Hermann took their other hands and we formed a circle around the small grave. Mr. Coffey caught my eye, and he bowed his head, as though waiting for words. I summoned all my strength, "Lily, child of my heart, it is not possible to let go of you. We will say *auf Wiedersehen*, but we won't let go of our memories. We loved you; we will love you. Good-bye, my darling."

Mr. Coffey took my arm and led Hermann and me off to one side; Fritz and Otto shoveled the dirt and laid the stones in place.

Mr. Coffey had three mules. He hitched two to our cart and tied the leads of our weak oxen behind. He helped me up onto the third mule. In this way, we left Lily's graveside. Hermann never left my side, his hand holding mine.

After awhile I asked Hermann to tell me about his trip; I was wondering how close we were to Lassen's Ranch and imagining how things might be different if we had reached that destination and engaged a doctor.

He began with a lament, "We should never have left you! I never even embraced my baby girl!"

He calmed himself and continued, "Before we reached the end of this ravine, snow started. The visibility became continuously worse; only by following the snow-covered shapes of discarded goods along the trail were we able to go forward, climbing the next mountain, picking our way around the obstacles and impediments in our path."

He looked around, "At least there's no snow on the ground today. It was hard going, and we were often breathless. Otto asked me at one of our rest stops, 'Will Lily be all right, Father?'

"It had been a hard climb. My shirt was soaked with perspiration, and I was chilled. I shivered and answered Otto that Lily would be all right. I told him that children are resilient and that she would bounce back faster than he and Fritz." He started to sob again. "He asked about you too, Frida.

"I told him I knew this trip has been hard on you and that it might take time for you to resume your healthful life.

"He answered that he didn't agree with me; he believed that Lily was weaker than I thought, and that you needed more than just time to recover."

"Otto was right, Hermann. But, tell me more about the trail."

"We climbed over rocks and boulders that first day, and we spent the night shivering in the open under a coverlet of snow. At dawn, when we could see where we could step, with only crackers for nourishment, we set out again. The snow stopped at mid-morning, and our progress was somewhat eased. Every thread of our clothing was wet from the snow. As the sun ascended, steam rose from our backs. We reached a creek - Antelope Creek - at midday. It was swollen from the storm run off, and at first we thought it unfordable. Several people were warming themselves by a fire, unwilling to attempt the crossing. Otto and I idled with them by the fire for some minutes, then lashed our clothes to our shoulders and forded the stream with setting poles. None of the others would attempt it. Although it was the hardest crossing I ever had, we made it across with nothing worse than freezing feet and legs. At four o'clock we arrived at Mr. Lassen's ranch."

Otto approached and walked with us, resting his hand on my shoulder. He took over the story, "What we saw in front of us was ludicrous! His dilapidated dwelling was made out of rough limestone, which would not have suited most farmers even for pigpens. His outbuildings – three sun-dried brick houses, in which are kept a tavern, a store, and some storage – were equally ramshackle and decrepit. All about were piles of filth: bones, rags, skulls, entrails, blood, rags, and the usual abandoned carts, wagons and stacks of belongings. Father and I knew immediately that Peter Lassen, this wily Dane, was not going to be our savior. We knew at once he had chosen his location solely to fleece emigrants, not to run a well-organized ranch. In fact, he appeared to do no farming of any kind."

Hermann interrupted, "My first thought was that it was very unlikely that we would find a doctor there to care for Lily."

He continued, "I took Otto into the tavern as we hoped for news of our friends. There was plenty of liquor there, if you were willing to pay twenty-five cents for a sip of whiskey or fifty cents for brandy! The place was filled with drunkards, though I could not imagine where they got the money to squander at Lassen's. We left quickly with just one useful bit of news, imparted to us not by a fellow emigrant, but by a true gold miner: The nearest diggings were but fifty-seven miles south on the banks of the Feather River."

"Remember, Father," Otto interjected, "We heard plenty of curses and abuses pored forth around Lassen's head!"

Hermann continued, "True. Nevertheless, I went to find Peter Lassen. I intended to demand that he lend me animals to fetch you and Fritz and Lily. I found him in his grocery. He heard my story and agreed, making it clear that I would have to pay for the privilege – one dollar per day for each mule. I told him I needed to think about it, and asked him the price of other provisions and was alarmed at his quotes. He poured me a glass of brandy with which I moistened my parched throat, thinking it a gift. Then he demanded fifty cents.

"I found Otto outside the grocery talking to a Negro and called him over to tell him of my conversation with the scoundrel Lassen. I opened my purse and spilled out my few remaining coins in one hand, showing Otto how few there were – only eighteen dollars plus some spare change. I thought I would try to bargain with him."

Then Otto spoke and told me that he asked his father to wait a moment. He brought Mr. Coffey over and introduced the two men. "I told Father that Mr. Coffey had three well-rested mules and had offered to help us, but Father was reluctant to burden a stranger with our problems."

"Otto's new friend was very persuasive," said Hermann. "He told me a long story. In fact it was so long and so seemingly beside the point that I almost brushed him aside. He told us that he started this trip as slave to a Dr. Bassett of Mason County, Kentucky, leaving his wife and eight children behind, not knowing if he would ever see them again. It was clear that he admired his master. Then he told us that when the doctor fell ill with cholera, he gave Mr. Coffey his freedom papers and told the rest of their group to leave them both by the side of the road with three mules and what medicines they could spare, saying that they would catch up with the group as soon as possible. His Dr. Basset did not survive, and Mr. Coffey was still grieving his loss.

"I can tell you, Frida, I was struck by his story as well as by the man's excellent elocution."

I had got interested in the story and asked, "But Mr. Coffey obtained his own freedom because of his master's illness and death; why was he grieving? And, I've noticed how well spoken he is too. That surprised me."

"Apparently Mr. Coffey had been assistant in the doctor's surgery for over twenty years; it sounded to me as though Dr. Basset treated him like a partner. He told me that several travelers stopped to assist Dr. Bassett in his illness and finally to help him bury him. It was that kindness of strangers that caused Mr. Coffey to offer help to Otto and me."

"He is a sensitive man. You would have hurt his feelings to refuse him," I said.

"Yes, I thought the same. I thought we were merely going to borrow his mules, but he said they were skittish and that he would come along to manage them. We were so anxious to get back to you, that our return trip took only a day and half."

Chapter 90

We would not have been able to make the journey back to Mr. Lassen's settlement without the assistance of Mr. Hamilton Coffey. That good man quietly took charge of our small family, brought us through the ravine, over the mountains, cooked for us, cared for his mules as well as our pitiful oxen, then found a patch of dry land under a sycamore tree. He set Otto and Fritz the task of finding another piece of canvas from the abandoned wagons around the settlement; then set up a sort of lean-to for us with our old canvas as a ground cover. I crept under the shelter, exhausted in body and mind.

Once again Mr. Coffey came and sat by my side. "This is a terrible place, Missus. People are arriving and leaving every minute. No one has time to help a fellow traveler. Let your family help you; don't let them move you too soon. Mourning takes time; so does getting well. My mules and I will leave in the morning. I shall hope to meet you again."

Everything made me cry. As he rose to go, tears soaked my cheeks. Mr. Coffey had seen tears before; I wasn't embarrassed to have him see mine. "Farewell. Thank you," was all I could manage.

I was suffering from diarrhea and cramps, as well as from grief. Hermann told me that I hallucinated at night, and sometimes during the day as well. He said that I once turned to him and said quite coherently, "I stood by the lake and shouted across, but the warm summer breeze carried away my cries, and they did not reach their destination."

Hermann asked around for a doctor. There was a man by the name of Dr. Applegate who had arrived just before us. He was very young and very dirty, and I am not sure he was a doctor. He asked for one dollar to examine me. Now I think that he created a title for himself in order to finance his continuance to the gold diggings.

He asked me about my condition, felt my head and neck, pulled a tattered pamphlet from his pants' pocket, considered its pages, then recommended that I purge with castor oil for one day, followed by drops of dysentery corrector. He told me I must eat nothing but gruel until the diarrhea stopped, then to add some rice boiled in milk. He cautioned me to rest, and suggested that Hermann put warm stones at my feet.

It was all sensible advice, and I agreed to it. He asked if there was anything else. I couldn't hold back and began crying and told him about Lily's death.

"Grief can be fatal, Madam," Dr. Applegate remarked. "If it is continuous, it is inimical to health. It will make your illness worse as it weakens you. Your functions will slow down, your energy will be sapped even more than it is now. I would worry about palpitations and even syncope. You must put it out of your mind if you wish to survive!"

I lashed out at him, "You think I can get over this! Tears of a weak, sentimental woman, you think! Here today, gone tomorrow! Be strong! You cannot imagine. I have had to live a life of getting over loss. What I cannot get over any more is the *getting over*! I cannot get over it this time. I will do as you say: purging, medicine, rest, diet, but I will not *get over* my baby's death!"

In spite of Hermann and Otto's opinion of Peter Lassen, Otto and Fritz begged work from him, and went out every day in the cold wet weather to bring wild and abandoned cattle from the surrounding woods that Lassen would then brand with his own mark, indicating his ownership. The bad weather kept many emigrants at Lassen's, and those that could went into the woods themselves to shoot the wild oxen for the meat. It was dangerous work for the boys, bullets often chasing after the same cattle that they pursued, but Lassen gave them one dollar for each head they brought in. In that way we were able to buy certain stores – beans, rice, flour, and bacon. We gave up drinking coffee and longed for fruit or vegetables. I knew from our bleeding gums, stiff joints, and weak condition that all of us were suffering from scurvy, and I suggested that Hermann and the boys collect anything green that they could find - leaves and weeds – and try making a tea. They did as I suggested and we forced ourselves to drink the vile concoction, relieving our symptoms somewhat.

One evening Otto came and collapsed down next to me. He was tired and filthy and stank of the mud and the animals. Uncharacteristically he wanted to talk.

"You know, *Mutti*, I see men come up the trail from the west, usually to meet a companion on a predetermined date. They tell me it's only three days to the diggings. I thought I could be there and back before anyone would miss me, with a bag of gold flakes tied to my belt."

"Yes, Son." I waited for him to continue, fear rising in my heart that he would leave us.

"I don't want to go there and back, of course. I really want to just turn around and go back to Jennetta's farmhouse in New Washington. I could be there by early spring.

"What do I care for the wealth that father longs for? Nothing. As for the adventure? I was a fool to think this trip would be anything but a disaster! At its best it has been boring and exhausting; at its worst it has been dangerous and sorrowful. Father should have foreseen the consequences of a family of city dwellers walking practically from Atlantic to Pacific. His greed has put us all at risk!"

He looked at me, judging my reaction, and continued, "I was proud of him in New York. He always had a new scheme, and as I boy I found it all quite exciting. When he caught a dose of gold fever, I caught it too. But I was a boy, and he was a man, supposedly.

"Thanks to Fritz and my efforts, we can now buy basic provisions; thanks to our skills with a rifle, we often have fresh meat; thanks to Fritz, meals are cooked. Meanwhile, he sits with this group or that, flinging his arms about, red in the face, undoubtedly bragging about his brilliant decisions, while you lie in a makeshift tent, mud oozing under the flap, with fever and stomach cramps."

"All that you say is true, Otto."

"It just makes me mad; that's all. I won't leave you." He gave me a quick kiss on my cheek and went to wash himself.

Again, the ready tears washed over my cheeks – this time in gratitude.

Chapter 91

Fritz had made a cot for me out of the bed of our two-wheeled cart. He filled it with straw, then covered the straw with a piece of canvas and set my bedding atop. I spent most of November in this nest, sleeping, dreaming, and trying to turn my thoughts away from our problems. Rain soaked us most days, but on the few sunny days, I lay with my head outside the flap, the weak sun warming my skin. Occasionally a stranger would stop to inquire after my welfare. Once I told a sympathetic visitor that my baby girl died. She patted my hand compassionately and answered, "We've all got our burdens." It was true, of course; no one was spared.

With so much idle time, I thought about time. Life's swift calendar had brought me to my fortieth year, had separated me from loved ones, and had possibly readied me for my own death in this inhospitable spot. Simultaneously an altogether different and slower calendar had marked the days since March 20 when we stood expectantly under the portico of the Astor Hotel. I could recall almost every detail of those eight months, and lying in our rough cart, I reviewed it all, my heart's beat substituting for footfalls. I couldn't discipline my mind to remember it all in chronological order, instead my thoughts roamed and leapt from one subject to another, always ultimately alighting on Lily: jouncing along on Silvester's back, finding toeholds on cliff faces, helping me pick berries or flowers, curling into my body for warmth. I remembered Felix Mittler's admonition to keep a journal as a means of controlling one's thoughts. I didn't think I could bear to set down my sad and anxious thoughts in a diary that might never be read by a single person; instead, I asked Fritz to find writing paper, and, pushing myself to a sitting position, I began a letter to Hermann's cousin, my sweetest friend Antonia:

Dearest Antonia,

> It is with deepest affection and sorrow that I write, sending love to you and Erich and your dear children from a place in California known to me only as Peter Lassen's Ranch.
>
> I cannot know where there will be a post office; perhaps a stranger will come along the trail

taking mail south to Sacramento and then to San Francisco for posting.

We are not all right. Much has happened since I last wrote. I have been able to endure it all, except this one thing: Lily died October 31 of pneumonia and dysentery. Her little body rests in a hasty grave under the wall of a canyon where her initials are incised. This canyon is only a few miles east of the Sacramento Valley. I send you these facts so that someone will know in case the rest of us do not make it.

Hermann and the boys are thin and weak. Hermann limps from an infection on his foot; Otto has a nasty wound on his neck from a boil that has not healed properly; all three have scurvy, as our provisions have not included fruit or vegetables. We own nothing, as we have abandoned everything that you and I lovingly packed together in New York. Some say a blind man could find his way to California by following the odor of abandoned dead animals, which include our milk cow and four of our six oxen, worn down by fatigue and hunger.

I am sick, Antonia. What food I can eat passes directly through me, leaving cramps and chills. My hair and skin are dry and papery; you would not recognize me. My weak legs will scarcely hold me up, and some member of my family must aid me to perform the simplest ablutions. It has been many months since I have been womanly. And my heart has flown out of my body; I don't know how to find it again or to find the strength to continue.

You were right not to come. You might have lost your child and even more, as I have. While I long for your companionship, I am also relieved that you are safe and away from this vile trail of woes.

We have rain every day and sometimes snow. I sleep in a cart under a wet and flapping piece of canvas. Hermann says we will move on as soon as the weather gives us a break, as this place is unhealthful and expensive, and he, true to his character, is anxious to strike it rich.

I close my eyes and see your rosy cheeks and long to feel your embrace at this time of struggle and lament.

Your devoted friend and cousin-in-law,

Frida Reinhardt

Herr Mittler was right. Setting our plight in writing served a purpose. I determined to get stronger; I had to get stronger to accompany and aid my remaining family. We had been at Lassen's Ranch nearly four weeks when I began getting out of my bed for a few hours each day, walking around our miserable campsite, using a stick as prop. By the third day, I could stand and walk without feeling dizzy; on the fourth day, December first, Hermann announced at dinner that he had negotiated for a new wagon, three additional oxen, and sufficient provisions for a month, using Otto and Fritz's wages as currency. "We will leave tomorrow."

"I can't walk, Hermann! How will I keep up?"

"The wagon is more commodious than the cart. You will go in with the provisions. We are through the mountains. Trust me: it will go easily."

One aspect of my weakened condition was that I seemed to cry all the time, and I began to weep as I thought of returning to life on the trail.

Fritz spoke gently to me. "We have to move on, *Mutti*. Here we are nowhere. If we are to get back to New York, we must first find gold to pay for our passage and then travel to a port to find a ship. If we wait here, we must wait all winter. Who knows how spring will find us."

"If we wait, Frida," Herman interrupted, "just imagine how many people will get to the diggings before us. There will be nothing left for us."

"Father's right," added Otto. "And, remember, we have less than sixty miles to go!"

"I know, Otto." I wiped my eyes. "But in sixty miles where will we be? Still nowhere."

Chapter 92

In the morning they loaded me into the wagon, along with our provisions and scant belongings. Before we were out of sight of the Lassen's encampment the road became a swamp, and the lead ox sank so deeply into the mud that he could not extricate himself. Hermann harnessed the other four to the back of the wagon and in this way freed the poor scared brute. The route did not improve. The November rains had left behind slick, slippery, and sometimes deep mud. Hermann and the boys slipped and lost their footing continuously; by the end of each day, they were covered with the filth of the trail. In four days we covered only twenty-five miles and reached another settlement. An American who had been there with his family for four years owned this one. Pens of horses and domestic oxen surrounded his poor sod house. His wife came out and stood by his side, watching as we approached.

"It'll cost you fifty cents a night to camp here!" was his greeting.

I called out to Hermann, "Please, Husband. I must have a day's rest!"

Hermann asked if there was a dry place for our tent. "She'll show you," said the man, indicating his wife. She shuffled off to one side, employing a gait more suited to a seaman. She pointed to a spot where grasses had been trampled flat, then turned to us with a dark smile, "A dirty cracked plate, that's what I am," she cackled, then shuffled, backwards this time, to her house.

I could understand how you could go crazy in a place like this, and I wondered which kind of illness was worse.

I begged to be left alone for a nap, but I heard Fritz and Otto outside our tent planning to scout ahead for a day or two. "No!" I cried out, loud enough to bring them both into the tent. "Boys, don't leave. Please don't leave. I will be strong in a day or two; then we'll go together."

They demurred. But it was not to be a day or two, as I became feverish. I begged Hermann not to take me back on the trail, and we waited at the American's for a week. Once more his wife came to our tent, this time barefooted. She smiled again and tapped the back of my hand with one finger. She jerked her head in Hermann's direction, "If I had a ladida like that one, I'd have drowned it when a pup!" Then she handed me something red that she had concealed in her hand. It was a rose blossom, crushed but fresh, and the sweetest gift she could have given. I squeezed her hand in thanks.

"Sadie was a lady!" she sang out and shuffled away, mud oozing between her toes.

On the thirteenth of December we started out again. The trail was still so muddy that our wagon and animals got stuck again and again. Three times Hermann and the boys unloaded the wagon, carrying our possessions across the swamps themselves. Each time Hermann took me into his arms, weak though he was, and bore me to dry land. Each time he would remind me that our reward would be at trail's end: achievement and prosperity.

When a man with four strong mules passed on his way back south to the Feather River after making a delivery of provisions to the settlements north of us, Hermann made an agreement with him to take our wagon to the Feather River. "I will," he replied. "But we will have to leave now; I have a schedule to make."

This stranger quickly hitched his more agile animals to our wagon, helped me onto the seat beside him, and we turned our backs on our oxen, not even giving a farewell pat to Silvester or Nikolaus who had been with us since Independence.

On December twentieth – exactly nine months after leaving New York - we arrived at our final destination: El Dorado. My sons set up our tarpaulin against the rain at Bidwell's, a sandbar jutting out into the Feather River, laid me on a pallet beneath it, and we awaited better times – after all, conditions couldn't get any worse.

Epilogue – December 28, 1900
By Fritz Reinhardt

I am sixty-seven now, a grandfather, with white hair and arthritis in my knees. I have enjoyed a remarkable and successful life. Now I have the leisure to reflect on my boyhood overland journey to California, to write about the events of fifty years ago, and to remember lovingly the courage of my mother. I know, without a doubt, that her mission was her family. She truly devoted her life to keeping us safe and together as our father's ambition took us across an ocean and a continent. Even in her final moments, she sustained and cherished my brother Otto and me.

I believe that profound emotions etch the deepest memory. Her last heartbreaking days are impressed indelibly on my heart.

I remember she and my father lying on their pallet under a tarpaulin stretched between trees to keep the snow off their sickbed. Both were weak and wasting with dysentery, scurvy, and the exhaustion of the rough-wrought road. She had been ill for a long time, languishing from fatigue, illness, and grief. He had succumbed too, but not until he had delivered us to the gold diggings, as he promised. In truth, we were all four worn out, too tired and disheartened to celebrate that moment which was the culmination of our arduous nine months on the trail.

It was Christmas time. We Germans regard Christmas as the great fete of the year, a time for merrymaking, good cheer, abundant food, and gifts. My mother begged my father to send Otto and me to the nearest town with his last coins to purchase something with which to celebrate the holiday. My father agreed, as long as we would also buy potatoes and vinegar against the scurvy from which we all suffered.

We borrowed a horse from another overlander. We would repay his kindness by purchasing his provisions as well, saving him a trip. We were each so thinned out that the horse could not have known it was carrying two passengers, and we rode foremost by turns.

Marysville was a real town, and we were excited to see women in dresses, houses with windows, and a few small businesses, including a store. We once-sophisticated city boys from New York were awed by its splendor. After purchasing the potatoes, vinegar, a very small jar of honey, and some other basics, and with ten dollars left in our pockets, we considered our mother's request and the approach of Christmas. We looked over the shelves and saw calicoes, kerchiefs, hunting knives, boots, and other sundries, but decided that nothing would be so welcome to our parents as some delicacy that would break the dull monotony of trail food. We considered a box of sardines or smoked herring, favorites of all of us. Otto reached over my shoulder and picked up something with a bright label, "This is it, Fritz! Peaches!" I agreed. Could anything be more delicious than peaches, canned in sugary juices?

The storekeeper had only one can, and he would take no less than ten dollars for it, regarding it as the most desirable thing in his store. We agreed, tied our bundles behind us, and rode back to celebrate Christmas at the Feather River.

We reached our campsite at Bidwell's Bar well after midnight; our parents were asleep, wrapped in their ragged blankets with a doubled-over length of canvas beneath them as mattress.

In the morning – Christmas morning – we greeted each other, kissing tenderly. Otto had cut a pine branch on our homeward journey, and he set this in the dirt that formed our floor. We put our blankets under the heads and shoulders of our parents so they could recline by the Christmas tree. I talked of past Christmas celebrations at Astor House, but the memories brought tears to all our eyes, and we fell silent.

"What did you get in Marysville?" my father asked. We showed him our meager provisions, holding back the surprise can of sweet peaches.

My mother wanted to cook Christmas breakfast, as she had all her life. We all knew she was too weak for that.

I remember that I told her to lie still. I would make flapjacks; she could watch and advise me. Otto helped with the preparations, mixing flour and water and a pinch of gunpowder, a common substitute adopted among the Forty-niners for salt. It gave savor to the food; I cannot imagine what it did to our stomachs. We set a box next to the pallet where our parents lay, and when everything was in readiness, we brought in the hot flapjacks and jar of honey and arranged everything neatly where Father and Mother could reach without getting up. Otto, as the eldest, had the honor of bringing in our gift, the can of peaches. I remember that he bowed theatrically, like a butler presenting the wassail bowl, placing the can with great dignity on the makeshift table.

My mother smiled and brought one hand out from beneath her covers to pat her stomach, but neither parent could swallow the delicacy; in fact, neither could taste any of the meal that we had prepared with such pride. Mother, characteristically, urged us to eat their share. Both lay back in their rude beds, exhausted with the effort of greeting Christmas morning. My brother and I divided the peaches, getting no pleasure from them or their sweet syrup, and ate what we could of the flapjacks. Christmas afternoon, while our parents slept, Otto helped me scrape the potatoes and soak the scrapings in vinegar; with this sour dish we hoped to save our parents' lives.

That was our Christmas in California in 1849 – a Christmas of bitterness and misery – on the banks of the Upper Feather River.

The day after our piteous Christmas celebration, our father, having ingested as much of the potato scrapings soaked in vinegar as he could stomach, was able to rise and to walk unsteadily around the small community of tents, greeting other miners and watching them at their work. I recall that he saw one poor soul digging with nothing more than a spoon and a jackknife.

Our mother had not been able to keep the disgusting concoction in her stomach, and her retching made her yet weaker.

She called to us that day and the next, between slumbers. I've thought of those moments so often that I believe I can remember every word of our conversations. The first time she called my name, she asked me to sit with her to talk about Lily.

"We can talk of Lily another time, *Mutti*. Now you should lie still and get well!"

"No Fritz." She insisted. "I may not have the time. Sit with me and listen."

With great effort she raised herself up on one elbow. Lily's hair ribbon, which she kept knotted around her wrist, was wrinkled and colorless. "There is a ritual I go through almost every day that helps me to stay calm. I say to myself: It is two o'clock in the afternoon, now imagine the rest, imagine everything. *She is skipping along next to Silvester, she is riding on Fritz's shoulders. She asks for an apple, a hat, a caress.* Then I imagine the place where she is doing these things. I *see* the ravine she is walking through, *smell* the rankness of the oxen, *taste* the dust in the air. I close my eyes and *feel* the tangles in her hair, the mud caked on her little boots. I imagine the sun beating down, and I think of her strong little body, warm, solid, alive."

I was weeping at her side, and she reached out her arm and took my hand, holding it tight in her own, but not crying. "The saddest thing, Son, is that I can't remember her voice. Can you?"

I wiped my eyes, remembering. "She was always talking, always commenting on the passing scene, wasn't she, *Mutti*? She would tell us about the flowers, the color of the sky, the amount of animal manure along the trail, what was hanging off the back of the last wagon that passed us by. If one of us wasn't around, well then, she'd talk to old Sylvester!" I was having trouble remembering her voice too; then it came to me. "Do you remember when she marched around the campfire singing 'Oh! Susanna?' She knew every word! When I recall that, I can hear her voice. Does that help you?"

Now my mother was weeping and nodding to me that she could hear Lily's voice too. She lay back in her blankets, turned on her side, and curled up into a ball, crying softly. She waved me away.

Later she called for my father, and I found him and brought him to her. I heard her say to him, "Hermann, although we never speak of it, our devil is always with us – our silent *Teufel*. You know what I mean. Now we must talk of it! We don't have much time."

I left them to their privacy, and when I came back several hours later, they were both asleep, wound up in each other's arms in a way I had never seen before.

She woke again at suppertime, drank a little water, and dipped a stale biscuit in it, eating a few bites.

"Are you feeling better, Frida?" asked my father.

"It's a hard task," she answered, looking from one of us to the others. "It is hard to release memories."

"What do you mean?"

"Letting go is not easy! Letting go of you, of the boys, of my sweet baby girl, and all my memories – it's hard work! My heart has a thousand misgivings, and my mind is tortured with anxiety!" She looked around, suddenly angry, "Don't tell me to have patience; I haven't time for patience!" She fell back into her bedclothes, spilling the remaining water.

"Are you afraid?" I asked her.

She whispered her answer, her eyes closed, "I've lived through everything there is to be afraid of."

Of course, she knew she was dying; it was we – Father, Otto, and I – who refused to contemplate such a thing.

On December 27 she slept most of the day, while the rest of us prepared to dig for gold. Every hour one or the other would come to check on her. At midday she asked for her toothbrush and comb and a wet cloth and soap to wash herself. I rushed to get the things she wanted then left her to clean up in privacy.

In five minutes she called to me, "I am in deep solitude, Fritz. It is a place I have not visited before. It's forced upon me, but also sought by me to some extent. Where will it lead? To madness, or worse?"

I stoked the small cooking fire and didn't leave her for the rest of the day, lying by her side, stroking her arm and face and reassuring her that she wasn't alone. I talked the way Lily did, non stop, telling her of our preparations, recalling incidents along the trail or in New York, reassuring her that she would get stronger, that she must get stronger to care for me, for us. When I ran out of conversation, I started over, and finally resorted to singing Lily's song to her. I don't know if she heard any of it.

The next morning her face was scarlet, her clothing soaked from night sweats, and her breath a dangerous rale. My father held her in his arms and patted her face and neck dry, crooning over her in German.

She woke and seemed to get control of her breathing. Her first words were, "Where's Lily?" Father told her, and she nodded that she remembered. "Where's my mother?" she asked next. Father told her, and she nodded again. "Fritz? Otto? Where are they?"

We kneeled next to her.

"Listen to me!" She closed her eyes, and I thought she had fallen asleep. "Listen! Too many good-byes, too many *auf Wiedersehens*. Promise me. Promise me. Stay together." Her voice was surprisingly strong.

"Frida, *Schwartzi,* what are you saying?" My father was sobbing, his tears falling onto her hair.

"I mean there has been too much separation and loss. Too much. *Zu viel,"* She whispered.

She closed her eyes again, slumped against my father. "Otto!" she said, after a moment. "Come closer." She pulled the rosy gold ring off her thin finger. "Take this to your sweetheart. Cleave yourself to her; hold fast to each other." She slipped it on his smallest finger, and held tightly to his hand. "Be kind to her."

Her eyes met mine. "Fritz. You are like me. You crave consistency, order. You will find a girl too. She will be a lucky one! Together you'll have a family, a big family!" She smiled at me the way she used to when I was just a boy. "Take my folding mirror wherever you go. Put it in your pocket for now. When you get back to New York, make it your talisman, as I have. Look into its glass when you want to remember."

"I'm tired," she said to no one in particular. Again, she spoke, but now her voice was not so strong. "What happens to the living? I wonder."

I was so intent on my mother and on hearing her quiet words, that for a moment I didn't realize that my father was speaking. "I can tell you what happens to the living," he said softly. "I can tell you, Frida. The living remember. The living stay together."

She turned her face to kiss him, closed her eyes, and fell asleep. He continued murmuring to her, more sounds than words. We stayed with her, watching the sparks fly upward. As her last breaths slowed then stopped forever, his voice became a groan, then rose in pitch to a long savage keen, as if to say all the things that needed saying.

We three stayed with her for several hours, stroking her arms, kissing her cheeks. In time her face softened, the lines of worry receded, and her body relaxed. When her skin began to cool, father washed her face and hands and attempted awkwardly to smooth her hair. Otto shook the dust out of our cleanest blanket, and together he and I laid her thereon. I crossed her hands onto her chest and put a small piece of the Christmas branch in one hand.

Aware of what had happened, the man with the horse walked over and respectfully asked my father if he could help. Father asked if he would dig a grave. Once again the kindness of a stranger helped us at our hour of dismal need. Otto and I lowered her light remains gently into the muddy hole; Father borrowed the other man's shovel. Choking and gasping for breath, he closed Mother's grave with dark wet California dirt. He turned his back to us for a moment, wiped his eyes, then turned and spoke: "Farewell my loving companion. *Auf Wiedersehen.* Sleep calmly and continue to be a comforting guardian to your sons and to your husband."

He tried to continue, cleared his throat, took a breath, but no more words came. He reached for Otto with one arm and for me with the other and folded us both into his heaving chest. We spent the afternoon huddled mournfully in our foul shelter as the continuous drizzle washed away the outward signs of the digging and chilled us three to our hearts.

By her last kiss, I believe my mother forgave him: for the travails of the trip, for uprooting her, for his bombastic, bullying ways, and even for Lily's death. I've always taken comfort in that belief. Of course, it was her nature to forgive, to take comfort from the next day's potential, and not to dwell on the setbacks of the past.

We three stayed at the diggings less than a year after Mother's death and never came close to finding the promised inexhaustible treasure. In the stifling heat of late summer 1850 we joined a company that would alter the course of the American River with dams and canals. On the day that we finished the two-month project, October 8, 1850, the dam broke, and all our investment of money and back-breaking work was for naught.

I cannot recall a single happy time during those months, not even September 9 when California became the 31st state, except perhaps for the moment when the dam burst, and my father threw down his shovel and announced that he'd had enough, and it was time to go home.

We left San Francisco October 31 for Panama aboard the *Northerner.* By poled canoe and mule we crossed to Chagres in six exhausting days, then took passage to New York on the small paddlewheel steamer *Falcon* arriving in New York on January 28, 1851. Otto and I had to support our father off the ship, as he was severely weak and tormented with chills, fever, and raging thirst – Chagres Fever, they called it. It had been nine grueling months from New York to California, but only three months to get home again.

When Father regained good health, he began planning his next great scheme: he would publish a newspaper in New York in both English and German.

"You boys will be my editors!"

"Not me, Father," said Otto. "I'm leaving for St. Louis to claim Jennetta." I think he never completely forgave Father for our ordeal.

Otto married Jennetta and began his own English language newspaper in St. Louis. They brought their four girls to New York once to spend part of the summer with my family at our cottage at Sheepshead Bay. He named his youngest Lily. She was a talkative little three-year old when I first met her – a beguiling little sprite who furrowed her small brow and asked if I would like to hear her sing a song. She climbed onto my lap and sang "Oh! Susanna," as lustily as Lily once had, not missing a single word or verse.

I settled in New York, finding a sweetheart, as my mother knew I would. Delphine and I have seven children. They are grown now and have families of their own. Six live in New York and one in Brooklyn. I like having them near; their visits bring me out of my occasional despondency. My daughter Frida calls these times my *dismals.* It is important to Delphine, as it is to me, and as it was to my mother, to keep us all together.

All attended us on this past Christmas day, glad for the *heringssalat* and goose, and perhaps for their Christmas checks as well. The Christmas tree remains in our commodious front hall where it will stand until Twelfth Night. Its crowning star is at my waist level when I look down upon it from the second floor landing. I see in its branches ornaments made over the years by all my children and three cornucopia still filled with colorful ribbon candy overlooked by our grandchildren.

I continue to go once or twice a week to the brewery that I founded, but now my eldest son, Frederick, is its president.

Today I have had a telegram from Otto in St. Louis, as I do every year on this date – December 28. He doesn't need to remind me of its significance. I am sure I speak for both of us: We vividly remember December 28, 1849, as well as the several days preceding. I take my mother's small folding mirror in my hands and look into its glass. It is always on the mantelpiece, not even displaced by the Christmas greens. I rub its wood with oil every Sunday night at the same time that I wind the clocks. And I reread my mother's diary. The ink has faded over the years, but as I have nearly memorized the words, I can read it easily. Her thoughts and descriptions help me recall much of our trip.

Otto's telegram and her diary take me far from my *gemütlich* New York home on a whirling trip of memories. My recollections always start in the foul weather of late March, when, at age sixteen, I left New York with my family on an escapade that became a tragedy. They reel themselves across the American continent, often in disorder, alighting on moments of joy and utter sadness. I remember gaily rolling down a springtime hillside with my mother, brother, and baby sister; then, barely able to stifle a groan, I recall the wail of despair from my sister when I inadvertently dropped her doll into a swift river. I will recall frightening river crossings as well as clear nights in the desert when the sky revealed every star in its bowl.

I can try to skip over the terrible events of October 31, 1849, when we buried little Lily; but I can't erase my memory of the shallow hole, dug by a stranger, into which Father lowered her swaddled body, and even now my pulse races. On a business trip to California ten or eleven years ago, I tried to find that spot, remembering that we had scratched the date and her initials onto the canyon walls, but a road had been built there, and the equipment had erased all traces. The spot I have always held as holy has vanished from earth. We never marked my mother's gravesite. At the time, none of us had the strength.

I remember a girl named Bess – another man's wife, actually – whose girlish charms stirred my boyish fantasies.

I shrink from recalling my father – his self-importance and rages – and how frightened of him I was during that trip. But I can't help but remember the shock at seeing him naked for the first and only time when we bathed in a faraway stream.

I think of my mother in a series of vignettes; each holds a kernel of a truth about her. She sits on a steamboat, still as a spider in its web, watching the shoreline for a glimpse of my missing brother. She is next to an Indian woman, holding out combs, smiling in the light of a cooking fire. I remember her doctoring our cattle, pushing animal fat down their throats to moderate the effects of alkali that had made them sick. I shut my eyes against the remembrance of her black eye and bruised arm, but my closed eyes do not diminish the memory. And I picture her on Christmas day, 1849, lying with my father under that crude shelter. When Otto and

I talk, we reinforce each other's memories; I'm no longer sure which are mine.

My father married again after returning to New York. Agnes was older than he was and cold in temperament. Dephine and I rarely saw them, but we saw him regularly; he liked stopping by our house, bringing candies to his grandchildren and testing their knowledge of German. Once, about fifteen years ago, I took him out for dinner. We took the ferry to Brooklyn and walked to a favorite German restaurant of his. I determined to talk with him about his insensitivity to my mother. I wanted him to know that I hadn't forgotten his brutish behavior. I thought to lay the blame for her death and Lily's at his feet. I believed that if I hurt him, I would release myself from the melancholia I experienced on and off throughout my adult life.

Before the waiter even brought our menus, he burst out with the news that he had been diagnosed with a tumor in his brain, and that the doctor gave him only months to live.

"Your mother's last wishes, Fritz, were for us to stay together. Do you think Otto would make the trip from St. Louis once again?"

Of course I never confronted him, and we ate our *sauerbraten* in sad silence. *Once again he has dominated the scene*, I thought to myself.

Our father deteriorated quickly, and Otto came east a month later. We went to his bedside together. His room and bedclothes were immaculate; Agnes was a competent *hausfrau*. She stayed downstairs to let us have our private time together. He was confused, and wasn't even sure which of us was which.

He listened to our greetings, and smiled his own back gently to us. He brought his hand out from under his blankets and opened his clenched fist. In it was a ragged colorless snippet of ribbon – Lily's once-pink ribbon that our mother had saved. He deliberately closed his fist on this treasured scrap and shut his eyes as though for a rest. When he opened them, he looked back and forth at Otto and me, wet his lips, and whispered his last words, "You remind me of your mother."